THE BUTTERFLY TRAP

Readers Reviews

'It was INCREDIBLE! I honestly loved it so much.'

'A gripping read that you will not be able to put down. A perfect sequel to Girl on the Beach.'

'Brilliant! It captivated a male audience from the start.'

'Anger, frustration, relief, love, fear and hope! J.V. Phaure's amazing ability to take you on a rollercoaster of emotions through the eyes of the characters makes this gripping sequel a page turner from beginning to end.'

'J.V. Phaure has done it again! A brilliantly drawn novel, I absolutely loved it!'

Also by J.V.Phaure

Girl on the Beach

THE BUTTERFLY TRAP

Dear Bruce,

Thankyou for everything!

With love and best wishes,

J.V.Phaure

J.V.PHAURE

A CIP catalogue record for this book is available from the British Library

Cover Design by Robin Freeman
www.robinfreemandesign.com

Cover Photo courtesy of mariusbphoto/pixabay.com

Paperback ISBN 978-1-913663-83-4

Typeset, Printed and Bound in Great Britain by Biddles Books Limited, King's Lynn, Norfolk

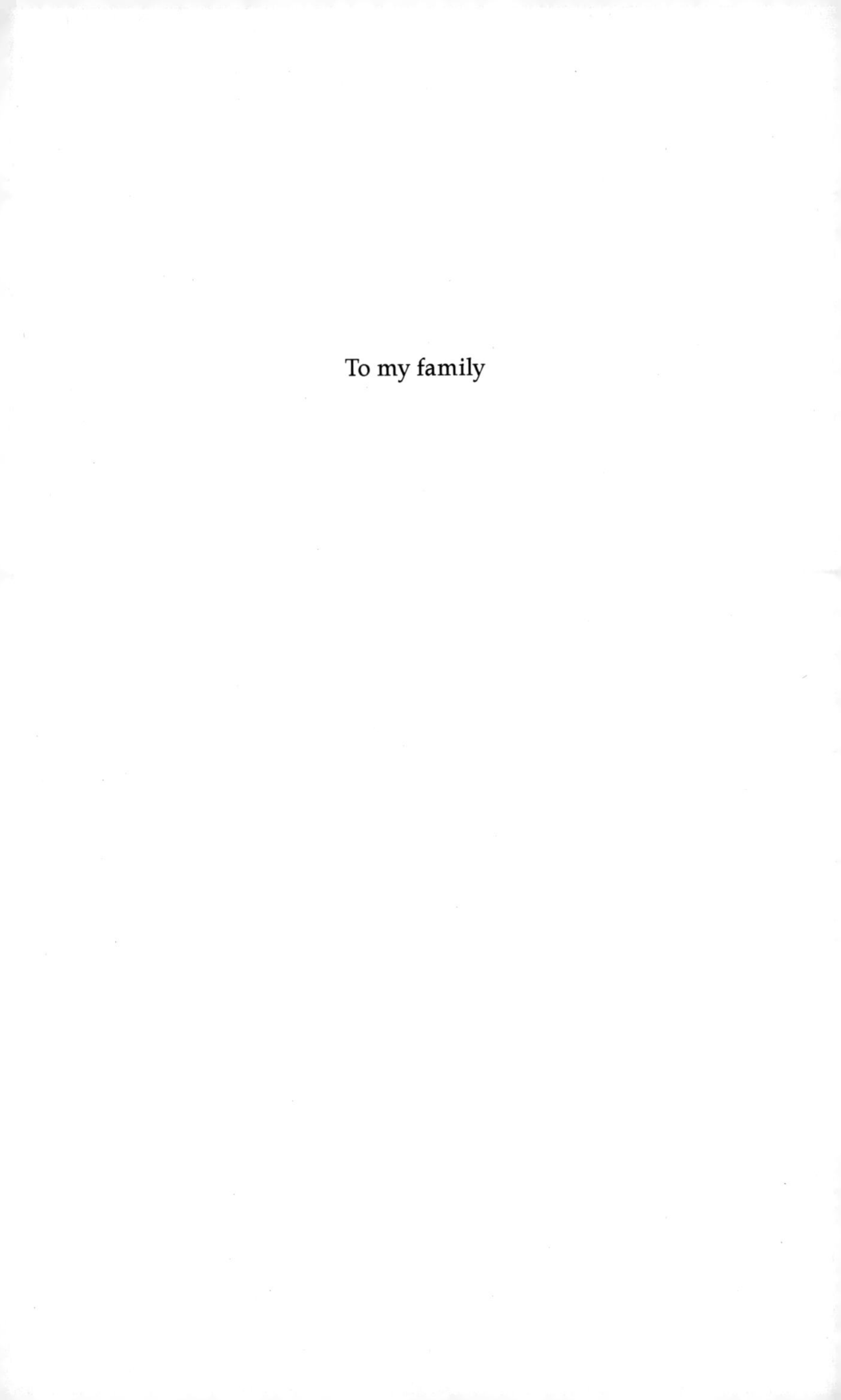

To my family

About the Author

J.V. Phaure is a British author, best known for her debut novel Girl on the Beach and The Butterfly Trap is its much-anticipated sequel.

Writing has always been a passion of hers and she takes her inspiration from the people she meets and the places and countries she has lived in. She loves nothing more than to sit in her favourite coffee shop or on the beach and people watch and write.

She lives with her family in North Essex.

To find out more about the author you can visit her website or find her on Instagram, Twitter and Facebook.

www.jvphaure.com

J_V_Phaure

@JvPhaure

Facebook.com/jvphaure

With thanks to all those who have made The Butterfly Trap what it is, my family, my friends and my readers.

Captain Gerry Northwood, a special thanks for all your naval knowledge, you were an awesome find. And to those others who have spoken to me behind the scenes, thank you from the bottom of my heart.

"If you can't look after something in your care, you have no right to keep it."

Enid Blyton

Prologue

'He was here in the room, he locked the door,' she stammered, the tears rolling down her face, her hands shaking. 'Then I saw the beach, I saw the beach, he dragged me.' Her breathing was fast and uncontrolled between each word. 'He was there, on the beach, it was him, it was him. Make it go away, make it go away. Get him off me, get him off me. He's here. There by the door.' Her screams of fear reverberated down the corridor. Her gasping wails echoed around. It was more than crying; it was the kind of desolate sobbing, wailing that comes from a person drained of all hope, terrified …

Chapter One

Saturday, 22nd February
Felixstowe, Suffolk

Two black BMWs, two squad cars and a forensics van were hemming in the abandoned black Audi, which was shielded by a white tarpaulin tent. The sound of huge container ships' horns blasted through the industrial port of Felixstowe. Giant blue Titan cranes obscured the seascape. They resembled monstrous transformers. Blue and white police tape fluttered in the sea breeze, cordoning off an area marked 'CRIME SCENE KEEP OUT,' securing the area so as to avoid any further evidence being changed or disturbed.

Jim Finlay - the Crime Scene Manager, part of the MO4 team - walked slowly up to the strip of tape. He surveyed the area slowly, measuring its perimeter, piecing together what must have happened during the 'golden hours' immediately after the crime, knowing that was when he was most likely to get his key evidence. A team of forensics officers - covered from head to toe, their white suits showing only their eyes - moved around the secured area. A coating of white dust lay on the steering wheel, door handles, boot and locks of the abandoned vehicle. Fibres taken from the footwells of the car had been tweezered into tubes and then into sterile polythene bags and placed in a crate on a table in the tent. An officer stood behind his camera on a tripod, taking stills of the area. Another took close-up photographic shots of the metal rail under the front passenger seat in the rear footwell and the footprints on the driver's foot mat. Particles of grit extracted from the mat were taken up and placed in a specimen pot, dated the 22nd of February 2019 and marked 'Driver's footwell'. Minuscule brown droplets of liquid, forming a crust on a rear metal rail under the front passenger seat, were swabbed and eased gently into another specimen pot dated the same and marked 'Rear footwell under seat rail'.

Three sniffer dogs, trained to pick up evidence, wagged their tails manically at each container and surrounding area of the port, picking up the scent the suspect had left after abandoning the vehicle. They sniffed unstoppably, trying to work out which direction the wanted person had made off in. Scamp, a springer spaniel, sat motionless by a container and barked once.

'We've got something,' shouted one of the armed officers.

Tony Phillips, the Detective Inspector, with greying hair and dressed in a charcoal grey suit, polished brown brogues and a blue mac, turned on his heels. They clicked on the tarmac as he approached the container. He signalled to Jim, who made his way over carrying a digital SLR camera. Behind him, another white-suited member of the team carried a white crate marked 'Evidence'. A pair of white Nike trainers covered in dry grit and particles of sand were tucked between the sides of two Maersk containers.

Jim's camera clicked rapidly as he took stills of the footwear, its flash lighting up the cramped space between the dark blue metal containers, picking up every minuscule detail. The forensics officer took up the trainers in a bag, placed them in the white crate and took them away to the tent. Scamp was rewarded with a chicken biscuit and instructed to find the scent picked up on the trainers and follow it. Phillips took out a packet of Benson and Hedges cigarettes and lit one.

'Anything?' Phillips asked as Finlay stepped back from the gap between the berths.

'Footwear, with what appears to be sand particles,' Finlay said.

'Breathe it in, Jim. We are dealing with an amateur,' Phillips mused as he took out his phone and dialled through to London.

'CID, DS Murphy speaking.'

'Murphy, what have you got in London, anything at the suspect's flat?'

'Afternoon, guv. We were granted a warrant to search the property. The apartment has been vacated. It looks like his passport and wallet are missing. There are no obvious signs to show he's taken any clothes. Looks like two pairs of shoes are missing from his shoe rack. The registration trace on the Audi is a hire company called Dobson and Peters Car Hire in Bow, East London,' Murphy said. 'Did a check on the company and a male matching the description of our suspect hired a black Audi Q3 2.0 TDI. The car was hired on Thursday the 20th of February, at thirteen-hundred hours, and was due back the next day. This coincides with the abduction time of Lucy Carter a few hours later. We've also retained CCTV footage of what appears to be our suspect, Charlie Wainwright, at Dobson and Peters. But it's not clear; he's shielding himself from the camera.'

'So, he's moved out of the West London vicinity for his plans, gone east. Clever. Easier for him to slip onto the M11 undetected. He's trying to outsmart us,' Phillips said, inhaling hard on his cigarette and looking out to sea.

'Just one thing, guv,' Murphy added.

'What's that?'

'The payment made by credit card - well, it's not in our suspect's name. It's a Mr C. Martinez.'

'Martinez? Are you sure?'

'I've got a copy of the receipt, terms and conditions and waiver forms. It's definitely not Wainwright's name.'

Phillips' breathing deepened as he mulled it over, and the sound of the horn of a ship being piloted into the port broke the eerie silence of the crime scene.

'What you thinkin', guv?'

'He's not in the country, Murphy. He's not in the bloody country. His car's been abandoned at Felixstowe. Why would you leave a car in a busy port? We need a Red Notice, so get on it! I'm back in London tonight. We need to speak with his neighbour again.' Phillips closed the call and kicked his cigarette butt into the swirling sea as it crashed against the sea wall.

'Where are you, Wainwright?' he said under his breath, as he scanned the mass of grey churning water. Charlie was on the run. Phillips turned on his heels and walked towards the tent. He watched the forensics team claiming their finds on the Audi as Jim Finlay came up.

'We've got a recovery truck for the vehicle at fourteen-hundred hours, Jim. It's to be taken to the examination pound in Acton. Anything else here?'

'We've pretty much got everything, Detective Inspector. We're ready for the car to be lifted and removed. We need to keep the area cordoned off, though,' Jim Finlay replied whilst shifting the crates into the forensics vehicle. 'We can do further examinations back at base and get the DNA results on the swabs we've taken. Should be with you within the next seventy-two hours – that's with the lab working at full pace.'

'Good work, though I'd prefer forty-eight hours. I'll call a meeting on Monday morning for the Major Incident Team. I need to talk to the operations manager here first.' Phillips took his phone back out of his pocket, but before making the call, he paused, then set off across the dockside.

At the entrance of the red-brick building where all the internal operations happened for the port, he flashed his badge to two burly men dressed in orange overalls. They moved aside and nodded, their yellow helmets displaying their names. He stood outside the building and watched the men walk towards a crane lifting a container onto a huge ship. Its immensity blocked the view of the horizon.

'Oi, Charlie, not like that, son. Swing it slowly, you'll take the side out,' a workman shouted down the walkie-talkie to the crane operator. 'Make sure it grips the rails or it'll be straight in the sea. Easy does it.'

As he finally pressed the speed-dial for the Major Incident Team, Phillips homed in on the crane and its operator. A man not clearly identifiable, his helmet shielding his face. He pulled the handle back and dropped the lever to slowly swing the crane towards the ship's side. Phillips stared at the cabin until his call was answered.

'Essex Police, PC Mackenzie speaking,' answered the familiar voice of Simon Mackenzie.

'Simon, DI Phillips here. I'm at Felixstowe docks at present,' Phillips said, keeping his eyes fixed on the crane's cabin.

'Afternoon, sir. Any news on Charlie?'

'Nothing yet. A pair of trainers have been found but there seems to be no further evidence outside the compounds of the port. The Audi has shown up as being hired from Dobson and Peters Car Hire in London, on Thursday, 20th of February, in the name of a Mr C. Martinez,' Phillips said. His conversation was interrupted by the bellowing of the ground worker.

'Jesus Christ, Charlie! Can you handle the lever slowly – are you certified to operate this crane?!' came the voice of the workman. Phillips looked back up to the operator, but he couldn't make him out between the glass windows of the cabin.

Phillips continued, 'Fingerprints taken from the car will be analysed and hopefully we will have a match with our suspect's. There could be any number of prints, due to it being a hire car, and these need to be eliminated. At the moment the necessary examinations of the vehicle have happened *in situ*. We've got MO4 on the vehicle to collect traces of saliva, blood or any other fibres. There'll be something here, without a doubt, that the suspect has unwittingly left behind. If he's been careless with his footwear, odds are he wasn't wearing gloves. Won't know for sure until we've got the results back from the lab. I'm going to need to speak to the operations manager here and ascertain what ships left in the last two days.'

'Do you think he stowed away on a container ship?'

'That I don't know. The area has been searched. Not sure how he's stowed away, though, as he'd have to get through the barriers and a whole heap of security. Like I said, all forensic evidence seems to stop here.'

'So, where do you go from here? What do I tell Lucy?' Simon asked. 'We visited her today after she came to properly. She's pretty frightened. Jo said she's already tried to answer the police's questions; she said it was DS Murphy with a female officer this morning, I believe a DC Milson. Ben hasn't left her side.'

'Understandably. DS Murphy asked some questions early this morning but is now back in London. I'll visit the hospital later this afternoon and have a chat with her. Not much else I can do, other than provide her with the assurance that we are on his tail. He's a couple of days ahead of us. In the meantime, look after Lucy once she's out. I'll organise a protection order for her, we can sort that. In the meantime, I have a manhunt on my hands, and I am going to find him.'

He closed the call and pulled open the door into the red-brick building.

'DI Phillips,' he said as he walked into the reception. 'Who's in charge here?'

A young girl in glasses, with a small hooped earring in her nose and chewing gum between her jaws, looked up from the magazine she was reading. 'That'll be Mr Roberts, Andy Roberts. He's on lunch now, can it wait?' she said turning the page, oblivious as to who she was talking to.

DI Phillips flashed his badge at the girl. 'No.'

The receptionist buzzed through. 'I've got a detective in reception, Andy, what shall I do? I've told him you're on lunch but he's ...' The internal line went dead, she hung up. 'He'll be out in a moment. Please take a seat, can I get you a coffee?' she said sheepishly.

Phillips looked at her then turned away. 'Straight black,' he said, moving towards the main door and watching intently the men crossing the dockside of the port, some wheeling huge trollies, others directing cranes by walkie-talkie. The crane he had been watching was empty. The receptionist disappeared and returned shortly afterwards with a straight black coffee, with two sachets of sugar on the saucer.

A door to the side opened. 'DI Phillips? Andy Roberts.' The operation manager extended his arm for a handshake. 'Please come through.' As the door closed, the girl at the desk went back to reading her magazine, sloppily chewing her gum and twizzling the hoop in her nose.

'I have to apologise for Tina, she's new. So, any news on the car?' Roberts asked, beckoning the DI to take a seat in his office.

'Forensics are working on it. It'll be taken by the recovery unit later today for further analysis at the pound.'

'Right, I'll inform the boys on the dockside,' Roberts said, stirring three sachets of sugar into his tea. 'How's the coffee?' he asked.

'Black and wet,' Phillips replied, pushing his empty cup away. 'I'd like to know the comings and goings of your personnel.' He pulled out his notebook.

'In what way?' Roberts asked, taking a file from his desk. 'I can give you who is on duty, if that's what you mean?'

'Their overalls, where are they kept?' Phillips asked.

'There's a locker room where overalls are hanging. Many of the men have their own, but there are also standby overalls for temps, onsite visits, spares, you know,' Roberts replied.

'Easy to gain access?'

'It's not monitored by cameras, if that's what you mean, and there's a trolley outside for used overalls. It's taken every other day for laundering.'

'Have you got a count for overalls used in this way?' Phillips asked. He mulled over the information. The only way Wainwright could gain access to a ship would be to blend in.

'Yep, I can show you,' Roberts said, opening the file. 'The laundry service is due tomorrow for a collection of the load. It's an external company based in Ipswich.'

'Cancel it! I want a count on overalls used and a count on those to be laundered,' Phillips said, taking the file and perusing the data. 'That trolley is to be left. I'll put one of my team onto it.'

'Right, not a problem. Is this linked to the girl found on the beach?' Roberts asked.

'Possibly.' He closed Roberts down. 'The containers – are they accessible?'

'Unlikely, highly unlikely. The only access would be through one of the men and that would be if they were being searched for smuggling. However, you can open a container from the outside, but then the seal would be broken,' Roberts replied. 'Security has really tightened up since that forty-million-pound haul of heroin found last year on a container. I can't let that kind of crime happen on my watch, I've got a wife and kids at home, need to get paid, not lose my job. The security is so tight on these shipments. That said, it could happen.'

'Understandably. Hypothetically speaking, could a non-crew member infiltrate the carrier?' Phillips pushed.

Roberts shrugged and shook his head. 'The only way – and this is hypothetical, right – is if there was an insider on the job. The boys wear ID passes, it's just not feasible …' He sighed and slurped his tea. 'What are we looking at, Detective Inspector? What's going on?' Phillips' deflection about the girl on the beach hadn't fooled him for long.

'At the moment it's a routine enquiry. I'd like a copy of the report of the used uniforms and all CCTV footage from the last two days. Also, the details of all shipments that left from yesterday to this morning.'

'That's not a problem, I'll email it over to you this afternoon,' Roberts replied.

Phillips stood up and handed over his business card. 'One thing,' he said as he turned from the door. 'You've got a crane operator called Charlie - when did he start?'

'Not that long ago, he's new,' Roberts replied.

'Surname?'

'You've got me there. It's not English, though. Greek, I think, might even be Spanish?'

'Right, you've got my card, email me and I'd like your new boy's full name too.' The girl at reception didn't look up as the door swished closed behind him.

As the operation's team recovery lorry pulled up into port, Phillips paced his way back to the fluttering tape. The driver climbed out from the cabin and pulled the lever to lift the vehicle to be taken away. The white tarpaulin tent had been dismantled and placed into the forensics van. All that was left was the blue and white tape cordoning off the area.

Phillips watched as the lorry left through the huge iron gates of Felixstowe. The forensics vehicles were next to file out of the port, then the police recovery lorry, sandwiched between two squad cars, and Finlay closing the procession in an unmarked black BMW.

The indicators of Phillips' black BMW beeped as it unlocked. He rested his hands on the steering wheel. He pushed the ignition button and the engine purred as he took out his phone and dialled through to Colchester Hospital.

Chapter Two

Saturday, 22nd February
Colchester Hospital, Essex

The smell of disinfectant hung heavy in the air. Neon white strip lights flooded the corridor with a bright unnatural light. Double doors swung open as trolley beds were pushed along by porters. Green paw prints on the floor marked the way to paediatrics, in a vain attempt to appease the mind of a child as they followed perhaps Shrek's very own footprints to a room or ward of smiling nurses and doctors. A woman pulled a heavy floor buffer along the corridor, adding an extra sheen to the already shiny floor. Phillips walked past her and took a left down the corridor, bearing away from Shrek's footprints. Doctors in blue scrubs walked past him and smiled. He arrived at the reception on Darwin ward and waited for the nurse to finish what she was doing. A policeman still stood outside the entrance to a private room off the ward's corridor.

'Can I help you?' came the friendly voice of a young nurse from behind the desk. Phillips flashed his card at her.

'DI Phillips, Met Police, I'm here to see Lucy Carter,' Phillips said.

'Sure, no problem. She's awake at the moment. Her partner is coming in soon, he's just phoned,' the nurse said and smiled as Phillips left the reception. He tapped the officer who stood at the door on the arm with appreciation, and the officer nodded respectfully.

Phillips knocked and gently opened the door. Lucy lay on the bed, her face bruised. A deep cut to her left temple was held together with stitches, brown crusted blood around it, and a larger wound on the right of her head was concealed behind white padding and gauze. Her lip split in several places, her eye swollen and unable to open, the skin around her eyes black and purple. Her wrists were bruised and red and she had marks around her neck that resembled a hard, tight grip on her.

'How are you. Lucy?' Phillips asked as he approached the bed. She shuffled up the bed a little. His face had lost the hard crime-fighting façade and his approach softened.

Lucy looked up at him and tried to speak, her eyes lost in a soullessness. She drew in a breath.

'I can see him in my sleep, when I close my eyes, I can see him,' she said. 'When will this end? When will I be free? When will my mind be free again? He's taken everything from me.'

Phillips listened like a father, like a friend, unlike a senior police officer.

'My head pounds.'

'Lucy, when you are discharged, I'd like you to have further protection,' Phillips said, drawing up a chair.

'Why? Because he'll come back?' she said as a tear fell down her cheek. Phillips passed the box of tissues from the bedside table. 'Is that why the police are still at my door?'

'We've recovered the car, Lucy. It has been taken back to London for further forensic examinations. Can you remember any more of the day, what he was wearing?'

'I've told the police everything I can remember.' Lucy tried to think but her head pounded, her body ached.

'His shoes - do you remember his shoes?' Phillips asked tentatively.

'I don't know, I didn't hear him approach, really I heard nothing. I can't remember what I heard. It was getting dark, I thought it was Ben, but it ...' She looked out of the window and watched the pigeons swirl around the sky, then perch and coo on the sill outside.

'Don't worry, we have everything we need,' he said reassuringly. 'Did he ever talk about his family to you?'

'Not much. I don't know about his father, I think he died or left. He never talked about him,' she said, holding the edging of the blanket tightly, curling it in her hands.

'And his mother?' Phillips coaxed gently.

Lucy sighed deeply. 'I didn't meet her. She came to London once, but he met her somewhere. I don't think she lives in the country. I don't know though. I think Spain. I feel stupid I don't know these things. Why don't I know these things? I should have known these things. Why is this happening?' Tears flooded her eyes and began to trickle down her face uncontrollably, and her breathing deepened. She began to gasp, trying to catch her breath.

'Lucy, Lucy, are you OK?' Phillips moved towards her hastily.

'I can't breathe …' She inhaled loudly, uncontrollably. 'I can't breathe … Help me, I can't breathe.' Lucy's eyes rolled to the back of her head, her hand fell from the bed. Phillips slammed the alarm button and a nurse and doctor barged into the room at speed.

'She can't breathe,' Phillips said, panicked. He swiftly moved away from the bed and stood back by the window, his brows knitted.

'I'm afraid you'll have to leave the room,' the nurse said as she pulled the oxygen canister to the bedside and put the mask up against Lucy's mouth and nose to help stabilise her breathing. She looked at her watch: it was five o'clock.

'Lucy can you hear me? It's Dr Thiroux, Lucy?' He opened her eyes and shone a light into them. Her pupils were dilated. 'We need to get another cannula into her,' he said calmly but urgently to the nurse. 'Lucy, it's Dr Thiroux, we are going to give you something to help you. I need to insert a small tube …' He lifted her head and removed a pillow from behind, lowering her body. She began to tremble violently.

'Quick, she's gone into shock, get the oxygen mask onto her again, we have minutes here.' He administered epinephrine.

As the hand moved around the clock, every second counted before vital organs went into failure.

Ben walked up the corridor with a bar of Green & Black's milk chocolate, a cappuccino and peppermint tea.

'DI Phillips, what's going on? Why are you here?' Ben asked. His face dropped and his eyes darted towards Lucy's door. 'Has something happened to Lucy?'

'The doctor is with her now. I came to make a routine visit before heading back up to London and she just ...' Phillips said, concern written across his face. At the moment he was heading up an attempted murder case. If she died, the man on the run would be wanted for murder.

'She just what? What's happened, is she ...' Ben's heart stopped beating for a moment, his hands clammy. 'She'd been OK when I left her at breakfast, she ate a little, she was tearful, frightened – but she wasn't on death's door, she was OK.' He'd kissed her goodbye just like he had the day before. Each day had seemed a little better in her recovery and the medical team were happy with her progress; it was slow but stable.

Lucy's door opened. Dr Thiroux came out carrying some notes.

'Is Lucy OK?' Ben asked hesitantly.

'She will be. She needs to rest, though. She's undergone a huge trauma, emotionally and physically. She went into shock – this can happen after such an event. It's crucial, though, that she's left to rest. We will monitor her closely, but no further investigation questions, I have to insist on that now. It's too traumatic. A flashback can send her into shock, and we have about three minutes to act. It's serious - I can't urge that enough. She has had a steady trickle of visitors all very close to her, but it can throw her back into the trauma. Ben, you can go and see her, she's possibly asleep now so don't be concerned. We've put another cannula into her along with the drip she has. We've administered a drug that brought her out of the shock. She's OK now.'

Ben's face was ashen. He couldn't handle the trauma and danger Lucy had been in and was now still going through. He scrunched his hands through his hair and shook his head in disbelief that this was even happening.

'She's OK, Ben, go and see her.' Dr Thiroux squeezed his arm and went to the reception to speak with Doris, one of the nurses.

'Let me call you tomorrow, DI Phillips,' Ben said. 'I need to be with Lucy now.' Ben shook the DI's hand and left him in the corridor. Phillips nodded to the nurse in appreciation for her swift and caring work and bid her a good evening. He left the hospital, concerned by what he had witnessed. Concerned that perhaps he had pushed Lucy too far.

Ben opened the door gently into Lucy's room.

She lay still on the bed, her eyes closed. Beneath the bashed-up face was a beautiful girl. He sat by her bedside and held her hand. He sat there until the lights dimmed, when he reclined the chair and took the spare blanket from the shelf. Kissing Lucy on the forehead, he lay in his makeshift bed and slept by her side.

***

The euphonious tones of the windscreen wipers swished across the windscreen, and Floyd's Comfortably Numb played in surround sound in the black BMW as it cruised down the M25 in the fast lane. Phillips' thoughts were on Lucy and what he had witnessed in her room that evening. He felt numb seeing her. For the first time in his career, he felt paralysed by it all. He had watched her in a courtroom, he had witnessed her being strong and fighting against a man who had beaten her, violated her, trapped her. A girl on the beach who had fought against the most brutal of attacks. A girl who had lain cold in the dark night on the beach's shoreline, left for dead. The image of her bruised and battered face in his head. Her inability to breathe, the speed of the medical team at her bedside. If he hadn't been there, would it have happened? Was he to blame? He pressed replay on his audio screen and indicated left, moving like a panther in the night, sleek and fast. His rear lights disappeared as he tailed off on to the slip road signposted London and West.

Phillips pulled up outside his west London terraced house in the leafy suburbs of Putney, the streetlights dazzling in the night air. He turned off the ignition and sat for a moment whilst Floyd ended.

Once indoors, he took out a tumbler and poured himself a large malt whisky in the dimmed light. *Where was Charlie?* His eyes narrowed as he swirled the whisky around the glass. He opened up his laptop and logged into his files. An email from Andy Roberts sat in his inbox. The files attached held the information of the personnel at the dock, with a cover note marked Charlie Theosis. Phillips logged out, placed his empty glass in the dishwasher, switched out the lights and made his way upstairs.

In North Essex, a guy who loved that battered and bruised girl sat by her side, watching her stir, tossing her head, listening to the cries, the heart-wrenching screams. His hand touched her gently to smooth away the frantic trauma in her mind.

Chapter Three

Monday, 24th February
Fulham Police Station, London

Monday morning and the criminal investigation department was buzzing. Phillips walked in, carrying a straight black coffee in his hand. He signalled to DS Murphy to come to his office.

'Morning, Murphy. Grab a pew,' Phillips said, taking the printout of Roberts' email from his printer's out-tray. 'Any more information on our suspect's next of kin? His mother?' Phillips sat down and threw his feet onto his desk. Reclining in his chair, he twiddled an unlit cigarette in his fingers.

'We're still working on that, guv. I haven't found anything on her in London yet. We've set the database search for further afield but nothing's flagging up,' Murphy replied. 'We've been onto the General Register Office this morning and should have something back on male babies registered under the name of Charles Wainwright, born on the 17th of July 1984.'

Phillips nodded.

'Anything at Felixstowe, guv?' Murphy asked, running through the papers he had from Dobson and Peters Car Hire, including the CCTV footage stills.

'A possible affirmative on suspect's clothing found. We need to run a DNA examination on them; we should get that back within three days. I've pushed for two. We're dealing with an amateur here,' Phillips said, still twiddling the unlit cigarette in his fingers. 'I'm going to call a meeting mid-morning. We need to close in on Wainwright and sharpish.'

Murphy left Phillips' office. As the door closed, the blinds rattled and the partition walls shook a little. Phillips watched Murphy walk over to the coffee machine; it spewed out a cup and the warm coffee filled it. He was a thorough officer, Phillips thought as he kicked the chair back from its reclined position.

Phillips perused the files that had come from Felixstowe docks. Five overalls had been used, but only four were accounted for in the trolley. A pair of workman's steel-cap boots, size twelve, were also unaccounted for and a yellow hard hat was missing. The name of the crane operator was Charlie Theosis, a trainee of Greek descent. It wasn't the right Charlie.

His external line rang.

'DI Phillips.'

'Detective Inspector? Tom Blakeney, Daily News. We're running a front-page cover on the girl-on-the-beach story. A Lucy Carter. Lover is a banker in the city. Headline "Lover is a W …"' Phillips slammed the receiver down and threw his pen at the phone.

It was time to bring the team up to speed. Phillips walked out onto the main CID floor, picking up a whiteboard marker pen, a mugshot-print of Charlie Wainwright, a print of the bruised and battered Lucy Carter and a blown-up still of the black Audi Q3. All these he placed with Blu Tack on the whiteboard. He turned to the desks of the awaiting officers; they fell silent.

'Good morning all,' he said, raising his voice above the general noise across the department. 'Can you gather around and listen up.'

DS Murphy and Kennedy perched themselves on a desk, while at least twelve detectives gathered around the DI.

'Right, you will be working as part of the Major Incident Team, or MIT, on code name "Operation Butterfly". On the 20th of February our victim, a Miss Lucy Carter, who we see here on the board, was brutally attacked and left for dead on Harwich beach, Essex. All links at the moment are pointing to her ex-fiancé, Charlie Wainwright, seen here.' He circled the mugshot of the suspect. 'Lucy sustained life-threatening injuries and is at present in Colchester General under police protection in a critical but stable condition. She suffered serious head injuries and further injuries across her body, which you can see on the image. A black Audi Q3 2.0 TDI was found abandoned at Felixstowe docks on Saturday the 22nd of February at ten-hundred hours. This car has been picked up on the A120 cameras leaving Harwich on the 20th February at 21.04.' He circled the blown-up image of the vehicle.

'Have we got anything on the car, guv?' one of the detectives asked.

'Yes. DS Murphy has located the car being hired from Dobson and Peters Car Hire in Bow, east London. Payment was made with a credit card in the name of a Mr C. Martinez.'

'Is Martinez connected?'

'DS Murphy is working on the details of that. My hunch is it is an alias being used by our suspect,' Phillips replied. 'The abandoned vehicle has had the SOCOs working on it at Felixstowe, and it was taken to the specialist unit in Acton later on Saturday afternoon. I expect to receive DNA profiles shortly. At present our suspect is on the run. Any calls from the media I want directed to me; no information is to be given. I've already had a reporter from the Daily News sniffing about today. Murphy, what have you got?'

Murphy stood up and addressed the plain-clothed detectives.

'As the DI says, I'm working on the identification used for the hire car. The name Martinez is of Spanish origins, but we don't yet know whether this is connected to our suspect's extended family. The General Register Office has been contacted for details on the next of kin to the suspect, primarily his mother. As the DI has said, Lucy was abducted and attacked on Thursday the 20th of February. Her body was found the following morning by a friend, Bob Henderson, aged fifty-five, former officer in the Royal Navy and a resident in Harwich. He raised the alarm at approximately nine-hundred hours. Lucy was taken to Colchester General unconscious and in a critical condition. On Saturday the 22nd, in the morning, Lucy was able to give a positive identification of her attacker to myself and

DC Milson, as a Charlie Wainwright. She can't remember anything from the point when she left her cottage, though. We think this is due to the blow received to her left temple. That's about all we've got, guv,' Murphy said, his hands in his pockets.

Phillips took the floor again. 'Thank you, good work, Murphy. As you can see on the image, our victim took a severe beating from the attacker. Extensive swelling and bruising on her face, wrists and neck. Lucy has a gash to her left temple, which would imply she was lying on the floor of the passenger seat footwell. No doubt traces of her blood or fibres from her clothes, even a strand of hair, will be in the Audi. We can't speculate until we get the DNA profile with a positive match to Lucy's. I've got a gut feeling with this one, though. The large gash to her right temple matches the DNA profile we have already received from forensics taken on the 20th of February from a rock on Harwich beach, the scene of the crime. It would appear that Lucy's body was dragged from this spot to the pier, where her body was later found by Bob Henderson as DS Murphy has already elucidated. DS Kennedy, I want you to pay an informal visit to Wainwright's neighbour, a Rachel Jones at Mansion House apartments. See if she can offer anything else on Charlie. She's known him for a few years. She has to know a little more about him.'

'I'm on it, guv.' DS Kennedy noted in his book: Rachel Jones, Mansion House apartments, Fulham.

'The files I have received from the operation manager show a workman's overall, boots and helmet unaccounted for. He could be on a container ship, blending in with the crew. But this is some feat for him to get on there unless he has insider help.'

'Does that mean we get Interpol on this, guv?' DS Kennedy asked.

'Interpol will be contacted, and a Red Notice request check has been submitted by a special task force. Dot all the Is and cross all the Ts to ensure it is compliant with our rules. We will get this circulating for wanted fugitives. However, I want to keep this under wraps and not publicise it internationally in the media or at home. If I am going to get him, he's going to walk into my trap. That's it, briefing dismissed, and remember, all media intrusion to be passed onto me. Good work guys.'

Phillips left the MIT and made his way to the coffee machine. He leant on the machine as the black coffee drizzled out.

DS Murphy walked over to him. 'How is Lucy?' he asked.

'Traumatised, went into shock last night when I visited. Ben was with her overnight. She's in a bad way, she's in a really bad way mentally and physically. This is a delicate operation with her. I want the media kept at bay. That Tom Blakeney is the scum of the tabloid press, I can't stand the guy.'

Chapter Four

Wednesday, 26th February
Colchester Hospital, Essex

A faint knock on the door and a rather plump joyful nurse came into Lucy's room, singing. She beamed as she opened the window blinds and swivelled the table away to the side. She leaned over Lucy and adjusted the drip that stood next to her bed. 'Hello me Lucy, me lovely. How are you feeling today? I've just come to do your obs and have a look at those dressings too. There now, that's better. Are you feeling a bit more comfortable?' She leaned Lucy up slightly and plumped her pillows. She smelt of lily of the valley and had a twang to her voice. She just bustled about Lucy with gentleness and talked, talked, talked with everything she did.

Lucy smiled a little as the nurse propped her up gently. 'Ahh there we are, me Lucy, here I go, chatter, chatter, chatter, I'm such a blabba mout'. Me grandmutta used to always say, "Doris will you take a breath child!"' Lucy's smile grew a little larger; she wanted to laugh a bit, but her sides hurt and her face throbbed.

'Where are you from?' Lucy asked as the nurse wrapped the blood pressure band around her arm. Lucy winced, as it pushed on her bruising.

'I'm so sorry, me Lucy, that must be uncomfortable. Jamaica, me lovely, I'll be back there for the summer with me Winston.' The nurse noted her blood pressure. 'How did you sleep last night, me lovely?'

'I was a little restless, I woke in the night. Ben said I was screaming, but I don't remember. Are the police still outside?'

'They are, me Lucy, I think your friendly policeman will be there until you're discharged,' she said, writing the obs on her notes and clipping them back onto the end of the bed. 'How's the pain and the headaches, are you managing? Or do you need a few more painkillers?'

'My head hurts and my ribs ache.' Lucy tried to wriggle up the bed, each small move sending a shooting pain through her body. 'When did Ben leave?' she asked, taking a sip of water through a straw. Her mouth was dry and her lips still stung. She could barely feel the straw against them.

'He left at seven, told me to tell you he was making a sail for you,' Doris said with a smile.

'He did? It was what I would say to him when he'd leave after staying at mine. I'd always ask him to make a sail for me. Did he say when he was coming back?' she asked. 'I can't find my mobile.'

'I'm not sure, me lovely. I can find out if you like. How does that sound?' Doris said. 'I'll be back in a jiffy.'

The room was quiet again, Lucy stared out of the window and watched the two pigeons cooing on the sill. Head pounding, she looked at her wrists: they were raw from his grip, bruised and cut. Her eyes glazed over and the room went dark.

***

Get in, you filthy whore. You wore that dress. What for? Get up, slowly. Get up! You bitch, you dirty bitch. You ruined everything. Look what you've driven me to! You played a game. Now I've beaten you at your own game. You wore that dress. You whore.

***

The cries from Lucy could be heard down the corridor.

'No, stop, please. No, you're hurting me. No please, no! I'm frightened … I didn't. Ben … Ben … *Ben!*' Her piercing screams had the police officer open the door hurriedly and enter the room. 'Lucy, it's PC Hughes.' Doris came running in as Lucy tossed and turned in the bed. 'Ben, help, somebody help.'

'Lucy, it's me, Doris, your nurse, I'm here, you're safe. Here, me lovely, have a little sip of water. Oh my, what has he done to you?' Doris carefully held the plastic cup as Lucy sipped from the straw. Her breathing was heavy and fast, her forehead wet from perspiration. Doris took a damp cloth and carefully dabbed at her face and forehead. 'There, there, me pretty.' The policeman on guard stood in the room, his own heart racing. He'd never witnessed at close hand the aftermath of trauma.

'He was here in the room, he locked the door,' she stammered, the tears rolling down her face, her hands shaking. 'Then I saw the beach, I saw the beach, he dragged me.' Her breathing was fast and uncontrolled between each word. 'He was there, on the beach, it was him, it was him. Make it go away, make it go away. Get him off me, get him off me. He's here. There by the door.' Her screams of fear reverberated down the corridor. Her gasping wails echoed around. It was more than crying; it was the kind of desolate sobbing, wailing that comes from a person drained of all hope, terrified. She lay in the arms of Doris.

'Me lovely, let it out, I'm here,' Doris said, rocking her in her cradled embrace. Lucy's breathing, ragged and gasping, began to slow and ease away, the gentle rock from the warm arms of Doris taking her to a place of serenity. She closed her eyes and dreamt of Ben. Then it came again, her breathing hard and heavy.

'Help me,' she cried. 'Make it stop. Get him off. Get him off me!'

Doris held her in her all-encompassing arms. Lucy could hear the melodic beat of her heart as her own heart raced, pulsating like a beating drum out of time.

'I keep seeing things and faces are muddled and sometimes it's Ben and then I think Ben wouldn't do that and then it's Charlie and I can hear the sea washing up and loud cries of the gulls but I can see nothing, just a bright light, and then I hear the children, their voices in the waves. And then it's cold and it's still and it's dark and I've gone.' The slow rock from Doris was like the ebb and flow of the sea's waves on the beach. There was calm once more.

The policeman left the room and closed the door quietly so as not to unsettle Lucy's current calm. He took out his phone, trying to steady his own shaking hand, and dialled through to London.

'CID. DC Palmer speaking.'

'Morning, it's PC Hughes speaking. Can I speak with the DI on Operation Butterfly?'

The internal line buzzed. 'DI Phillips speaking.'

'Sir, it's PC Hughes on Operation Butterfly at Colchester General. It's Lucy Carter, she's had another trauma attack, only this time she's mentioned the beach, sir.'

'What did she say?' DI Phillips asked, taking his pen and notebook.

'She screamed, "Get him off me." She mentioned a locked room, then, "Help me," again and again. She then screamed, "He's at the beach, get him off me, help me." She said something like "I heard the children in the waves". Sir, she's beginning to relive it all,' PC Hughes said, as the tea lady clattered her trolley past him, with an urn of hot water and a tin of biscuits, the cups and saucers rattling as she passed.

DI Phillips listened intently as PC Hughes recounted the hysterical moments from minutes earlier.

'She is indeed. Thank you, Hughes. Keep me up to date with any further information on Lucy's well-being.' DI Phillips closed the call.

'Children? Who are the children?' he said to himself. 'Possible eyewitnesses?'

The red light on his external line lit up.

'DI Phillips? Jim Finlay here. We've got some results from Felixstowe.'

Phillips stood up and pressed the speakerphone button.

'I'm listening.'

'The particles found on the trainers match those from the particles of sand taken from Harwich beach on Friday the 21st of February. The shoe size is a ten, which matches the suspect's size. This has been confirmed from his records at Wandsworth Prison. We've also got a positive DNA match on fingerprints taken from the steering wheel and the Audi's boot latch; a particle of hair found in the boot again matches the DNA profile taken from our suspect,' Jim Finlay said.

'What are your thoughts?' Phillips asked as he stared out of the window across Fulham Broadway.

'My guess is he had a bag that was in the boot. A small fibre was found on the boot's latch, probably got caught as he's removed the bag. A black bag, possibly a rucksack, maybe a change of clothes, shoes, water, I'd say.'

'Anything else?' DI Phillips said, turning to take another file from the drawer behind the desk.

'Particles of blood and hair were found on the rear rail of the passenger seat. The blood and hair match Lucy's,' Finlay said.

'So, she struck her head on the rail. She had to have been lying in the rear footwell,' Phillips said as he took his pen and noted the findings.

'The evidence is leaning that way. Another thing you might be interested in: a fibre taken from the trainer matches that of a fibre found in a space where a container had been. The profile for this DNA ends there,' Finlay said.

'So, he was in a container?' Phillips said. 'Which had already left the dock?'

'Exactly. Either side of the container are two blue Sealand containers on our still shots; they're in berths nine and seven,' Finlay said. 'We are still running profiles but that's what we have at the moment.'

'Good work, Jim, many thanks.'

'Just one other thing. There was another residue found on the trainers. It flummoxed us a little, as most of the DNA has been human extractions or sand.'

'Another residue?' Phillips' brow furrowed.

'Yup, residue from what appears to be the firing of a handgun. Either already on the trainers or used that night?'

'A handgun. So, he's armed?'

'Potentially, can't be sure, but it's likely.'

'Your thoughts, Jim?'

'To break a lock, air holes, maybe. It's a clean residue.'

Phillips ended the call and mulled over the conversation. Not only was he dealing with a fugitive, he potentially had an armed man on the run.

He took up his notes and called Andy Roberts's direct line.

'Andy, good morning. DI Phillips here. I'd like some information on a container in what appears to be berth eight in our stills. How long has that been a vacant berth?'

'One moment, Detective Inspector.' Phillips could hear Roberts as he tapped in and pulled up the screens for cargo shipped. 'Berth eight are Maersk's sister company Sealand's shipping containers. Normally it's dry goods being exported, such as mechanical, medical, plastic supplies. The container was for a private haulage company and contained household goods, tables, chairs, that type of thing. Probably a relocation. That container was marked as being shipped to Valencia.'

'Is it scanned before it leaves the port for thermal body heat?' Phillips asked, piecing together the movements of Charlie.

'Not unless something looked wrong to the boys on the dockside or we were suspicious of its contents. The containers are airtight and loaded pretty much immediately for shipment. Berth eight was set to depart the docks on Saturday as the first shipment out.' He paused for a moment, scanning his screen. 'Let me see, yes here we are, a shipment confirmed at 4 a.m. on Saturday the 22nd of February.'

Phillips scribbled the dates down. 'And how long is the trip to Valencia?' He had him - Charlie had to be inside the container.

'Valencia is a six-day crossing, direct with no stops. However, it was a private shipment so it would then be picked up by a private haulage company and we wouldn't have had any further information on its whereabouts once it left the port at Valencia.'

'Right, OK. Many thanks for this, Andy. I'll be in touch.'

Phillips ended the call and looked out of the window. He could see the business of Fulham Broadway from his fourth-floor office. Pedestrians milling around, the same face of the Big Issue seller outside the tube station trying to get a few pounds for his hours on the street until he returned to his lodgings. North End Road was a hive of activity as the market traders got into full swing selling fruit and veg. The honking of a horn as a pedestrian dared to cross the road on a green light for the traffic, sticking his finger up to the irate driver. A typical Wednesday morning on the Broadway with the hustle and bustle of London's streets.

Phillips stared out and sighed reluctantly. 'He's trying to get to Spain,' he said to himself. 'Martinez is Spanish, his mother is Spanish. I'm closing in on you, Charlie, I'm closing in on you. You are going to walk right into my trap. My Butterfly Trap.'

Phillips' door swung open.

'Right, gather round please,' he said. The team of twelve detectives working on Operation Butterfly stood close to the board.

'Right guys, we have positive results on our suspect, Charlie Wainwright, who is currently on licence after three years being served at HMP Wandsworth. He is a white British male and confirmed DNA as abducting Lucy Carter on Thursday the 20th of February. We have a profile match of the sand from Harwich beach found at Felixstowe in and around the abandoned Audi Q3. The white Nike trainers found are those of our suspect. Interestingly, forensics have picked up the residue of a small firearm on them. A positive DNA match to Lucy Carter's has been found in the rear of the hire car. Evidence has shown that she was more than likely gagged, most definitely bound by her wrists due to the injuries sustained. I believe that during her journey from her home at number 3 Lambourne Terrace she would have been hidden in the footwell, bound and gagged. The injury sustained on her left temple has been caused through the immediate impact of a sharp metal object – in this case, the front passenger seat's rail. Traces of blood and hair were taken from it and the DNA profile matches that of our victim. Her body was left for dead, with the suspect's view being it would probably be washed away by the incoming tide and never found. However, that evening was a low tide, hence her body remaining on the beach unconscious, presumed dead by our suspect.'

'What about the suspect, guv? Where would he have gone? Is he armed, then?' DS Kennedy asked.

'I'm coming to that.' Phillips turned to DS Murphy: 'Any more on his mother, Murphy?'

'I do, guv. I think I have a positive lead on our suspect's parents. What I've got so far is that Charlie Wainwright is the son of a Robert Wainwright, now deceased. He died in June 1992, after losing power in his own light aircraft and crashing into the Mediterranean. The plane's wreckage and his body were recovered from the shallow shores on the coastline of Valencia, no foul play recorded. His body is buried at Brompton Road cemetery. His mother is Sofia Martinez – married to Robert Wainwright but never took his name. She's a non-UK resident who holds a dual nationality passport: British and Spanish,' Murphy said confidently.

'Good work. So, this leads me onto your question, DS Kennedy. Where has he gone? Where has he gone indeed. On Saturday the 22nd of February a container holding household goods was shipped to Valencia. It left Felixstowe at 4 a.m. on a non-stop route to its destination. The residue found on his trainers would suggest he is armed,' Phillips continued.

'Guv, how many days will the shipment take?' DC Parker asked.

'Good question. It's a six-day crossing, arrival time Friday the 28th of February.'

'So, we can stop the ship in its tracks, get the RAF to scramble and intercept it?' DC Parker piped up.

Phillips threw a look at him and sighed, 'This isn't James Bond, Detective Constable.' The team laughed at the satire of Phillips and the stupid innocence of a young detective. The comedy of Parker's naivety lifted the seriousness of the briefing and allowed the team to relax for a brief moment. Scrambling jets did seem like a rather thrilling experience and they doubtless all fancied themselves in the shoes of James Bond, although none of them would have admitted that on the CID floor. The Major Incident Team was about as Bond-like as it would become, without even a snifter of a Martini, shaken not stirred.

'Simmer down.' Phillips flashed a look across the team.

'If he's on a container ship, sir, he's a day ahead of us, and still at sea potentially?' a blonde DC said, looking at her scribbled notes. She was new to the department.

'Absolutely, which is why our only chance of getting him before the container is unloaded onto its haulage lorry would be to call in backup,' Phillips said. 'We'd have to call in the Navy. The container's in international waters.'

The female officer asked again, 'What's the feasibility of that, sir? I mean, the Navy wouldn't necessarily have jurisdiction, would they, unless the shipping container was flagged as a UK vessel?' The men in the room turned to the DC, who scribbled more on her notes. She looked up and blushed a little under the gaze of a dozen eyes on her, all men. She cleared her throat. 'I mean, sir, wouldn't we have to involve the Home Office - Whitehall?'

Phillips turned to her. He liked her enthusiasm and acute grasp of the facts of the operation. 'DC ...?' he said, probing for a name that might follow.

'DC Milson, sir.' Her cheeks took on a hue of pink and she wriggled back in her seat.

'You seem to know a lot about military operations?' Phillips quizzed gently.

'Fancies her chances as a Bond girl,' another detective joked. Phillips threw him a look. 'Reel it in. You're not indispensable on my team.'

'Guv,' the officer said, looking down.

'We potentially will need to call in for support from the Navy. Whether the Home Office will be forthcoming is another story. I can push with the knowledge he is potentially armed. Support from the MoD is crucial in the ship's interception. The risk we have is a dead man arriving in a container, and I want him alive.'

'Sir, what about the coastguards, could they not assist?' DC Milson asked.

Phillips' look flashed back to Milson. 'Normally, this would be a very positive means of interception, Milson. However, the coastguards are not armed and if we have a fugitive with a firearm any amount of damage could be done. Lives lost. He's stuck in a container, and his mind is going to be somewhat imbalanced, delirious, unhinged. A frenzied attack could happen.'

'So military interception, sir.'

'Yup, if I can swing it. Right - DC Banks, I want you to locate the grave where Robert Wainwright has been buried, see if there's been any recent activity there. DC Milson, I'd like you to work closely with DS Kennedy for the interim. I'd like you to visit Miss Jones; I need a female to coax further information from her. She might engage better with a female officer. Murphy, I want you to look into Wainwright's work habits, see whether he has any accounts in different names. DC Parker and Milson, you will be assigned to work on undercover surveillance and the protection of Lucy Carter in Essex once she is discharged. You will be residing at 10 Lambourne Terrace. Parker, you own your own graphic design company working from home. Milson, you'll act as his partner. Keep it real. Right, that's it, MIT dismissed.'

Phillips left the team and went back to his office. He logged into his PC and read the file Andy Roberts had sent on the shipment. As he did, he pressed the speaker phone and dialled out. He took a cigarette from his Benson and Hedges packet and twiddled it between his fingers. The line rang out.

'Good morning, Home Office, how can I direct your call?'

'DI Phillips, Met Police. Can you put me through to the Secretary of State.'

'Certainly, sir. Can I ask what the call is regarding?' replied the operator.

'MACP. I'd like a direct call, not the PA,' Phillips replied.

'Military Aid to the Civil Power, sir. Which station are you calling from?'

'Fulham.'

'Thank you, sir, I'm just putting you through.'

Phillips listened to the obligatory, hackneyed caller-waiting music. The Home Office had opted for Eric Coates's The Dam Busters March.

'Sir, the line is busy, would you like to keep holding?'

'Yes, I'll hold.'

There was a beeping sound and the line rang through.

'Andrew Peters,' a well-spoken voice said.

'Good morning, Secretary of State, Detective Inspector Phillips, Met Police, speaking.'

'DI Phillips, good morning, how can I help you?'

'I'm working on a covert operation with the Major Incident Team. You may have seen the news in Essex of the brutal attack on a female left on the beach?'

'I'm aware of it, yes. How is the victim?'

'Stable. The female attacked is a Miss Lucy Carter and had moved from London and taken up residence in Essex to escape an abusive relationship. She was left for dead by our suspect, a Mr Charlie Wainwright from London, Fulham to be precise.'

'Lucy Carter? As in the author of The Defence?'

'Yes, sir. Lucy Carter the author.'

'Right, terrible news, but how does this involve us? I have here you've requested an MACP?'

'That's correct. The suspect is believed to be on a container shipment to Valencia and I require military support.'

'Are the coastguards not adequate support?' Andrew Peters responded.

'We believe the fugitive to be armed. The coastguard for this operation is obsolete. I require naval assistance to intercept the ship in order for me to make an arrest. We just don't have the means within the Met to handle this alone.'

'Can you not wait and make an arrest when the ship docks? These ships are gargantuan steel beasts. I mean, it would just be hazardous at sea. We can't just go storming onto German or French sovereignty vessels. We have fraught relations as it is with these countries and Brexit. This is just another upset to add to the list.'

'Understood, Secretary of State, but I need to act rapidly. If I wait for the ship to reach Valencia, I will have a dead body on my hands, and I want him alive. There is reason to believe that not only is he armed but he is a potential danger to women.'

'Right. Where is the shipment at present?'

'I believe steaming in international waters. It's due to dock in Valencia on the 28th February.'

'And the vessel is UK sovereignty?'

'It is, Secretary of State.'

Andrew Peters sighed heavily and tapped his fingers on the desk. 'I'm not convinced this is an MoD operation. I mean it just seems a little far-fe ...'

Phillips closed him down. 'With all due respect, I have been a serving officer with the Met for a number of years. We have an armed, potentially dangerous criminal on board a British shipment. I need to make an arrest and I cannot do that without the aid of the MoD. As I have said, if I leave this vessel, I will have a dead man on board. I want him alive. I don't need to remind you of the field day the press will have with this. She's a much-loved author and guaranteed I will not allow this to become my department's problem when I have made it very clear to you what is needed. I cannot stress enough the support that is required and at this stage I would expect the call to be made to the Ministry of Defence and communications to become an open dialogue. Without question.' The line went quiet.

Phillips wasn't going to let a politician be the deciding factor in a criminal case. A man who had very little experience in the real world of crime. A politician who pushed paper and policies around with ambiguity at the best of times.

Peters' breath was heavy on the line. 'I'm going to have to enlist support from another department and contact the MoD. Leave it with me. I'll have a call back to you later this afternoon – I feel time is of the essence here, is that correct?'

'It is. Many thanks for your time and co-operation on the matter.' Phillips closed the call. 'Bloody politicians ...' he said under his breath as he took his cigarette pack and Zippo lighter from his desk and made his way across the department.

He passed DS Kennedy's desk. 'Kennedy, take Milson now and visit Rachel Jones.'

'Guv.'

Phillips stood at the coffee machine and pressed the espresso image. A plastic cup dropped down and the sludge-like coffee poured out. He left the department to smoke his cigarette in the car park.

DS Kennedy and DC Milson waited in the squad car at the junction of Munster Road as the shrill piercing beeps sounded for pedestrians to cross, ricocheting off the beautiful Victorian terraces, with clean white shutters masking their windows and elegant front doors with brass numbers. Small children crossed the road, covering their ears from the abrasive sound, whilst being pulled along by their nannies as they stopped mid-road to point and stare at the waiting police car. It all looked far too exciting: a police car with an angry-looking grille, blue lights unlit and bright yellow and blue markings. Kennedy flashed the blue lights and smiled at the children as their faces lit up with the excitement of seeing the flashing light as a morning treat.

The squad car pulled up outside the apartment block behind a silver Jaguar parked outside with a layer of London's grime and dust on it. At the main door of Mansion House, DS Kennedy held his finger on the buzzer of flat four.

'Hello,' came a female voice.

'Miss Jones?'

'Yes.'

'Miss Jones, it's DS Kennedy and DC Milson from Fulham police station. Could we come in please?'

The door buzzed and unlocked.

The first-floor corridor was clean and freshly carpeted. The two officers knocked at Rachel's door.

'Miss Jones?' said DC Milson.

'Yes, come in.'

She led them through to the sitting room. It had huge great double-aspect sash windows which overlooked Waldermar Avenue and Colehill Lane. She looked nervous, unsure of why she needed to be contacted again after so many years. She had already told DS Murphy all she could remember when they first arrested Charlie. She knew then something wasn't right, something had happened to Lucy. She remembered her saying she'd fallen, split her lip. She hadn't seen or heard from Lucy for years now. Why were they coming back to question her? Was she a suspect? She gripped the cuffs of her sleeves.

Both officers took a seat on the sofa, adjusting the cushions behind them.

'Please don't be nervous,' DC Milson said, sensing Rachel's anxiety. 'We just need to ask a few questions about your neighbour, Charlie Wainwright. Is that OK?' She took her notebook and pen from her bag.

'I'll try to help. Is Lucy OK? I heard the terrible news. How is she?' Rachel asked.

'She's in hospital at the moment. She's in a stable but critical condition and under police protection,' DS Kennedy said.

'I feel terrible,' Rachel said.

'You feel terrible? Why?' DC Milson asked. Her tone was soft and engaging. Although she was a police officer, she had a reassuring manner, conveying that she was on Rachel's side.

'I knew things weren't right at home for her, I knew she was hiding something. But I didn't do anything.'

'Didn't do anything,' Milson coaxed. 'What could you have done?'

'I don't know, something I guess, anything? Where's Charlie now? He hasn't been here since the attack. Nobody has been to his flat.'

'You told my colleague, DS Murphy, when he first arrested Mr Wainwright that you'd known Charlie for a number of years – seven, I believe,' DS Kennedy said, reading the notes Murphy had given him.

'Yes, that's right, I knew him before Lucy moved in. We were good friends.'

'And how well did you know his family?' Milson asked, her head tilted slightly, her body leaning forwards a little.

'I knew his mother a little, I'd met her a few times, but Charlie rarely spoke about her otherwise. Their relationship I think was slightly fraught.'

'D'you know why?' Milson asked, again noting each word Rachel said, her eye contact engaging but soft.

'I don't know … he was angry with her. He didn't ever say much, just that she drank, and he blamed her.'

DC Milson looked up from her pad, her eyes narrowed. 'Blamed her? For what exactly?'

'I don't know. His dad, his school – honestly, I really don't know.'

'Do you know where his mother is now? Does she live in London?' Milson asked, pushing a little harder with her questions but still keeping Rachel at ease.

'No, she doesn't live in London. She's Spanish.'

'Do you know her name, perhaps?' DC Milson wrote a little more on her pad.

'Sofia Martinez. I remember it because I've always loved the name Sofia. But that's all I know.'

'Rachel - can I call you Rachel?' DC Milson quizzed.

'Yes.'

'Did you ever know Charlie in any other way?'

'What d'you mean?'

'Were you always just friends?'

'Meaning?' Rachel felt herself blush a little and played with her hands. DC Milson watched her hands and her body language. She leant forward a little more.

'Were you ever romantically linked to Charlie?' Her eyes were still on Rachel's hands.

'Oh God, I was drunk. It meant nothing. Once. It happened once.'

'Once?'

'We slept together. We were a bit drunk. It was long before Lucy was on the scene. Umm, it just wasn't my thing.' She squirmed a little in her chair and her eyes darted to the window.

'Wasn't your thing?' DC Milson coaxed gently.

'He was just a little rough. I guess I put it down to alcohol. It didn't happen again, though, and we didn't ever mention it again. He just wasn't my type.'

'Rough, you say. Like S&M?'

Rachel could feel the warmth flush through her cheeks. She wriggled in her chair again. 'Umm ...' She looked out of the window, avoiding eye contact. 'No, he was just a bit rough, just ... umm ... he held me down quite tightly?'

'Consented?'

Rachel took her glance back to DC Milson. 'Yeah, I guess. I didn't stop him, it was just rough.'

'Did you consent, Rachel?' DC Milson's approach was more direct.

'Yeah, I think so. I was drunk. I don't remember.'

'OK. Did he hurt you?'

Rachel squirmed in her chair, her hands knotted themselves, her fingers twisting around each other.

'Oh God, he used tape, we were both drunk and high ... I took some coke with him. I don't do drugs, really, I don't even smoke. I don't know why I did then. I don't remember if I said yes. I just don't remember.'

'It's OK, Rachel. Are you OK? Do you need some water?'

'No, thank you, I'm fine.'

Milson wrote a little more and looked at DS Kennedy.

'You mentioned his father, Rachel, what do you know about him?' Milson asked, reading her notes and knowing he was dead.

'Very little. Charlie really didn't talk about him. I think he died when he was a little boy. But I really don't know. I'm sorry. I just don't know.'

'Rachel, you've been really helpful, thank you,' DC Milson said as she stood up and straightened her trousers, brushing them down.

'We've got everything we need at this stage. Thank you for your co-operation, Rachel,' DS Kennedy affirmed.

As Rachel opened the front door for them, she stopped. 'Please, will you tell Lucy I send my love and I'm thinking of her.'

'I will,' DC Milson said. The officers left the apartment.

The sun was high in the sky in Fulham and the buds on the tree-lined avenue were just beginning to show. The noise of the traffic hummed around them. The sound of a siren blared through the streets. Kennedy unlocked the car and got into the driver's seat.

'What do you think?' Milson asked. 'The DI's got to be right about this. He's in Valencia, isn't he?'

'I reckon. I liked your style, by the way. You had a gut feeling there had been a sexual relationship between them.' Kennedy turned the engine on and pulled out slowly, heading back towards the station.

'Woman's instinct. He's a good-looking guy, regardless of what he's done, she's an attractive girl. I had a gut feeling. But it looks like he has some kind of dislike towards women. You're not normally rough on the first time.'

'Dunno about that. Have you read Fifty Shades of Grey?' Kennedy joked.

She looked at him and smiled, but rolled her eyes. 'No.'

Back at her desk, DC Milson pulled up the screen for Operation Butterfly and added the information she had collated from Rachel Jones.

DS Kennedy made his way straight to the DI's office and knocked on the door. Phillips beckoned through the internal window for him to come in.

'How did your meeting go with Rachel Jones?' he asked, twiddling an unlit cigarette in his hand.

'Good, guv. She gave us quite a bit of information. She didn't know much about his father, other than she thought he died when Wainwright was a boy. But she'd met the mother a couple of times. She confirmed she was Spanish and lived in Valencia and her name is Sofia Martinez. She said she hadn't seen Charlie since his release or the attack, and nobody had been to his flat.'

'Right, good work.' The DS turned to leave the office, but Phillips ruffled the notes on his desk and called out, 'Kennedy?'

'Guv?' He turned, leaving his hand on the door handle.

'How was DC Milson?'

'She asked most of the questions, guv. She knew how to approach Rachel Jones. She got her to open up. She was good.'

'Open up?'

'Rachel Jones admitted to having a sexual relationship with Wainwright. He was rough with her.'

'I knew it. I knew there'd be another Lucy, who escaped his clasp. Thought Milson would be good, she's following her gut. Right, follow me.' Phillips moved towards the door and led Kennedy out onto the department.

'Guys, gather round,' Phillips said, his voice raised above the banter of the department. The MIT gathered around him.

'Right guys, we have further information on Charlie Wainwright. Rachel Jones has confirmed she had a sexual relationship with him prior to his relationship with Lucy Carter. One which shows him taking a dominant role, a possible threat and a danger to women. We've also had further information to suggest that our suspect is heading out of the country with Spain as our main country lead. Sofia Martinez has been confirmed as his mother and she resides in Valencia, we think?

'I want to get as many leads as we can on Martinez's exact whereabouts. It's his obvious destination. I want her address, and all authorities primed and alerted at passport control and all surrounding countries' border controls.

'Murphy, I want you to contact Interpol again and speak with the police in the area. I want a mugshot of Wainwright circulated with the Spanish police and border controls. Keep the media at bay - we need to run this operation covertly. If he gets a whiff of us on his tail, we will lose him.

'DC Barratt, I want you to work closely with DS Murphy, find what other bank accounts he has in his name or an alias, see if there have been any movements in his equity. Lucy mentioned he had equity clients; dig deeper with that. Money laundering, whatever, find it. DC Palmer, I want you to now work alongside DS Kennedy and get more information on the mother, her circle of friends etc. DC Hobbs, find out what private haulage companies took delivery of a container from Felixstowe to Valencia containing household goods. We are on his tracks and we're going to bring him in. Parker and Milson, start to prepare for your undercover surveillance. I have spoken with the Secretary of State about getting an MACP. His approval will hopefully be confirmed this afternoon. Richard Havers, top brass, has approved at Met level.'

Phillips paused and took a deep breath. 'Briefing dismissed.'

Chapter Five

Wednesday, 26th February
Fulham Police Station, London

Phillips' internal line rang.

'CID, Detective Inspector Phillips speaking.'

'Sir, I have Andrew Peters, Home Office, on the line,' came the voice from the police switchboard.

'Put him through.' Phillips switched to the speaker phone. 'Detective Inspector Phillips.'

'Good afternoon, Detective Inspector, Andrew Peters here. I will make this brief. I have spoken with the MoD and the governing bodies on your requirement for an MACP. I've also received confirmation from Richard Havers that he's sanctioned your request and has pushed for the MACP to be forthcoming without further delay. I have acknowledged your concerns in-line with the Met and specialist operations, and due to this I have called an urgent Cobra meeting at six o'clock this evening. I'd like you to come along. Contact has been made with Richard Havers - the Assistant Commissioner for Specialist Operations at the Met police, no introductions needed there - he will be present. Also in attendance will be the Royal Navy's Lieutenant Commander Smith-Jones, along with Captain Robertson from the MoD and myself. A car will pick you up at 5.15 p.m. and drive you to Whitehall. I trust this meets with your approval.'

'It does, I'll be there.' Phillips hung up. He looked at his watch: it was four-thirty.

He knew Richard Havers well. He also knew that Havers despised thinly veiled humans who had used their kudos, power and privilege to allow them to go undetected as liars and bullies. Havers had come from Essex police, where he'd worked his way up through the ranks straight from school and transferred to the Met as a Superintendent. A little like Phillips himself, with no privileged background but just with a strong set of values, morals and loyalty to the people he worked with. Phillips a few years younger and lower-ranking, had learnt much from working under him. Havers was an outstanding officer and his connection with Essex had made Phillips' case even stronger.

Phillips buzzed through to DS Murphy's phone.

'Guv?'

'My office.' Phillips beckoned through the window for the DS to enter. 'Murphy, what are your plans this evening?'

'Nothing, guv.'

'Well, you now have plans. I have a meeting at Whitehall with the Secretary of State, Richard Havers, the Royal Navy and the MoD for an MACP.'

'Interception, guv?'

'Exactly that. I need you to attend with me. Whitehall are sending a car for 5.15 p.m., so can you make damn sure you are up to date on your files on Wainwright and bring them with you. Havers, I know from old, and he'll support this request for military support. All our leads are pointing towards Wainwright being on a container, and if the ship isn't intercepted, he will without a doubt be dead on arrival.'

'Guv.' Murphy left his office.

Phillips pulled up the files on Charlie Wainwright and pressed print. His printer whirred into action and darted out fifty-six pages on Charlie from his arrest over three years ago to date. All DNA files collated and reports and statements from key witnesses and acquaintances.

After flipping through the papers one last time, he took the file and placed it to one side on his desk. The internal line buzzed through.

'DI Phillips.'

'Sir, I have a government car waiting in the car park for you.'

'I'm coming down.' Phillips took his keys, case file, navy blue mac and his packet of cigarettes and Zippo lighter and left his office, signalling to Murphy to join him. Together they left the department.

A black, armoured, custom-built Jaguar XJ Sentinel supercharged with a five-litre engine purred quietly in the car park amongst the squad cars. An officer from the Metropolitan's specialist protection walked around from the driver's side and opened the rear passenger door.

'Nice car, guv,' Murphy said as he straightened his jacket and adjusted his cuffs.

'Savour the moment, Murphy.'

'Sir,' the officer nodded from the specialist protection branch.

The car was sleek inside, not too dissimilar to Phillips' BMW in its streamline beauty. The spec perhaps somewhat different. Phillips' BMW, an unmarked police car with a few impressive toys, wasn't a patch on this vehicle. It offered 13mm explosive-resistant steel plate underneath the body, something that the BMW didn't come with. It had titanium- and Kevlar-lined cabins, armoured windows with bullet-resistant polycarbonate toughened glass and run-flat tyres. From the back seat, Phillips peered at the front panel systems. There was a self-contained oxygen supply to protect the passengers against a chemical or biological attack.

Murphy looked at Phillips, his eyes wide, his eyebrows raised. His mind was working overtime like a small boy's. This was his James Bond moment. He spied the button that, when pressed, would release tear gas and other crowd dispersants, and gestured to Phillips.

'Some car,' Phillips said to the officer driving.

'That it is, sir. A little different to our squad cars. A few more added extras,' he said wryly, his eyes looking in the rear-view mirror at his passengers.

'Like?' Murphy asked, running his hand along the smooth lines of the interior.

'It can withstand the blast of fifteen kilos of TNT. Not your normal car, sir.'

'Bloody hell, wouldn't mind seeing this on Top Gear. Jeremy Clarkson would be all over this,' Murphy said, totally engaged in the small talk about a governmental car, which was giving him the James Bond moment of the day.

'He certainly would, sir. It's got a five-litre supercharged engine, top speed of 121mph, absolute dream.'

'And from stationary?' Phillips asked.

'Sixty miles per hour, in about 9.4 seconds.'

'Fast then, impressive,' Phillips said, enthralled by the specifications of this car.

'Certainly is, sir.'

The officer drove through Knightsbridge, a wealthy part of London's west end. The streets were still busy with shoppers milling about. The lights in the immaculately dressed windows began to illuminate as the sun dipped in the sky. A throng of pedestrians filing down the stairs to the underground clutched bundles of designer shopping bags and the obligatory green Harrods bags with tourist gifts inside. Black cabs performed U-turns as they were hailed by random pedestrians. Couriers on their bikes wove in and out of the traffic like snakes through long wild grass.

The Jaguar moved so smoothly and rapidly that it seemed like only moments had passed before they pulled up in Whitehall. The white, smooth stone building, dirtied from the exhausts and general dirt and grime of London, had a greyish cast. Huge great sash-styled windows flanked its walls from top to bottom, high enough to shield the inside from any curious eyes peering in from the passers-by. It stood majestically, a building untouched and unscathed in wartime England adjacent to 10, Downing Street. The pillared balustrade-style wall gave it a sense of importance and grandeur as the huge yellow markings on the road demarcated the bus stop for the modernised Routemasters and the simple life of normal people to-ing and fro-ing in their normal everyday lives.

A huddle of Japanese tourists stood and busily clicked away with their cameras before they made their way up to Westminster. The officer got out and nodded to the security guard at the entrance. He held the car door open for DS Murphy as Phillips let himself out roadside, pulling his mac in as the breeze caught under it, blowing it into the oncoming traffic. His files were tucked away in a leather pocket file. The government car indicated and pulled out, slinking off into the traffic.

They stood on the pavement and looked out across the main thoroughfare. The tip of Big Ben's bell tower popped up above the tree-lined Westminster street, and a myriad of Union Jacks flapped lightly in the evening breeze.

On either side of the blue double doors, screwed into the wall, were two brass plates, highly polished and buffed and engraved in large black capital letters. The left one read Cabinet Office and the right read 70 Whitehall.

DI Phillips and DS Murphy both flashed their badges and were let in. The building's interior gave a sense of old and new. The walls leading off the main reception hall were a simple brickwork and the floor a terracotta and dark blue patterned tile. The reception area had a highly polished white floor overlooked by the glass-lined balconied atrium.

They waited in the atrium until a petite girl with mousey-brown hair greeted them and guided them along the tiled corridor. She led them to Suite A, the meeting room that was assigned for COBR. (The A had been added by the media over time.)

A carved oak banquet table sat in the middle of the room with at least twenty chairs around it. The walls were adorned with portraits of political dignitaries. The deep red and blue, swirly patterned carpet was laid corner to corner and hoovered meticulously with not an ounce of dirt or fluff on it. A room full of pomp that neither police officer had seen the likes of before.

Phillips caught Murphy's eye, and they both knew they were thinking of the same thing. Their CID department, which was a million miles away from this austere, decadent room of grandeur and opulence. Its grey felt-like flooring, with a partition wall and internal windows that shook whenever a door was closed. Its plastic white blinds that rattled from any draft that caught them. No luxurious Hildon water, only a large water cooler that spewed out crinkly plastic cups. And a few accolades of the best of the Met adorning one wall. Rather than huge gilded frames of ministers been and gone and historical figures of importance, there were instead mugshots of the most wanted criminals. One of them being Charlie Wainwright.

A tray holding six tumbler glasses and three large bottles of Hildon water sat in the middle of the table. Phillips brushed his hand along the table; not a speck of dust came up on his fingertips. He could almost see his reflection in the highly polished surface. He walked around the table to observe the world outside from the windows. The traffic outside moved without any sound. The room was totally soundproofed.

'Nice joint, guv,' Murphy said as he took in the immense portraits on the wall.

The door opened and a lady in a white blouse and a straight black skirt carried in a tray with a pot of tea and fresh coffee, a jug of cream and milk, and six cups and saucers. She placed them in the centre of the table.

'The Secretary of State will be here shortly. Please do help yourself to tea and coffee.' She left the room, the door closing with a soft cushioning sound.

Phillips looked at his watch: it was three minutes to six. He stood with his hands behind his back, still wearing his mac. The door opened again, and a man entered the room: tall, dark hair, slightly greying at the sides, clean-shaven. In a black uniform decorated on the epaulettes and breast.

'Tony, good to see you.'

'Sir,' Phillips replied, extending his hand. Their handshake was firm. 'This is DS Murphy. He's working on Operation Butterfly with me. Murphy, this is Richard Havers.'

'Good to meet you, Detective Sergeant. How is the victim, Tony?'

'She's stable, sir, left for dead on the beach, not a nice operation to be working on. Domestic violence at its worst.'

'Well, you have my total support, Tony. I will push this through. I have already sanctioned it at paper level, hence this meeting. My wife was particularly saddened by the events, she likes her books. An avid fan.'

'Thank you, sir.'

The door opened and two officers joined the table.

'Lieutenant Commander Smith-Jones,' said the first officer, extending his hand to the three men. 'Royal Navy, but please call me Henry.'

'Captain Robertson, MoD,' said the second officer.

'Pleased to meet you, sir,' Phillips said as he shook his hand.

'Please call me, Tim, sod the formality,' Robertson said.

'Coffee, gents?' Captain Robertson poured the freshly made hot black liquid from the silver percolator pot into the porcelain cups. 'Is Andrew Peters coming? He's late.' The punctuality of the Force and Forces was still acutely precise. The carriage clock on the marble mantelpiece that framed the large fireplace ticked, its gilt hands at five past six.

The door brushed open. Andrew Peters entered the room, dressed in a blue suit, white shirt and blue tie. His blond hair was slightly ruffled at the front with a short back and sides.

'Gents, sorry I'm late. I got caught up with another meeting, ran overtime as these things do. I see you've all made your acquaintance and have a coffee each, so shall we set to and begin without further delay?' The six men sat in close proximity around the table.

Peters began rustling through the papers that had been requested from Phillips and stamped and signed by the Assistant Commissioner of the Met.

'So, what do we have here? A request for an MACP with your stamp of approval to sanction it, Richard,' he said as he turned to Havers. 'I mean, for this sort of operation it's very short notice, is it not? It's just it doesn't seem feasible, a little absurd perhaps to the taxpayer. I'm not sure the PM will ever agree. And you know all too well if I back this and it goes wrong, I've got some serious explaining to do.'

Havers interjected, 'Unfortunately, Andrew, with criminal operations, we don't have the luxury of time. Every part of a criminal investigation is driven by immediacy, and the Met - in fact all of the Force nationwide - work with the ethos, "time is of the essence". It's what we call in the Force "the golden hours". For the record, the PM doesn't need to approve this. It is your remit as you well know, and I, as the Assistant Commissioner of the Met, have sanctioned this as paramount. To not comply or ignore this would be foolhardy on your part. As for the taxpayer, well, any money spent is absurd to them.'

Peters cleared his throat and ruffled his hair. He shuffled the papers in front of him as Richard Havers pulled his rank a little. Peters was a rather small chap with a voice that owed much to elocution lessons, grammar-school educated, who liked to run in the circles of the high-end scholars from Eton, Harrow and Winchester who'd then gone on to St Andrews, Oxford and Cambridge. He had gained a 2:1 in Maths from Durham University and worked for a large London accountancy firm before becoming an MP and councillor for his local ward of Buckinghamshire and cementing his post in the PM's Cabinet after his predecessor had sadly died. A huge blow to the party at the time. He was no match for the minds of the five men surrounding him in terms of military operations.

Phillips smiled inwardly at the way in which Havers mastered a politician, and with genius style manoeuvred him back into the box that he'd popped out of, a little like an unwanted, irritating jack-in-the-box. Peters had no idea how criminal investigations worked and what was required to solve a crime, when it came down to the nitty-gritty. He was relatively new in the Cabinet and hadn't quite fine-tuned his smooth demeanour yet.

Captain Robertson took a slurp from his coffee cup and placed his hands on the table, twiddling the pen between both hands. 'Tony, where do you see our role in this?'

Phillips leant forward. 'I need an interception of a container ship. We don't have the ability within the Met to intercept, we simply don't. That's our biggest problem. We have a fugitive who has committed a heinous crime and left our victim, a Miss Lucy Carter, for dead on a beach. The suspect, Charlie Wainwright, recently released on licence, is on the run and we believe him to be armed. You'll see here in our forensic reports that residue from a firearm was found on his trainers.' He pushed the forensics file towards Robertson for his perusal.

'Who was the judge on this case, Tony?' Havers asked, picking up a Cabinet Office pad and pen.

'Lady Scott,' Phillips replied.

'Tough cookie, but fair.' Havers noted on his pad. 'What was his sentence?'

'Five years, to serve three, two on licence. He was charged with sexual harassment, false imprisonment, common assault, controlling and coercive behaviour and stalking. He was granted no bail and served his sentence at HMP Wandsworth.'

'So, he's now on licence?'

'Indeed.'

'When was the attack?'

'The 20th of February.'

'And his release date?'

'The 17th of February.'

'His conditions of licence have not been adhered to,' Havers said, rubbing the smooth bristles on his chin.

'Exactly,' Phillips replied. The other men listened intently.

'And our victim?' Havers pushed.

'Found unconscious on the beach by an ex-naval officer and friend, Bob Henderson.'

'A charge of attempted murder,' Havers mused.

'Bob Henderson? I know that name. It's Robin Henderson, he trained me. He left the Navy under compassionate grounds, lost his family in a fire. Brilliant officer, highly regarded,' Lieutenant Commander Smith-Jones interjected. 'So, we are dealing with quite an unpleasant character and have an armed fugitive on a ship?'

'Exactly,' Phillips replied.

'The Navy can help with the interception. This isn't a problem at all. It would be the Royal Marines we would deploy. Trained for this type of action, the bloody best. We would deploy six, maybe eight men on a Merlin helicopter, which would be assigned to one of our destroyers or frigates. Where exactly are we talking, assuming the vessel is British sovereignty? I mean, what seas are we in?'

'Lieutenant ...' Phillips began.

'Please, do away the titles, please call me Henry.'

'Henry, the shipping container left Felixstowe at four-hundred hours on the 22nd of February. Its destination is Valencia and it's due to arrive on the 28th February. Our suspect is holed up in one of the containers holding household goods.'

'So, it has been at sea for four days already and will be steaming ahead through the English Channel, the Atlantic and then the Mediterranean,' the Captain stated. 'It will be somewhere on the Atlantic at this stage, by tomorrow crossing onto the Med. So still in international waters. There won't be much chance of us pulling him out alive without interception, that's for sure.'

'Exactly, and I want him alive.'

'What ships are in the vicinity?' Captain Robertson asked.

'We've got a frigate and a landing platform dock vessel on high seas at present,' Lieutenant Commander Smith-Jones replied, noting on his pad the timings of the shipping container. 'I'm assuming we would want to board the ship without the knowledge of your fugitive, correct?'

'Correct,' Phillips replied. 'Your take?'

'With the Royal Marines, it's very simple. You won't hear them coming and you won't hear them leave. They are the elite, whether it be warfare or as a raid to aid a civil case. I'd deploy 42 Commando. My only concern is that your fugitive is armed. Obviously, the deployment of my men would mean their safety is of the utmost importance. By that I mean, I wouldn't want to lose or put any of my men at risk for a civil operation. This isn't warfare or combat. They need to be safe. That said, we can assist. We would need to bring you on board to make the arrest, which again is tricky as my men would be roped down from the Merlin. Again, we could manage this by bringing you on board by a Royal Marine RIB. Nothing is impossible for the Navy.'

'So, when are we talking?' Peters intervened.

'Immediate action, I would say.' Smith-Jones replied. 'Time is crucial. Wouldn't you agree, Tony?' he said, turning to Phillips.

'Absolutely. I have a team of twelve working from the CID department on this operation. I can leave DS Murphy in charge in my absence.'

'Isn't HMS Albion in the Med at present?' Captain Robertson said.

'Yup, she is. She was sent out to protect allies in the Mediterranean waters and also for the commandos to practise their operations before she comes back in to assist

HMS Queen Elizabeth on her maiden deployment. She's well suited to this type of operation and a carrier for air defence.'

'So, we use her and what, deploy six to eight of 42 Commando? Walk in the park,' Robertson continued. 'Obviously, we need to look at the logistics of getting Tony onto the ship but again we can fly him out on the Merlin from RNAS Culdrose. What are your movements, Tony? Can you get to Cornwall tonight?' Robertson asked.

'Yup, not an issue.'

'So, there we have it, don't you agree, Henry? The flying squad are prepped and ready at Culdrose; deploy the Merlin. Seems like the best option. They can be briefed early before heading out.'

Peters ruffled his hair at the front, 'I'm sorry, I'm sorry. Are you trying to tell me that a Merlin helicopter can fly from Cornwall to the Mediterranean without stopping? This just sounds bonkers!'

'Secretary of State, the Merlin can fly 1,400 miles without a problem. You do realise what a Merlin is, don't you?' Robertson asked dryly, bemused by Peters and his naivety about military operations.

'Of course I do,' Peters chirped. 'It just sounds a little far-fetched. Richard, what are your thoughts on this?'

Havers looked at him dead on, his eyes drilling through Peters' skull. 'I sanctioned it, Andrew. I think you have my answer.'

'Well, it would seem I have little choice in this matter.' Peters gathered his papers together and shuffled them into an orderly pile. He knew he was cornered by all five men in the room: the Met, the MoD and the Navy. It was almost full combat at the table.

'I will sanction this and leave it to the MoD to sort out the necessary logistics. However, I want a full report on all of this and to be kept up to speed without fail. I'm not a hundred percent on this operation. As I said before, if anything goes wrong, I have a lot of explaining to do to the PM.'

'Naturally,' Phillips replied. 'Thank you, Secretary of State.'

Bring back Ben Clark as Secretary of State, Smith-Jones said in his head, *God rest his soul.* 'Right, so the operation – Butterfly, isn't it?' he said out loud, pouring another coffee.

'Correct, Operation Butterfly,' Phillips said.

'Richard, will you be accompanying Tony?' Robertson asked.

'No need. I just need to be kept up to speed and our fugitive brought home without any casualties. Your men or indeed my man,' Havers said.

'My suggestion,' Robertson continued, 'is that, Tony, you hole up at a local B&B in Mullion, that's a nearby village about five miles from RNAS Culdrose. If you arrive at the base for 6.30 a.m. we can get the commandos briefed and a Merlin launched and head over to the Med with yourself and the commando unit. If we come in from behind the vessel, they won't hear us. The element of surprise is better with these ops. Depending where the container is, our fugitive could potentially hear us from above, if we came in from port or starboard side. Can we get a location on the household container itself?'

'Yup, I can get that,' Phillips replied.

'Perfect. Well, I think we are there. I'll get your information sent over to Culdrose and for them to expect you at 6.30 a.m. Henry, Richard, do you have anything else to offer at this stage?'

The two senior offices shook their heads.

'I'll have the paperwork sorted and any necessary reports on your desk, Andrew, in the morning,' Robertson finished. 'I think we can leave this meeting here.'

'Don't let this go wrong,' Peters said, shuffling his papers and shaking the men's hands before leaving the room.

The men left Suite A and made their way out of the Cabinet Office. Robertson and Smith-Jones shook hands and walked towards Westminster.

Richard Havers stood with Phillips and DS Murphy.

'Well, Tony, all the best and keep me up to date.' Havers shook both officers' hands and hailed a black cab.

'That was a result, guv,' Murphy said as he viewed the street ahead.

'Indeed. I need to get my bag sorted and catch a train to the Southwest. I'm leaving you in charge of the team, Murphy, whilst I close this part of the operation,' Phillips said as he walked to the curbside and whistled down a black cab. 'You coming?'

'No, guv, I think I might take a walk around Westminster. Stay safe, guv.'

The black cab pulled away, leaving Murphy alone.

Chapter Six

Thursday, 27th February
Mullion, Cornwall

In a hangar that also harboured a briefing room, eight commandos and two pilots sat in full marine combat uniform. The briefing was short, accurate and simple. Each commando knew their role and that they would at all times shield and be with DI Phillips, who was unarmed.

The helicopter's subdued grey colour blended into the tarmac. Its blades whirred into action, mimicking a mini tornado outside. The two officers got into position, adjusting the controls, ready to take their special cargo to the Med. Eight men, dressed in combat uniform and holding their weapons, sat shoulder to shoulder. Phillips climbed into the Merlin and buckled himself in. They acknowledged him.

'Sir,' they said. He nodded his head in response.

The two officers in the cockpit waited for their signal. The helicopter slowly lifted itself from the grey tarmac, dipping its nose slightly as it began to take height before leaving behind the base and the flight control tower. It hovered slightly before picking up speed and rising high above the treetops and fields of the idyllic surrounding villages. As the patchwork of fields and greenery began to disappear, a mass of blue was all that could be seen.

Its estimated arrival time at HMS Albion was 11 a.m. with a lily pad fuel stop on RFA Tideswell, which was stationed on the Atlantic ocean.

They would approach the container ship from behind, unnoticed and unheard.

Phillips would be deposited on the landing platform dock vessel and a Royal Marine RIB would be launched into the sea with Phillips on board.

The sky was grey and cloudy as the Merlin flew low across the Channel and veered in a southwesterly direction. The hum of the blades sounded like a machine gun in slow motion pummelling through the air. It manoeuvred through the skies over the Atlantic before landing to refuel on RFA Tideswell.

The sun beat down on the helicopter as it crossed the aquamarine water of the Mediterranean. It flew low across the sea, its sound enticing the playfulness of a pod of dolphins. The water below formed white crests from its flight. The dolphins leapt through the sea's waves, playing along with the sound of beating blades. Phillips sat quietly whilst the Merlin approached the landing platform dock vessel. His stomach tightened a little and a small bead of sweat formed on his forehead as he drew closer to his target. The helicopter dipped its nose to make its descent. It approached from astern and stationed portside before it manoeuvred to the centre line and descended on the spot of the vessel. A man in uniform handed Phillips a buoyancy vest. HMS Albion moved across the sea before positioning herself ahead of the container ship, close enough for the RIB to be launched.

From the bridge of the container ship the RIB could be seen, but the crew thought nothing of it. Many times a practice operation would be held at sea and this was like any other. The landing vessel then steamed ahead and slowed her engines until she rested over the horizon. The Merlin's blades whirred into action and lifted itself from the landing platform dock. It flew in from over the horizon with the six commandos on board, ready for their mission.

As the helicopter flew lower in the sky and came into sight, the RIB moved closely behind, tailing the British shipping container. No one on the ship was aware of the 42 Commando tracking it. Two ropes dropped from the Merlin as it hovered above the bridge of the container ship.

Charlie sat inside his container, huddled in a corner, cold, tired and hungry, a handgun and rucksack by his side. His eyes had become accustomed to the darkness, The helicopter was silent; nobody noticed the commandos rope down like small ants as they took either side of the bridge masterfully. No one saw them. No one heard them. They were not supposed to. They moved with precision and speed, undetected. Five men dropped one by one with stealth and accuracy, two making their way to the bridge. The commandos took the bridge by surprise and the crew fell to their knees with fear as they were confronted by two officers head to toe in combat uniform. They held SA80 A2 ACOG weapons which allowed them to deploy quick and accurate fire at close range.

'Royal Marines, 42 Commando, where's the Captain of this vessel?' one commando demanded.

'In his cabin,' replied the second officer.

'Call him up,' instructed the commando.

An able seaman called through to the Captain's cabin.

'Sir, we have 42 Commando in the bridge, can you please come up.'

'Royal Marines? What the hell, I'll be right there. This better not be a joke!' The Captain looked out of his porthole, but there seemed nothing untoward. He then spotted a Royal Marine RIB and a Merlin hovering portside. He hurriedly straightened his attire and left his cabin with speed.

'I'm Captain Ryman. Is there a problem?' he asked.

A Royal Marine stepped forward. 'At present you've been commanded to stop this vessel. We require the papers for your crew and their identification passes.'

'Not a problem.' He went to the desk and pulled out the sheet which had all the details of the enlisted crew.

The second officer began to slow the ship until her engine stopped two miles from where they had been ambushed. There were no intruders on the list.

'Can I ask what has happened – is it piracy?' the Captain asked as the sound of the engines diminished.

'We are here on an MACP operation. We believe there to be an armed fugitive stowaway on board. Can you please order your crew to remain inside their cabins or the mess and not exit onto the outside decks until it is safe to do so,' the commando ordered.

The Captain gave the orders through the internal communications system. The crew of the container ship downed tools and took shelter as authorised.

Once stationary, the RIB pulled up alongside the ship, portside, and a pilot ladder was thrown down for Phillips to embark. His blue mac lashed about in the wind as the water churned around the ship. He clung tightly to the rope edging as the wind buffeted and billowed him. His leather sole slipped on the wooden slat of the ladder, and a Royal Marine put his hand up to stabilise him. Phillips looked down to the churning water below.

'Don't look down, look ahead,' bellowed the marine. The sweat on Phillips' brow began to run. The Merlin hovered above the ship with a sniper on board. It moved starboard side, the sniper's weapon marking the target's container at the stern of the ship. The sniper's eye closely watched the commandos as they crouched low on the container ship, ready for their unsuspected ambush of the private haulage container. They shielded Phillips. He was unarmed.

They moved slowly along the deck up against the cargo, signalling to each other which direction to go. Two commandos scrambled over the containers stacked on top of each other and stayed low as they crossed along the tops of them. As a commando's direction changed, another commando moved forward, crouched low towards another position, his comrade covering his back. Another signal and another position taken by a Royal Marine. No sound came from the men. They crept towards the container that hid Charlie. Its seal had been broken. The two commandos crouched in position above on the containers, their weapons aimed below.

Then the noise came, the shouts, the orders. The door of the container flew open and the sunlight flashed in. Charlie cowered in the corner, unaware of the commando only feet away from him. The pungent, rancid smell of human excretion, urine and bodily odours permeated the container.

'42 Commando, Royal Marines. Come out with your hands in the air,' hollered a commando. Charlie scrambled under a table and belly-crawled nearer to the entrance. Three commandos entered the container, backs against the walls, stealth-like in their operation. Charlie silently moved a little under the furniture, still unseen. His rucksack still lay in the corner where he had hidden for days. The commando moved like a wildcat stalking its prey, low, hunched, until he reached the corner where the rucksack was. He signalled to his commando unit. Charlie hid and watched in the dim light as the feet moved around the container slowly but with agility. He scrabbled a little closer to the entrance. The commando signalled to below the furniture. He stopped. Charlie moved up a little and ran out of the container and across the deck of the vessel.

'Target out!' a commando yelled from above the container. The sniper aimed his weapon, ready to engage fire, the infrared light following his target. His men blocked his aim. It was too dangerous to take the shot. Charlie stumbled towards the edge of the container ship. Phillips shouted, the sea's wind carrying his voice. Above, close to the bridge, the crew watched from their cabins, their noses pressed up to their portholes.

'Put your hands in the air, Charlie, you're cornered,' Phillips said, his voice raised but calm. The sniper aimed low, ready to take him out – injured, incapacitated, not dead.

'Charlie, give up. You've nowhere to go, come quietly. Don't be a fool.'

Charlie stopped and turned, Phillips was right: he had nowhere to go. The ship was approximately fifteen miles off the Spanish coast. There was no escape. Only the deep blue sea surrounded him. His run was over. He faced Phillips. He moved his hands to the back of his soiled trousers.

'Raise your hands in the air slowly, Charlie, come quietly. Don't make this any worse for yourself. You can help yourself. I can do you a deal. Lessen your sentence. If you co-operate, I'll see you right.'

Charlie's fists clenched behind his back. His eyes darted to the men in front of him. Their eyes looking down the tunnel of a machine gun. Their weapons ready to fire.

'You must miss your father, Charlie.'

Charlie stared at him, the same look he'd given when he was arrested. Yet this time, he was unsure. Was this a trick? How did this man know his father? A man he'd adored.

'Tell your men to drop their weapons,' Charlie shouted above the winds of the sea.

'Do as he says.' The commandos relinquished their target, still ready to fire with precision if need be.

Charlie began to walk slowly towards Phillips. Surrendering. He took one arm and raised it in the air.

'Both hands, Charlie.'

Charlie stopped in his tracks. He looked up at the helicopter and could see the sniper as he knelt at the ledge of the Merlin. The commandos surrounded him with Phillips ahead, his mac flapping in the wind. He was hungry, he was tired. He took three steps back, his body now closer to the stern's edge.

'Charlie, think about it. Come quietly and I will see you right with the CPS. You didn't mean what you did - you were pushed, weren't you? Your mother, Charlie, she abandoned you, didn't she?'

What did Phillips know of his mother? His left hand shook behind his back like an uncontrollable rattle. As he took his right hand out from behind his back, the sound of a bullet exiting a gun went off.

'Man down, man down,' a commando shouted. His weapon fired.

'Man overboard!' shouted another commando. 'Starboard side!'

As Charlie's body hit the water, he gasped. The sudden gasp filled his lungs with water. His body disappeared beneath the waves. He stayed under the water, gone. A shot of red disappeared in the aqua blue.

His arm throbbed with pain as he tried to thrash at the water. His body was fatigued and exhausted after days without food. He had no strength to bring himself up to the surface and be rescued. He saw the life ring thrown down; he tried to grab it, but a wave took him down again. He heard himself screaming inside, like the sound of a hyena, animalistic, yet unheard. Gradually his body began to slow down and drift below the waves, splayed out in exhaustion. A boy's voice inside him was screaming, 'Daddy!' The life ring just too far, his body just too weak.

Phillips lay on the steel deck of the vessel. Blood began to seep through his clothing and form a small pool on the floor where he lay.

'Rob, what's going on, how serious is the casualty? I've lost vision on the target,' the sniper radioed down to the commando medic.

'We've got a fucking bleed out, Johnny, upper shoulder, get the Merlin down, we need to get him on it and back to base. I'm stabilising the casualty, get the fucking Merlin down.' The helicopter dipped its nose before moving above the container ship and swooping out and over the ship before hovering starboard side on a level with the container ship's deck. The commandos were kneeling around the casualty.

A commando took out his Gerber knife tool kit from his belt and ripped open the buoyancy aid, moving quickly and with precision to Phillips' sleeves, tearing them to reveal his upper body. He threw his medical Bergen from his back.

'Fuck, we've got a bleed out. Locate the fucking exit wound. Tim, hold his neck stable. On my count, three, two, *turn*! Dan, pack out the exit wound, I need to get a fucking line in.' The DI groaned with pain as the commando rammed the exit wound with quick clot.

'I need to get the fucking line into him! On my count, turn him back, three, two, *turn!* Dan, get your fucking thumb in the entry wound. I need to get a line in.' Phillips inhaled hard as the commando's thumb plugged the wound, stemming the bleed. His eyes rolled to the back of his head, his body succumbing to the pain.

'Look at me, buddy, keep your eyes open, buddy. We'll square you away, mucka. Keep talking, look at me, buddy. Eyes, open,' the commando said, his thumb pressed into the wound, the wet warm flesh around it. Phillips' eyes were opening and closing as he drifted in and out of consciousness.

The commando medic grabbed the fold-up stretcher from his Bergen. 'On my count we need to lift him. Three, two, *lift*! Tim, hold his neck.'

'Hold him fucking still, keep him fucking talking, come on, buddy. Dan, quick clot the entry, thumb out.'

'The line's in, come on, buddy. Look at me, look at me. Come on, buddy, you've got this. Tim, hold his head, Dan, Pete, top and toe. On my count, three, two, *lift!*'

The commandos ran the stretcher, with the medic alongside holding the plasma bag, to the edge of the container ship. The waves buffeted below against its side, the blades of the Merlin pummelling the air. It hovered low with the ship as each of the commandos left the edge with a CASEVAC. 'Hold him steady, stay with us, buddy.' Nimble, fast, precise, they left the edge of the ship and boarded the Merlin.

Moving out, the Merlin circled the ship, the pilot radioing ahead to HMS Albion.

'Foxtrot 10 inbound, your location figure 5 with casualty. Gunshot wound, left shoulder. Casualty is friendly non-military callsign.'

'Roger, standing by. Out.'

Below, on the water, the RIB still bobbed portside. Three commandos boarded it by pilot ladder. The high-powered boat turned on the water with accuracy, and the commandos began their search for the body in the water.

'Did you hit him?' a commando said, his eyes on the water.

'Nah, scuffed his shoulder.'

The waves moved around them, leaving a wake as they tracked the water. It was not a Royal Marine, at least, that they were looking for. Still no body had surfaced. There was no sign.

The RIB hit the waves with a pounding force towards HMS Albion. It slowed as it approached its naval ship. The arms of the crane overhung the vessel and its straps hung over the RIB, swinging violently in the wind. Two commandos pulled them and locked them onto their vessel, signalling to be drawn up. The RIB steadily made its way back up into its storage place on the ship.

The commanding officer called through to the MoD.

'Tim Robertson,' came the familiar voice.

'This is Captain Sanderson, of HMS Albion.'

'I read you, Captain Sanderson,' Robertson replied. 'Was the operation a success, do you have the fugitive?'

'Negative. We have a casualty and a missing person,' Sanderson replied. 'We have called VHF 16 for the coastguard to assist in the search.'

'Jesus, a Royal Marine down?' Robertson replied. This was not what he needed.

'No, DI Phillips was taken down by a gunshot wound. Our commando engaged on the armed fugitive. His aim was precise, to incapacitate not kill. However, the fugitive's body went overboard. It has not been recovered.'

'So, he's dead?'

'He was wounded not shot to kill. The crew from the RIB have searched the waters but there is no trace. The commandos tried in vain to rescue the man overboard.'

'And DI Phillips?'

'Gunshot wound to his shoulder. He was stabilised by our medic on the container ship and was stable on arrival. He's now in the operation suite. He should recover well under R and R.'

'How bad is it?' Robertson asked.

'The commandos were fast; they acted on instinct, immediate pressure used and a tourniquet to stop the bleed. Once the casualty was stabilised they operated with a CASEVAC straight onto the Merlin. He went into surgery as soon as he was brought back onto the ship. He's in capable hands. Once the surgeon has operated, he will be taken to a medical suite to recover and we will then fly him back to Blighty.'

'Right, I'll inform DS Murphy, Havers, Peters and Lieutenant Commander Smith-Jones. Bloody hell, Peters is going to be all over this. Keep me posted, Captain Sanderson.'

It wasn't until three days later that Phillips was deemed fit and well enough to be flown home. He'd received the best medical treatment on HMS Albion, and now needed to rest from the wound. His arm in a sling, he sat with 42 Commando on the hours-long journey back to RNAS Culdrose with a lily pad fuel-stop on RFA Tideswell. He thought only of Charlie. Not having him with him in handcuffs was not the result he wanted. The fact that they hadn't found his body left Phillips unsure of the operation. He didn't believe Charlie to be dead, and if he was, did that bring closure for Lucy? He needed to see a body of a wanted man to believe he was really gone, that the operation was really closed. He was not going to close it until he had seen proof of a dead man at sea.

What he'd seen on the ship stayed in his head for the journey. Charlie had looked fatigued, unkempt, lost. There was no longer the stare of a man who was defiant or cunning. He had shrunk in his posture. Phillips had thought he had him, he thought he was going to give up, surrender, realise the game was over, realise he had been outwitted. And now their suspect had outsmarted them by disappearing into the sea. 'Damn Charlie Wainwright,' he said in his head. 'Damn him!'

As the helicopter touched down on the tarmac of RNAS Culdrose, the blades slowed until they finally stopped. The commandos climbed out and helped DI Phillips out.

DS Murphy, Assistant Commissioner Havers, Lieutenant Commander Smith-Jones and Captain Robertson greeted him with firm handshakes before taking him into the building opposite, where they could be debriefed.

'Guv, good to see you,' Murphy said, gripping Phillips' hand longer than the rest. Phillips walked across the tarmac with the men.

They sat together in a meeting room, normally used for debriefs on assignments of combat and training.

'How are you, Tony? How's the shoulder?' Havers asked.

'I have another at least,' he said. He hadn't lost his satirical humour through the injury sustained.

'We'll need to fill out the required forms for a man overboard and unrecovered,' Smith-Jones said.

'I'm not closing the operation,' Phillips replied. 'I don't think he's drowned.'

'The commando unit said they had lost sight of the body. A wave came over him and that was the last they saw of him. He didn't come back up, Tony. The vessel was fifteen miles off the coast of Spain. It's highly unlikely he would ever survive.'

'I don't believe him to be dead, I don't know why. But I don't think he drowned.'

'Tony, a coastguard was alerted by the Royal Navy and the area was searched for twenty-four hours.'

'I don't disbelieve that, Henry. But I've got a gut feeling with this, and until I see the body, I believe Wainwright is still alive. I need to get back to my department and bring them up to speed. I am not closing the case until I have proof and a missing person is not proof. You need to trust me on this.'

'Tony, you'll need to sign the forms,' Richard said. He understood Tony's reasons; he'd had a case once before where his gut ruled his head.

'I'll sign the forms as missing. I'm not confirming he's dead.'

Phillips left the room and walked to DS Murphy's car, the image of Wainwright in his head. Pitiful, frightened, reckless, the gun fired. He stood by the car door and waited.

Murphy walked side by side with Havers.

'He's going to go mad, sir, with the case,' Murphy said.

'No, he won't,' Havers replied. He knew Tony well.

'He will, sir. This one's got under his skin.'

'He's following his gut. Let him. He's too good to get it wrong.'

Murphy shook Havers' hand and drove Phillips the long journey back to West London.

'D'you listen to Floyd, Murphy?' Phillips asked as he stared out of the window at the passing fields.

'Coldplay, guv.'

'You should listen to Floyd.'

'Guv.'

Chapter Seven

Wednesday, 5th March
Peñíscola, Spain

The dishevelled figure walked up the winding steps to the whitewashed villa. Each step was a little laboured, his shirt drenched and soiled. The steps were uneven and craggy, with only a rope as a handrail. A spray of pink bougainvillea rambled along the pergola with a glint of blue skies peeking through, the scent infusing the air as the figure clutched the rope. His gait was that of an old man, weary and without strength. His hands, cut and grazed, rapped on the door and his breath caught as the pain ran through his red raw knuckles. He waited. There was no answer. He stood awhile, taking in the view of the aquamarine crystal-clear sea below, clean and fresh, a stark contrast to his drawn, unshaven face blackened by soil. Weary and unsightly, he turned to knock again.

'Hola?' A voice came from behind him. *'Puedo ayudarte?'*

The figure turned and faced the voice. It was familiar, softer in age. Spanish.

'Hello, Mother.'

She stood and stared at the figure in front of her. Her hands muddied from the salad plants she'd been tending to. Sweeping her hair away from her face. Her eyes a deep chocolate brown, her face framed by loose strands of hair caught up slightly at the sides. She wiped her hands on her tatty, muddied jeans.

'Charlie?' Her Spanish accent soft.

The two looked at each other; life stood still. The waves brushed the shores of the small Spanish beach below, and the breeze murmured through long ornamental grasses. Olive trees, old and gnarly, enveloped the grounds of the villa that nestled in the mountainous terrain. She stared at him, long and hard.

'Charlie? Is it you? It is you?' She moved forwards. 'Are you ill?'

He exhaled with scorn. 'Ever the welcome, Mother,' he said, his voice laced with cynicism. 'No, I'm not ill. I need to stay here for a while.'

'Is everything OK?' She moved forward, brushing the hair from her face.

'Meaning what, Mother? Since when? Since school? Since university? Since life?'

'Charlie, please …' She held out her hand. He moved back, not wanting to feel her touch. 'Please, Charlie, come inside, we can talk.'

She left her trowel on the swinging chair and opened the mesh door into the villa. The floor was covered from corner to corner in white porcelain tiles, the whitewashed walls adorned with two pieces of modern art.

He stood and watched while she took a jug of freshly made lemonade from the fridge.

She drew up two chairs at the table and beckoned to him to sit with her.

He slumped into a chair and downed a glass of the crisp, refreshing liquid in front of him. His body ached, his mouth was dry, his lips chapped. He drank as if he hadn't drunk for days, weeks, shoving his glass forward for a refill.

He was unkempt and emitting unpleasant bodily odours.

'Are you hungry?' she asked as she placed a basket of bread and a dish of oil on the table. He dismissed the oil and stuffed the bread into his mouth. Eating like a savage animal ripping the meat from a carcass. The crumbs stuck to the sores on the sides of his mouth. He pushed his glass forward for more lemonade. He spoke not a word.

She poured another glass for him and walked away from the table. From where he sat, he could hear the water rushing from the taps. The scent of camomile drifted through to where he was sitting. He watched his mother glide from one room to another, carrying white towels and a bathrobe. She walked back to the table where his glass was now empty, and the bread had gone. There was just a man who seemed unrecognisable.

'Charlie, the bath is running. I have left towels on the rail and a clean bathrobe on the door. Leave your clothes outside the door and I will wash them. I have nothing here. Then we can talk.'

Charlie pushed the chair back along the tiled floor. The screech was like nails on a blackboard. He stared into her eyes, this woman who should have loved him, protected him, but was simply now just a woman – older, with small lines on her face and soft tanned skin - but never a mother until now. His body moved slowly towards the bathroom, his head held low. He undressed and left a pile of damp, soiled clothes outside the door, their stench pungent.

She heard the door lock behind him, and the water stopped running. She picked up the bundle of clothes with an intake of breath. She sat and watched as the washing machine whirled around the soapy suds, removing all the dread and fear that had been worn by the man who now lay in a bath in her villa. Where had he been? Why had he arrived now? What had happened?

Opening the mesh door, she walked back out onto the veranda. The sea's waves lapped gently onto the beach below her villa tucked away on the Iberian slopes. The sound of cicadas filled the air, their gentle clicking sound warm and soothing. She rested her hands on the veranda's railing. What had happened to her son? She heard his steps behind her and turned.

His face was clean, still with a dark stubble shadowing it. His hands and nails looked softer now from the camomile water. They were still grazed, though. His hair was clean. He wrapped the bathrobe tightly around his waist and sat on the chair swing. She watched him as he looked out to sea, his eyes distant, his breathing slow.

The washing machine gave a shrill beep and broke the silence. She left him whilst she tended to his laundry. He watched her as she pegged out his clothes, the breeze catching them and swishing them gently in the air. He could feel the gentleness of the sea breeze on his face, the salty taste of the air on his tongue. It took him back to his childhood. As if in a time warp, he closed his eyes and could hear his father laughing. It was a memory now, a distant, forgotten memory.

'May I?' she said as she came to sit beside him. He shrugged. 'Talk to me. What's happened? Is it Lucy?'

He sighed heavily and looked out to sea. 'I need to stay here a while. Who do you know here? Nobody must know I'm here – nobody.'

'OK, but why? What's happened? Are you in trouble?' She pushed. 'I am your mother.'

'You're Sofia. You've never been a mother to me. I'll call you Sofia.' His voice was stony.

Her eyes followed his face. His words were unloving, cutting, but she was his mother and she would never not be his mother, whatever hatred he had for her.

'Charlie.' She paused, her voice soft but forthright. 'To my friends I am Sofia, to my therapist I am Sofia, to you I am your mother. I don't know why you are here but if you want to stay here with me, I will not be Sofia. The choice is yours.' She could see in his eyes his angst, his hatred for her. She knew that the mistakes she had made had probably led him to this feeling. Her maternal love should have seeped into his veins, but it had now evanesced. She watched as he gazed outwards, his thoughts captured by the landscape of billowing white clouds and a sea that could hide the memories that haunted him. She was a mother who, wrapped up in her own life, had forgotten the son who now needed her. But why? Why would he come to her, when she had barely been a mother?

'Charlie, you can either take your dried clothes and leave and never return, or we can begin again.'

She wasn't like Lucy: she had a fire in her belly. She was Hispanic after all. Men didn't rule her life. She hadn't taken her husband's family name, she'd kept her own. Lucy had once had that fire, but she had been squashed by Charlie. Sofia stood her ground. Charlie had not been in her life for many years, and she would survive if he walked away now. He sat contemplating her words. He got up and walked to the veranda's edge.

'I have to stay here, but you can tell nobody, and I mean nobody. Do you understand?' he said.

'Why? I will tell nobody, but I need to know why. What have you done? What are you hiding from?' Charlie stared out to sea. He heard her words but said nothing. 'You can stay here,' she went on. 'When you feel ready to talk, I will listen, but I will not shelter you without knowing. At some point you will have to explain. Now I must tend to the garden.' She walked down the stone steps, then turned back to him. 'The room to the left of the bathroom is made up. You can sleep there.'

Her graceful figure disappeared around the side of the villa, leaving him alone on the veranda. The thoughts of a cell flooded his mind, the stench of disinfectant from the corridors, the sinewy-yellow, nicotine-stained walls, the small barred windows, the taunts from the other inmates. He got up from the swing chair and walked back inside, to the bedroom. There was a double bed dressed in crisp white linen with square pillows laid along the headboard, perfect and plump. The white walls held black and white prints. In the corner an old school trunk with the large red initials C. W. printed on the front sat cushioned on the floor. He sat beside it. Tightening the cord around his waist, he opened the trunk. His left arm still rested against his chest, bent, aching.

***

Haphazardly hopscotching with stolen chalk in his hands across the craggy rocks, the sun beating down on a hazy Spanish day. The wind whispered through the waves as they ebbed and flowed into the shallow waters of the rock pools. A hand strong and firm rested gently on his bronzed, brown shoulder. There was the scent of aftershave behind him. 'It's time to leave.' The words that hung heavily in the air.

He hugged his father so tightly, never wanting to let him go. He grabbed the cotton shirt tightly in his hands, made a snuffling sound into his waist.

The loud sounds of a jet engine, the rumbling noise of take-off.

She drank champagne until the patchwork of fields became close again.

Through the nights he had lain in his bed listening to the sound of raised voices. She would shout. The sound of another bottle being opened. He pushed his face into the pillow, wrapped the perfectly crisp covers around him, drew in his soft, scruffy brown bear closer. Now they were gone, the summer heat a memory.

The sound of a door opening into a room of old, oak-framed windows. A blackboard at the front with white chalk marks scribbled across it. 'Amo, Amas, Amat …' The stern figure in its frame holding the brass knob. 'Wainwright, my office!'

The sorrowful coffin that consumed him.

The strong, firm hands gently resting on his shoulders, the soft cotton shirt he'd hold tightly to, only ever a memory now.

***

He took out the bear, its fur a pale brown colour, a little worn in places, musty with the scent of childhood. He held it close to his chest and wept. A broken man.

She stood at his bedroom door and watched him. He hadn't heard her come back in. 'It's your school trunk,' she said softly.

'You kept it?' he said as he turned, holding the bear against his chest.

'You're my son. Of course, I kept it.' She placed his folded clean clothes with a note on the table by the door, where a single white orchid stood in a sleek white pot, then left the room again. Charlie replaced the bear, nestling it against his soft, tartan cotton pyjamas from boarding school, and closed the lid, closed away the memory. He went to the door and picked up the note. It read; Ana Pérez, Cueva Cascada, 12598 Peñíscola, followed by a mobile number. The address belonged to a rambling old villa tucked away on the coastal tracks of the Mediterranean, its name meaning *waterfall*. Charlie dressed in the crisp, fresh clothes. He left the room, leaving the note on the bed.

As he walked into the open-plan living area, he saw Sofia tending to the wild trout she had bought from the market the day before. A huge pan of boiling water bubbled away on the hob and the potatoes, with their skins still on, tossed and turned in the water. The clattering of the lid sounded like cymbals clashing off the beat, an obtrusive noise in a silent room. She chopped delicate sprigs of fresh parsley and thyme she'd picked earlier from the garden and two bay leaves picked from her laurel tree close to the veranda. Charlie watched as she diced the trout. Onions sweated in a shallow cast-iron pan with carrots caramelising and garlic infusing the air.

'Are you hungry?' she said as she tossed the trout into the pan. Steam floated into the air from the potatoes as she drained them and set them on the side. 'I'm making a fish casserole; it was your favourite as a child. Do you remember?'

He watched her move around the kitchen like he had as a small boy, the aromas familiar and warming.

'I am hungry,' he said. 'I remember this dish. The name and address you left with my clothes, Ana Pérez – who is she?' His tone had softened.

'Ana is my therapist. Maybe you should see her? Talk with her?' She covered the pan, leaving it to simmer and produce the most sumptuous, warming meal. She knew the depth of his pain would never come to her in words. He was angry with her and she could never change the past.

Charlie stood at the counter; his throat tightened, his face flushed. He slammed his fist down on the worktop and picked up the knife, then slammed it into the wooden chopping board. The point pierced through the board. The sunlight shone on its blade, flashing in her eyes like a shard of glass. She looked at the blade. She looked at him. She bit her lip.

'Your therapist! You think I need a fucking therapist!? You think I'm mad? Is that it?'

Sofia gulped and she stood back, her eyes turning back to the knife she'd used for the trout, her heart racing. She turned to the tap. The cold water came gushing out and she filled a glass, her hand shaking. She took in another breath, her eyes still fixed on the knife near Charlie, and exhaled slowly. One hand rested on the counter, the other clasping the glass in her hand tightly. She would use it if she needed to.

'I ... I ... I believe you need to talk, unravel, let go of your demons. And if not with me then with Ana. I don't understand why you're here.' She bit her lip again, her hand still clutching the glass. 'You need my protection, that's clear, but will you ever be open with me? I don't think you will, and I understand that. I'm not deserving of that. But I'd like to try. I'd like to be given that chance.'

He moved towards the knife. Her breathing hastened. 'Please, Charlie. Please leave the knife alone.' He took the handle and pulled it from the board and laid it on the counter.

'I need a cigarette.'

'There's some tobacco in the potting shed. It's Roberto's, my gardener.' Her grip on the glass slackened.

Charlie left the room and walked out onto the veranda, down the craggy steps to a small wooden shed tucked behind the olive grove. The smell of tobacco was sweet. Lighting his rolled cigarette, he slumped onto the bench at the end of the grove and watched the sun peek through the treetops as it relinquished itself to the early evening sky. His breath flowed fluidly once again. She came out with a pashmina thrown around her shoulders and found him sitting on the bench, 'Charlie,' she said. He looked at her. Her arms opened and he placed his head on her chest, hearing the sound of her heart beating softly. She wrapped her arms around him. Her only child. Her arm rested lightly on his shoulder; he winced. A crudely mended wound lay hidden beneath his shirt. The sweet staleness of the tobacco enveloped her. He was shivering. Her pashmina fell onto his shoulders, her hands brushed through his hair, smoothing away the heavy burden that lay in his body and mind. He wept.

'Will you call Ana for me?' he said.

'Yes, I will call her.'

The birdsong lessened in the trees, the petals of the flowers began to slowly close, and droop a little as if nodding to their own sweet slumber.

'Come inside now, supper is ready.' She took his hand and led him back up to the villa. The candles on the porch were flickering now, shimmering a soft glow in the darkening skies. The sea below was calm – just the gentle swishing of the deep dark blue waves and the white foamy crests as they broke and washed against the shore. The rattle of shells and pebbles taken by each wave and the clickety-clack of scuttling crabs that passed across the golden sand.

The villa now had a dulcet tone, the whitewashed walls bright and sparse with only the modern art flanking them. The lights cast a soft hue over a faux fur throw lying across the white, cube-style leather sofa. With the mesh door closed, the hum of insects filled the air outside. The sumptuous smell of the fresh fish casserole funnelled out from the kitchen. Two linen placemats, a jug of water and a bottle of Rioja stood on the table. Together they ate. Occasionally he looked at her as she cut a hunk of olive bread to mop up the rich, garlicky juice. A sense of calm encompassed them, an unravelling of forgiveness, tentative but present.

Chapter Eight

Wednesday, 5th March
Colchester Hospital, Essex

The sounds of the trolley rattling along the corridor and faint voices outside the door woke Lucy.

'Me lovely Lucy, how are you feeling?' Doris clattered in with the trolley, the rustling blinds opening to let light flood into the room. 'Dr Thiroux is very happy with your progress, me lovely. Dat lovely young chap of yours is going to take you home today. How does that sound, me lovely?'

'I'm going home? What day is it?'

'It's Wednesday, me Lucy. And a beautiful day it is. Me Winston dropped me at work today and do you know what I saw, me Lucy?' Her voice had a joyful ring to it, every word with a singing sound.

'What? What did you see?'

'I saw me first daffodil, shining bright and yellow, as yellow as the sun in Jamaica.'

'That's nice. I've never been to Jamaica.'

'Oh, me Lucy, tropical fruit, spices, the hot, yellow sun. Sandy shores, a paradise, me Lucy. Me Winston would say, "And Marley, me Doris. Don't you be forgettin' Marley, me girl."'

Lucy smiled. 'I like Bob Marley.'

'Well, you'll be having to go to Jamaica, you'll be hearing him all 'thee' time. He's always being played.'

'How long have I been here now?'

'Well, a little while, not far off two weeks, me lovely? You be doing so well now. And your head wound is looking nice and clean, oh yes nice and clean, nice and clean. How were your dreams, me pretty?'

'I don't know, I don't seem to remember when I wake or sleep. Am I really ready to go home? I don't think I'm ready. I don't want to go home. Please don't make me go home. Please don't make me.'

Doris straightened the blankets on Lucy's bed and lifted her gently to readjust the pillows. Her full bottom perched on the bed. Her scent of lily of the valley clung in the air.

'Now listen, me Lucy, you will be OK and you will need support. Me grandmutta used to say when I was little girl and was sad some days. She'd sit me on her lap on the chair that rocked on the veranda of her house, and she'd braid and bead my hair and she'd say, "Mi deh yah, yuh know." Yep that's what she'd say, I remember it as clear as day.'

'What does it mean?'

'It means, me Lucy, "I am here. Everything is OK."'

'I'm frightened.'

'I know you are, me pretty.' Doris smoothed her hair and tucked it behind her ears. 'Now no more tears, your fine chap will be here soon.'

Brushing down the covers once more, she added Lucy's obs to her notes and clipped them back on to the end of the bed. The sound of Doris's trolley clattered around the room as she wheeled it about. She opened the door to leave and as she did, she turned and smiled, 'Mi deh yah, yuh know.'

Two pigeons cooed on the window ledge outside. Lucy watched them as they snuggled into each other. Her thoughts went back to her cottage and her writing room and Jim and Peggy and the story she was writing. She thought of her time with Bob on the beach and the peppermint teas she shared each morning with him. She thought of Jo, her literary agent who had become such a valuable friend, and Matt, the police constable - how they were beginning to embark on their new relationship. She thought of Simon and how he was always there as a policeman and friend and how he'd helped her baste a turkey for the first time at Christmas. She thought of Ben and how she thought she'd heard the motorbike that night and how it went dark. The figure behind her was never Ben. She tried to put Ben in her thoughts, but the acrid smell of stale cigarettes flooded her mind. Each time she opened the window in her cottage, the smell was there. The smell of him, the familiar smell of his cigarette smoke. Yet she hadn't realised he had been there watching her.

Her windows had stayed closed in the hospital. She couldn't smell him there. It was her sanctuary.

At home he'd be there again. The police hadn't found him; he was on the run. He'd come back, he'd come back for her. What if he came back, what if this time she lost the fight? What if this time the skies would turn black? The sound of waves stopped. The cries of the gulls silent. What if this time it ended?

The soft, sweet tones of the pigeons' coos let her eyes slowly close and the trauma in her mind began to drift away. The memory of the sounds of the waves brushing onto the sand and catching the pebbles in their wake. The clinking of halyards in the sea breeze.

The door opened, and a figure stood at her bed. He walked around to the side. He bent down and pulled her covers a little further up, smoothing the creases with his weather-beaten hands. His scent was clean and fresh, his footsteps silent. He brushed his hand along her bruised face and bent down to kiss her forehead. She murmured in her sleep. He left the room.

Outside the room, Doris stood with Dr Thiroux, deep in discussion.

'How was Lucy emotionally today? Her obs are looking very positive,' Dr Thiroux said, perusing her notes and turning the page as the file rested on the reception counter.

'Well, you know, she's a little frightened, but she's doing better. She's ready to go but she needs time. I think she'll need a lot of emotional support. You know, someone to talk to. Someone to let go with. But she has a fine young chap, in fact speak of the devil, here he is.'

Dr Thiroux turned around, picking up Lucy's notes and holding them close to his body, his hand tucked around them. Dressed in blue scrubs, a stethoscope around his neck, he smiled at Ben.

'Ah good morning, Ben. We were just talking about Lucy and her progress. I feel it's the right time now for Lucy to go home. She's doing very well, and her wounds have healed perfectly. Originally, we'd hoped she would be much better after a couple of days, but as you know we've had a couple of relapses and shock attacks, and it just wasn't safe to send her home at that stage. She needed immediate medical attention to bring her back into a calmer place. We haven't had any attacks for a couple of days now and I think it would be better to try and introduce her back into her home environment. There is a risk it can trigger a shock attack, but with baby steps we can hopefully reduce the chances of that happening. There are no signs of any permanent physical damage in the scans we took of her head injuries. Which is a huge relief. I really am very happy to discharge her today.'

'Right, OK. And Lucy, does she know this yet?'

'Doris, her nurse, had a chat with her this morning and although there is still the trauma and flashbacks, these will need to be addressed by a psychological therapist. There's little we can do with this medically, as such. It's a little like PTSD. She will struggle, that's a certainty, but any emotional support we can give her will be there. But I am very happy with her physical progress, I can't stress that enough.'

'And DI Phillips, does he know?' Ben asked. The news that she could come home again was perfect, but was she really ready? What if she relapsed?

'I spoke with DI Phillips this morning. He is still putting her under police protection, potentially a safe house. But like all these things, there are hoops to jump through. Her attacker could still be at large and that will no doubt frighten Lucy. But we will make sure that medically she will be OK, and in terms of her safety, the DI has assured me that no harm will come to her. We will do everything, Ben, I give you my word as her doctor. But from now on in, it will be a slow process for Lucy mentally. It could take weeks, months, years for her to get past this. She may never get past it. But with you and her friends, and the home that she knows, it is the best place for her.'

'Could still be at large? You said still? Where's Wainwright?'

'I don't know, Ben, I'm just her consultant.'

'Right, OK ... so what time can she leave? I saw her just now, but she was sleeping. I didn't wake her, she looked so restful.'

'When she wakes, Ben. We will finish our notes on her and fill out her discharge form and I'll give you the medication she needs to take. One will be for pain relief, which to be honest she is managing very well at the moment, and the second drug is for her trauma. Side effects of that could include insomnia or even the reverse, sleepiness. It affects people differently. Coupled with this, though, Lucy will need psychological therapy. That is paramount.' The doctor cleared his throat. 'I'm sure this perhaps sounds a little daunting, and Lucy has a long road ahead of her. The simple fact that she is a writer will help her hugely; it will allow her to write her feelings and fears down. I'll fill in all the forms for you and Doris will help Lucy dress.'

'She doesn't have any clothes, though. When she came in, she was wearing the clothes she was attacked in and the police have those,' Ben said, 'I can't get into her house, either.'

'We have her keys here; they were found in the gutter by her house. The police left them here with us. Perhaps you could grab some clothes for her. There's no rush, Doris can help her shower whilst you're gone.'

Ben left the hospital, hardly able to believe Lucy would soon be back with him. He pulled up outside the cottage in Lambourne Terrace. The gate squeaked as he opened it and the rambling rose snagged at his hoodie. He looked around and went to open the door to the cottage, but the key jammed in the lock. Over the road, the curtain twitched. The yellow door of number 8 flew open and Gladys Pope stormed across the road.

''Ey you! That's private property!' she hollered, waving a frying pan in her hand. 'My Stan is onto the police, don't you move an inch! I've got a ferocious dog inside me 'ouse too, my Stan will bring 'im, savage you 'e will.'

Ben jumped. 'Jesus Christ, Mrs Pope! It's me, Ben, Lucy's boyfriend. I've just come to get some clothes for Lucy. I'm bringing her home today.'

'She's coming 'ome, oh dear Lord. Well, why didn't you say, boy? And don't you be taking the Lord's name in vain, d'you 'ear me.'

'Er ... you didn't give me a chance.'

'Well, if you don't mind, I'll be sure to 'elp you. Poor mite, she's going to want something warm and snug. Come on, love, out me way, let's see what we can find. It's no bother.'

Gladys Pope's mighty figure barged in front of Ben, waving the frying pan as she went. She turned the key in the lock.

Ben led her up to Lucy's room and opened a drawer.

'What do you think she'll want?'

''Ere, let me.' She rummaged around and pulled out clean underwear, a pair of grey leggings, a snuggly warm sweatshirt and a pair of socks. She opened the cupboard and pulled out a pair of Ugg boots. 'There, that should do it. Now you make sure she's warm and you make sure you don't let 'er out of your sight too. D'you 'ear me!' Gladys picked up her frying pan and left Ben with a pile of clothes, with a spray can of deodorant and a hairbrush on top.

'You'll be wanting to clear up this post, too, before she gets 'ome,' Gladys bellowed up the stairs. The front door closed behind her.

He stuffed the clothes into a rucksack and took them downstairs. He picked up the post that lay scattered across the mat and placed it on the side table in the hallway, balancing Lucy's mobile on top.

He closed the door of the cottage and tucked the rose back on itself before driving back to the hospital.

Lucy was sitting in her chair in a clean hospital gown when he arrived, her hair washed, and the dressing now removed from her head. He smiled at her as he plonked the bag of clean clothes down onto the bed.

'Shall I help you dress?' he asked, opening the bag. 'Mrs Pope helped me gather some clean clothes. Man, she scared me half to death with her frying pan, I couldn't refuse.'

Lucy watched him as he placed the clothes on the bed and put the Uggs on the floor. She didn't know what to say. He hadn't seen her body since before the attack and now it was bashed and bruised and aching.

'Can you …?' Her voice was just a soft whimper. He helped her stand up, wobbling a little. He slowly untied the hospital gown and let it slip gently from her shoulders. She held it close to her so as not to let it fall. Her ribcage more prominent and defined. 'Can you turn around?' she said as she tried to put her bra on, struggling with the clasp. Ben turned back. 'Here let me,' he said, taking her hands away from the clasp and carefully doing it up. His touch gentle across her back, a vague touch of the bones that he could now feel, with an ugly yellow and black bruising across them. She felt the touch of his skin and she flinched. Walking away, he took the socks, pants and leggings from the bed and placed them on the chair, then left the room, leaving Lucy alone.

'Jesus Christ,' he said under his breath as he flumped onto the plastic chair in the corridor. The tears streamed down his face. His hands shook with the unknown. She had flinched when he touched her. His touch on the bare skin he had caressed the night before the attack now frightened her. His touch along the streamlined contours of her body now repelled her. The plastic chair in the corridor was cold and hard. With his head in his hands, he cried.

'Me lovely, how's me Lucy, you not helping her?' His eyes red from the tears, his hair ruffled from pushing his hands through it, Ben wiped his nose on his sleeve.

'I repulse her. She flinched at my touch.'

He felt the warmth of an arm around him. 'Me lovely, you don't repulse her. Listen to me: Lucy is scared, she was attacked, a brutal attack. She's a woman. You've never seen her body looking touched by strength and violence, only ever beautiful. Her own body will scare her. Give her time, give the girl time.' She patted his knee. 'I'll go and help her finish dressing. Sometimes in life the emotions become too much. She's in that space now. Be there for her, that's what she needs. And one day she'll be able to touch you again and enjoy your touch. Give her time, me lovely.' She pushed herself up from the chair and squeezed his shoulder with reassurance. 'You'll have her back and she'll shine brightly again, just like the yellow sun in Jamaica.' Ben sighed and mustered up a smile of hope.

Hands in his hair, head held low, he waited outside the room where Lucy was dressing. He hadn't waited on that plastic chair since the day she was brought in, the day he thought he'd lost her forever. He couldn't lose her because of that man. He wasn't ready to lose her.

The door opened and Doris led Lucy out, carrying her bag for her. She passed it to Ben and gave him the discharge forms and a paper bag full of an assortment of drugs.

'Now, me Lucy, this lovely young chap will take care of you at home, d'you hear? Dr Thiroux has referred you to a psychological therapist. I'll make an appointment for you to see Dr Hawkins next week, a wonderful therapist, ahhh, just wonderful. Now remember what I said: "Mi deh yah, yuh know."' The warmth of Doris' arms around Lucy felt safe and secure, and she hugged her tightly. The pain in her ribs subsided momentarily. Ben and Lucy left Darwin ward behind them.

Sirens screamed down the road outside the main doors of the hospital. Visitors bustled by, knocking her as she walked. The bright sunlight blinded her a little; cars, people, noise came at her from every direction. She began to feel disoriented. Her head swam with anxiety and fear. Her breathing, heavier now, became more audible. She stopped for a moment and watched. A man came too close to her, and she took an intake of breath, startled by his closeness. The shrill sound of the pedestrian crossing jarred in her head. She turned to Ben. 'Here,' he said, 'take my hand, Lucy. I'm here.' Slowly she took his hand and let him lead her across the road to the car. He threw the almost empty bag into the back. Lucy sat in the front passenger seat, and Ben helped her as she struggled with the buckle.

He pulled out of the car park. At each junction the cars weaved in, as seamlessly as a shuffled deck of cards. She stared through the window at the passing pedestrians. The pavements were littered with people, dogs, joggers, mothers and pushchairs. Every colour outside was brighter, every noise louder, every stranger on the pavement a trigger to make her heart beat more fiercely. The sun struggled through the murky cloud but even in its weakness stung Lucy's eyes. She turned her face away from the window, her fists clenched, her nails digging into her palms. Ben fiddled with the radio but the silence was deafening.

The A12 was humming with cars, huge freight lorries destined for Parkeston, Harwich and Felixstowe. Ben indicated left, slipping off onto the less busy A120. The countryside sprawled further, and the view was more subdued and calmer. The familiar sight of the water tower at the roundabout for Clacton and Manningtree, which Lucy always used to think resembled a giant concrete rook from a game of chess or a huge white salt mill, was a sight that told her she was nearly home. Back home in Wrabness, the village with far-reaching views of the estuary.

As she waited for the agent to arrive, she walked down the road: there were fields and, just beyond, the most amazing view of sailing boats on a huge expanse of water. She wasn't sure what river it was, but it was breathtaking. 'Hi, I'm Jack Williams from Parker and Lovell. Hi, I'm Jack Williams from Parker and Lovell. Hi, I'm Jack Williams from Parker and Lovell. Hi, I'm Jack Williams from Parker and Lovell.'

'Lucy ... Lucy.' The sound of her name broke her trance.

'Are you ready?' Ben said, unfastening her seatbelt. 'Come on. I'll light a fire and make you a peppermint tea and you can rest on the sofa.'

The hinge of the gate squeaked as Lucy turned to close it. The curtain of number 8 twitched.

'She's back, Stan,' said Gladys to her husband. 'Our young Lucy is back, ahh, back where she belongs. I'll make 'er a nice chicken pie. Take it over later, I will.' Stan grunted in his chair and turned the telly up.

Ben opened the front door. The clock ticked in the kitchen, the unopened post sitting neatly in a pile on the hall table. The smell of a burnt-out fire in the sitting room, untouched for weeks. The gentle humming of the boiler and trickling of water running through the radiators. An empty mug sat on the table in the sitting room with a line of mould forming on the top of the unfinished peppermint tea.

Slowly Lucy pushed the door open a little more into the sitting room, the sun's light catching particles of dust dancing in its ray. She took off her boots and lay on the sofa, her head resting on the cushions. She wrapped the throw around her and stared into the fireplace. A fireplace as cold and as empty as her feelings inside. The sound of the cupboard doors opening in the kitchen and the kettle boiling were the only sounds she could hear, the only sounds that felt familiar. Ben appeared at the sitting room door holding a warm peppermint tea, which he placed on the table. Kneeling by the fire, he began to clear it out, brushing away the ash. He scrunched the newspaper into tennis-ball-sized clumps, and they gave a crinkling, crunching sound. He laid them in the hearth and dotted about pieces of kindling wood, arranging them like miniature wigwams. He took a match and lit it. Small red flames licked around the jagged ends of the wood as it caught alight. He stood up and lit the scented candle on the window, another familiar scent for Lucy to feel at home again.

'How are you feeling?' he asked as he handed her tea from the table. She sat up and took it, her hands wrapped around its warmth.

'Tired, my ribs ache a little. Where's my phone? I need to message Jo.'

Ben left the room, taking the weeks-old tea from the table, and retrieved her phone from the hallway.

'It'll need to charge for a while, it's totally dead. Where's your charger?'

'There's one on my bedside table, next to the lamp.'

Upstairs, her bed still had the duvet thrown haphazardly across it from their morning of tenderness and passion. He pulled it up and tidied it a bit. Her underwear was still lying on the floor where he'd taken it off. He unplugged the charger and put the underwear in the laundry basket by the stairs and went back down to the sitting room.

Lucy watched the flames as they darted around the wood, small sparks flying off each piece with a crackle and a pop. He plugged her phone in and placed it on the table. The screen lit up and the Apple image shone brightly, a neon white. It pinged and jumped as message after message came hurtling through. Her hand trembled as she swiped across to unlock it, scared of the messages she might see. Thirty missed calls from Ben, three voicemails, numerous text messages.

'I've got voicemails. Ben, are they from him?'

She handed the phone to Ben, who listened to them. 'No, they're from me. I called you and left messages the night you disappeared. Shall I delete them?'

'Are they horrible? I mean, are they cross messages?'

'No, how could they be cross? They're concerned messages. Shall I delete them?'

'No, leave them … Ben?'

'Yes?'

'You're staying with me, aren't you? You're not leaving me?'

'I'm staying right here. I can bring some clothes over tomorrow. Jo is coming down to stay with Matt and see you. When she arrives, I'll get my things. How does that sound?'

'Ben …?'

'Yes?'

'Have you seen Bob at all, is he OK?'

'Bob is fine and yes I've seen him. He sits on the beach most days with Archie. I think he's been keeping your stone step warm for you. He misses you.'

'Ben …?'

'Yes?'

'Will you promise you won't leave me on my own?'

'I promise. I will need to go to work but Simon and Matt are on hand too and Mrs Pope, well, I think you might be seeing her a lot more often.'

There was a rap at the door, 'I'll get it,' Ben said, looking out of the window. 'Speak of the devil. It's Mrs Pope, what do I say? Do you want to see her?' Lucy shook her head.

Ben opened the door to Gladys.

'Right, now then love, I thought I'd make this for young Lucy, to get 'er strength up. It's my Stan's favourite, a chicken pie. Didn't know whether she'd 'ave any food in, so I brought a dish of mash too. Freshly made today. There's plenty of gravy in the pie, you won't be needing no more. I've got a broth on the go from the stock, I'll be bringing that over tomorrow. No bother. Now, you tell that Lucy from me I'm just over the road. I'll be walking my Barry later for 'is last whoopsie of the evening and will be sure to keep an eye out. I won't bother you any longer.'

With that she turned and took her hefty frame down the path and back to number 8.

Ben stood at the sitting room door, balancing the dishes in his hands. 'It looks like it's chicken pie and mash tonight. Are you hungry? Shall I warm the oven up?'

'Yeah, I'm hungry – in fact I'm starving.'

The sun began to drop in the sky and the small birds outside in the trees quietened their babbling tweets.

'Shall we have supper on our laps?' he said, nudging the door open with his foot.

'Sounds good.' He left the sitting room, returning with a beer from the fridge. The sun began to dip in the west, making way for the moon to light the darkening Essex skies.

He drew the curtains, the aromas of black pomegranate from the burning candle infusing the room.

Together they ate the chicken pie on their laps. Gladys Pope certainly was a good cook and made a mean pie, chunky and wholesome and every bit as stodgy as her figure. It was the most Lucy had eaten in days. Hospital food wasn't up to much at best, but she had never felt hungry and would simply push her food around her plate. For the first few days she had been on a drip and most of the time she was in and out of sleep. Each mouthful hurt when it touched her fat split lip, and her ribs ached almost all of the time. The clock in the kitchen ticked: its hands sat at eight-thirty.

'I feel like I need to go to bed now. I'm tired.' She lifted the throw that was tucked around her feet and made her way up the stairs. As she reached the top she stopped, her hand on the bannister.

'Ben!'

Ben hurriedly left the sofa to find Lucy motionless at the top of the stairs.

'What is it?'

'The door, it's closed. Ben, the door, it's closed. Why is the door closed?' She crumpled to the ground, her head in her knees, her sobbing hard and unstoppable. 'The door, Ben, the door, he's been here, he's been here.'

'Hey Lucy, come here.' He shielded her in his arms, rocking her backwards and forwards. 'What door, tell me, what door?'

'The door. The door to the room, it's closed. He's closed my door. My room. My writing room door. He's been here. He's been here, Ben, he's been in my writing room. He's been in my room.' She sobbed into Ben's chest, his top wet with her tears. Her nose streaming, the salty tears falling down her cheeks and over her lips. He lifted her face, brushing away the tears, wiping her runny nose with the cuff of his sleeve, unfazed by the slug-like slime trail it left.

He gently lifted her from the stairs and prised open the door.

'See, it's just how you left it.'

She stood and stared at her desk, and then at the cabinet that was full of five books by an author she knew well, 'Lucy Carter.' And a row of books she hadn't known the author of, but whose house she had lived in. An author who wrote about love, hope and fear. An author who had written through her own heartache, the heartache of losing Jim, the man who loved her and protected her and her country. A room Lucy had begun to love being in - and now once again her head, her heart, her mind were full of dread and fear. Slowly she walked to her desk and brushed her fingers along the old typewriter that sat next to her laptop. She pressed down on a key, then another, then another, then another. The roller whirred along until it pinged. A coating of dust lay on her sleek laptop. She swept her finger across it, leaving a lightly cleared trail.

Turning away from it, she left the room and went to her bedroom. The tree's branches tapped on the window, the moon, now high in the sky, throwing a glow on her window and casting shadows against her walls. She turned the side light on and undressed, leaving a pile of clothes on the floor. Ben sat on the side of the bed.

'Shall I stay in here tonight?'

'Er, yeah, I'd like you to.'

Her head rested on the pillow and slowly the night stole her away.

He pulled the duvet around her shoulders and kissed her forehead, then left her sleeping. He turned on the light in her writing room and sat in her chair at her bureau. He rolled the paper up to see what she had typed. It read: – *Affliction.*

Chapter Nine

Thursday, 6th March
Wrabness, Essex

The familiar sound of the morning chorus woke Lucy. She hadn't heard the birds' shrill song for a while, and it felt good to hear it once again. She rubbed her bleary eyes gently. The swelling had gone down a little, though they still felt bruised. She turned to find her phone to see what the time was. It wasn't on the side. She lay in bed listening to the sounds coming from the kitchen. She could hear Ben whistling whilst he clattered about in the cupboards. She leant across and pulled the curtain a little to let in some more of the sun's morning light. Its early morning rays, soft and diffusing, gave way to the opera in the tree's branches, which became louder and more powerful, as if the golden rays were a conductor's baton.

Ben appeared at the door, wearing his boxers and T-shirt.

'Peppermint tea, gorgeous?'

'I'd love one.' She wriggled up the bed and adjusted her pillows. He placed the tea on the bedside table.

'Are you not working today?'

'Not today. I've taken the day off to be with you. They're fine about it at the yard. We are working on a pretty awesome yacht in the dry-dock, she's going to be a dream when we've finished her. Some rich guy from St Helen's commissioned the build of her. It's still early days, Rob's working on her with me. They know you're home now, so Pete's good for me to be with you.'

'Right, OK. Have you heard from the boys and Jo? When is she coming down?'

'Matt's picking her up later, I think he said after lunch. They're coming over later to see you.'

'That'll be nice. I need to get up, I guess.'

'There's plenty of time.' He sat on the bed next to her and passed her tea. The muscles in his arm flexed.

'Right, I'm going to have a shower and then make you some breakfast. We need to get your strength back up again.' He left her with her tea. The pump of the shower kicked in and she could hear through the wall the sound of the water running.

The bathroom lock unclicked, and Ben emerged with a towel wrapped tightly around his waist, revealing his bare chest rippled with a six-pack and the tattoo she so loved that circled around his upper arm like an intricate inked bracelet. She watched him as he dressed, the taut, strong lines in his back. He pulled up his jeans, threw on his T-shirt and left Lucy alone. She heard the curtain across the front door being pulled open.

Now he was downstairs, she could muster up the courage to shower and dress herself. She slowly rolled the duvet off her and carefully swivelled her legs out, steadily easing herself out of the bed. She padded across the bedroom floor to the bathroom. She smeared her hand across the steamed-up mirror and looked at herself in it. It was the first time she'd seen her face since the brutal attack. A reflection she didn't recognise stared back at her. The two gashes on either side of her temples, her cheekbone a yellowy-blue colour and her lip still a little swollen. Her eye now almost open and the swelling not as prominent.

How could Ben love or want a face like this? She touched her neck: the lines where it had been gripped were fading away. As she lifted her top, she saw the bruising on her ribs was still purple. She could feel her ribcage. For days she'd been fed by a drip simply because of the pain to her mouth and jaw. She stood on the scales; the dial hovered and swung until it settled on 44kg, so she'd lost 10kg whilst in hospital. Her body felt weaker as she leant across to turn the shower on. Her legs threatened to buckle beneath her. The water gushed out, steaming up the bathroom again and hiding the smear she'd made on the mirror. Hiding what she didn't want to see. Hiding the ugliness that had stood in front of it.

She climbed into the shower. Her toes curled as they touched the cold ceramic of the bath. She let the water drench her tiny frame. It trickled down the nape of her neck and down her back. She lifted up her head, so the sprays of water splattered across her face, soothing the bruising that still showed. Opening the bottle of shampoo, she lathered up the suds. She could still feel small particles of sand in her hair, and she scrubbed at it, trying to wash away that night, her scrub more aggressive and manic. She crumpled to the floor of the bath and cried, cried until the tears blended with the sprays of water that hit her body.

Ben could hear the humming of the boiler and the shower's pump buzzing. She'd been in the shower for over twenty minutes. The eggs fervently knocked together in the boiling water, nudging their fragile shells in the pan. The toast popped up – smoke funnelled into the air. The kettle boiled noisily. A small plate fell to the ground and shattered. He caught his shoulder on the kitchen door. His hand swung around the newel at the end of the bannister. Taking two steps at a time, his feet hit the stairs.

'Lucy!'

She didn't answer, the sound of the water drowning out her name. He knocked on the door.

'Lucy, can you hear me?' He knocked again with more panic. 'Lucy, can you hear me? Are you OK?' No reply came. The water of the shower still running. He stood back and then heaved his shoulder into the door. The catch broke. He barged in. The steam hit his face like a hot mist. Lucy sat huddled in the bath with the water pummelling her. Her arms were clutched around her bent legs. Her teary face on her bent-up knees. Ben turned the shower off and took a towel from the rail, then wrapped it around her and gently lifted her from the shower, her hair soaked and clinging to her face. Slowly he carried her from the bathroom and into the bedroom. He sat on the edge of the bed, her crunched-up body in his arms. The water dripped from the strands of her hair and soaked his T-shirt through. He smoothed away her hair as it stuck to her face. He kissed her forehead and head as she shivered in the warmth of the soft white towel. Her eyes closed over and over again, each time showing her the images like a Polaroid photograph. Her mind in shreds; she would never get the picture out of her head.

He held her tight as she lay still in his arms. Gently, he lifted her from his lap and rested her on the side of the bed. She shivered. Her toes on point as they barely touched the soft carpet under them. He opened the drawer and found her clothes. Lightly he dried her, lifting her arms to aid her with her bra. Tenderly cupping it round her smooth curves. His hands touched the skin of her back as he did up the clasp. Her back arched abruptly at his touch. With care and affection, he dressed her, trying to ignore her arched back from his unwanted touch. Taking her hairbrush from the dressing-table, he pulled it slowly through the drenched strands of hair. He'd never brushed a girl's hair before. Was he hurting her? The sound of the hairdryer was noisy and obtrusive. Its heat blasted in her face.

Clutching her shoulders, he helped her to her feet. Taking her in his arms, he carried her down the stairs and laid her on the sofa. He left her alone.

The clock in the kitchen ticked. The sound of a dustpan and brush sweeping up the smashed pieces of china. The clang of the bin lid shutting as the broken plate tumbled into it. The toast in the toaster now stale and cold. The soft-boiled eggs now hard-boiled and fizzing about on tiny bubbles that were clinging to the bottom of the pan. The gas hob burning a hot, blue, angry flame. The saucepan now with a white stain from the dried, evaporated water.

He flicked on the kettle and made a peppermint tea and a cafetière of fresh coffee. Fresh toast popped up and he slathered butter over it. It seeped into the small air pockets of the warm golden toast. He smoothed a sliver of Marmite over the toast and cut it in half.

He took it into the sitting room and left it with Lucy. Then he went back to the kitchen to make a call, closing the kitchen door with a soft cushioning sound. He dialled Jo's number. The morning had been lost.

'Hi Ben.'

'Hi Jo.' The line went silent.

'Ben? Are you still there? Sorry, I've got a really bad line, I'm on the train.'

'Yep, I'm still here.'

'How's Lucy?'

'What time are you arriving?'

'Umm, the train gets in at 11.56. Matt's picking me up. How's things?'

'I brought Lucy home yesterday evening.'

'Well, that's good news. How is she?'

'I found her in the shower this morning, a crumpled mess,' Ben said, leaning on the worktop.

'Right ... and now?'

'She lay in my arms like a small child.'

'Oh gosh ... I'll be there soon, Ben, I'm about twenty minutes away if that. I'll come straight to you. Matt's got the day off today. I'll get him to drop me straight over. Where is she now?'

'In the sitting room, with some toast and tea.'

'How are you doing?' Jo asked tenderly and with concern for the guy who'd spent every waking hour with her bashed, bruised best friend.

'I'm OK. Maybe Matt could stay too, go for a walk or something with me. This is hard, Jo.'

'Sure. Listen, I'm in the quiet carriage and I've got some old goat giving me the evil eye. Take care of yourself and Lucy and I'll see you very soon. You're doing OK, Ben.'

He placed the phone down on the table and went back to the sitting room. Shifting the cushions from Lucy's feet, he sat next to her and cupped her feet in his hands, softly rubbing them.

'That was Jo on the phone,' he said. 'She'll be here in twenty minutes or so.' He didn't know what to say or how to make Lucy better. He didn't know how to control the feelings he had inside of him, and yet it wasn't about him. It was about Lucy. He wanted to take Charlie by the neck and wring every inch of breath out of his vile, horrible body.

'I'd like to see Jo,' she said as she stared into the hearth. 'I've missed her. Is Matt bringing her over?'

'Yep.'

The letterbox clattered noisily as the post fell to the floor. The whistling of a happy go-lucky postman could be heard as he sauntered along down the street.

'The post,' she said. 'I like that sound, don't you?'

'Yeah, I like that sound.' He got up to retrieve it.

'Anything important?'

'Looks like junk mainly and an NHS letter. D'you want to open it?'

'I'll open it later.'

He popped the post on the table and began to clear the fireplace.

'Shall I make a fire for you?'

'Yeah, that sounds like a good idea. I feel a bit cold. You're pretty much a pro at it.' A faint smile showed on her face. 'Ben ...'

'Yep.'

'The door in the bathroom, you'll need to fix it.'

'I know, and I'll have a look at the lock on the front door, too, and the squeaking on the gate.' He turned and smiled at her, a reassuring smile.

'Ben ...'

'Yep, gorgeous.'

'I'm sorry.' A single tear fell down her cheek.

He wobbled up from his knees and sat on the edge of the sofa, stroking away her tear.

'You've got nothing to be sorry for. D'you hear me? Nothing.'

She watched him as he went back to the fire and scrunched the newspaper into balls, dotting kindling around it before resting an old dried log on the top. The fire caught and the flames sizzled around the dried wood.

After a time, the knocker on the door rapped loudly and two voices outside could be heard. Ben got up and opened the door.

'Jo, hi!'

Jo threw open her arms and hugged Ben tightly. She let go of him and stood back. 'Is the patient in here?' She gestured towards the sitting room door.

He nodded. Matt shook Ben's hand, 'Sod it, mate.' He pulled his hand in and gave him a manly embrace. 'Come on, let's go for a walk. I think you need one. The girls need some time together.'

'See you in a bit, boys!' Jo closed the front door behind them.

Jo popped her head around the door and beamed. 'Hey, gorgeous girl. Look at you! You're looking so much better. Peppermint tea? Any coffee on the go? I'm gasping.'

'Am I? I saw myself for the first time in the mirror today and it frightened me. I didn't recognise myself. I don't know how to recognise me anymore.'

'Right, listen, hold your thoughts, I'm going to make your tea and a coffee and then I am right here with you.'

Jo left Lucy for a few minutes and came back with a freshly made strong coffee and a peppermint tea. She placed them on the table.

Jo then moved over to the sofa and bent down to Lucy, balancing her hand on the sofa's arm. 'You saw yourself in the mirror?'

'Yeah.'

'Listen to me. You are the most beautiful girl in the world. Your face, your mind, your body, your writing. Just you. Don't ever doubt that.'

'But …'

'No buts. What Charlie's done is horrific. But the bruising will go. You need to focus on the now. Charlie is your past.'

Lucy pulled herself up a little.

'Ben tried to help me dress in the hospital when I was being discharged yesterday.'

'OK, that's good isn't it?' Jo asked coaxingly.

'His hand touched my bare back and I flinched. I squirmed when he touched me. He placed my clothes on the chair and he left the room. And I knew in that moment he was hurting from what I did. But I didn't know how to stop it, to say come back, don't go. Doris, my nurse, came in and helped me finish dressing.'

'OK, but Lucy, listen …'

'Wait – let me finish. When I stood in the corridor, I could see he'd been crying. I've hurt him, Jo. I pushed him away. I couldn't let him touch me and he felt that. I gave him that feeling.'

'Oh my gosh, Luce.' Jo stood up and sat by Lucy and held her head against her heart. She smoothed her soft dark hair. She just held her softly, saying *shhh* as she did.

'How are you doing, Ben?' Matt asked as he lit a cigarette.

'D'you know what, mate, I don't smoke but I want to bloody smoke right now. I found Lucy in the shower today, I had to break the door down. She was on the floor, just a mess. Every time I touch her it feels like I make her skin crawl. I don't think I can deal with this. I want to but I don't know how to. I want to break his fucking kneecaps and punch his face until his mouth is throbbing like Lucy's, pummel him until his scrawny body stops breathing.'

'Mate, you, me and Simon all want to see him suffer. But promise me you'll keep that to yourself. Like Simon said in court, you'll be done for GBH and it doesn't help Lucy. That tosser has hurt a person we all love, but the police will deal with this. DI Phillips is on him. CID phoned the station yesterday. Phillips is pretty sure he's in Spain. A Red Notice has been requested and Interpol are now on it too. Phillips *will* find him! He hasn't let go of this. He's on it and he'll get him. And I swear to God he's one of the best in the Met.'

'How long's that gonna take, though? He could be anywhere – Spain's a big country. How the fuck's he got to Spain? Surely, he wouldn't have got through passport control. How the fuck has he escaped?'

'Phillips knows he stowed away on a private shipping container that was due to arrive in Spain. With any luck, he rotted to his own death in it. Simon mentioned something about the Royal Navy but didn't go into any details,' Matt said. 'DS Murphy has searched for his next of kin. His mother is Spanish, and Rachel Jones, his neighbour in London, has corroborated that. They think she lives in Valencia. If he's still alive he's probably on his way to her. CID just need to locate her. Give it time, mate, give it time. They'll get him. They'll get the fucking bastard! But for now, keep doing what you're doing. Lucy needs you.'

'The Royal Navy? What have they done? Is he still on the container?'

'I don't know, I'd tell you if I did. But just remember Lucy needs you.'

'She might need me, but she doesn't want me. Something's happened, hasn't it?'

'I don't know. Simon spoke with the DI and something went down with the "dark blues" – I don't know what, though. Listen, she's been to hell and back. She does want you! She just needs to work that bit out for herself. I know it's hard. I can't even begin to imagine how you're feeling. But me, Simon and Jo are here for you. Don't give up, mate. Don't give up on Lucy. Don't let that evil shit win.'

'I can't believe I'm even thinking of throwing in the towel. What kind of guy does that make me? To leave a girl after this. It makes me as bad as him. As worthless as him.'

'No, it makes you human. Come on, let's get back to the girls. I wouldn't mind a beer, too – any Buds in the fridge?'

Matt threw his arm around Ben and squeezed his shoulder.

The gate squeaked as Matt opened it. He turned to Ben and smiled.

'You need to sort that squeak out, mate, it's bloody irritating.'

The door of number 8 flew open.

'Young Ben!' came the holler from Gladys Pope, rollers in her hair and a duster in her hand. 'I've got that broth for you! Come and get it, would you, love.'

'Here Matt, the keys, I'll see you back inside.' He tossed the keys to Matt and crossed the road to Gladys's cottage.

'Afternoon, Mrs Pope.'

'Wait there, love, I'll go get it.'

Ben stood at the doorway. The television inside her cottage was booming in the background.

She waddled back down the hallway and handed him a huge great saucepan of still-warm chicken broth. 'I see you've got that lovely Officer Willis and Lucy's friend over too. There's enough to feed you all. Fresh vegetables and chicken in the broth, just needs warming, me love.'

'That's very kind of you, thank you.'

'No bother. 'ow is Lucy? She was such a strong lass in court. I'd take two rolling pins to that rat if I could.'

'She's OK, we're getting there.'

'Well, you make sure you send 'er me best, d'you 'ear me.'

'I will and thank you again, Mrs Pope.'

'No bother. Always ready to 'elp in the community.' Ben turned to cross the road.

'Will you turn that wretched telly down Stan, for gawd's sake! You old sod. I'm sick and tired of the darts.' The door of number 8 closed, but not before Ben heard Stan grunting from his chair and turning the telly up.

Ben smiled to himself. Would he and Lucy ever be at that stage.

He placed the pot of broth on the mat and rapped on the door.

Chapter Ten

Thursday, 6th March

Ben carried the warm pot of broth into the kitchen and lit the hob on a gentle flame. Matt followed him through and opened the fridge to extract a couple of beers. 'Want one?' he said, handing Ben a bottle of Budweiser.

'I'd love one. I'll go and see if the girls want anything. Keep an eye on that soup!' Leaving his opened beer on the side, Ben went to the sitting room and poked his head around the door.

'Hey, d'you fancy a drink? We're having a beer.'

'Ben, I would love a drink!' Jo exclaimed. 'How about you Luce, do you feel up to it?'

'To be honest, I don't think I do. It might give me a fuzzy head. But you have one, I don't mind. There's white in the fridge and red on the wine rack.'

'OK, let's go white.' Jo said, rummaging through her bag for her Marlboro Gold cigarettes. 'I'm just popping out for a quick ciggie, I'm gasping for one. I'll be right back.'

'Can I keep you company?'

'Of course you can, gorgeous girl. You just looked all snug on the sofa.'

Lucy's Uggs were still by the sofa. She winced a little as she put them on.

'Still sore, Luce?'

'Yeah, a little. Dr Thiroux said it would take a while for the pain to really go. He said he was expecting to see broken ribs and a fractured cheekbone from the bruising. Nothing showed up on the X-rays, though.'

'Well, that's good news. Here, let me help you.'

Lucy eased herself up and walked cautiously to the kitchen. Each step felt like she was walking on ice. The two boys were leaning against the worktop, chatting with a bottle of beer in their hands. The soup was still gently simmering away. The homely aroma of Gladys Pope's cooking wafted around the cosy kitchen.

'I've popped a couple of those ready-to-bake baguette things in the oven,' Ben said as he unlocked the back door for Jo. 'You going out for a smoke?'

'I am indeed. The obligatory smoky-Jo,' Jo laughed.

Lucy stood outside whilst Jo blew a plume of smoke into the air. It caught in the spring breeze and floated away.

'Are you OK standing – shall I grab that chair for you?' Jo asked, moving towards the folded, dilapidated old garden chair that rested against the tired-looking fence, overhung with ivy.

'I think I might end up on the floor with even more bruising if I sat on that!' Lucy said with a laugh. It was the first time she'd laughed since her time in hospital. It was the first time that life didn't feel quite so dark. She'd missed Jo and now she was here. Life was beginning to feel a little more normal with Jo being at the cottage. It was the first time she'd smelt a cigarette and didn't feel dread, too.

'How's the wine?'

'Like sweet nectar. D'you know I haven't had a drink since … Oh my God, Tuesday!'

Lucy cracked another smile. 'Jo, it's only Thursday! That's like, two days ago?'

'I know! Get me! How good is that? I missed a whole day out from drinking. How amazing is that? I am certifiably not an alcoholic.'

Lucy laughed. Her laughter could be heard inside by the boys. The most wondrous sound that day in the garden.

'Jo, you just missed Wednesday out?'

'I know! Fuck me, how did that happen? Call the press, this is frontline news! And look what else, Lucy Luce …'

'What?'

'You're smiling.'

'Come on, let's go back in and see what those boys are up to.'

Lucy walked over to the fridge and took out the chilled bottle of Sauvignon Blanc. 'Can you grab me a glass, Ben?'

Lucy poured a minuscule glass of wine for herself. Something inside her had shifted. She was back in the home she so loved, where she belonged. Holding her glass in her hand, she walked over to Ben to rest her head on his shoulder. But before she could get close enough, there was a knock at the door.

'I'll get it. Are you expecting anyone?' Jo said, walking down the hallway. She opened the front door and put her finger to her lips. The front door closed behind her. Jo pushed the kitchen door open.

'Simon!' Lucy exclaimed.

'Come here, gorgeous.' With the gentleness that he oozed, he hugged Lucy. 'How's my favourite author?' It was so good to see Simon. He'd sat with her as a policeman when she'd first arrived. A tea-no-sugar kind of chap. He'd taken her statement, escalating it to the Met because he knew something wasn't right. He was your typical police officer who had an inner depth to him that didn't give up. He was never going to give up on Lucy. He was the friend who'd basted a turkey with her, watched her in a courtroom, willed her on. She'd caught him unawares with her simplicity and openness to life, and now he was bewitched by her.

'I'm OK,' she said, smiling and looking up at him. 'Beer?'

'Well, it would be rude not to.' She took a beer from the fridge and handed it to him.

She brushed past Jo and Matt and went straight back to Simon, and rested her head on his arm. Matt caught Ben's eye as he took a swig from his bottle. The five together again in a kitchen that brought warmth and happiness and Gladys Pope's homemade soup.

'Who's hungry?' Ben said as placed his almost empty bottle down on the worktop. 'Not sure how we're going to do this; there's only four chairs. I wasn't expecting you, Simon.'

'Half day at the station,' Simon said.

'Easy! There's a chair outside in the garden. I knew you were coming but I forgot to say,' Jo said with a glint in her eye and casting a mischievous look at Lucy. Matt went outside to get the old garden chair propped up against the fence. He opened it and popped it up by the table. Simon went to sit on it.

'No, don't!' squealed Lucy, smiling. 'You'll end up on the floor!" The two girls laughed childishly. 'Ouch! my ribs. Don't make me laugh, it hurts too much.' Slowly, the Lucy they knew and loved was beginning to show herself again. As much as they didn't want her ribs to hurt, it felt good to see. It was a good kind of hurting because behind the mask of bruising and swelling, she was happy and smiling.

'OK, I'll volunteer myself to not have a chair. I'll sit on Matt's lap – haven't sat there for a while and I'm missing it,' Jo said as she wiggled her bottom down onto his lap.

'You're so bad, Jo. But I like it,' Matt said as he squidged her sides.

Simon got bowls from the cupboard and Lucy took five spoons from the drawer. Ben began to ladle the steaming hot soup into bowls. He took the ready-to-bake-baguettes from the oven and cut them into uneven hunks of bread. They were golden and crispy, the steam from the soft doughy insides escaping into the air. The sound of the chatter in the kitchen reverberated around the old brick walls of the cottage. For weeks it had been an empty shell of a house, free of noise and laughter. And now, as if the two weeks had never happened, it became a little reminiscent of their first Christmas, which they had all shared together, now with one newcomer to the table, Ben.

In the sitting room, Lucy's phone jumped and buzzed along the coffee table.

'Your phone's ringing,' Jo said.

Lucy left the others to answer it, but as she reached it, it rang off. She stood at the low-slung table and disconnected it from the charger. Bold red letters read: *Missed call – no ID number.*

Simon left the kitchen, with Ben's eyes followed him. He pushed the sitting room door open a little to find Lucy holding her phone, staring at the withheld number.

'What is it, Lucy? Everything OK?' he asked, moving towards her.

'A missed call.' Her voice was faint and apprehensive.

'Who from?'

'I don't know. It's him, isn't it?'

'Could be a cold caller, could be a wrong number. Could be anyone.'

The phone pinged to announce a voicemail. Her hand trembled. 'Er, can you listen to it?'

'Sure, pass it here.'

Lucy, good morning, DI Phillips here. I just wanted to make sure you were OK and safely home. Could you give me a call on my direct line, 020 7368 1283. Many thanks.

'It was DI Phillips,' Simon said. 'There, feel a little happier?'

'What did he say?'

'He'd like you to call him. Would you like me to stay with you whilst you call?'

'I'll call after lunch. But yes please. Come on, our soup will be getting cold.' She left the phone on the table with the unwanted words *No ID number* in red on its screen.

Ben watched as Lucy took a seat opposite him. Simon pulled out a chair and sat down.

'Who was on the phone?' Ben asked, breaking the sound of hungry slurping.

'DI Phillips,' Simon said, throwing a reassuring look at Lucy.

'Right, that was a quick call,' Ben said, taking a swig from his bottle.

'It was a voicemail,' Lucy said. 'I'll call him back after lunch, Simon's going to call with me.'

'That's good of you, Simon.' Ben took another swig from his beer and placed his bottle down with an audible thud.

Simon looked at him quizzically, a little perplexed by his attitude. 'I guess.'

There was an awkward silence across the table. Ben scraped his chair across the floor.

'Right, if it's OK. I'm going to go and get some clothes whilst Lucy's got company.' He took the last swig from his bottle and left the four of them. The front door slammed shut.

'Did I say something?' Simon asked, unsure why Ben had left so abruptly.

'Leave him, he'll cool off,' Matt said, opening another beer.

'Cool off?' Lucy questioned.

'Touch of the green-eyed monster,' Jo butted in.

'Jo!' Matt pinched her sides.

'What?! Just stating the obvious. Why else would he leave? He hasn't even finished his soup. I mean, come on, it's obvious, isn't it?'

'Obvious …? Meaning?' Lucy pushed.

'Dunno, ignore me. Grab the wine, Matt.'

Lucy shrugged and tipped her bowl to get the last dregs of the soup from the bottom.

'Right, I'm going for a cigarette, you coming?' Jo said, swivelling round to Matt.

'Sure, babe.'

Lucy left Simon alone in the kitchen to clear the table. She came back holding her phone in her hand.

'You wanna call?' he said kindly.

'Yeah, can we?'

'OK – do you want me to talk or d'you want to talk?'

'Umm, can we put it on speaker phone and then you can join in too. Am I allowed to do that?'

'Sure, away you go, dial through.'

Apprehensively Lucy pressed the keypad.

'It's ringing,' she said.

'No shit Sherlock, it's on speaker phone,' Simon joked.

'Oh yeah, I forgot that.'

'DI Phillips, CID.'

Lucy froze. Simon threw a nudging glance.

She took a deep breath.

'Umm … DI Phillips, it's Lucy, Lucy Carter.'

Phillips reclined in his office chair, his feet on his desk, his arm in a sling. 'Lucy. How are you?'

'I'm OK, I'm home now.'

'Yes, Dr Thiroux called me to say you'd been discharged. How's everything?'

'Umm, good thank you. Simon is here with me now.'

'Ah, good job. Now, are you happy to talk?'

'Er, I guess. Simon's right by my side.'

'Good work. Now in terms of your safety, I don't want you to be alarmed but I have arranged for two plain-clothed officers to move in close to you at Lambourne Terrace.'

'Plain-clothed?'

'Yes, to blend in with the village community.'

'Right, OK. Do you think he's going to come back for me?'

'I don't know what his moves will be, but I don't want you to be alarmed. You will be under close surveillance.'

'OK.'

'At present we have him tracked as being in Spain – Valencia, to be precise. DS Kennedy and DC Milson have spoken with Rachel Jones, your ex-neighbour here in London. We have Interpol on this with a Red Notice alert. I am in close contact with the local Spanish police and we believe he has probably made his way to his mother's.'

'So, you know where she lives?'

'That, Lucy, we don't know. Yet.'

'What if he comes back?'

'He will be arrested at passport control, but to be honest I don't think he will try. What I need from you is to act as normally as possible. You are in safe hands now and we will not let any harm come to you. The undercover surveillance officers will mingle and blend, so act as you would as if they were members of the community. Don't draw attention to them or yourself. They will follow you everywhere until we have further word from Interpol on Charlie's whereabouts. We're keeping you safe, Lucy.'

'Right.'

'Can I have a word with Simon, is that OK?

'Sure.' Phillips kicked his feet down from his desk and walked to his window. He scanned the streets on Fulham Broadway.

'And Lucy, take care of yourself. Don't forget I'm wanting a signed copy of that novel you're writing.'

'Yep, OK.' She handed the phone over to Simon. 'He wants to speak to you.'

Lucy left Simon and went into the garden to join Jo and Matt.

'Afternoon, sir,' Simon said.

'Simon, I expect you heard most of that.' Simon turned the phone's speaker off.

'I did, sir.'

'How's Lucy bearing up?'

'She's good, actually, she's been smiling today.'

'Good job.'

'You mentioned Valencia, sir.'

'Yup. DS Murphy has tracked his mother to Valencia, so we've got some serious combing of the area to do with the help of the Spanish police. We are concentrating on the province of Castellón. Our leads are pointing us to Peñíscola.'

'So, he was on the container ship then?'

'He was.'

'You said *was*, sir. And now?'

'We had a covert operation with the "dark blues", Simon.'

'The Navy?'

'Royal Marines, to be precise. I was on board HMS Albion in the Med, had him in my grasp.'

'Had him?'

'He took me out, gunshot to the shoulder. The Royal Marine commando took him down, his body went overboard.'

'So, he's dead?'

'I don't believe so. I believe him to be in Spain.'

'If he was shot, sir, and went overboard, isn't he likely to have drowned?'

'I don't believe him to be dead. I have a gut feeling and it tells me he's not dead. He'd like me to believe it.'

'And you, sir. You're injured?'

'A scratch,' Phillips said, brushing off his own wound.

'Right. Shit. Matt said you had news on his father.'

'Deceased – plane crash in 1992.'

'He also said Rachel Jones had been interviewed.'

'Yup, she's co-operated with our enquiries and has confirmed that his mother is Sofia Martinez and lives in Valencia, we think. My gut says he's drifted onto land. Chances are he's hiding out. Miss Jones has led us to believe that his relationship with his mother is pitted with holes and they are estranged. That said, we are not ruling the mother out as a safe house.'

'That's some gut feeling, sir.'

'I know. I need a dead body to prove me wrong. I don't have one.'

'He definitely can't get through border control then, sir.'

'Not a hope in hell. He's wanted as a fugitive. Interpol have fingerprints, DNA, eye colour, the lot. He's on their wanted list. Unless he's about to morph into John Travolta's "Face Off", he's cornered. That's if he's still in Spain.'

'And the plain-clothed officers, sir?'

'From the Met, I'm keeping this tight. DC Milson and Parker. Male and female officers. They are located at 10 Lambourne Terrace; it was up for rental. I have twelve officers on the Major Incident Team. Need to keep it closed in.'

'Right, and the press?'

'Press are being kept at bay. The operation is too sensitive, and with the internet and social media, I need to let Charlie think he's safe.'

'And the operation code name, sir?'

'Operation Butterfly. Right, Mackenzie, I need to brief the team. Look after Lucy and keep vigilant.'

'Sir.'

'Good work. You'd work well in the Met, Mackenzie.' Phillips closed the call.

Simon left Lucy's phone on the table and opened the door into the garden.

'Any news?' Matt asked.

'Only that he's not in the country. And Lucy is under police protection.'

'Well, that's good.'

'Yeah, it is. I like this DI Phillips.' Simon moved over to Lucy and put his arm around her, giving her an encouraging rub on the arm. 'You OK?'

She nodded with a smile.

'He's a top officer, Phillips, isn't he,' Matt said, throwing his cigarette butt into the flowerpot.

'Thorough, bloody thorough. He's not left any stone unturned.'

'Right, I'm going back inside,' Lucy said, opening the door. 'I need to see where Ben is. He's been gone ages.'

'Yep, I'm coming too, it's not very warm out here,' Jo piped up.

Lucy took her phone into the sitting room and stoked the fire. It had almost gone out, with just a layer of red-hot ashes glimmering in the hearth. She threw on another log before settling down onto the sofa. She opened up her messages on her mobile and began to type.

Hey …

The dots below bubbled whilst she waited for Ben to reply. They stopped bubbling. She sighed to herself and took the post from the coffee table. Sifting through, she found the NHS letter and opened it. It was referring her to see Dr Hawkins, a psychological therapist. The appointment was for Wednesday, 19th March at 10 a.m. The voices of the others came bounding down the hall.

'You OK, Luce?' Jo said, perching on the sofa's arm.

'Yeah, I'm good. I've got an appointment.'

'For?'

'A therapist. A Dr Hawkins.'

'Hmmm, male or female?'

'Dunno, I guess I'll have to wait and see.'

'So, you're gonna go?'

'I've never been to a counsellor or therapist before. I'm not sure. I feel like I want to go to the beach first.'

'So why don't we go? We could go now, if you feel up to it.'

'Ben's not back, though.'

'So, text him.'

'I did.'

'And ...'

'And nothing, he's read it. Just didn't reply.'

'Matt, you went for a walk with him, was he OK?' Jo asked.

'Yeah, he seemed fine, a bit stressed, but you know, all things considered – he's a bloke, he's fine. He's just getting his stuff. Tell him we're at the beach.'

'No. I'll wait. I can do the beach tomorrow, maybe with some peppermint tea. That sounds like a better idea.'

The roaring noise of a motorbike's engine stopped outside the cottage. Simon looked out. 'Speak of the devil,' he said.

The knocker on the door rapped hard. Matt got up to open it.

'Sorry, I forgot to take a key.'

He brushed past Matt with a rucksack on his back and his helmet tucked under his arm. He hung the helmet on the newel of the bannister and took his bag upstairs, leaving it by the door of Lucy's writing room. He sprinted back down the stairs.

'Anyone for a beer,' he said as popped his head around the door, repressing the feelings he felt inside.

'Love one, mate,' Simon said.

'Make that two,' Matt chipped in.

'Would love a top-up, Ben.' Jo handed him her glass.

'I'll help him,' Lucy said, getting up from the sofa.

'You need to be resting,' Jo said.

'I need to do something to help, and I need to see Ben.'

Lucy left the three friends in the sitting room and made her way to the kitchen.

'Are you OK?' she asked as she leant on the worktop.

'Yeah, I'm cool, just needed to get my stuff.'

'But you left without finishing lunch.'

'I needed to get my stuff.'

'Right, but couldn't it have waited until after lunch?'

'Probably, just figured it would be a good idea to go.'

'Ben?'

He opened the fridge to take out three Buds and a top-up for Jo.

'Ben?'

'Yep.'

'Stop.' She held his hand on the fridge as he opened it.

'What's the matter? I'm just getting the drinks, Lucy.'

'You're acting strangely.'

'No, I'm just getting the drinks.'

He balanced the drinks in his hands, then brushed past Lucy. 'You coming?'

'Yeah, sure.' *And no, I didn't want a glass of anything,* she said to herself, sighing and shaking her head in disbelief.

Jo was still perched on the sofa's arm. Matt had shifted next to her on the sofa, with Simon slouched on the old leather beanbag. Ben went and sat in the armchair, leaving space for Lucy on the sofa next to Matt.

'Jo, how long are you down for?' Lucy asked.

'A week or so. I've taken annual leave. I'm staying at Matt's, but I'll be here for you mainly.'

'Cool – and you'll be back at work, Ben, won't you?' Lucy said, glancing at Ben. She felt awkward.

'Yeah, I'll be back at work, but here at night. I'm on the bike, though. I can get there and back quicker.'

'Perfect. I think I'm all covered, then, with you all. Are you guys going to order a cab later? You've had a couple of beers.'

'I'll call Dave's taxis,' Simon said. 'However, we're not going anywhere yet and I think tonight we should have a curry. Who's game?'

'I'd love a curry, I haven't had one in yonks,' Lucy said. 'D'you fancy curry, Ben?'

'Yeah, whatever, I'll get the menu.' Ben left the room. He still seemed a little short with her. Lucy threw Jo a glance. Jo shook her head: *Leave it, he'll be good,* she telegraphed with a smile, reassuring Lucy.

Chapter Eleven

Friday, 7th March

Lucy woke in the morning and turned towards Ben. His side of the bed was empty and cold. She leant over to her bedside table and looked at her phone. It was only seven o'clock; she'd slept right through the night without stirring. She crawled over to his side of the bed again and peered over the edge. His bag of clothes wasn't by the bed. Nor had the pillows been disturbed. They still lay perfectly by the headboard, untouched. The white duvet was still pulled high up to them, uncrumpled. She could hear the sounds of the boiler humming and the shower running.

She felt so wretched and ashamed that she'd pushed him away. They'd never spent a night apart. She rolled the duvet off her and tiptoed to the bathroom, the lock on the door still broken. She teased the knob around and opened the door.

In the bathroom, he stood with his back to her. He hadn't heard her come in. She watched him as the water soaked his body. She stripped off her top and pyjama shorts. His eyes were closed as he washed his hair. She climbed in and stood behind him, letting the water beat over her head in steamy rivulets. She closed her eyes as the water soaked into her skin. It cascaded over her and down her body. She touched his back, his muscles tight and strong. She moved her hands over them in a soft massage. The tips of her nails brushed gently on his skin, in small circles and swirls. The sensation of the steamy water calmed her.

He turned and faced her. His concerned eyes flashed down her bruised body. He touched it tenderly. Slowly she raised her arms and cupped his face in her hands. How she had fallen in love with him. She felt his hands glide over her smooth, soft skin. He lifted her chin and kissed her lips gently. The water drizzling over their faces and between their touching mouths. He stopped and looked at her. She bit her lip as the water ran from them.

'Hey, I'm sorry about yesterday,' he said.

She smiled back at him. Grabbing a towel, she left the bathroom.

She sat on the bed in her underwear as the warm air from the hairdryer buffeted through the strands of her wet hair. Her eye was still a little bruised but the swelling had gone down.

The bathroom door opened, and he stood in the bedroom doorway with a towel wrapped around his waist.

'Peppermint tea?'

'Love one.' She watched him as he sauntered out of the room and down the stairs. She clicked the hairdryer back on and curled her hair under as she dried it. Seeing Jo, Simon and Matt had filled her with good vibes. She needed to feel Ben close to her again too; she'd hurt him. Yesterday had been odd. He'd treated her distantly, maybe the same way she had treated him. Maybe she deserved it. She never wanted to hurt anybody, least of all him.

Holding two mugs in his hands, he placed them down on the dressing-table. As he walked behind her, he leant over the bed and scrunched her shoulders and nuzzled into her neck.

'What time are you working?' she asked, pulling on her leggings and a polo-neck jumper.

'Need to be at the yard for nine. What are you doing today?'

'I thought I might go to the beach.'

'Are you ready for that?'

'I don't know, but I need to go. I need to go and write again.'

'What about Jo?'

'I'm meeting her for lunch at The Pier and then I need to pop to the supermarket on the way home. There's pretty much nothing in. What time do you finish work?'

'About 5pm? I'll be home for you, though.'

'That'll be good.' Picking up her mug of tea, she went into her writing room, leaving Ben to dress.

The paper was still in the typewriter. She leant across the bureau and opened the curtains. The sun beamed through the small square panes of the window and threw a ray of light through the silk lampshade and onto the glass doors of the cabinet.

She took out the journal from the cubbyhole and opened it. Her leg was bent up and her bare foot rested on the edge of the chair. As she began to read it, the milk float rattled past along the road. She watched as the milkman stopped and delivered two milk bottles each to the cottages opposite. The door of number 10 opened and a young blonde woman appeared on the step. She looked up the street and then over to the door of Lucy's cottage.

The curtain of Gladys Pope's house twitched.

'The milkman's delivered next door to number 10, Stan. They've never 'ad milk delivered before,' she said, leaving the net curtain to fall again.

'Will you come away from that bloody curtain, woman,' Stan grumbled from his chair as he tucked into his black pudding and fried eggs, on his lap.

The milk float accelerated a little past Gladys Pope's and up towards the Hungry Hound pub on the corner. But Lucy's eyes were fixed on number 10. It was a cream painted cottage with one step leading straight from the pavement to the front door, which was painted pale blue with a brass knocker dead-centre. The curtains were open, and an empty vase stood on the sill inside. A midnight blue BMW hatchback was parked outside. She hadn't noticed the car before. She hadn't noticed the blonde woman either. She was young, maybe late twenties or early thirties.

'Hey,' Ben said breaking her thoughts from the road and the activity of the morning. 'I'm going to work now. Are you going to be OK?'

'Yeah, I'll be fine. I'm going to head to the beach soon.'

He leant over her and kissed her head. 'See you later, gorgeous.'

She tilted her head back and smiled at him. He kissed her lips gently. She was intoxicated by the divine scent of his aftershave.

'Ben.'

'Yep,' he said as reached the door.

'Make a sail for me.'

He winked at her.

She heard the front door close and watched him as he put his helmet on. He straddled his bike. The engine purred loudly as he pulled out of the space and opened up the throttle. He turned right at the T-junction, past the church, and headed in the direction of Harwich. Lucy's tummy somersaulted a little as she thought of Ben on his bike. He looked gorgeous and sexy and he was all hers - she just didn't know how to be touched by him.

She went back to Peggy's journal and turned to the diary's next entry.

Wednesday, 10th May 1942

Today, the sun is trying to shine here in the valleys. But there is a feeling of greyness and ominousness that clouds this once green land, and my heart skips a beat as I think of you. There is still a smell of burning ash and rubble that carries in the wind. York was bombed through the late April nights. The Rowntree's Factory where cousin Eleanor worked is now unrecognisable. She is safe. The primary school no longer stands and the church where we were to be married is now a pile of stone and rubble. I'm not sure how many lives the Germans took that night. They say hundreds. The skies were full of unwanted sounds, like an invasion of giant swarms of bees humming through the silence, overpowering, deafening, frightening. Then the sounds of whizzing and wheeling as another bomb could be heard dropping in the dark, black night. The screams of people running to another shelter. The air raid sirens piercing the skies with a menacing sound, unwanted. It terrifies me, that sound. My blood runs cold when it shatters the silence. Eerie and haunting. Places that were once old and beautiful and full of childhood memories ripped from the very ground. Now just a smell of lost lives. And you, my love in a split dark, dank trench. I despise that thought of you cold and wet and muddied. At least for now, I am safe, and the family are well, and we busy ourselves. But my world is no longer with you and I so want for you to be near again. I wonder if it will ever end. If I will ever see your face once more. And I know in my heart that the valleys will wait for us to wander freely in them once more. But my wait is long, and I miss you, I miss you every day. My heart aches.

Lucy rested her hand on the page where the ink had dried and faded a little. She placed the journal back in its cubbyhole and opened her laptop. She began to type her story, her story of Jim and Peggy, the love story that she would give a befitting end to, a story that deserved a fairy-tale ending. A story that was so far removed from her own life.

She looked at her phone. 'Shit,' she said out loud. It was half past ten and she was meeting Jo at The Pier for lunch at one, and she'd wanted to sit on the beach for a while. She needed to sit on the beach for a while.

She saved her work and closed her laptop. Leaving her writing room door, open she walked carefully down the stairs. The pain in her ribs was beginning to subside and every day felt so much better.

She went to the kitchen to make a flask of peppermint tea. Whilst the teabag infused in the hot water, she went back upstairs to get her satchel. It wasn't in her writing room. She went through to her bedroom - maybe it was in there? It wasn't. She went back downstairs and looked in the sitting room, but just her Uggs sat by the sofa. She searched the kitchen too. It wasn't on the worktop or hanging on the door handle. She went back to the hall and picked up the post from the mat and placed it on the side table. She lifted her car keys. She stood and stared at the keys.

Her satchel was in her Mini; she'd gone out that night to get it. She closed her eyes and began to relive the moments before it happened. As the memories edged their way back, she sat on the bottom step of the stairs, staring at the front door. Knowing she had to go to the car anyway if she wanted to drive to the beach.

Come on Lucy, she said to herself, *be brave, he's not here, he can't hurt you.* She pushed herself up from the stair and made her way around the house, grabbing what she needed – flask of tea, keys, Peggy's journal, her phone.

Closing the front door behind her, she opened the squeaky gate. The curtains at number 8 twitched. Lucy didn't notice the voyeur in the top window of number 10. The young blonde woman.

She balanced her flask of peppermint tea on the car's roof as she opened the door. Her satchel was still lying on the floor of the passenger's side. A few seconds passed, her hand still holding the key in the car's lock.

Footsteps behind her ... Ben? 'Hello Lucy.' 'Open your curtain, open your curtain, please open your curtain. Please no you're hurting me. Where's Ben, hurry, please hurry.'

A small dog yapped at her ankles and she jumped.

'You alright, love? Don't mind her, she won't hurt you,' said the passer-by.

'Oh, it's fine. Sorry.'

She placed the flask, phone and journal on the seat. Then she sat silently in the car for a while, trying to catch her breath before turning on the engine. It rattled and spluttered a little. The air billowed out noisily and a powder of dust flew into her face. She hadn't noticed the pale blue door of number 10 open and a young couple get into the midnight blue BMW opposite. She indicated and pulled out. Gladys Pope's curtain twitched as the BMW slowly drew out of its space and, keeping its distance, followed Lucy.

'Not seen that blue flash car before, Stan,' she said as she shook the pot-pourri in the glass bowl on her sill. 'I'll be walking Barry for an evening whoopsie. I'm going to watch it.'

Lucy turned to go past the police station in the direction of Harwich. The BMW turned off too. Her drive to Harwich was steady and slow; she hadn't driven since the attack and she felt a little anxious alone in the car. The flask on the seat beside her rolled from side to side as she took the country road's bends, the BMW still tailing her. She turned off at Ramsey, towards the huge great cranes she so loved seeing. The view took her thoughts and memories seamlessly back to London and the Embankment. She drove past Trinity House with its great buoys standing in the yard and snakes of chains wrapped in piles. She remembered when she'd first driven past it all and had no real idea of what it was. There had been a ship that read THV Patricia moored at the quayside. Ships she knew nothing about, only that they were perhaps Merchant Navy but nothing more than that. THV, she'd learnt, stood for Trinity House Vessel. She knew Trinity House from London and Trinity Square.

Now she knew from her times with Bob that the ships belonged to Trinity House and had helipads on them. Once Bob had been flown onto one of them from his naval ship in British waters to bring him back home. For him to run to his home, Artillery House, which was burning to the ground with his young family still inside and sleeping in that house forever more. Never waking.

Now the views and buildings and landmarks were part of her life, as much as Battersea Power Station, Big Ben, the London Eye had once been. No longer just a view, but a landscape that made up where she so loved being. The quaint RNLI museum was just ahead of her, with the jolly paintings on its walls of a rather large bather, which always made her smile. She pulled up and parked. She took her satchel and mobile, and tucked Peggy's journal into the satchel before taking the flask of peppermint tea and locking the door.

The blue BMW slunk past her and stopped a little further away. The couple got out and crossed the road, still keeping a distance. Lucy made her way down past the sailing club. It was locked up and looked like it had had a lick of paint over the last few weeks. She stopped short of the wall just by an old bench. Her hands felt clammy. She wiped them on her leggings. She looked out to the giant blue Titan cranes that stood on the horizon. The Maersk container ships were still there. She still wondered how they never sank under that enormous load. Her breathing slowed as she stared at the beach, the sand a dirty golden colour with tiny specks of black running through it, probably shards of blackened broken shells. The seaweed straggled across it, untidily sprawling its long, spindly fronds over the beach as if grasping at something. The wind whistled through the halyards of the small boats bobbing on the water. The seagulls wheeled in the sky, a frenzied mass of grey and white feathers. An upturned boat still lay on the beach, looking tired and unloved.

She ran her hand through her hair. It was smooth and clean, no longer pitted with particles of sand. She tucked it behind her ear and took a couple of steps towards the stone steps where she used to sit. She swallowed and brushed the wall with her hand, leaning over to see the sand running up to it. It felt rough and scratchy like coarse, hard sandpaper. Scratchy like the sand that rubbed against her and the shells that cut at her jeans. She listened to see if she could hear the children's voices in the waves. She heard nothing.

The clouds, a mass of grey, floated by, allowing the sun every now and again to peek through. She took another deep breath. The breeze caught her hair and blew it into her face. Fine strands catching on her nude lipgloss. She brushed it away and looked to her right. In the distance she could just about make out Dovercourt. She cast her glance to a rock that rose jaggedly up from the sand on the shoreline.

Get up you bitch. Get up. You played your game. You tried to ruin me. You whore.

Her breathing deepened and she shook her head, trying to dispel the memory. The ebb and flow of waves as they brushed onto the shore captured her breath. Heart racing, she could feel the clamminess in her hands again. Small beads of perspiration formed on her forehead and upper lip. She wiped them with the cuff of her jacket. The angry, high-pitched call of a gull as it swooped past her head. She jumped.

I didn't ruin you. You did, Charlie.

She tried to control the feelings that were bubbling up from somewhere deep inside her. Bubbling like an exploding volcano, her breathing becoming harder and her knees trembling. She took slow breaths to try to bring herself back to a place of normality. Letting the cold sea air into her body, to reach the depth of her lungs. She breathed in slowly and exhaled, staring at the jagged rock on the beach. The words of Doris flooded her memory, first as a chant in her head and then as a faint whisper in the breeze: 'Mi deh yah, yuh know, mi deh yah, yuh know, mi deh yah, yuh know.'

His hand on her shoulder stopped her thoughts, stopped her words. She didn't know whether she was imagining it – had he found her again?

The flask of peppermint tea slipped out of her hand.

She inhaled.

'Lucy?'

An old collie sat by her feet where she stood. Bob stood by her side and took her hand and led her to the stone steps, picking up her flask as he went. Together they sat, silent: not a sound but the whistling wind, the wheeling gulls, the gentle wash of water flowing on and off the beach.

He brushed the grit from her flask and opened it. He poured two cups. Together they sat still, not a word. A silence that was needed, a memory that needed to be left in the past. He knew her pain.

The warmth of the cups penetrated through to the palms of their hands. As she sat and watched the horizon, he took her hand once more and clasped it tightly.

'My dear Lucy, welcome home, you brave, brave girl.' She swallowed and placed her head on his shoulder, he still clasping her hand with tender firmness. Together they sat, just the two of them and Archie by their feet and a flask of peppermint tea. Bob was like a father to her.

Chapter Twelve

Friday, 7th March
Harwich, Essex

The stairs leading up to the restaurant in The Pier seemed like a mountainous climb for Lucy.

'Can I help you, madam?' came the friendly voice of the receptionist from behind the sleek counter adorned with a huge vase of white lilies, their fragrance permeating the entrance.

'I'm OK, I'm just meeting a friend for lunch, Jo Segal.'

'Ah, yes, she's at the table by the French doors overlooking the pier - she arrived a few minutes ago. The restaurant is straight up the stairs.'

'Yep, I know, thanks.'

Lucy left the receptionist and instead bore left to the loos. She pushed the door open and listened to the mellifluous voice of a broadcaster through the surround-sound speakers playing the shipping forecast. She'd never heard it until she'd moved to Wrabness, and since coming to The Pier both she and Jo had found it rather comical. Today, however, it gave her an overwhelming feeling of calm. The melodic tone of the broadcaster's voice as she read from a transcript.

"Low north Biscay nine, nine, five expected south Biscay nine, nine, one by 0600 tomorrow. Thames, northeast four or five, occasionally six at first. Slight or moderate. Rain or showers, fog patches later. Moderate or good, occasionally very poor later. Dover ..."

Lucy still didn't understand it, but it was as good as white noise. She looked at herself in the mirror and applied a touch of foundation to her face around her eyes and lips, to conceal what little was left of the bruising. She applied a little more nude lipstick and gloss, smoothed her hair and pulled the door open to leave the loos, leaving the lilting voice from the shipping forecast behind.

As she approached the main entrance to the restaurant, she spied Jo already with a glass of white wine on the table and a bowl of Mediterranean olives.

Jo got up from the table and held out her arms for an all-encompassing hug.

'Hey, gorgeous girl, how ya doing?'

'Good. I've just been to the beach.'

'Have you? Why didn't you tell me – I would have come down with you!'

'I know. I just needed to do it on my own, just to try and work my head out. Untangle everything.'

'And did you?'

'Kind of. I was nervous, and I found it hard to breathe, but I kept remembering what Doris said to me.'

'Doris, that's your nurse, right?'

'Yep. She told me this phrase her grandmother used to always say to her when she was sad. It sounds like something from The Lion King to be honest,' she smiled.

'Seriously, that's hilarious – The Lion King! Tell me it.'

'OK, so it goes "mi deh yah, yuh know."'

'And what does it mean?' Jo asked, taking a sip from her glass.

'It means, "I am here. Everything is OK." It's nice, isn't it. It's weird, though, because I kept saying it in my head, like a chant, and I kept hearing him and the rock and the fight and then like …' She stopped. 'And then it was like the words from Doris were real, because Bob stood by my side and it was real, I am here, everything is OK – it became real.'

'Luce, it's perfect. Doris sounds like a wonderful nurse.'

'Oh my, she was just lovely. She talked all the time of Jamaica and Bob Marley and her Winston and the yellow sun. She was amazing, just a life of happiness that glowed around her. I think that's what I miss about London, if I'm honest.'

'What d'you mean?'

'I miss the cultural side of London, just that melting pot of difference.'

'I guess down here is different, Luce, and it's your home now. Matt asked me again if I'd move in with him.'

'And what did you say? I'd love you to be closer, Jo, you know that, don't you.'

'I know, but I need to work out whether I rent my flat or sell it. I can't really afford to keep it just for me to stay in when I'm in town. I'm not ready to sell it and I don't want to rent it either. So quite frankly I'm screwed,' she laughed, taking another mouthful of wine.

'Can I get you anything to drink?' said the waitress as she hovered over them with a tray, balancing two water glasses and a carafe of iced tap water.

'Umm, I'd love a soda water with a wedge of lime if that's possible. Oh, and some more olives and perhaps a couple of menus,' Lucy said, pouring the water into the glasses.

'I'll have another Picpoul de Pinet please, large,' Jo said, finishing her glass. 'So, what about you and Ben? He seemed a little off yesterday. Not-so-cute Ben anymore?'

'I don't know what that was about. He was off with me when Simon arrived, and you said with all your normal tact that he was a green-eyed monster.'

'Well, he was. It was bloody obvious! Couldn't you see it? Every time Si said anything, it was like, "That's nice of you Simon," or "That was a quick call." It was layered in sarcasm. Bloody obvious.'

'Why would he be jealous of Simon? Simon's just a friend.'

'Simon dotes on you, Luce, he adores you.'

'Yeah, but not like that. He was there for me when Charlie messaged and stuff, both him and Matt were.'

'I guess, but you don't see it when it's staring you straight in the face. I reckon Simon's mad about you. And I don't know – if you haven't been close to Ben or you've pushed him away recently, then he probably saw Simon as a threat as well as everything else. Not to mention you put your head on Si's arm?'

'Yeah, but I was going over to Ben to snuggle him and then the door went, and it was a lovely surprise to see Simon.'

'Still, you put your head on Simon. I mean, what's Ben going to think? You flinch when he touches you and then you choose Simon's arm over his.'

'I guess. But it wasn't like that.'

'But that's not what Ben saw," Jo pointed out. "He loves you, and he's struggling with Charlie and what he has done to you. But he's a guy and, yep, he had a chat with Matt about it.'

'And ...?'

'He's finding it hard. He wants to be near you and for you not to push him away. That's going to be tough for any guy to try and get their head around.'

Lucy sighed. 'I know, but it's hard. I knew I'd hurt him. But I didn't know how to stop pushing him away. I just feel damaged and dirty and shit and I can't help that. I think he slept on the sofa last night – he wasn't in bed this morning.'

'And now? D'you still feel that way?'

'I feel damaged and I feel shit inside.'

'You're not damaged, Lucy, and neither are you shit. You're facing your fears. Today was a really big step for you and you did it on your own. You came to the beach for fuck's sake. A beach where you write, where we cartwheeled, where you first clapped eyes on Ben. And now a beach that Charlie brought you to, in his sick mind, to hurt you.'

'I know, you're right. Anyway, it was good to see Bob today at the beach.'

'How did that feel?' Jo said, resting her hand on Lucy's.

'It was good. I was losing my mind a little as I watched the sea and the sky and the gulls. I couldn't even take myself as far as the stone steps. I can remember thinking *I'm going to fall, I can't breathe.* I could feel myself sweating and my heart racing and the clouds no longer floating but spinning. Then there was a hand on my shoulder. For a split second I thought it was Charlie and he'd found me again. It was Bob, though, with Archie on a walk. He stood for a while with me and then led me to the steps, as if he knew I wanted to get there but didn't know how to. It's like he knows me inside or my thoughts or my fears. It's like he hears me screaming inside and wanting to escape and not being able to.' Lucy sighed and drank some water. 'He took me gently down to the steps without a word – he knew that was where I wanted to be but couldn't put one foot in front of the other by myself. And we just sat there together and shared my flask of peppermint tea.' Lucy's eyes shimmered with tears as she recounted the morning. She brushed her eyes before any fell. The people at the next table huddled closer together, whispering behind their hands, perhaps recognising from the pictures in the local papers the girl on the beach.

'Bob found you on the beach. Do you remember that?'

'He didn't mention that today. We didn't say anything, we just sat.'

'And Ben? Where does he fit in all of this? Remember, he's still the guy on the bike that you were smitten with.'

'I still am! I'm just struggling, and I can't make it go away. I heard him in the shower this morning and luckily he hadn't fixed the lock.'

'So ...'

'I took a shower with him and showed him I loved him.'

'Like really showed him?' Jo said with a glint of mischief in her eyes.

'Listen, I'm not ready for that. I'm not sure when I will be. I let him see me naked, I let him touch my bruises for the first time. I think he was happier.'

'So, is everything back on track and OK now?'

'I'd like to think so.'

'You're gonna be OK, Luce,' Jo said, squeezing her hand reassuringly.

Lucy sighed heavily and gazed out of the double doors, which opened up onto a small balcony that would hold a few covers in the warmer weather. The THV Patricia ship had now left the quayside and a few men in orange overalls walked up the gangway. A young couple sat on the bench close to the real-life 'Boat that Rocked'.

'Penny for them,' Jo said as she fanned the menu in Lucy's face.

'I was just thinking of our first time here. D'you remember it? We drank a bottle of Sauvignon Blanc and demolished a couple of lobsters.' She smiled wistfully at the memory.

'Yep, I remember, we sank a bottle of chilled white, it was nice. Talking of lobster, whatcha gonna order?'

'Hmmm, I don't know, I'm toying with the moules marinières or the roasted halibut,' Lucy said, almost drooling over the menu. 'I love the menu here. It's just so bloody hard to choose. I could eat it all.'

'Yeah, I quite like the idea of mussels too, but the pan-fried fillet of salmon with chive and parsley butter sounds pretty divine. That's me, I'm sorted. I'm going for the salmon. I'm not dithering. Job done.'

Jo beckoned politely to the waitress and the girls placed their orders.

'Is Matt picking you up later?' Lucy asked as Jo steadily drank her way through her second glass of wine. 'That's your second.'

'Yeah, he's on duty until three and then he said he'd swing by here. What time does Ben finish?'

'He said he'd be home for five.'

As Jo took a sip of her wine, the waitress appeared with two perfectly dressed white square plates with salmon and halibut and a side order of steamed courgettes and baby asparagus.

'Why don't you get him to swing by here?'

'I'd love to. But I desperately need to get some food in the fridge and cupboards, they're pretty bare. Maybe we could do something tomorrow night? Samuel Pepys, see if Simon is up for it too?'

'Sounds like a plan.' As the two of them chatted away, the hands on the clock turned and life for Lucy became a little more normal again.

'Hey, you two,' came the familiar voice of Matt. He bent down and kissed Jo before drawing up a chair. 'How many have you sunk?'

'Only two, but I wouldn't mind one more and then you can take me home and lose me forever,' she said with a sparkle in her eye.

'Right,' said Lucy, 'I'm going to leave you two lovebirds to it. Text me about tomorrow.'

Lucy paid the bill and left Jo and Matt together.

The breeze was picking up outside and she pulled her jacket around her more tightly. The couple sitting on the bench threw away their paper coffee cups and followed in the same direction as Lucy. She walked past the Old Bank and along the mews, remembering how Ben had stopped her and asked her for her number. She'd been cross with him for not calling her name and making her jump. She walked past the café where he'd first taken her for a coffee when she was freezing cold, and she'd left him without even touching her drink. She hated coffee. She smiled as the memories flooded her thoughts. A Coke can scuttled past her, its tinny sound startling her.

'Sorry, love, didn't mean to make you jump.' A burly workman walked past her, picking up the can and lobbing it into a bin.

She crossed the road and walked over to her Mini as the couple walked past her. She pulled out of her parking space. She didn't notice the blue BMW slink out too and veer off in the same direction. The BMW kept its distance as she drove towards Colchester, her car's heaters frantically blowing out warm air. When she turned off at the roadside services, the blue BMW filed off too. It parked next to a police car and waited whilst Lucy filled up and came back out with two bags of shopping.

Lucy drove home, while the BMW pulled in as it approached the police station. She didn't notice it stop. She parked outside her cottage and unloaded her bags, going back to grab her flask and satchel. The curtain at number 8 opened. Ben's bike was parked outside. He was home already, waiting for her, just as he'd promised.

'She's back, our Lucy,' Gladys said from the window as she dusted the Barry hound lookalike ornament in the window and ruffled the curtains a tad. 'I'll be dishing up stew and dumplings and mash for dinner. Turn that telly down, would you. I can't 'ear myself think,' she said as she shoved Stan's feet off the pouffe and knocked him on the head with her duster.

The door of number 3 closed and the midnight blue BMW pulled up outside number 10.

The couple looked up the road and went inside.

'Ben,' Lucy called from the doorway as she sifted through the post. 'Ben?' Only the clock in the kitchen ticked in response. She walked up the hallway, the floorboards creaking beneath her footsteps. The kitchen was empty. She switched the kettle on and placed the shopping bags on the table.

'Ben?' she called again. The kettle boiled noisily on the worktop. She pushed the handle on the kitchen's back door. It was locked. She poured the water into a mug, and the teabag bobbed down as the water splashed onto it. The breakfast plates still sat on the side from the morning. The cafetière, now full of cold, sludge-like coffee, sat on the table.

The bin lid clanged as she put the teabag in it. She left the kitchen, the clock still ticking.

'Ben.' She went into the sitting room. The hearth was just a mound of ashen dust and the faint smell of the burnt-out black pomegranate candle. The throw was unfolded, left in a pile on the sofa, three cushions bundled in a heap on the arm, to form a makeshift pillow.

'Ben.' She went upstairs. Her writing room door was open, how she'd left it. She drew the curtain back a little and peered out of the window. The gate was closed.

'Ben, where are you?' The bathroom door was open, the lock still broken and the window ajar. She pushed open her bedroom door, her heart beginning to beat a little faster. The dipping sun shone through the window. The bed neat and tidy. The pillows placed squarely by the headboard. The boiler humming in the cupboard. The sound of the water trickling through the radiators. She went back downstairs, her tea now tepid in the sitting room. She walked down the hallway again and stopped at the cupboard under the stairs. A thud came from the kitchen. She stopped. The boards beneath her feet creaked as she pushed the kitchen door, a little. An apple rolled on the floor, the bag tilted on the table. She turned. She swallowed and stared at the door under the stairs. The clock ticked. Her hand slowly went to turn the knob. She was shaking. 'Ben …' His name stuck in her throat.

The gate squeaked. Her breathing quickened. The window in the bathroom thumped against the frame. Her mobile was in the kitchen. She looked at the clock: a quarter to six. The floorboards creaked with each footstep as her hand slowly clutched the newel, each stair a silent step. Trepidation swelled through her. Lucy's heart twisted and sank. She pushed the bathroom door a little, the window knocking against the frame on its hinge. She pulled the latch shut. She went back down the stairs, each step slow and quiet.

'Ben.'

She stood in front of the door of the under-stair's cupboard. She swallowed again as she went to turn the knob. The knocker on the front door rapped loudly. She jumped. She went to the kitchen and got her mobile phone. She called Ben, but it went to voicemail. Her hands shook as she dialled Simon's number. The door rapped again. She dropped her phone, the line still ringing. Her heartbeat quickly surpassing the rhythmic beat coming from inside her.

Simon answered, his voice sounding tinnily from the phone's speaker. 'Lucy. Lucy are you there?'

There was no answer. 'Lucy.' A pause. Then the line went dead.

She stood in front of the under-stair's cupboard door. Her hands gripped the cuffs of her sleeves. Her hand went to take the handle ... 'Ben.'

Tyres screeched outside her front door, and then the gate squeaked. The front door shook with the hammering on the knocker.

Inside, Lucy froze.

'Lucy, Lucy, it's Simon, are you there?'

Lucy opened the door. Her face was pale, her hands shook. Simon stood there, his walkie-talkie crackling. He turned it down.

'Bravo November Five. Stand down. I repeat, stand down, over.' The door of number 3 stayed open.

The curtain at number 8 twitched. The young woman at number 10 watched from an upstairs window.

'Lucy, are you OK?' She looked like she'd seen a ghost.

'Simon, the cupboard,' Lucy said, her hands shaking.

'What d'you mean, the cupboard?'

'He's in the cupboard. Ben, he's in the cupboard.'

Simon gently moved her away. His hand slowly turned the handle and he edged the door open, his grip shaking a little, a bead of sweat forming on his brow. The Hoover stood at the front.

'He's not, Lucy. There's nothing there, just your cleaning stuff and the Hoover,' he said, holding her shoulders.

'He's somewhere - Charlie's killed him - I know he has, his bike's outside. He's not here. He said he would be here. He said he would be here at five. He's not here, Simon. He's gone. Where's he gone?' The tears streamed down her face. 'He's taken him, he's taken him, Simon. Find him, find him. You have to find him.'

'Lucy, listen to me, I will find Ben.' He guided her to the sitting room. 'When did you last see him?'

'This morning.'

'And he said he would be home at five.'

'His bike's outside - I saw him leave on his bike this morning. Where's he gone? Where's he taken him?'

'Lucy, Charlie hasn't been here, you have police protection. Seriously, I will find Ben, but nothing has happened to him.'

'Phone him?'

'OK.' Simon dialled Ben's number. It went to straight to voicemail.

'See, he's not answering, is he. You have to find him, Simon. Something's happened.'

Just as he was about to radio Matt, the gate squeaked and Ben came in the front door.

'Lucy!' He rushed straight into the sitting room, worried by the squad car outside and the open front door.

'Ben!' Lucy cried and ran to him.

'What's going on – has something happened, Simon?'

'No, Lucy called, she couldn't find you,' Simon said, turning down his walkie-talkie again.

'I couldn't get in,' Ben said, holding Lucy in his arms. 'I don't have a key. I went to the pub to wait.'

'Your phone went to voicemail,' Lucy said, still in Ben's arms.

'It's out of juice. I couldn't message to say I was in the pub.'

'I thought he'd got you.'

'Who, Charlie? Babe, no, I'm here. I saw the squad car outside and the door open and panicked.'

'Listen, guys, I'm going to leave you alone,' Simon said, edging towards the door. Ben followed him.

'Is Lucy OK?' Ben asked as he walked with Simon to the car.

'She was frightened, she was frightened of the cupboard. Where has she been today? I thought she was with Jo?'

'She went to the beach and then met Jo for lunch at The Pier.'

'Did she go to the beach on her own?'

'Yeah, d'you think that's the problem?'

Simon sighed and rested his hand on the roof of the car.

'I don't know, mate. It's probably triggered something. Nothing's going to happen to her here, though, she's got protection.'

'Protection?' Ben quizzed. 'I can't watch her twenty-four-seven.'

'No, I mean DI Phillips has put protection in place. She's safe, that's all I can tell you. She'll be safe wherever she goes. At some point she was bound to go to the beach. It's just where she would have gone - she writes there. It's been her safe space since she first moved here. Her life with him blows my mind.'

'When she first made a statement, what did she tell you?' Ben asked.

'I can't tell you that, you know that, mate, but it wasn't a great morning. Both Matt and I were present, with Jo too, and that was when we barely knew her. But her story was pretty crushing and she's frightened.'

'Did she tell you everything?'

'Ben, I can't tell you what she said. You know that.'

'So, this protection, where is it?' Ben asked. 'Like today, where was it?'

'She didn't need protecting, she was OK. I can't give you the information; it's a covert operation. But believe me, it's there. Nothing is going to happen to Lucy. I give you my word.'

'He's still out there, isn't he? He's going to come back for her. She wouldn't need protection otherwise, would she?'

Simon's silence spoke volumes. He got into his car.

'For a moment I did think you were in that cupboard. I was pretty relieved when I saw a Hoover and not a dead body! Go in and see her, she needs you.'

Ben walked back up the pathway, taking the parcel that had been left on the doorstep along with a scribbled delivery note reading, 'Parcel left on doorstep at 5.46.'

Simon turned the engine on. *What did Ben mean by 'everything'?* he thought to himself as he pulled away.

Chapter Thirteen

Saturday, 8th March
Peñíscola, Spain

The waves brushed onto the beach below the villa. A silver convertible Beetle drove down the winding track of the Iberian slopes. The tracks were parched and crumbly, with tired mud and stones forming dirty red clouds in the air as Sofia drove towards the small coastal town of Peñíscola. She approached the small roundabout where a pack of dogs moved wolfishly together, unfazed by the passing cars and humans. Their brindled coats merged with the arid, dappled colours of the ground, where their bodies hunkered low. Sofia turned onto the main drag of the town, following the narrow road towards a small turning that led to a cobbled street. The street was lined either side with shuttered windows and small balconies with pretty window boxes overhanging each. Children played along the narrow pavements, dodging the cars as they passed. Scraggy, wiry-coated feral dogs padded the streets, looking for scraps of discarded food. She indicated left, leaving behind the line of pretty, whitewashed walls of the Spanish houses.

'We could perhaps stop in the town later, to buy you some clothes,' she suggested, as the car climbed the steep ascent to a villa that lay cocooned at the top of the mountainous red terrain.

'I have no money,' Charlie said.

'I know.'

'How much will I need for Ana?'

Sofia pulled up outside Cueva Cascada, a small whitewashed villa tucked away on the slopes. A mountain spring flowed freely down the slope, cascading into a small waterfall nestled at the bottom. She took her bag from behind her seat and pulled out her purse.

'Here, take this, that should be enough. I will return in an hour.' She handed him a fifty-euro note.

She left Charlie and drove away. He watched as the dust from the track flew up from behind her tyres. He turned and walked up the stone steps leading to the front door of the villa. A hammock swung between two olive trees, and a small dog ran out and yapped at him, jumping and scratching at his legs. He bent down and stroked its head. He pulled at the rope bell outside the door.

'Ya voy,' came a voice from inside. The door opened and a woman stood smiling. 'Is it Miguel?' Her voice was soft and kind.

He nodded.

'Please, come through, my room is just here.' She led him down a small corridor into a room with a view of the mountains and stream, with the waterfall that glistened like tumbling diamonds as the sun caught the flowing water. The shutters were open, and a cool breeze sifted through.

The floor was tiled in red stone, and a mahogany-coloured leather chair sat by the French doors that opened out onto the balcony, with another opposite. A carved, dark wooden cabinet rested at the edge of the room.

'Please take a seat.' She beckoned to the seat by the French doors.

The leather made a squidgy, crackling sound as Charlie sat in it. The frame of his body was upright and rigid, his hands clasped.

'Miguel, my name is Ana - would you like me to call you Miguel?'

'Yes.'

He stared out to the mountains. The small of his back pushed into the chair.

'Why are you here, Miguel?' Her body was angled forward, her arms open and resting on her lap.

He stared at her. Her eyes were a deep dark brown, her hair long and dark with a ringlet running through it. She'd caught it up in a messy chignon so that the ringlets fell around her face. She wore long, dangling, feather-like earrings. Her skin an olive colour. Her eyes didn't leave his face. He stared at her face and then her eyes. She smiled gently. He looked away from her, his hands gripped together. He looked down to the floor and said not a word. They sat in silence while the wall clock's hands slowly moved around its face.

'I am here, Miguel. I am here with you.' She said nothing more, her eyes never leaving his face. 'Tell me why you have come.'

'I was a curious person,' he said, 'but I lost it.'

She searched his face. She watched his hands as they gripped each other more tightly.

'Curious? Tell me about your curiosity,' she coaxed, her head tilted to one side, her face soft and telling.

'I was a boy in Spain once.' His eyes caught hers for a moment until he looked away again.

'Once? Tell me about that time.'

There was a pause. She let him sit in silence, she said nothing, she waited.

'I lived here,' he said, rubbing his hands on his legs to dry the wetness inside his palms. 'I found my school trunk when I arrived.'

'When you arrived? You mean now, when you arrived?' she asked, her questions tentative, allowing him time to unravel and share his thoughts.

He let out an audible sigh and shook his head.

'Your school trunk, Miguel – was it just an empty trunk?'

'No.'

'What was inside?'

'Hugo.'

'Hugo?' she questioned cautiously.

'My bear, my scruffy bear. My father bought it for me.' He paused, his gaze taken by the mountain view once more. His body moved a little in the chair, becoming more cushioned. 'I remember, we walked around the shops when I was about four, maybe five, and I saw it on the shelf. I took it out of the shop in my hand. She tried to take it back and I cried. I remember crying on the street. My father went back to the shop and paid for it and I took it home. My bear – Hugo is my bear.'

'It sounds like Hugo was much needed,' she smiled gently.

'I guess,' he said, wistfully.

'You guess?'

'She never acknowledged it.'

'She? Who is "she"?'

'Any woman.'

'Any woman?' Her approach was soft, she said very little, just gently handed back his words for him to unfold. The noisy clicking of cicadas outside, a bee buzzing about the early spring flowers. The soft white clouds billowing through the bluest of skies. His gaze followed them until one gelled with another. The air was steeped in the sweet-smelling scent from the blossom of the almond trees that lined the craggy descent of the terrain from the villa. He breathed in the infusion of aromas, filling his lungs to capacity, yet still watching the bee busying itself. He shifted a little in his chair.

'Yeah … she never acknowledged my needs … my feelings.'

'What were your feelings, Miguel. To be acknowledged?'

'Acknowledged or loved.'

'And now ...?'

He sat motionless, staring out to the view. His thoughts of his childhood – he so knew the far-reaching views ahead of him. The warmth of the sun as it rose in the sky. The sound of cicadas. He knew them all, caught in his memory of his childhood. His grip slackened, his body sank a little more into the chair. She gave him space, time to let go. The silence was important.

'Miguel ... Let's look at the little boy. If you began to give Miguel attention, what would that look like?'

His eyes dropped.

'Drawing, hopscotch. The touch of his hand,' he said, dolefully.

'Hopscotch ...' She left the word with him again, for him to take it back and unleash his childhood memories.

'Hopscotch on the rocks with chalk, playing in the surf with him. Being loved. Being loved rather than being right.' He paused for moment. 'I loved my father,' he sighed. 'I adored him.'

'And the woman in your life? Did you love her too?'

'I tried to.'

'Tried?'

'She didn't ever love me. She was always right.'

'And your father? Was he – always right?'

'Love was worth more than being right,' he said.

'I hear the word "was". Where is he?'

'Dead.' The hands of the clock were approaching the hour.

'In your heart or in your head, Miguel?' she asked with care.

'In my head – he will always be in my heart. But now he will be ashamed of his son.'

'Why? You are his son.'

'He is dead and if he knew me now, he would probably wish himself dead.'

'I sense there is a lot of hurt in your life. Shame, guilt?'

'In my life,' he sighed. 'I don't want to talk anymore. Tomorrow, can I return tomorrow?'

Her eyes reached his. She felt the depth of his pain.

'Tomorrow is Sunday. I do not work on Sundays. I can do Monday.' A gentle smile formed on her face, her head nodding slowly. 'I will see you at ten.'

He handed her the money and left the villa.

Sofia had already arrived and was waiting in the car.

He got in, blenching slightly as the seat belt caught his shoulder. The radio presenter blabbered away in Spanish in between continental-style pop music. He looked at his mother as she turned the engine on. She looked beautiful, simply dressed in an off-the-shoulder blouse with small ruffles at the front and a long chiffon gypsy-style skirt, pretty diamante sandals and painted toes. Her dark sunglasses hid her eyes. She smelt divinely sweet.

'I must go to the market. Shall we go to the town for some clothes?' she asked. She said no more; she made no enquiry about his morning and pushed for nothing.

'Sure. I need a suit and shoes, and a shirt too.' He said nothing more.

They drove to the small town centre without a word to each other. He watched as the narrow streets busied themselves with market traders selling an array of food and goods. The cheerful sound of a busker filling the streets with his guitar's melodic tones.

'I'll wait in the car,' he said, as she stopped in the parking spaces by the central square. 'Don't tell anyone I'm here.'

He watched from the car as she stood at each stall one by one, each market trader knowing her by name, their faces a caricature of bubbly friendliness. She weaved through the crowds, edging through a dense throng of people milling about as her basket got fuller.

The air was perfumed with produce, the nose-tingling aromas of the hessian sacks full to the brim of the deepest rust-coloured paprika and saffron spilling out from their rolled-over tops. Sweet scents came from the florist on the corner, while a stream of water meandered through gaps in the cobbles as the flower girl emptied out another bucket. Plump golden chickens turned on their skewers in rotisserie ovens. The warming smell of paella cooking in colossal skillets, ready to be taken and eaten. Vegetables spilled onto the ground, knocked down by the grabbing hands of the mothers hustling and bustling. Feral dogs snatched at the smashed food: they were unfussed by it, it fed them.

Charlie watched the children squeal and laugh as they splashed in the florist's discarded water. They hopped and skipped along, carefree, small, childlike. He smiled gently as he saw a young boy, maybe seven or eight, throw a pebble and hopscotch along and then run to slip his hand into his father's hand. The man gently ruffled his hair before throwing him onto his shoulders, like a giant overlooking the tops of the throbbing crowds. The boy's mother, ahead, shouted back to them in Spanish to stop dawdling. What would that little boy become? Would he become like him – bitter, cruel, a monster?

The car door opened and jolted his thoughts. She threw the bags into the back and rested the basket of market produce on the seat.

'I remember the market,' he said as they approached the winding track back to the villa.

'Yes, it is the same, the faces a little older perhaps,' she said, with a smile. The savoury smell of a roasted chicken seeped around the car. She parked the car and got out. Charlie took the bags and walked up the steps to the villa.

'I have a roasted chicken for lunch. Are you hungry?'

'Yes. I need to transfer some money from my accounts to pay for the clothes and Ana. Do you have internet access here?'

'The money is not important, Charlie.'

'I'm seeing Ana again on Monday. I must transfer my funds. The money is important to me. Do you have a laptop?'

'I do, but really, the money is not important.'

'Please, I want you to take the money. It's important to me. Did anybody ask why you were buying men's clothes and toiletries?' he asked, as Sofia began to make a salad with the fresh produce she'd bought. She sliced the deep red, plump tomatoes, the seeds and fleshy juice oozing out of them. She drizzled them lightly with oil and threw some torn basil leaves over them and cracked a little sea salt on top.

'No, nobody asked,' she said as she pushed the salad to one side. 'Why don't you try the clothes on, whilst I finish preparing the lunch. I got you some shoes too. I thought perhaps you were the same size as your father was. I hope I am right.'

He took the bags and began to walk to his room. Then he turned, resting the bags on the floor.

'Thank you,' he said.

He turned away and continued to walk to his room, where he closed the door and placed the bags on the bed. What had his life become? How had he got to this place of such desolate despair and hatred? Would he ever be able to make it right, to right his wrongs, to be forgiven? He slumped onto the floor, his back against the soft linen of the bed. His shoulder ached. He placed his head in his hands. How could he ever be normal again? Life would never be normal again. If he was found, his life would be behind bars - he had killed a girl. He had killed Lucy.

He leant forward and opened his school trunk once more, this time knowing what to expect as he prised open the lid. He took out a small box and opened it. There were letters inside on airmail paper, watermarked Basildon Bond. His memory drifted back to the building he spent his childhood in.

Two stone lions sat majestically at the pillars of the wrought iron gates. A gravelled driveway swept around the manicured lawns that led up to the grandeur of a Georgian building. Below, in the valley of the grounds, was a cricket lawn bordered by enormous elm trees and a pavilion for after-match teas. Stone steps led up to the double oak doorways of St Edmund's Preparatory School for Boys. Huge great oak sash windows flanked the walls, letting the light stream in. Along the wood-panelled walls inside were placards with the names of three houses. The grand hall's walls had landscape photos of pupils old and present. One important framed board gave the names of those who had become Head Boy over the years. Another was etched with names of the alumni.

It had been pompous and bewildering to a small boy who simply wanted to play with the children by the sea. A million miles from where his heart should be.

Charlie held the wafer-thin envelope in his hand and took out the letter inside.

1st June, 1992
Casa Bendita
Peñíscola, Spain

My Dearest Boy,

Charlie, so today I took the plane for a wonderful flight high above the sea. I thought of you and how you would enjoy seeing the clouds float by and the sea so blue. The sound of her engine humming through the winds. The clouds as soft and white as candyfloss. I think I might have even spied a mermaid playing in the surf.

I would so love to come and watch your cricket match, but I am unable to come this time. I promise I will be there for the next one and the next one and the next one. I hope your tuck box is still full of all the goodies we bought from Santiago's fishing shop by the beach and you haven't snuck them away and eaten them all for a midnight feast. Your time at school will speed by, my loveliest boy and when you are home, we will play once more and collect some more crabs caught in the rock pools. I have bought you a new bucket and spade, a net and some more chalk for hopscotch. I have popped it by your bed waiting for you. When you are home, I will tell you more of the fishing tales of Santiago.

I would love so much to wake you in the morning with a kiss and a cuddle, and for it not to be a school bell. Make sure you work hard, and I will write again in a few days. And win that match for Daddy. I will be cheering you on whilst I work hard here in Spain.

I love you, Charlie, and hold Hugo close at night.

See you soon my dearest boy.

Daddy xxx

Charlie put the letter back into the box and tucked it beneath Hugo. His hand gently stroked the soft ears of his bear. Daddy hadn't ever watched the next cricket match, nor the next one, nor the next one. He closed the lid to the trunk, to the memories.

He undressed and tried on the clothes Sofia had bought that morning. Leaving his old clothes on the bed and wearing a fresh new T-shirt and jeans, he went back to the kitchen where Sofia was preparing lunch.

'Ah, so they fit,' she said as she poured two glasses of freshly made lemonade.

'Yes, thank you. Can I use your computer now? I need to transfer some funds from London.' Leaving the kitchen counter, she opened the lid of her laptop and signed herself in. Charlie released funds from his account in London to his Spanish account.

'Can we go back to the town on Monday? I need to go to the bank to withdraw some money and also see Ana at ten. Can you drive me there?'

'Of course. Shall we sit on the veranda for lunch? It seems pleasant enough outside.'

They sat together once more and tucked into the sumptuous roasted chicken and salad, mopping up the juices with some olive bread.

Chapter Fourteen

Monday, 10th March
Peñíscola, Spain

Ana settled into her chair and poured two glasses of mineral water. The ice from the jug fell through the spout and plopped into the glasses with a clink.

'How are you today, Miguel?'

'I'm good.'

'How did you feel after the last session?'

'I felt tired. Emotionally tired. Does that make sense?'

'It does, it makes perfect sense. And today, do you still feel tired?'

He didn't answer. 'I went to the market on Saturday and watched from the car.'

'Did you feel safer in the car?'

'I guess. There was a small boy with his father. He reminded me of myself as a young child. He played hopscotch with a pebble as he dilly-dallied along. He was with his parents, although his father held his hand and then threw him onto his shoulders.'

'How did you feel watching him?' she asked.

'Warm, tender, loving at first. I wondered what he would become. Whether he'd be normal and happy or whether he'd be like me, full of hatred and resentment.' His words sat with him. Ana let them.

'You mentioned your father. When did you lose him?'

'I was nine, away at school, a boarding school in England. Miles away from here. Miles away from what I knew and loved.'

'Is that why you are resentful?' she probed.

'Not at my father, no.' He paused. 'I read his letter yesterday. I can remember reading it in my bed in my dormitory, under the sheets with a torch. Keeping it safe with me and Hugo, letting no one else know his written words to me. "I couldn't come and watch the cricket match," he wrote, but he promised to come to the next one.'

'And did he come?'

'He would have come. I know he would have come.' Charlie's thoughts meandered to the open doors of the room. The far-reaching view was still the same, still as breathtaking. The aquamarine sea in the distance glistened. 'Do you believe in mermaids?' he asked, his look still on the sea as it reached the sky and blended into the horizon.

'I'd like to think mermaids are real. It makes the sea a more wondrous place.' She smiled, her approach soft.

'He said he'd spied a mermaid playing in the surf. And then he went.'

'Where did he go, Miguel?' she coaxed.

'Maybe to meet the mermaid. If you believe in mermaids.' His voice trailed off as his eyes flooded with tears. She sat with him, holding him in a space that brought sorrow to his heart. She said nothing. He could feel her presence, he knew she was there with him. He swallowed. 'He never watched my cricket match. I never saw him again. I never saw my father again. And I want to see him – he was taken from me. Why? Why would that happen? Why would I be left with her? A woman who didn't love him and didn't love me. A woman who drank champagne and let a headmaster tell me my father had died in his plane in the sea. Alone in the water, drowned. I know that feeling, to drown. What person does that? What woman does that? Why? Why take the person I adored? I wonder if God is a woman. D'you hear me?'

'I hear you.'

'She was meant to make things better. Isn't that what parents do? I was nine. When I cried, the matron would send me to be flogged. Is that what you do, to a child who is grieving? To a child who is homesick. To a child who just wants to be at home with their father. Each time the slipper hit me, I cried, and the more I cried the more I was hit. Is that evil, or was I evil?'

'You were a child, Miguel, I don't believe children are born evil.'

'So, what happened to me, then? I tried for such a long time to forget. I wondered for many years why she did what she did. Boyfriends came and went with her, never the same one. I was just a pest. In the way. A nuisance.'

'That must have been hard,' Ana said as she leant forward a little, catching each word and holding it with tentative care.

'Were the dinner parties, cruises, weekends away worth it? The men, the lovers - were they so much better than him, than us? Perhaps it was convenience to keep me locked away at school. She could live her immaculate life, quaff her champagne, forget her child. She could do what she wanted. That must have been nice. The dysfunctional wreck of the family she didn't need to bring up. Does she feel remorse, does she even care?' His voice was cynical.

'And now, Miguel, where does that sit with you now - as a grown man?'

He sighed.

'I want to forgive her, but it feels so hard to do even that. When the feelings of abandonment have leaked into every part of my life, ruined every part of my life. Have stripped me from being able to love a woman, any woman, without feeling resentment towards them. I became like her. Unloving, cold, heartless ... a monster. Children are not born evil. I wasn't born that way. D'you hear me? I wasn't born that way.'

'Any woman?' she asked. She watched as his posture reverted back to how it had been the day before, rigid and unwanting. He had relaxed as he talked about his childhood but now his body moved back into the chair and tensed once more. His hands, which had been resting gently on the arms of the chair, moved back to his lap and clasped each other with a tight grip. He turned the signet ring on his finger. He adjusted the cuffs on his shirt.

'I'd like to finish now,' he said abruptly.

'That's fine, Miguel, let me know when you'd like to come again.'

'Tomorrow, I'll come again tomorrow at ten.'

He paid her and left.

Sofia was waiting in the car, the engine on. The Spanish radio was noisy and obtrusive in the background; it jarred with his thoughts. He turned it off with a swift move.

'Shall I take you to the bank?' she asked.

'Yes, and then I must go back to the villa,' he replied.

They drove to the town without a sound. His thoughts were on the morning and the woman who now sat next to him, shielding him, with no knowledge of his life. She parked the car in the small square and waited whilst he walked to the bank. There were no market traders in the square that day, and the streets were quiet. A man sat on a bench shaded by the palm tree that sprawled above it, its shadow of jagged leaves looking like the tentacles of an octopus on the cobbled ground below. He appeared to be reading a newspaper, which hid his face a little. He almost belonged but not quite.

Charlie quickened his pace as he passed, turning his face away. The gentleman looked up, flicking his eyes over Charlie as he brushed past. Charlie locked his gaze straight ahead on the door of the bank, his heart beating fast. The bank was cool inside, the cashiers behind the desk counters waiting, smiling for a customer. The cashier smiled as she spoke in Spanish and he replied with fluency. Her eyes travelled down his figure as she counted the notes quickly. He was dressed in a neatly pressed grey suit and white shirt, the collar open. It was a suit that perhaps you'd only see on a highly paid lawyer or gangster. He had a fortnight's worth of stubble that shielded his wanted face. A gold signet ring on his little finger. She smiled and passed the envelope under the glass screen. He turned and walked away, diverting his eyes from the overhead cameras that swivelled to face him like a Big Brother watching you. Charlie took in the room with a single sweep, his grey eyes settling on nothing, expressionless.

Sofia waited in the car for a while, the engine still running, watching the door of the bank until it opened, and Charlie was visible once more. He crossed the road hurriedly, the envelope tucked in his inside jacket pocket, stuffed with crisp new euros. As he approached the car, he turned back to the bench; the gentleman had gone. El País, the newspaper, rested on the top of a bin nearby, neatly rolled, barely crumpled or touched. As Sofia pulled away, Charlie checked the alleyways as they drove past, scanning each one for the figure of a man, now perhaps without a newspaper. He saw no one, least of all the gentleman on the bench.

It was midday, and the sun was now high in the sky, casting its warmth on the town of Peñíscola. The sea lapped onto the beach, the waves glistening like diamonds, twinkling with each shot of sunlight. Charlie walked up the steps towards the veranda. A man could be seen in the garden of the villa. His hands were soiled, his shirt clinging to his sweat, his shorts muddied. Charlie turned to Sofia.

'Who is that in the garden?'

'It will be Roberto. He comes every Monday.'

'Does he know you have a son?'

'He knows of you, that you exist, yes. You are known here, you lived here once – you remember that, surely?'

'I haven't lived here since I was a boy, d'you forget that?'

'No, I haven't forgotten that, but you are like your father. People will see that. Why are you hiding?'

'Who does Roberto know?'

'Me, the people in the village, why?'

'It doesn't matter.'

'Are you Charlie to him, or do I call you a different name, is that what you want?'

'I will speak in Spanish and you will call me Miguel. Yes, that's what I want.'

'Miguel?' she scoffed. 'And who are you to me and why are you here? What is this for?'

'I'm your godson, and I'll be staying a while. That's all he needs to know.'

Charlie went indoors to his room and closed the door behind him. He took off the suit and shirt and laid them on the bed. The wound on his shoulder was now an untidy, unpleasant-looking scar. His torso, though, was defined once more after it had been nourished again with the Spanish meals; he had been fed well. His olive skin was smooth and scented only with a natural odour of a man. He pulled on a polo shirt and shorts, kicking off the brown leather shoes he had worn and slipping his feet into the leather boating shoes. From the envelope he took out six hundred euros and laid the notes on the bed. He placed the rest in his school trunk and left the room.

Sofia was already in the kitchen, preparing an ice-cold drink for Roberto, when Charlie returned. In his hand he carried the money for his clothes, toiletries, cigarettes and the sessions he had already had with Ana. He placed the money on the side.

'I'll be on the beach,' he said, holding the cigarettes she had bought him.

'I am making lunch. Will you not be eating with us?'

'Us?'

'Roberto is a friend and will eat as well.'

'I'll eat later if that's OK. I'm not hungry right now. May I take a beer?' She handed him a San Miguel from the fridge. 'Please, remember my name is Miguel and I am your godson.' His eyes like steel cut through her. She said nothing.

He took off his shoes and carried them in his hands. His bare feet sank into the golden sand, soft and warm between his toes. He walked towards the rock pools in the jagged cream rocks and sat on the sand, his back against the rock. Taking a swig from the beer bottle, he watched as the waves came along like sun-warm loving rascals up onto the sand

– perhaps that was why, as a child, he loved to play in them so much. And now, as an adult, it was something he should have held onto. His lips bore the semblance of a smile, just enough to remind him that his thoughts were good and enjoyed.

Lucy moved closer, close enough that he felt her presence, yet she stayed quiet. Lost in the moment but allowing him his thoughts. He closed his eyes and blinked several times. It wasn't real. Lucy wasn't there, that feeling wasn't there.

That feeling had never been there. Yet it was a wanted feeling, a wanted need, a wanted thought. But unreal, like the mermaids in the sea. He unravelled the film from the unopened cigarette packet, screwing up the paper and silver foil. He lit the cigarette and inhaled hard on it, blowing the grey smoke into the sea air. He watched the gentle roll of the waves forming as they came into play. He thought of Ana and how she listened to him, her dark mahogany eyes never leaving him. Her restfulness in the chair opposite him. The small child who played hopscotch in the market square. Taking a pebble from the sand, he felt the smoothness of it in his hand. He ran his thumb along it – no jagged edges, smooth curves perfectly round. He flung his arm back and flicked his wrist and watched it skim across the water.

The touch of a firm hand on his shoulder, a reassuring touch, the familiar scent of cologne. He turned to look, there was nobody there. Just his thoughts, vivid and wanted.

In a small café on a narrow street in Peñíscola, a gentleman made a call through to London.

Chapter Fifteen

Monday, 17th March
Harwich, Essex

On the beach, the sky was the bluest Lucy had seen it since she had returned home from the hospital. The saltiness of the sea air filled her lungs. She'd been home for twelve days and had weaned herself off her drugs for almost a week now. She had cancelled her appointment with Dr Hawkins, the hospital's psychologist, making up some excuse that she had to meet a deadline for HarperCollins.

Dr Hawkins would never know whether that was true or not. She simply wasn't ready to sit with someone and tell her story. Jo had tried her hardest to get her to go but in vain. Lucy knew Jo would relish the idea of lying on a couch with a therapist. Her gazelle-like legs hanging off the leather chesterfield or totally Freud chaise-longue, smoking her Marlboro Golds and letting everything out. Not that she would be allowed to smoke – but with Jo, anything was possible. She was made for a therapist. She was of Jewish descent, her father a hard-hitting New York financier, her mother an agent within some celebrity circle. Therapy was the norm in her daily life.

Therapy for Lucy wasn't the norm. She told her stories in a novel: she let her emotions unfold in a story, a fictional story but one where she could let go. Her feelings and regrets she'd write in her journal daily and that was as good as any therapist. Dr Thiroux was right: her writing would help her. She didn't need to spend hundreds of pounds raking up her past. She knew why she was messed up, damaged. She didn't need to ask a therapist to tell her why. She didn't need to sit in a leather chair and tell some stranger that she wasn't strong enough to walk away. She couldn't tell some stranger who knew nothing of her life that the man she shared a bed with had raped her. A man she'd tried to love had thrown her to the ground, split her lip, locked her away, jeered at her, taunted her. How could she tell somebody she had been weak, she had allowed it to happen? Why would she want to allow a stranger to maybe judge her? Would they judge her? Charlie was right: she had played the game, a bet for a free drink, a game she and Jo played, still played.

She could realise her own destiny and make her own pain subside. She also had Bob and her peppermint teas with him. He was like a natural tonic to her. He was her therapy, along with the sea and her writing and Ben, of course, who she desperately needed to feel close to again. Would a therapist tell her how to manage that? Probably, but so would time.

The briny grey of the water washed up onto the sand. She could sit for hours and forget, although today she didn't have hours, because she was meeting Jo later at Samuel Pepys. The gigantic dark blue shipping cranes overhung the docks of Felixstowe on the horizon. They reminded her how life was still the way it was. They had remained in place, waiting for her to return. A stark reminder of the deep-rootedness of where she now was. She took from her satchel her notebook and pen and unscrewed the flask. Cupping the warm tea in her hands, she gazed out to the horizon. The container ship never changed; it was always there, as if giving her a constant focus on life. Remaining there to keep the calm and remind her of what life was like before the horrors she had endured.

Lucy looked around her. A young couple sat on the bench by the sailing boats in the dinghies' lock-up. They were busied by their mobile phones. Behind them the beautiful renovated Artillery House stood important and grand on the seafront. A house that had once belonged to Bob and now perhaps had another family living in it, enjoying it, knowing nothing of the horrors that had gone before them.

In the distance she watched as the mother she had seen before walked along the beach. Now that little child with chubby hands picking up seaweed was no longer a toddler, but a little girl with long blonde plaits and a splattering of freckles on her nose. Her mother walked behind now, carrying a small bump in front of her, tenderly holding it as she bent down to take another shell for the bright red bucket in her hand. The upturned boat on the beach became a small climbing frame and slide for the little girl. The simplicity of the wooden boat allowed the playfulness of a child to imagine and use its smooth curves to carry her down with a squeal and a giggle. The mother's gentle hold on the beautiful bump cocooning the growing life of a sibling for the playful little girl. Lucy contemplated her own life. Would she one day hold her hand tenderly on a small precious bump? Would the man behind her who rested his hands on hers be Ben? Would they grow old together like

Gladys Pope and Stan? Would that give her the fairy-tale ending to the novels she would write? The fairy-tale she didn't seem to live.

A huddle of raggedy-looking men congregated outside the sailing club, accompanied by a couple of scrawny dogs. They had a few cans of Woodpecker cider and Special Brew between them. They reminded Lucy of the homeless men who would meet outside the Chelsea Potter on King's Road, a leafy, affluent suburb of west London. The landlord was always giving them a free pint and a sausage roll from the hot plate. They weren't bad people, just people whose lives had taken a different turn, maybe running from a violence they couldn't withstand, losing a person they loved, failing a person they loved because they couldn't meet their needs, simply not being able to give more. Giving everything but it never being enough. Maybe veteran soldiers who had nowhere to turn to, yet they'd fought for their country, put their own life in front of a machine gun to protect a person they'd never meet. Maybe the streets and those who lived on them provided more comfort, care, love and protection than the people already in their lives. Maybe that's what the landlord saw when he offered his kindness daily with food and a cold beer.

They were harmless, with unwavering politeness and graciousness in response to his kind gesture. They were always cheerful, even though their bed for the night would be in a shop doorway in one of the wealthiest boroughs of London. The stories they told were no doubt a little like the tales of the men behind her, hardened by the cold, dark nights and the alcohol to knock away the bad memories, numb the feeling of abandonment of a life they shouldn't be living. Which no person in a first world country should be living. Did the landlord at the Harwich local give them a free pint and a warm sausage roll, she wondered? Yet her life was marred and scarred by a man who had everything. A man who had wealth, a home, no worries, yet he controlled, bullied, violated.

A black and white collie ambled along, cocking his leg at every spot, and behind him she spied in the near distance, with his stick and a limp, Bob. She waved as he approached.

'Ah, my dear Lucy,' he said as he neared her.

'Hello, Bob,' she said, pouring him a cup of peppermint tea.

'How's the story coming along?' He took his seat on the stone step next to her and watched a small sailing boat launch from the sea's edge, the gentle wind billowing in the sails, taking it out further onto the water. A young windsurfer ducked and dived in the surf. Bob sighed as he took a mouthful of the warm tea. 'The sea has so many stories and secrets yet to tell. Here we explore, admire the wonders and learn.'

'You said that before,' she smiled.

'You remembered, young Lucy.'

'Yes, I remember everything. I've never sailed before,' Lucy said, catching Bob's words in her own.

'Sailing is a wondrous pastime. I would have taught Robin and Lottie to sail if they were here now. To dance over the white-crested waves, to cleave a path through the wind-whipped waters. A freedom like no other, to simply leave the duties of the land behind you. Forget a little.'

'You make it sound so wondrous and effortless. Here …' She handed him her notebook with a little of the chapter she had been writing. 'I should have been seeing the psychologist on Wednesday, but I cancelled it,' she said, staring into space and cupping her tea.

'And why are you not going?' he said, opening the page to his next chapter to read.

'I don't know - fear of the unknown. Fear of sharing my past. Fear of being judged.'

'Judgement, well, there's a fine word we humans like to use and adopt. Judgement and assumption - two words that I have come across in my life, many times. You might never need or want to speak with a psychologist, but to be judged is hard to learn how to deal with. My dear Lucy, I will tell you a secret. The Navy wanted me to speak with the naval doctor after the fire and my request to leave. It was barely equipped to deal with trauma and fear. Today it's now commonplace with PTSD, you wouldn't not have it. But I was a relatively young naval officer with a career ahead of me and I turned it down. I never wanted it. Do I regret it? I don't think I do. Should I have gone, who knows.'

'What rank were you, in the Navy?'

He sighed deeply. 'A lieutenant commander.'

'Is that quite high? I mean, is it like a major, I mean higher?'

He smiled and held her hand. 'Major is the Army. Our equivalent to a major would be a lieutenant. So, I was one above in the "dark blues". I was on my way to becoming a commander and then I would have been a captain. But my life took a change of direction and for me to continue was impossible. Not to have a wife at my side for the military occasions was something I couldn't do. Sailing is like the Navy: you leave the duties of the land behind you. I left my duties of the land and was dealt a hard price, loss like no other.'

'What are the dark blues? What do you mean?'

'The Royal Navy. The RAF are the light blues.'

'Oh, I see. I like that,' she said, smiling fondly at how Bob would tell his story.

'And now, would you not sail now, if you had talked to somebody?' she asked.

'One day I might, Lucy. But talking to someone wouldn't have made me do that. Only I could have brought that about. Although my injury would hinder me: I'm not as nimble, and to tack and jibe would be hard. Not impossible. Nothing in life is impossible.'

'Do you miss not being in the Navy? I mean, you had got so far.'

'I often think of my time spent travelling the seas and the world, seeing sights that captivated me and sights no man should ever see. I could never have returned, though, not after the fire. I blamed my time away from the family for the reason they're no longer here.'

'But you can't be blamed, it was an accident, Bob.'

'That it was, but I lost all that I loved that day. A part of me died. Now, enough of me – your book, tell me more before I read this chapter.'

She smiled and leant into him.

'Well, Jim didn't return from the war in Peggy's diaries. His last letter was written on the 2nd February 1945. I'd hoped he would return but I couldn't find any more letters. Hoping there might be one I'd missed. I think he must have died whilst in action. There's no way of me really knowing, I don't know his name other than Jim. But Peggy's diary speaks of her love for him and the hope that she had for him to return. I can't write about the sadness she would have endured, I simply can't, and at the moment my head doesn't feel like I can be sorrowful – too much has happened over the months for me to do that. Does that make sense?'

'It's a wise decision, to focus on the good. And your past, Lucy, where is he?'

'Do you mean Charlie? I don't know. On the run somewhere, waiting to come back. That's my fear, my past, my present and now my future.'

Bob listened to her like he understood every word and every fear in each of those words. He took her hand in his, not dismissing any of it but not allowing her to think of it either, or it would consume her like a huge volcano waiting to erupt.

'If you need any tales of the sea and wartime experiences, I can tell you mine, although they're a little different to the

World Wars, which were a little before my time, too.' His voice reassured her that her future would be hers, what she would make of it.

'What wars did you serve in?' Lucy asked, her head resting on her hand, her body turned in towards his.

'My experiences are of the Persian Gulf War and the Iraq War. But war is war, and hope is hope, and fear is fear. And a seaman's story is one of many such. Just a different time, a different location, but the feeling is the same.'

'When were they?'

'Seems like a lifetime ago. Another dictator, a man who wanted power, who ruled by tyranny. These men exist, be it war, be it normal life. They exist; control is a powerful thing.' He'd heard her words and without her realising it, he had let her know that control can come from anybody. It didn't need to be a dictator, it just needed to be a person who wanted power.

Lucy watched the small sailing boat as Bob read from her notebook and turned to the chapter she had begun.

Lines and lines of trestle tables stretched along the streets of York, covered in white crepe paper. Children tirelessly cut out bunting from cardboard and coloured it with crayons of red, white and blue. They set to making Union Jacks and streamers to decorate the tables and streets. The Women's Institute busied themselves baking and dressing the tables ready for a party that had had no announcement. No bells clanged to celebrate the end of the war and the return of men and women who had enlisted and fought for their kingdom and country. Two radios sat side by side in the open window of Peggy's front garden, relaying the music from the BBC. The streets were bright and full of noise. A surge of Canadian troops whisked the single WIs off their feet to dance all day and night.

She stood admiring the street as the merriment of music rebounded between the walls of the houses. Laughter reverberated through the streets. He would be home, he had to come home. She watched the GIs warmly as they embraced the girls they'd fallen in love with.

'He'll be here,' Emma said, squeezing her arm as she brushed past her, laughing and giggling with her soldier who had returned. Peggy watched her smile as her beau lifted her into the air and kissed her as she came back down into his arms to the sounds of Boogie Woogie Bugle Boy.

Would he return? Her eyes searched every murky-coloured flannel uniform, each one either holding his sweetheart or joyous with a comrade. Her heart beat faster and faster. It was as if the arm of a record player lifted and moved into place: the intermittent crackling sound and the needle softly dropping, and then there it was, Vera Lynn's We'll Meet Again. Goose bumps trickled across her as she felt the arms snuggle around her. Jim's arms held his sweetheart closely, the fragrance of her auburn hair infusing his lungs with a feeling of euphoria. He was back. She turned and kissed him long and slow.

'So, Jim has returned, and the war is over. How utterly delightful. Now, my dear Lucy, I must take leave and return tomorrow for another peppermint tea.'

He got up with a slight stagger and shook his lame leg back to life. She watched him as he walked across the beach and waved his stick in the air. 'Until tomorrow, young Lucy. Fear is a reason to be brave. Remember that.' His words caught in the wind as he whistled to Archie who ambled behind, still cocking his leg at every spot.

The small sailing boat had returned from its jaunt on the water and Bob stopped to chat to the young boy who had sailed alone, patting him on the head as he hauled his dinghy up the slipway and onto the nearby trailer. The windsurfer was still out, planing across the crests of the waves, jibing out of the way of the incoming sailing yachts and larger ships.

Lucy took up her notebook and began to scribble on the clean page, her thoughts untamed by the story she would tell of Jim and Peggy. He had returned and now their love story would truly begin. Her tummy rumbled a little; she was meeting Jo for lunch and the morning had run away with her. It was half past twelve and Jo would be on her way.

She packed up her satchel, tipped away the unfinished tea and left the stone step. The quaint RNLI museum's doors were open for business and a small queue of young, excitable children waited patiently outside. She crossed the road and walked along the narrow mews towards the wine bar, passing the café where she'd once sat with Ben.

The familiar smell of the wooden floors hit Lucy as she entered the bar. The cheery face of Sheila behind the bar welcomed her.

'Gin and tonic, love?' she said with a broad smile on her face. She never forgot a face or the tipple of her punters and Lucy was no exception.

'I might skip that today. Just a soda and lime would be good.'

'Haven't seen you in a while, you been away, lovely?'

'Yeah, I've been away.'

'Anywhere nice, love?'

'Oh, you know, just here and there, London mostly.' Lucy's stomach tightened, the butterflies somersaulted. She twizzled the glass in her hand, hoping the door would open and Jo would come swanning in. She was late. *Hurry up, Jo,* she pleaded in her head.

'So how long were you away, love?'

'Oh, umm, two weeks, maybe three.' Her stomach tightened even more as she tucked her hair behind her ear and bit her lip. *Bloody hell, Jo, where are you?*

'You would have missed the terrible goings-on at the beach. Poor girl left for dead. Rumours are it was a crazed lover.'

'Sounds terrible. I'm just going to grab a table.'

'Something I said, love?'

'No, just thought I'd grab a table.' Lucy moved away from the bar, holding her satchel closely to her. The door of the bar flew open and the sun caught on the sheen of Jo's silky sleek bob. Her face looked thinner and her features more defined. Her lips were slightly plumper and poutier than normal. She sauntered over to the table, a black denim jacket flung over her shoulder.

'Hey you! Whatcha drinking, kiddo, gin?'

'No, I'm on soda water.'

'Seriously?'

'Yep, seriously.'

'Right, well, I'm not. I've been on the phone all morning with HarperCollins and there's some woman taking over from Giles. She's a right head-up-her-own-arse bloody egotist. Just pushing from every angle, thinking she could tell me what's what. Let me get a drink and the menus and I'll fill you in, I'm about to burst.'

Lucy smiled. Having Jo for a literary agent was like having a pitbull fighting your corner. 'I thought you were on holiday?'

'Yeah, so did I. Stupid bloody woman.' Jo tossed her head and made her way directly to the bar, her eyes fixed on the large green bottle of Gordon's. She'd much prefer a Hendrick's or even a Tanqueray but after the morning she'd had, she wasn't fussy. If the bottle had gin written on it, she didn't much care.

Jo tapped her charcoal-painted nails on the wooden bar, tutting that in an empty bar, she was still standing there with a much-needed gin not yet poured. The door of Samuel Pepys opened and a young couple came in. They conferred for a brief moment before the young blonde made her way to the table in the window and the guy, in jeans and a long-sleeved T-shirt, joined Jo at the bar. Jo tossed him a look, he smiled. Sheila reappeared from the cellar.

'Sorry, who's next?' she asked, her pink lipstick still as bright as when Jo had first clapped eyes on her.

'The young lady,' the man said as he took out his wallet. Jo smiled appreciatively.

'Large gin and slimline tonic and a soda and lime, please.'

'Ice and a slice, love?'

'Yeah, sure, that would be great. Do you have a menu for lunch?' Jo asked, handing her a fiver and getting no change.

'That I do. The crab pâté is off the menu today, and the treacle tart, but everything else is available.' She smiled and turned to the young man, leaving Jo with the well-pawed-over menus.

'What can I get you, love?' Sheila said, leaning on the beer pumps, her attention now diverted to the young chap at the bar.

Jo carried the drinks over to the table. She eyeballed Samuel Pepys' portrait as she sat down. Flicking the hair from her lip, she leant forward to take a mammoth slurp from her gin.

'Man, I needed that.' She watched as the young man took his drinks and menus over to the blonde in the window. 'That guy reminds me of Matt.' Lucy turned to look.

'I don't see it myself.'

'No, it's not his look, he just reminds me of Matt or even Simon. Just weirdly, he seems the same. Don't you see it?'

Lucy turned again, inconspicuously. The blonde caught her eye and smiled. Lucy turned away and then darted a look back. The blonde was busy with her phone again. Lucy took a sip from her soda and lime. Was there something in what Jo had said? The blonde looked familiar, but she didn't know why.

'Anyway, your diva at HQ – so she's taking Giles' position?'

'Yeah, fuck, he got offered a bloody brilliant position and snapped up by Random, bloody sod's law. Anyway, this Clarissa is one hell of a B-I-T-C-H! Jesus, man, I thought my tongue could be harsh, but this woman can whoop your arse and make you feel two inches tall in the time it takes for a bloody adder to let its tongue out. I've only ever known one person like her in my life and that was the sister of a guy I went out with from boarding school, Angelica Vaughn. To the adults, she was this picture of perfection, but man she was vile. Her tongue was made of acid, I'm sure. Nothing angelic about her. Satana would have suited her better!'

Lucy burst into fits of giggles at Jo's utter honesty, the way she just said it how it was.

'So, what about my novels? Is my contract in jeopardy?' Lucy asked.

'Nope, you've hit the novels they wanted. We can just go now. They've no hold. I think we get this novel out, manuscript finished, primed, and move with Giles. He loves your work and to be honest cow-face Clarissa will make both our lives a misery. We've given Harper's enough to fulfil their contract; we simply terminate it. Random House will love you, that's a cert. And Clarissa can go shove it where the sun don't shine. Right, let's order some grub and talk this through, I'm starving!'

Jo took the menus to the bar and ordered two baskets of scampi and chips. She swaggered back towards where Lucy was sitting, but instead veered off to the table by the window.

'Hi, sorry to intrude. I just had to ask, do I know you? You look really familiar.'

The guy looked up from his phone. 'Don't think so,' he said.

'That's weird, you just remind me of my boyfriend.' She threw a glance over to the blonde. 'God, I'm sorry, I mean not looks-wise, just he's a policeman. You've got a familiar kind of look. Uncanny really.'

'Nope, don't know any policemen. I'm a graphic designer. A little less exciting.'

'Graphic designer, wow, that's cool. With a London firm or independent?'

He squirmed a tad in his chair. 'Yep, independent, work from home,' he said, trying in vain to close her down.

'Nice. So, what do you design?' She rested her hand on the back of a vacant chair. Lucy watched: was Jo playing the game? Was she trying to get a free drink from what appeared to be an already-taken guy?

Parker shot a look towards a nearby table, which had an array of tourist leaflets and pamphlets about where to go in Essex whilst on holiday.

'Leaflets,' he blurted out. He hadn't been expecting to be asked about his job in a pub by a beautiful girl who seemed to know what she might be talking about.

She looked at him, her head tilted to one side, her eyes narrowed.

'Leaflets, interesting. Right, yeah. Sorry to barge in on your lunch.' She turned and sashayed back to Lucy, her own self-assurance seeping out of her pores.

Jo sidled back into her chair and crossed her long legs. 'He didn't look much like a graphic designer,' she muttered.

'What were you doing?' Lucy asked, 'were you playing the game?'

'Nope – although I should have put a bet on it. I just asked if I knew him. He looks familiar.'

'And do you?' Lucy quizzed.

'Ummm, nope. Reckons he's a graphic designer.'

Lucy smirked at Jo's indignant response. 'Take it you don't believe him.'

'Do I fuck. Leaflets – who the fuck says they're a graphic designer for leaflets? Right, manuscript,' she said, swiftly changing the subject. 'Let's head out of here after lunch, go back to yours and talk Medusa. Sorry, did I say Medusa, I meant Clarissa.'

The young blonde looked at Parker. Had their cover been blown? A text came through to her phone and she read it anxiously, then passed it to Parker.

Possible sighting of our suspect in Peñíscola, call London.

Chapter Sixteen

Monday, 17th March
Peñíscola, Spain

The shadowy feral dogs cowered down low, swallowed by the encroaching darkness. Hiding from the humans that passed them by, tempted by the bats as they swept silently ahead. A cool breeze came off the sea, swept through the cobbled streets.

In a dimly lit bar, a scattering of tables were occupied by Spanish revellers. The dulcet, velvety tones of a jazz singer rang softly through the room from her stool in the corner behind the door. Her silk blouse was cut low. Dark hair caught up, red lips plump, her eyes a deep chocolate brown. One leg rested on the step of the stool, a large split opening up the skirt and revealing the smooth brown legs beneath, her hand caressing her neck as she sang, oozing a sultry, sensual appeal.

A gentleman sat in the corner, with the glow of an amber light above him. A carafe of red wine and a half-filled glass. The door opened and a young couple, no doubt lovers, came in. They sat close by, their hands unable to refrain from touching each other. He watched them and waited, his hand resting on the wineglass in front of him. The candle in the netted round bottle on his table flickered. The door opened and a man dressed simply came in, his face weather-beaten with a mop of thick grey curls. The gentleman at the table took out his empty packet of Ducados and placed them on the table. The man glanced at the packet and made his way over to the table.

'Is it Pedro?' he asked, his voice low.

'It is, please sit.' He beckoned to the patron for another glass.

'Do you have the money?'

'I do, but first the information,' the gentleman said, pouring a glass for his guest.

'I do not want to be in any danger. I have a wife and grandchildren. I must be left alone afterwards – you must promise me that, no harm must come to me.'

'Nothing will happen to you. We are not underground criminals. But I want the information and the money is a simple reward. Now tell me what you know?'

'I don't know much. He was delirious when we found him, his eyes bewildered and frightened, like a wild man. His face was badly sunburned and blistered, his hands white like the blood had been drained from them. His face looked like he had been pecked at by the seagulls.

'His name, I don't know – I think he said it was Miguel, but I don't remember. Like I said, he was delirious, he mumbled through dry, cracked lips. We fish for sardines, tuna, lobster. It's a simple life we lead. I have a simple fishing shop, that's all. To find a man at sea, it's unexpected. But he was there on a piece of driftwood as we hauled in the first nets. At first, we thought it was just driftwood, but as we drew in closer, we realised it was more than that. One of my men called and shouted, "A body!" We thought he was dead but as we drew him in, we realised the person clinging to the wood was alive, clinging to his own life. We gave him water and tended to his face. He struggled to drink at all. We used a sponge at first, because he could barely open his mouth. His lips were dry, chapped and cracking with blisters. When he did speak, he said his sailing boat had sunk, had taken on a leak that overpowered him before he could get back to shore.'

'He was Spanish?'

'It was difficult to understand him, as when he spoke, he hardly opened his mouth, it was too chapped. But yes, he spoke Spanish like a native. Yes, he was definitely Spanish. He slept in the berth for a night until we returned home.'

'Did he speak with you?'

'No, he asked for some fishing wire and a hook and that was it. He said nothing more. He slept the whole time we sailed back to the harbour.'

'Did you not ask him where he was from?' the gentleman asked.

'I asked no questions. A sailing boat to become overpowered by a leak – it seemed reasonable.' The man took a large mouthful of wine and pushed his glass forward for another.

'What did he look like?'

'Olive skin, grey eyes, like a Spaniard. It was his eyes that were familiar. But his name was Miguel, so it couldn't have been …'

'It couldn't have been what?' the gentleman said as he took a sip from his glass, and then poured another for himself.

'Roberto.'

'Roberto?' the gentleman questioned. 'Who is Roberto?'

'The husband of Sofia. It was like his ghost. But Roberto died at sea. He was English but we called him Roberto, he liked that. He was a kind man, a gentle soul, but his body was found at sea in the wreck of his plane. But this man looked like him, like he had returned from the dead. He wore a gold signet ring on his little finger, it reminded me of Roberto. I remember telling my wife that evening that I had seen a ghost. And then the other night, after two weeks maybe had passed, my wife said that it was strange, as Sofia had been in her shop and had bought men's clothes. Sofia lives alone. And this is why I phoned you.'

'Are you sure of this?'

'I am very sure of this. Please, I have given you the information, now the reward.'

'You say Sofia: what is her family name?'

'Martinez, it is Sofia Martinez. She was the wife to Roberto, they had a son. His father's joy. He'd crab in the rockpools, play hopscotch, search for mermaids. A sweet boy - he'd visit my shop for sweets - yes, Charlie, the sweetest child.' He smiled fondly.

'And where does she live?

'On the Iberian slopes in a villa tucked away. It's the only villa on the track, Villa Bendita.'

The gentleman pushed the envelope across the table. It had one hundred and fifty euros inside.

The fisherman went to take it, but as he did, the gentleman put his hand over it.

'One last question.'

'What?'

'Where did you leave the man when you came in to shore?'

'At the harbour. We arrived back at 5 a.m. ready for the market traders to buy from the quayside. It was the market that day. But he had already gone. I didn't see him leave the boat. We were busy with the nets and the catch. I haven't seen him since. I know nothing else. My memory is hazy.'

The gentleman took his hand from the envelope and slid it further along the table. The fisherman finished the remnants of his wine and stuffed the envelope into his pocket.

'Please, can I ask you one question?' the fisherman asked.

'Of course.'

'Why did you phone me and ask me to call you back? Why did you think I would know anything? I am a simple fisherman.'

'That's precisely why. I am a detective, working with the British police, and a man has been lost at sea. What better person to ask than a man who works at sea, Santiago? It is simply *el golpe de suerte* that you were able to help.'

'You think it is Roberto?'

'No, Roberto is dead.'

The fisherman took one last drop from his wineglass. '*Buenas noches*,' he said and left.

The gentleman gestured for the bill. He placed twelve euros on the table and walked out, leaving his empty packet of Ducados. He walked down the cobbled streets towards the market square, veering off into the shadows of a narrow street and letting himself into the apartment above the bakery, leaving the nightlife of the Spanish streets with lovers and music below. He took out his phone and texted a message.

In London, Phillips sat in his kitchen, the lights dimmed, a scotch on the rocks poured. His mobile screen lit up and a message buzzed in. He twizzled the phone nearer to him and swiped the notification to open.

Your suspect is alive. A man was picked up half dead by a fishing trawler. I believe him to be at Villa Bendita, on the Iberian slopes. The villa belongs to a Sofia Martinez. His name is Miguel. The message was signed off by Pedro Rodriguez, Detective *de la Policía.*

Phillips read the message again. He moved the knight on his chessboard and took out a black bishop, pondering it before placing it on its square. He rattled the ice cubes around the glass and finished the last drops of his scotch before turning out the lights. He could do nothing more now until the morning.

***

DS Murphy was already at his desk when Phillips entered the department. He looked up as Phillips neared him.

'Guv.'

'Murphy,' Phillips replied, before going into his office and shutting the door. He sent an internal email to the department. It read: *MIT briefing 9 a.m.* Just as he pressed send, his direct line rang.

'DI Phillips.'

'Sir, it's DC Milson. We received a message from DS Murphy yesterday to call, saying there had been a possible sighting of the suspect.'

'Correct., that's now been confirmed. What's happening in Essex?' Phillips asked.

'Nothing much, sir. We've kept a close eye on Lucy. She's mainly been to the beach to write. Nothing untoward or suspicious has arisen here. Do you suspect we might get a visit from the suspect?'

'I can't be sure. Our lead has come through from the Spanish police. Keep her in your sights at all times, she's not out of the woods yet. Our suspect is masquerading as a Miguel at the moment. So there's a chance he could get through passport control under an alias. I'm not ruling anything out at this stage. Keep Lucy safe.'

'Will do, sir.'

'Good work.' Phillips closed the call. The blinds rattled as the door closed behind him and he made his way to the coffee machine.

As per their orders, the MIT began to gather around the briefing desk and whiteboard. The pictures of Lucy Carter, Charlie Wainwright and the abandoned Audi were still Blu- Tacked on the board, with timings and arrows on each print. The team sat facing the steely face of their Detective Inspector, his arm now out of the sling.

'Morning guys,' he said, leaning on the desk behind him. 'To date we have Lucy living back at home and under police surveillance. This was the best option rather than a safe house. All is well with her. She has been out to the beach and continued her daily life as normal. She seems content.'

'What about the sightings of our suspect, guv?' Murphy asked.

'Our Spanish plain-clothes police operator met with a local fisherman yesterday. A man was picked up by a fishing trawler about ten miles from the coast and brought back to the harbour, some days ago. By all accounts he appeared to have been out at sea for a few days, staying afloat on a piece of driftwood. His spiel to them was that he had been out on his dinghy and it had taken on a leak which overpowered him.'

'And they believed him?' DS Kennedy quizzed.

'They had no reason not to. He spoke Spanish fluently and his story added up.'

'So how do we know it's our man?' Kennedy asked.

'His mother was seen at the market,' Phillips replied.

'I don't get it, guv. How does his mother being at a market prove it's Wainwright - was he with her?' Kennedy probed further.

'No, he wasn't, or at least he wasn't seen. She was seen buying clothes for a man in one of the boutique shops. We know that her husband died some years ago, and the shopkeeper is the wife of the fisherman, so she knew a man had been rescued at sea by her husband.'

'How do we know it's our suspect, guv?' one of the detectives asked.

'The fisherman who picked him up said it was like seeing a ghost.'

'Not surprised, guv, he must have looked half dead.'

'Not because he looked half dead. The fisherman said he spoke Spanish like a native and was the image of Roberto,' Phillips cut in.

'You mean his father - Robert Wainwright?' Murphy interjected.

'Exactly, Murphy, but they called him Roberto,' Phillips said, his hand in his pocket, his ankles crossed as he leant further onto the desk. 'The same undercover operative noted a guy matching the description of Wainwright accessing the local bank. He was seen leaving in a small Spanish registered car, with a female driver. It would seem he is being aided and abetted by his mother, because he was dressed in a finely cut suit, bought by her. Murphy, what have you got on his accounts?'

'Funds were moved from his account in London to a Spanish bank in Peñíscola. A large sum of money was withdrawn as cash from inside the bank on Monday the 10th March at 11.43 a.m. But there have been no other movements or transfers on his accounts. That's been the only one, guv.'

'How much was the large sum of money?' Phillips asked.

'The transfer was twenty-five thousand pounds. He withdrew four thousand euros.'

'Right. Why would he need so much cash, that's the question. What information have we got on the father's grave?'

'A fresh bouquet of flowers was left around the time of his departure from London, but no more flowers have been left since,' DS Kennedy said.

'He seems to have had a strong affinity with his father, this is clear,' Phillips said, piecing together the relationship. 'The fisherman has said the father was a kind man, liked, a gentle soul. Wainwright has tended to the grave, yet his relationship with his mother is fraught and estranged. He barely saw her.'

'Right, so we go in, guv,' one of the DCs piped up.

'That's exactly what we don't do.' Phillips replied. This young DC had much to learn.

'So, what's our next step?' Murphy asked.

'Outwitting him. Like a game of chess. Murphy, I want you to get two flights to Peñíscola. We'll fly out and meet with Pedro, our Spanish operative. Sort accommodation, too. Kennedy, I want you to man the department and take over from Murphy on the bank account monitoring. Also, keep in touch with DC Parker and Milson in Essex. We're closing in. Team dismissed.'

Phillips left the team and Murphy followed behind him.

'Shall I get accommodation in the town, guv?'

'Yup, and a car. We'll fly out this evening.'

'You were right. He didn't drown.'

'If I can teach you anything, Murphy, it would be to stick with your gut instinct. I knew he hadn't gone under, I just knew it. I'll get my man. I'll get him.'

He closed his office door and watched from his window as Fulham Broadway busied itself with people milling about. An internal email came into Phillips' inbox from DS Murphy, notifying him that the flights had been booked from Stansted at 17.45 and arriving in Valencia at 21.15. A hire car and two hotel rooms in Peñíscola had also been arranged. He closed down his PC and left his office.

Phillips lit a cigarette on his patio and made a call.

'Essex Police, PC Mackenzie speaking,' came the voice from Wrabness station.

'Simon, DI Phillips here. How's Lucy?'

'Sir, afternoon. She's doing OK. She's been to the beach several times now and is never really alone in the house for too long.'

'Good job, and her flashbacks?'

'It was difficult at the beginning, sir, but each day becomes better for her. I had to attend in an emergency not so long ago as she thought Ben had been killed by Charlie.'

'Why would she think that? And where were DC Parker and Milson?'

'In their cottage, sir. They didn't intervene because they knew Ben hadn't been killed.'

'So why did Lucy think that?'

'He wasn't home when she got back, but his bike was there. She just got herself into a state about it. That's all, sir.'

'Where was he?'

'Waiting at the pub – he didn't have a key to get in before Lucy. Like I said, sir. It was something of nothing.'

'Right, keep me posted, Simon. I'm flying out to Valencia today with DS Murphy.'

'So, you think he's still alive?' Simon asked.

'I know he's still alive. We've had sightings of him and a positive description of him being brought in from the sea. Money has been transferred from his account to Spain.'

'What do I tell Lucy?' Simon asked.

'At this stage, nothing. I'll be in touch once I've settled in to the town where he has been seen,' Phillips replied, drawing on a cigarette.

'You're closing in, aren't you, sir.'

'That I am, Simon, that I am. Take care of Lucy.' He closed the call and tucked the chair back under the table.

Before heading up the stairs, he closed and locked the concertina door. The king on his chessboard remained in the same place - not checkmate yet. He packed a suitcase, then grabbed his laptop case and stashed his passport and powerboat identity card inside. Then he went out hailed a black cab, giving his destination as Liverpool Street station.

Liverpool Street was full of passing people dashing for trains. The huge screen displaying train times flickered constantly, ever-changing. Phillips and Murphy met outside Costa coffee on the concourse before making their way through the barriers to the Stansted Express.

As the train pulled out of the station, Phillips mulled over the days and weeks that had passed. The image of a frightened Lucy in a hospital room. The strength of a victim in a court room. The dead flowers now at the grave of a father who perhaps should never have died.

'Guv?' Murphy said, breaking Phillips' thoughts. 'Can I ask you a question?'

'Sure.'

'Why is this case so important to you?'

'Meaning what?' Phillips replied.

'With every case you find the wrong and you make sure you solve it. But this one, guv, you haven't let go of. Even when the military were adamant Wainwright had drowned at sea. You didn't believe it.'

Phillips pursed his lips and drew in a breath. 'I didn't believe him to be dead.'

'I get that, guv. But why Lucy? Why is this case one you won't let go of?'

Phillips pushed his phone to one side. 'I saw a girl in a hospital room with fear in her eyes. A fear that hit me head-on like the bullet that hit my arm. Punctured me.'

'But, guv, this is different, it's like this is more,' Murphy said. He was a good, kind officer who he knew Phillips well and how he operated, and he knew his DI was damn good at his job.

As the train swept past the suburbs of London and out into more open spaces, Phillips sighed. 'I've seen that fear before, Murphy. I saw it in the eyes of my sister when I was seventeen years old. My uncle put that fear into my sister.'

'And your uncle now?'

'He hanged himself. Why?' He took an intake of breath. 'Why, because of guilt, shame, a worthless man. A wretch of a man.'

'You've never spoken about it, guv.'

'Never needed to. But the day I saw Lucy, that day I realised this was what I saw in my sister.'

'And your sister now? Is she OK?'

'She'll never be OK. The damage was done by his years of unnoticed abuse. Justice wasn't seen because the man who did it took the easy way out. Justice can be done for Lucy and it will be.'

'I'm sorry, guv.'

The two detectives' eyes flicked rapidly as the scenery passed by, the train too fast for them to keep a steady stare on the world outside. Both with the same focus: to catch a wanted man.

Chapter Seventeen

Tuesday, 18th March
Peñíscola, Spain

The Bonita Rosa was an old-style boutique hotel sandwiched between the pretty walls of the houses, shops and tapas bars that ran in a Spanish-style terrace on either side. Above the old wooden door was a sign that read Hotel Bonita Rosa, with intricate red roses painted around the words. On each small window balcony hung a wrought iron window box with a few spring flowers already beginning to blossom. Every window was framed and flanked by artisan shutters. On the wall by the front door hung a blackboard with a simple menu of the meals served daily.

Opposite the hotel was a taberna, its sign reading Taberna de José. Its windows were small panes of glass and inside the light was dim but the sound of music reverberated around the intimate space. It was just gone eleven o'clock at night and the feral dogs were on their nightly prowl. Phillips and Murphy entered the small foyer of the hotel. The two detectives spoke little Spanish between them.

'Buenas evening,' Phillips said taking out the confirmation slip of the rooms booked.

'Buenas noches,' replied the receptionist.

'I … am … Tony … Phillips … and … this … is … Sean … Murphy … we … have … a … booking,' Phillips said in a slow laboured way, in a meagre attempt to communicate with the Spanish girl.

'That is great,' the receptionist replied. 'Could I see your passports and the credit card used for the booking?' Her English was perfect, only accentuated by her Valencian accent. Coughing a little, Phillips complied.

'That is perfect,' she said. 'Your rooms are numbers fifteen and eighteen and located on the third floor. The stairs here will take you straight up. Maria will clean your rooms daily and breakfast is served in the dining room just here along to the left. It is served from 7 a.m. until 10 a.m. If you would like lunch or supper, please just book in at the reception with me.' She handed them both the keys to their rooms.

'Good job,' Phillips said, taking his passport and room key.

'Enjoy your stay and *buenas noches,* gentlemen.'

Phillips nodded, and he and Murphy climbed the narrow, curving wooden staircase.

'Shall we grab a beer, guv, before we hit the sack? I wouldn't mind a chilled one. It's been a long old day.'

'Sounds like an idea,' Phillips said as he pushed the key into the lock. 'Let me unpack and I'll meet you in the reception in fifteen minutes.' He closed his door behind him. His room was simply furnished, with golden silk lampshades on each of the bedside lamps. The French-style windows were open and the soft muslin drapes fluttered a little in the night's breeze. The sky was an ebony black and the stars as white as white, dotted about the sheer blackness. The air held a salty freshness from the sea that enveloped the shoreline of this fishing town.

He unpacked and changed into his chinos and a pale blue polo top, and swapped his brogues for a pair of simple deck shoes. Retrieving his keys, cigarettes, wallet and phone, he left his room. It looked as empty as when he had arrived. The only giveaway that there was a human presence was the pair of highly polished shoes left neatly by the mirror.

He made his way down the stairs where Murphy was already waiting in the foyer.

'Thought we could go opposite to José's, easy to get back,' Murphy said, smiling.

Before leaving the foyer, Phillips took a strip of hotel matches from the bowl on the counter. They left the hotel and walked not even two metres across the cobbled passageway to José's Taberna. The feral dogs paced the passageway. Through the windows of the taberna could be seen an amber glow of light. It was warm and inviting, and the noise inside was that of melodic Spanish music, laughter and chatter.

Inside, Phillips scanned the bar and took a seat in the corner at a table made of dark mahogany, with a candle in a bottle. He caught the eye of the patron and a waitress came over. They ordered a bottle of San Miguel, a scotch on the rocks and a bowl of nuts. The waitress left the drinks on the table along with the bill. Phillips paid.

'Guv?' Murphy asked as he took a swig from his bottle. It tasted like pure nectar as it slid down his throat.

'Tony, whilst we are here,' Phillips replied.

'Tony,' Murphy continued. 'How are we going to trap him?'

'I need to locate him and watch and wait. He needs to come to us. We can't arrest him here, we're on Spanish soil.'

'How are we going to do that, though?'

'Entrapment,' Phillips said.

'Entrapment?' Murphy questioned.

'What do we know of Charlie?' Phillips said as he swirled the ice around his glass.

'That he is an abuser, dominant, a control freak, an animal,' Murphy continued.

'Right, but apart from that, what do we know about him?'

'Well, he's wealthy, a banker, clever … I don't know,' Murphy said.

'We know that he tends to his father's grave. We know that he never talked about his father or mother. Or at least when he did, according to Rachel Jones, he said she was a drunk and didn't care. Yet he tends to his father's grave … paint the picture. A son who tends to his dead father's grave and yet has no care for his living mother. A man who by all accounts wanted a little rough sex with his neighbour and a man who abused and hurt Lucy and wanted her dead. What does that tell us?'

'He wasn't a mummy's boy, he hates women,' Murphy said, musing on what his boss was saying.

'The fisherman said Charlie's father was a gentle soul, likeable, a kind man.'

'And ...'

'And just that,' Phillips said.

'I don't follow.' Murphy checked the contents of his bottle before taking another swig.

'If a man treats women badly, why would that happen?'

'Because he's seen it happen,' Murphy said, taking a stab at the answer and hoping he might be right.

'But his father was a gentle soul, well-liked, a kind man. His son tends to his grave,' Phillips responded.

'So, his mother?' Murphy questioned, unsure of his answer.

'Exactly. The hatred he has for women has stemmed from his mother.'

'And yet he's hiding out at his mother's.'

'Why not? He owes her nothing, he doesn't care whether she gets tangled up in this. He has no apparent love for her. Yet he loves - loved - his father. I'd place money on him adoring his father and being smashed to pieces when he lost him as a little boy.'

'So, you think he now hates women because of his mother?'

Phillips nodded his head and took a large sip of his scotch.

'But entrapment, Tony. I can't see how we'd make that work.'

'When my sister was abused, I did nothing. Why? Because I didn't really know myself. Fifteen years ago, I realised I should have done something - believed her, helped her. A sense of guilt lay with me for years, until I spoke with someone.'

'A therapist?'

'Yup. It was the best thing I ever did.'

'And Charlie?'

'He'll do the same.' Phillips' eye was caught by a group of Spaniards entering the taberna. He looked at his watch. It was half past midnight.

'Murphy, I'm going to turn in now. I suggest you do the same. We've an early start tomorrow.' They finished their drinks and headed back to the hotel. Before going in, Phillips lit a cigarette.

'Mind if I join you?' Murphy asked.

'I didn't know you smoked.'

'I don't. I'm that once-in-a-while old college boy smoker. But I quite fancy one.' Phillips flicked the bottom of his pack and a cigarette shot up. Murphy took one. Phillips ripped a match from the strip and struck it across the packet. The cardboard match bent in his fingers a little before it fizzed and lit up, giving off an instant smell of sulphur. Shielding it from the night's breeze, he lit Murphy's cigarette and then his own.

'Are you beginning to feel sorry for Charlie?' Murphy asked as he drew in on the cigarette and felt the nicotine in his throat and the slight head rush it gave him.

'I'm beginning to understand him. There's always a motive, and my hunch is the mother. I've dealt with some monsters in my time, but invariably those monsters weren't born evil. Someone made them that way.'

'Right,' Murphy said, blowing the smoke into the air.

Together the two men stood outside Bonita Rosa and smoked their cigarettes before heading back inside to their rooms for the night.

Phillips lay in bed, musing over the conversation he'd had with Murphy that night. He took up his phone and searched boat hire in Peñíscola. Only three kilometres away along the coastal path was Peñíscola Marina, an established sailing company that hired dinghies, jet skis and powerboats. Phillips had brought along his powerboat ID, which he'd gained from working as an officer on the Thames. He could use this internationally to charter a motorboat. He filled out the necessary booking forms on the website and pressed submit. He set his alarm for 7 a.m. before switching out the bedside lamp. The balconette windows were still ajar, but the shutters were closed, pushing away the huge silver orb in the sky. Phillips let the night steal him away.

The clattering of bottle crates and bins being emptied into a small, narrow wagon woke Phillips. It was six forty-five. His alarm would go off at seven. He pulled the crisp white sheet back and stretched, then cancelled the alarm on his phone, leaving it on the bedside table whilst he took a shower and shaved.

Downstairs, Murphy was already sitting at the corner table tucking into a continental breakfast of pastries and artisan bread and jam. Phillips poured himself a large black coffee from the self-service table and joined Murphy.

'Morning, guv, I mean, Tony,' Murphy said as he polished off the last piece of bread on his plate.

'Murphy,' Phillips replied as he glanced over at the young girl who was making a fresh pot of percolated coffee.

'So, what's the plan today?'

'We're going to take a boat out and sail along the coastline, see what villas run along the shoreline, and watch from the water. I've messaged Pedro to let him know we're in town. We'll need his eyes and ears too.'

The two detectives left the hotel and drove to Peñíscola Marina. Along the quayside sat four large, elegantly beautiful, glossy white yachts. Their streamlined sides gleamed in the early morning sun, each one with a name along it. A row of jet skis bobbed on the water and as each small wave came in it knocked them gently onto the quayside. A handful of sailing boats swayed and rocked amid the clinking sound of halyards beating in the wind as it whistled through them. Two cream and blue RIBs were moored below a small wooden office. Phillips went in first, whilst Murphy swooned over the yachts, wishing they could hop on board one for their coastline detective jaunt.

'Good morning,' Phillips began, taking out his passport and powerboat ID. 'Do you speak English?'

'Good morning, yes, how can I help you?'

'I've booked a powerboat for a day's hire for today,' Phillips continued.

'Do you require a skipper?' the sailor behind the desk asked. 'The RIBs all require a powerboat certification to cruise them, or you will need a skipper which is one hundred euro for the day. I will require two forms of identification too, please.'

'I have certification.' Phillips placed his ID on the counter, along with his passport and Metropolitan Police card. The sailing assistant took a copy and returned it. Phillips signed the necessary forms and waivers.

'If you follow me, I will take you to the RIB.' The pontoon swayed a little on the sea's gentle waves as the three men walked along it to the RIB that was moored at the end, buffeting up against the jetty's edge.

'Here is the key for the boat. It is all very simple. The power lever is the same internationally, the kill cord must be worn at all times, and the fuel tank is full. There is a full tank also under the back seat. The day return is six o'clock; each hour after that, you pay. The RIB has an anchor, medical box, high lens binoculars, two flares and a VHF channel 16 radio, if you need help.' He handed each detective a life jacket to put on and untied their mooring, still keeping hold of the rope. 'If you go south, you'll see a small taberna that sits on the coastal path. It's Taberna As de Copas. There is a jetty where you can moor up and eat lunch, or in the evening some supper, maybe tapas. In summer there are many divers, waterskiers. Now, it is less busy, you will not need to book. Maria is the *patrona el la taberna,* I don't know how you say that in English, and her husband is the cook. You will know it when you see it because it has a card like you play with on the jetty as a sign for it. Tell them I sent you, my name is Juan. They will look after you, although their English is not good, but their food, well, it is great.' He snaked the rope in a loop before throwing it into the boat. 'Have a good sail,' he said, as he pushed the boat away from the edge with his foot.

Phillips let the engine throttle out a little as he reversed the boat slowly out of the marina, before turning the wheel and spinning it out over the waves towards the hills that sloped back from the coastline. He slowed the engine down and turned to Murphy: 'Make a note of the private beaches and villas.' Murphy sat on the edge of the RIB as Phillips slowly cruised along the beaches.

A scattering of villas came into sight along the slopes as the town of Peñíscola became a distant landmark behind them. Some of them had long trails of sandy beaches, while others were small and private. A few with small shacks built into the slopes to house sailing equipment and beach furniture. Nowhere was there any sign of life.

The speedboat knocked against each wave, a spray of salty water splashing up onto the detectives' faces. Murphy noted the villas and beaches as they passed each one at a steady pace. As they veered around the craggy rocks of the slopes, the scattering of villas lessened. They had cruised no more than three kilometres when they spied the jetty and the taberna tucked up high above the water. As they motored past it, they could see three more villas dotted along the coastal path. Phillips steered the RIB a little closer in to the shore and slowed the engine. Its gentle humming was the only sound as it neared the beaches. He pulled the lever back into neutral and turned to Murphy.

'Under the seat are some binoculars. Can you pass them to me?' Murphy lifted the rear seat and took them out. Phillips scanned the three villas.

To the left of them was what looked like a fishing shop. It was open. A dog sat outside with a bowl close by. He twizzled the wheel on the nosepiece and zoomed further in. The walls of the shop were whitewashed and the board above the door read 'La Tienda de Santiago'. He could make out a splattering of buckets and spades outside and fishing rods and nets. A little higher, on a lone track, was a villa tucked away. He could see the steps that led up to a veranda, and down to a private beach below, nestled between rocks on either side. He zoomed out a little and turned his body to the left: an olive grove surrounded the villa to one side. He turned back, and as he did the door on the veranda opened. He zoomed back in on the figure. It was a woman. He watched her through the binoculars as she walked along the veranda and disappeared around the side of the villa, out of sight. She came back around the side and hung out what appeared to be washing line. She went back into the villa. The door closed. Was that Sofia, he wondered.

He started the engine and cruised the RIB a little further in before stopping again. He brought the binoculars up once more and fine-tuned them so he could see the track that ran up to the villa. He honed in on a silver car that was parked under a pergola, overhung with vines and a gnarly old olive tree.

'Murphy, take down this number plate,' he said as he intensified the vision of the binoculars. 'Silver Beetle, 2620VAP.'

While Murphy scribbled the number plate down, Phillips took out his phone and began to text a message to Pedro Rodriguez.

We have located a villa on the Iberian slopes. Parked outside is a silver Beetle. Can you confirm this as the car you saw in the market square. DI Phillips

Below Phillips' message, the bubbles began to move he waited for the response.

Sí. PR

The woman, is she in her late fifties?

Sí.

We have their location, are you in Peñíscola?

Sí. Where are you?

On a powerboat, on the shoreline of the beach close to the villa

What do you want me to do?

I need you to stay in Peñíscola. If they leave the villa by car, I want you to follow them. You will need to be close to their track. How far away are you from Taberna As de Copas?

Approximately 1.5km

Can you find the track that leads to their villa? It is three villas in from the taberna, due south, to the left is a fishing shop called 'La tienda de Santiago'

I can do that. I know this shop

The bubbles disappeared and Phillips took up the binoculars again. The RIB drifted a little further out to sea, so he turned on the engine again and pulled her in a little more. As he watched the veranda door, it opened and the female figure came out. This time she held a basket, which appeared empty. She left the door open and began to descend the steps. As she reached the bottom, he zoomed his vision back up to the veranda and the open door. A male came into view; he twizzled the focus to bring him up closer. 'Got you!' he said under his breath.

Phillips tracked him down the steps. He lost sight of him behind an olive tree. He scanned the car. He could make out a figure in it, but only one.

Are you in place, car is on the move?

I am

I have lost sight of the companion. I believe only one person to be in the car. Follow it

I can see the car coming down the track behind me, there are two people in it. The female is driving. It has just passed me. I am leaving now

The messages finished.

'Was that Charlie?' Murphy asked.

'Yup, Pedro is now on his tail.'

'What now, guv?'

'We wait,' Phillips replied. 'They can't be going far. Maybe to the town – she has a basket with her.' Phillips and Murphy sat in the RIB as it drifted back and forth on the waves, waiting for a message from Pedro. Phillips looked at his watch; it had just gone ten. His phone beeped and a notification alert came in. It was Pedro.

The car has driven to a villa close to Peñíscola. I know the villa it has gone to

Where are you now?

I have stopped on a nearby street that has access to the road leading to the villa. If I followed the car I would have been seen. It is better that I wait

Who lives in the villa?

Ana Pérez

Who is she?

A local therapist and healer

Do you have an exact address?

Cueva Cascada, 12598 Peñíscola

Wait a while and see if the car comes back

Pedro got out of the car and walked a little way from it before lighting a cigarette. As he smoked his cigarette, he could hear a car coming along the rocky track that he'd stopped shy of. As the car passed, he looked up. He flicked his cigarette and went back to his car.

The car is on the move again. Only the female inside. The driver I know, I recognise her

Is it Sofia Martinez?

Sí

Can you access the Taberna As de Copas from the coastal road?

Sí

Meet me there now. I will be with DS Murphy

Chapter Eighteen

Wednesday, 19th March
Wrabness, Essex

His arm pulled her into his body, and she could feel his lips on the nape of her neck. Her hands were tucked under her head, her pillow cushioned around her. She moved her hand down and nestled it inside his hand. He was warm and she felt safe in his arms. The birds babbled outside on the tree branches that gently tapped against her window. The sky still grey and unwelcoming to the morning chorus.

'What's the time?' she asked.

'Seven-thirty.'

She felt him move in a little closer, his arms pulling her closer into him. She could feel his breath on her, as his hand rested on her tummy. His fingers moved slowly and gently across her tummy, mapping out the lines of her body. She closed her eyes and let his hands wander, feeling every touch, but she didn't flinch. His hand slid through her hair and he kissed her neck tenderly. He breathed in the sweetness of her tousled locks as he curled his fingers through it. She wriggled back into him a little more, feeling his body press up against her. She felt his hands slide under her cotton vest and onto the smooth curves of her breasts. He caressed the silky softness of her skin and breathed in the freshness of it. His hand rested on the roundness of her breast, cupping it, kneading it softly. He needed to feel her again, touch every smooth line of her body, he wanted her. He moved steadily up to her neck and onto her shoulder. Lucy's head swam with thoughts of Ben's touch. She had craved his touch yet hadn't known how to let go, how to let him back, and now every inch of her body wanted him, yearned for him.

Tenderly he moved her shoulder, so she lay on her back. She turned her face to his and let her hand touch his face again. He lifted her vest top and moved his lips onto her tummy, every kiss soft and wanting. He looked up at her, his face cracking a gentle smile. She bit her lip. He brushed away the strand of her hair that caught on her lips. His fingers trailed down her temple, across her cheek to her lips, he outlined them with his fingertips. She kissed them as they brushed against her lips, her gaze not leaving his face. He said not a word; her body was telling him it was ok. Shivers ran through the whole of her supple body as she ached for him, her deep chocolate brown eyes looking into his dotingly.

He kissed the softness of her earlobes tenderly, moving down her neck, each caress amorous and soft. He moved his lips onto her collarbone and took her wrists in his hands, lifting them above her head, resting them on the pillow. His hands moved back to her vest top and he peeled it slowly from her body, letting his lips glide across every inch of her skin. He slid his hand over the curve of her hip and slipped the lace down over it, his fingers sliding between her thighs.

He drew the lace away from the other side. Lucy lifted her hips as she let him.

Then she lay naked beneath him. There was nothing between them now, just skin on skin. He trailed a lazy finger down the length of her sternum and her skin prickled with his touch. He wedged a thigh between her legs, gently pushing them apart on the cotton sheet as he moved further onto her. She let out a small whimper as she felt him inside her, gently moving between her legs. The backs of his hands stroked her face and his fingers linked into hers. His gaze lingered as he smiled gently, staring into her eyes. She was bewitching, her allure irresistible. He moved into her harder. She gave a soft sigh as she felt him again. Her hand let go of his linked fingers and trickled down his back as he moved more deeply into her, pushing slow and hard. She closed her eyes and let him take her, her back arching as he went deeper, every part of him making love to her. Their bodies moved together.

She could smell the salt on him and woodsmoke from the fire, the sweat of the day and the anticipation of his night in her bed. He gazed into her eyes and moved his lips onto hers, smiling into his kiss, tenderly kissing Lucy until his tongue plunged between her lips and found hers, tasting her, the sweetness she gave. She placed a hand upon his cheek, her thumb gently grazing the contour of his mouth. The tips of her fingers ruffled through his hair, drawing him in harder on her lips as they became entwined. The need to be touched overwhelmed them. Her legs wrapped around him and his eyes looked into hers for a long moment before the tension left his body and he became the man she had wanted so much. A much-needed smile formed on her face as her legs squeezed around him tightly, holding him there, in her. She inched her lips closer to his ear and whispered, 'I love you, Ben.' She melted beneath his body. His mouth was harder on hers, tasting her sweet pureness.

'I love you too, Lucy Carter.'

They lay in bed with their bodies entwined, neither one of them wanting to leave. The gentle brushing of the branches on the window, the rhythmic gurgling of the water running though the pipes in the cottage. He rolled his nakedness off hers and lay propped on his elbow, his hand gently stroking her abdomen and circling the perfection of her breasts. Her eyes staring into his, not leaving his face. She cupped her hand on his face and brushed her thumb across his five o'clock shadow.

'Do you have to go work?' Lucy asked as she snuggled closer in to him, breathing in the scent of his chest, the salty sweat of their love-making.

'I do, Lucy Carter,' he said as he kissed her forehead and then her nose.

'That's a shame.' She scrunched her nose, he kissed it again. He left her in bed. She watched his naked body pad across the bedroom and listened as the bathroom door closed. Her arm stretched out to touch his side: it was still warm. She pulled his pillow close and breathed in the scent of him from it. She listened as the hum of the boiler kicked in and the sound of the water fell from the shower. She closed her eyes and let thoughts of his body on hers take over in her head, consumed by every touch on her naked body. Her tummy somersaulted as she let her mind drift back to the moment they had just shared, a soft, warm, gooey feeling inside her tummy that she'd thought she'd lost forever. She pulled his pillow in even closer to her and smiled into it. She adored him.

From across the road the net curtain lifted slightly, and a thick, bright yellow duster moved hastily around the ornaments on the windowsill. Lucy watched from her writing room window. Mrs Pope was fervently spring cleaning at number 8. Ben had left on his bike just after 8.45 and Lambourne Terrace was quiet below. The familiar sound of the postman whistling in a happy-go-lucky way could be heard as he opened Lucy's gate. He looked up and winked as he spotted her in the window. She smiled back. She'd never even clapped eyes on her postman in London, yet since she'd moved to Essex he'd become a familiar smiling face in her morning. She knew he was called Toby from the signed cards he'd leave to let her know where a parcel had been hidden. The brass letterbox rattled and he dropped a couple of letters through her door. Her gaze followed him as he disappeared behind the neighbour's hedgerow and out of sight, his whistling still audible along the street.

The morning sun struggled through the murky clouds. The darkest of clouds were threatening rain; today she would stay at home and write. Today, she had a warm gooey feeling inside her, that feeling where she just wanted to snuggle with a cushion close to her and think over and over again of her morning with Ben. He had made love to her in a way that, every time she thought about it, made her tummy wriggle and jump, and she smiled. A smile on her face that she couldn't let go of. She opened her journal and began to pen her own words.

With her head gently resting on her hand, the words flowed onto the new page. She had not seen the therapist she had been referred to. Instead, her feelings and thoughts she left in ink on a clean page daily. To write would heal her broken mind, she knew that. Although her life had been taken in a direction she could never have anticipated, it was a direction she hoped she would one day forget.

She was happy, happier than she thought she could have ever been, and this morning had been the best morning ever. She thought about her days at school and the friends that she had made, and her life at university that had become part of her life in London. They were all high-fliers, career-savvy, wanting the best. Lucy had never been that girl. She'd left university with a modest 2.1 in Classics and her ability to write had got her noticed. She had shunned the high- flying career, instead opting for the stories she would tell. She didn't have a fancy car, only her Classic Mini that her grandfather had given her for her eighteenth birthday. It was one of the most expensive things she possessed and something she would never let go of.

She had no more friends than she could count on one hand, and now to that she added Simon and Matt. Her relationship with Bob was one of a father and daughter, almost. But she was happy.

She had fallen in love again and loved her job and her tiny little cottage on Lambourne Terrace in a quaint untouched village in North Essex. It was eclectic, with a mish-mash of the cast-offs she had kept from its purchase. She had always thought she would replace them, but she never did. They were hers now and the cottage was hers and why would she ever eliminate the charm that had been bestowed by another author? There was a piece of Margaret Arthur living alongside her.

She sat in her writing room and watched as a few people passed her window, catching her gaze and her thoughts. Here in this special place, she had the freedom to create entire new worlds, and characters whose conflicts she could solve for them, in her own unique way. Her ink pen glided across the page as she began to write.

Her phone pinged in a message. It was ten o'clock.

Hey gorgeous, are you up yet?

Of course, cheeky! ☺

Whatcha doing?

I'm writing, silly x

Soooo, this morning…

Yeaeeesss…☺

You were sensational

Ben!

What?

I'm writing…

And I love you!

Ben?

Yup, gorgeous x

I love you too ☺

The bubbles on her phone disappeared but the smile on her face stayed. She placed her mobile on her desk and skipped down the stairs, with the thought of him telling her he loved her in her head. It was like that first-ever feeling she had had when he first texted "I love you" as she sat on the stone step on the beach. Her heart had skipped a beat then. She'd raced home that day, too, to snuggle up with him and eat pizza with extra pepperoni and olives. Her thoughts of him swirling, his face etched in her mind, his text she read over and again until she finally kissed him. Today, she had that very same feeling.

She picked up the post and drifted in a lovestruck way to the kitchen, flicking on the kettle. Once she had a mug of peppermint tea, she went back upstairs with her unopened post.

She sat back down at her desk and opened the post: a statement from the bank and a letter from HarperCollins letting her know that Giles Metcalfe had now left the company and she would be working with Clarissa Jones. She picked up her phone and called Jo.

'Hey, gorgeous girl, how's it going?'

'It's going perfectly,' Lucy said through a beaming smile.

'You sound particularly upbeat. Shall I come over or are you busy writing?'

'Well, I am writing, but come over, I'm almost done. I've had a letter from Harper's, too.'

'Ooooh, from Medusa?'

'Her PA.'

'PA, blimey! I'll be right over. Matt's on duty, I'll take his car, give me five.'

'No probs, see you in a bit.'

As she closed the call, the door of number 8 opened and Mrs Pope bustled out in a plastic raincoat, wearing a transparent polka-dot rain scarf to protect the rollers beneath it. She yanked at the lead and Barry, her basset hound, trotted down the step of her cottage, his belly nearly grazing the ground and his ears flapping in the light breeze. She looked up at Lucy's window and waved. Lucy waved back. She watched as Mrs Pope waddled up the road with Barry pulling her along, sniffing at the hedgerows and cocking his leg before stopping for his mid-morning whoopsie. Lucy liked Mrs Pope; there was something rather endearing about her.

When she'd moved to Wrabness, she'd learnt very quickly from the boys that Gladys Pope was Neighbourhood Watch at its best, and ready with the gossip from the village. Yet her gossiping and incessant need to curtain-twitch had saved Lucy. Mrs Pope had looked out for her when she had been discharged from hospital, made her the meanest chicken pie and warm chicken broth that had fed a table of friends. She had a warm heart, a very warm heart. Every village needed a Gladys Pope, Lucy thought to herself.

As she tapped away at her keyboard, Jo pulled up outside. Dressed in a figure-hugging black polo-neck jumper, fitted black denim jacket, ripped skinny jeans and black biker boots, she wore her hair in a perfect bob with an even more perfect fringe, plus a deep red lipstick and huge great Jackie Onassis sunglasses shielding her eyes from the non-existent sun. She flung the car door shut and zapped the fob to lock it, then swaggered around the car, adjusting her oversized glasses as she did. She flicked her hip around the front of the car and sized up the street. Lucy bounded down the stairs and opened the door before Jo had a chance to knock. Jo stood in the hallway, looking striking with an urban-style cool about her. She peered over her huge black shades.

'Hey gorge. Right, strong coffee first, cigarette and spill the beans. You've got a smile on your face that would give the Cheshire Cat a run for his money.' The girls went straight through to the kitchen where Lucy made a cafetière of fresh coffee. Jo unlocked the kitchen door and sparked up. Lucy stood there with her peppermint tea, watching Jo as she puckered up and blew a trail of smoke into the garden.

'Come on then, the smile, what's with the smile? You haven't stopped grinning since you opened the door – you've bounded down the hallway like a little spring lamb. It's Ben, am I right or am I right?'

'You're right, it's Ben!' Lucy's smile was intoxicating. 'It was just ... Oh my God, like, every touch, it was, oh my God.'

Jo smiled. 'You let him back in?'

'Jo, he made love to me like nothing I've ever had before. I mean the first time was magical, but this morning. I couldn't breathe from his intensity and touch. I fell in love all over again, which was weird, because I've never stopped loving him. But this morning, oh man, I can't explain it.'

Jo beamed as Lucy recounted the morning to her and how every touch sent goose bumps up her spine, and how she had missed his touch and now it was like it had never gone. Jo put out her arms and hugged Lucy.

'You see, it was time. Whatever that line was your nurse said, it was time.'

'I know – just everything was perfect, his messages like the ones he used to send. It's like we've begun again. I'm so in love with him Jo, like I want to shout it from the rooftops. I've never felt like that before.'

'That's the best, Lucy, Luce.' Jo's smile was as huge as Lucy's. To see her friend back in that happy place again was amazing. 'Now then, moving on from Ben and his sensual powers … Medusa. Show me the letter. God, those names really shouldn't be in the same sentence.' She stubbed out her cigarette in the flowerpot and blew the last drag of smoke into the cold air.

'I'll go get it, I'll be right back.' Lucy ran upstairs whilst Jo poured another mug of warm fresh coffee with a slug of a milk in it, and closed the kitchen door against the draft. Lucy came back into the kitchen and handed over the letter. The sides of Jo's eyes creased as she read.

'What's she talking about, wanting three more books from you? Stupid cow. Harper's have had five and that's the contract. I mean, listen to this sentence.' Jo put on a snooty stuck-up voice and read out loud whilst she sauntered around the kitchen table. '"I will be taking over from Giles

Metcalfe and will be expecting from you over the coming period a selection of four new novels to complete the existing contract and continue our relationship with you." I mean, who the fucking hell does she think she is? And a selection of four novels, what planet is she on? I swear to God she reminds me of one those Roger Hargreaves characters from the Little Miss range. She is absolutely Little Miss Up-Your-Own-Bloody-Arse, with her nose in the air.'

'Jo?'

'Yup,' Jo replied as she swanned indignantly around the table, swishing her bob into even more perfect position.

'I don't think there was a Little Miss by that name,' Lucy giggled.

'Well, there bloody should have been! Is it too early for wine?'

'Yep! OK, so what do I do?'

'We tell her to sod off! Who the hell does she think she is? Jeez! Anyway, I've spoken with Giles and he's absolutely given the green light to jump ship. We're totally on-line with our contract: *Hold My Hand* was your last novel to complete our ties with Harper's. Your new one can go straight to Random and let the money roll in, ch-ching. They are chomping at the bit for you. Also, they're as tight as anything with Pete Harvey, the new drama producer at the Beeb. We're done with Harper's and Clarissa can go bloody jump.'

'Are you going to tell her, or am I?' Lucy asked.

'I'll tell her. I'll have great pleasure in telling her where she can stick her four books. How bloody dare she. She needs to learn a thing or two. That letter should have come to the agent, not the author. She's punching way above her belt.'

'OK, I'll leave it with you. I've finished the first draft of my manuscript, by the way, d'you want to read it?'

'Wow, that's amazing Luce, what's it called?'

'War Torn,' Lucy said, simply.

'Love it! Absolutely! Ping it over to me and I'll mark off tomorrow as a read only day. I've lost Matt for the week and then I'm heading back to London on Sunday, need to touch base with Giles too and sort out your contract with Random. I can't believe you've finished the first draft, that's awesome!'

'I know, I can't quite believe it either. But I had a drive and a need to just get it done and forget everything. I wrote the last sentence this morning. Like, all that bad crap, I just channelled it and just kept thinking, I'm going to beat this.'

'Charlie?'

'Yeah. You know, for ages, I thought it was me and maybe I deserved it. And then I figured, when I read Peggy's journals and the love she had for a man who had the courage to protect her and his country – it just gave me this fire in my belly to prove I could do this without therapy, without moping, without drugs to numb the pain. I had to do it on my own. I've never written a manuscript that fast, but something snapped in me. The picture changed. I woke up and wanted a different picture.'

'Lucy, you're amazing. Truly.'

Lucy snorted softly through her nose and a slight smile glimmered on her face.

'This morning with Ben, I just needed him, I was tired of pushing him away. And now, I can't stop smiling. I bloody love the guy and never want to lose him again. I almost lost him, I almost lost him, Jo. For what?'

'And what about Charlie?'

'They're still looking for him, but you know, if they find him, I feel only pity for him. Yeah, he almost killed me, but he didn't. I lived. I'm here to tell the tale, and one day, Jo, one day I will tell that story of how to walk away from a damaged mind, damaged heart and find love. One day I will tell the world how someone I loved hurt me. But at the moment, I've just finished the first draft of my manuscript and I finally got to write "The End".'

As the girls chatted about the men in their lives, novels and the excitement of switching over to Random House, Lucy's phone rang upstairs. She raced up to grab it before it rang off. It was a No ID caller. She stared at it and went back downstairs.

'Was it Ben?' Jo asked, pouring another coffee from the cafetière.

'No, it was an unknown call,' Lucy said. She reminded herself of what Simon had said when she'd received the same after being discharged. It could be anyone, she told herself. Her hand shook a little and then the phone rang again. She threw a glance at Jo.

'Answer it,' Jo said reassuringly. 'I'm here.'

With a little unease, she pressed accept.

'Hello ...' Her voice was soft, unsure, with a sense of trepidation.

'Lucy, DI Phillips here.'

Her heartbeat slowed back down to a normal pace.

'Hello, DI Phillips,' she said.

'How are you?' he continued.

'I'm fine, thank you.' She gripped the phone tightly in anticipation of what he was about to say, the plastic edge biting into her palm.

'Lucy, I'm in Spain with DS Murphy.'

'Right – is Charlie in Spain?'

'He is, yes. Has Simon filled you in?' Phillips asked.

'Umm, only that you believed Charlie may have stowed away on a container ship and that he was missing.'

'Right, yup, that's a fairly concise version of events. Charlie was on the container ship as I had suspected, and the Royal Marines were used to intercept the ship.'

'The Royal Marines, wow. So, you have him?'

'No, he was lost overboard, with a gunshot wound.'

'I don't understand – he's dead?' Lucy's voice dropped as she said the words. She had suffered hugely by him, but she didn't want him dead. She looked at Jo, her face expressionless. Jo's eyes scrunched in confusion as she tried to interpret Lucy's side of the conversation and the word 'dead'.

'No, he's not dead.'

'OK, good, that's a relief,' Lucy replied. Jo gestured a hand across her neck as if to ask: *is Charlie kaput?* Lucy shook her head.

'He was found in the water, close to the shores of Peñíscola and Valencia, by a fishing boat. The fishermen brought him in as he hung on to a piece of driftwood, half dead by all accounts. He said his name was Miguel and he spoke like a native.'

'That's right. His mother is Spanish, he speaks the language fluently.' Lucy pulled out a chair and sat at the table. 'But Miguel? I don't understand. Are you sure it's him?'

'We are very sure, Lucy. We have an operative working undercover in Valencia. In fact, Peñíscola, to be precise. He met with one of the fishermen, who told him it was like seeing a ghost.'

'A ghost? I really don't follow, Detective Inspector. So he is dead?'

'No, Lucy, he is very much alive. The ghost was the image of his father, Robert Wainwright. He was killed at sea many years ago.'

'Right, I see, so Charlie is alive? Where is he now?'

'He is with his mother, Sofia Martinez. Miguel is an alias,' Phillips continued.

Lucy's voice dropped. 'And now? What do you do now? Are you sure it's him? I mean, how could he have survived?'

'That I don't know. But it's him.'

'I don't want him dead. I didn't want him dead.'

'We've confirmed sightings of him, and today, we had his mother's car followed and he was with her. My hunch is he's looking for forgiveness.'

'Forgiveness? From who – me, his mother, who? Will the Spanish police not just arrest him?'

'Not without my order. We sit and wait, Lucy. His mother is shielding him, but I don't want to go in with guns and police. I want to do this sensitively, carefully, strategically. I'd like you to assist.'

'What do you mean?' She darted her eyes at Jo.

'I need you to come to Spain.'

'When?'

'As soon as possible.' The line went quiet. She said nothing. She could hear the breathing of Phillips as he waited for her to respond.

'I can't. I can't do that.'

'Lucy, we need you to, it's our only option.'

'I'm not ready to do that. Please don't make me do that.'

'I know it's hard after everything you've gone through, but think about it, and call me back.' The line went dead.

Jo looked at her quizzically. 'So, what was that about?'

'He wants me to go to Spain. I can't do that. He wants me to call him back.'

Jo shook her head in disbelief. 'Talk to Simon, before you call him back.' Lucy pressed the keypad.

'Wrabness Police Station, PC Willis speaking.'

'Matt, hi it's Luce, is Simon there?'

'Yeah, sure, hold on a sec.'

'Lucy, you OK?' came the familiar sound of Simon's voice.

'Not really.'

'What's up, gorgeous?'

'I've just had DI Phillips on the phone.'

'OK? And, what's happened?'

'He wants me to go to Spain. I don't know why.'

'Right, on your own?'

'Well, yeah, Ben won't be able to come and what happens if something happens to me? What happens if ... what happens if I don't make it? What happ ...'

'Shh, shh, wait, Lucy. Call the DI, tell him you'll be there and I'll come with you. Nothing's going to happen to you, he wouldn't put you at that risk.'

'How d'you know that?'

'Because I'm a police officer and I wouldn't let anything happen to you. Call him back and tell him you'll do it.'

'Right ... I'm frightened, Simon.' Her voice trailed off

'I know. I'll be there, Luce.'

Lucy ended the call and stared at the screen.

'What did Simon say?' Jo asked.

'He said to call back. He said he'd come with me.'

'OK, so call, I'm here, do it now.'

Her fingers slowly pressed the keys on her phone.

'DI Phillips – CID.'

'OK. I'll do it.' Her voice dropped to almost a whisper.

'Good girl, Lucy. Do you have a pen?' he asked.

Lucy gestured to Jo for a pen and paper, Jo scrabbled around in her bag until she found a pen, and then she turned the letter from Clarissa over and waited for Lucy to say the address.

'I need you to get a flight to Valencia. I'll have a taxi pick you up. The address is Hotel Bonita Rosa, Calle San Ignacio, 24 Peñíscola, it's just off the market square. I'm staying there with DS Murphy.'

'OK, I have the address,' she paused, 'I need to speak to Ben and then I'll arrange my flight. I'll let you know as soon as I have sorted everything.'

'Lucy, you will be safe, I promise you that. Believe me when I say that to you.'

'I believe you.' The line went dead.

'What?' Jo said taking the paper. 'They've found Charlie?'

'Yeah, he was found at sea by a fishing trawler. He's with his mother.'

'And who's Miguel?' Jo quizzed.

'Charlie. Phillips wants me to go out – I don't quite understand why. He said something about forgiveness.'

Jo sighed, 'Entrapment, Lucy. He's bringing him in with you as bait.'

'I really don't want to go ...'

'I know but you have to. Take Ben with you. I can't come; I have to be back in London by Sunday.'

'Ben won't be able to. He's pretty busy at the boatyard,' Lucy said, totally thrown by the morning's phone call.

'Then Simon, Lucy, take Simon. He's a policeman, he'll protect you.'

'Simon said he would come but what about Ben?'

'Ben loves you. He'll understand.'

Chapter Nineteen

Wednesday, 19th March

The roar of Ben's bike pulling up caused Lucy to look up from her writing desk. She'd spent the best part of the day searching flights from Stansted. She wanted Ben to come with her, but she knew he wouldn't get the time off work. She closed the tab in her browser. It was five o'clock. She hadn't told him yet of the call she'd had with DI Phillips. She needed to find the right time to even broach the subject with him. Was Jo right - would he understand?

She flipped her laptop closed and went downstairs. Ben was already standing in the hallway by the time she reached the bottom tread of the stairs. He hung his helmet on the newel and wrapped his arms around his girl. She cupped his face with her hands and kissed him tenderly on the lips. He lifted her so she hovered above the stair she was standing on. She felt her tummy turn over as he found her tongue with his.

He took her in his arms, her legs wrapped around his waist, and carried her upstairs, still with his lips firmly on hers. Opening one eye to spy where he was going, he nudged the bedroom door open and laid Lucy on the bed. His biker jacket strewn on the floor by his feet, he knelt above her. He undid the belt of his jeans. He pulled her legs closer to him, while she grabbed at his T-shirt and tugged him towards her. He stripped it off until he was on top of her again, his bare chest close to her. She arched her back as she felt his hand reach under her top and pressing his palm across her abdomen. Taking his hands behind her back, Ben undid the clasp of her bra. She smelt the saltiness of the sea in his hair as he nuzzled into her. His nose tickled her neck as his tongue licked slowly down it, savouring every scent of her smooth, soft skin. He looked at her and smiled. Lifting her hips, he peeled off her leggings. He knelt with one knee on the bed, smiling at her as he let his jeans drop. Her eyes sparkled as he came closer to her and kissed her nose. Then he moved his tongue slowly over the contour of her mouth, before letting it find hers once more. He slowly dropped back down to her, tasting her. He'd thought of nothing else all day. Clock-watching until he could make love to her again. They moved together, her hands stretched over his back, feeling the tightness of his muscles as he writhed on top of her. She inhaled the smell of sails and cloth that lingered on his body. He pushed into her until she arched her back and let out a sigh with him. She breathed deeply into his ear as he lay still on her, his eyes closed. He kissed her gently.

'Ah, Lucy,' he whispered faintly in her ear. She lay beneath him, enjoying every minute of that welcome home. She squeezed him with her legs.

'Was that nice?' he asked as he teased her with his tongue and fingertips, tracing circles around her silky skin.

'Yeah,' she said faintly and then he went back pushing into her again. She closed her eyes, her back arched once more, her spine prickled with his touch. His body on hers.

Her breathing deepened, her lips on his neck as he pushed harder. He held her arms above her head until they came together. In that moment her body flushed warm. She bit her lip as her eyes searched his face. Enjoying every part of their bodies together.

'Fuck,' he said as he lay heavy on her. 'God, I want you.'

'Have me,' she whispered as she moved her lips around his ear.

'I just did. And I'm going to have you again later, Lucy Carter.'

She scrunched her nose and a huge beam lit up her face.

'Are you now?'

'Aha.'

'You need to work for it.'

'Oh yeah, like what?'

'Hmm, let me see ... order pizza, with extra olives and pepperoni, and whilst we are waiting you can take me for a bike ride before the sun goes down.'

'Done. Get dressed, gorgeous. I need to take a shower first, then I'll call for a pizza.'

He prised himself away, kissed her tummy and left her totally wanting more of him. Her gaze of doting yearning for him followed his nakedness. In that moment he turned at the doorway and caught her eye; before she could turn her head away, knowing he'd seen her look of desire for him, a genuine grin spread across his face, turning it from handsomely gorgeous to divine. He winked at her. She pulled a pillow over her head. This was the guy she could love forever.

As the shower drenched Ben and washed away the day of canvas sails and the woody smell of boat-making, Lucy went back to her writing room and flipped open the lid of her Mac. She opened the browser to the flights she had been perusing from Stansted, and scanned the screen looking at her possibilities. There was one tomorrow at 5.35, arriving in Valencia at 9.05 Spanish time. She hovered over it, swirling the cursor as if making invisible doodles on her screen. The sound of the bathroom door opening jolted her, and she felt him behind her. The scent of his fresh clean body around her, his arm naked and wet, wrapped around her waist. She closed her eyes and inhaled him.

'What's with you, naughty? You've just had me …' she said, brushing her hands through his wet hair.

'I know, you're irresistible.' He pushed her back against her writing desk. Her hand shifted the laptop away from her resting bottom.

His towel still wrapped around his waist, his arms flexed, she ran her fingers along the ripple of his muscles, smoothing the intricate inking on his bicep. His hands wandered under her top again.

'Uh-oh, no Ben, pizza, bike ride … come on.' He adjusted his towel.

'OK. Pizza, bike ride and then pudding.'

'Pudding? Like what?'

'Something smooth, delectable, incredibly bad for me.'

'Chocolate chip ice cream?' she teased.

'More than that,' he said as he twizzled a strand of her hair in his fingers and kissed her neck.

'Hmm, maybe double chocolate chip ice cream, with cookie dough,' she said tantalisingly.

'Still not bad enough,' he said as he pulled her hair back and stretched his hand across her ribcage.

'Sounds intriguing, this pudding ...'

He placed a huge smacker on her lips, slapped her bum cheekily and said, 'I'll order the pizza. Put some trainers on, I'll take you for a quick spin, babe.'

He left her to get her trainers, but she turned back to the laptop and viewed the flights. Her attention was caught by the door of number 10 opening and a young couple coming out. Lucy watched them intently. They looked familiar. The indicators on a midnight blue BMW flashed and the girl walked around to sit in the passenger side. The guy looked up the street and then towards Lucy's house. Lucy caught his eye. He looked away hastily, ducking his head to get into the driver's seat. The car pulled out of its space, heading for Harwich. Lucy's eyes trailed the street where it had driven, then darted back to the house. The vase on the windowsill, still devoid of flowers. Where did she know their faces from - why did they seem so familiar? She mulled it over for a little while before leaving her laptop and finding Ben already downstairs on the phone to the pizza delivery company.

'Quick spin, pizza will be here in thirty mins?' he said, pushing the menu back into the kitchen drawer.

'Sure, let's go,' she said, snatching her jacket from the stairs.

Ben wobbled the spare helmet onto Lucy's head and secured the strap, giving her head another wobble to make sure she was safe inside it. He pinched her nose and winked at her, then flapped the visor down. Her tummy somersaulted.

Ben straddled the bike and waited for Lucy's petite frame to climb up behind him. He tilted the bike a little so she could lever herself up. The curtain of number 8 twitched, but neither Ben nor Lucy noticed Gladys Pope's watchful eye. The engine roared and Ben turned the throttle more. Lucy tucked her knees in and clamped her legs into the side of his buttocks and thighs, wrapping her arms around his waist, clasping her hands together in a lock. He held her hands in his gloved hand as he pulled out, turning towards the A120 and Harwich. He only had half an hour but could really open up the engine on the dual carriageway and give Lucy a little bit of fun with speed.

Ben took the country lane slowly, riding low on each bend, Lucy moved with him as he leaned into each corner. The sun was beginning to dip in the sky, with dusk coming all too soon. As they rode past the police station, out of the corner of her eye she spied the midnight blue BMW. It was the same one she'd seen pulling out from 10 Lambourne Terrace. Both squad cars were there, too.

Ben let out the throttle, and she gripped him more tightly. He held her hands reassuringly as he felt her grip tighten around him. He pushed himself back on the seat into her groin. This time she let him without moving back herself out of embarrassment. She liked it. She was no longer the shy girl he was taking out on a date; she was his girl now. The quietness of the soft rattling waters of the estuary meandered in and out of view as the bike snaked along the lanes, freeing the horsepower in the fast twisting corners. The bike hunkered low around each bend. He slowed his speed as he rode through the small village of Ramsey, then turned left on the roundabout and let the throttle really have it.

He hit a bump on the road and Lucy's bottom left the seat. She grabbed him more tightly. Her heart was racing and the cold wind snatched at her body as they rode fast down the A120 towards Harwich. The road was clear. The noise of the engine was deafening but it only intensified the thrill of the bike. The cold wind whipped at her hands, and she clutched them more tightly together. Her helmet hit Ben's as he pushed the speed and power of the bike. She could see the cranes of Felixstowe ahead of them; she'd never seen them before from a bike. Ben eased off the throttle and slowed as he reached Harwich, and cruised past the huge great buoys in the yard of Trinity House, turning back on himself on the mini roundabout. The road was clear as they rode back the way they had come, overtaking great haulage lorries: her heart raced, hoping they'd pass in time. His body went lower towards the bars and he pushed further back in between Lucy's legs. She shifted back a little and held tightly as he overtook one, two, three cars. The dimmed lights of a lorry approaching them left her heart somewhere in her throat. She squeezed her eyes closed and clung to Ben. Was this it – would they make it? She daren't look.

The bike swerved in as the lorry rumbled past. She opened her eyes and swallowed hard. The road was clear ahead. She'd never ridden so fast with Ben before, and her breath was ragged. As Ben took the lanes steadily, she tightened her clamp on him. He touched her leg and rubbed it. They rode past the police station: the BMW was still there.

He pulled up outside the cottage and tilted the bike for Lucy to clamber off. Her legs were shaking beneath her. He kicked the stand down and took the keys from the ignition. She stood watching him like a tiny weeble-wobble, totally off balance with a helmet on her head. Ben shot the visor up for her and undid the strap so could wriggle it off her head. She looked petrified, her face drained of all colour, her hands like ice cubes.

'Come here,' he said, 'you're shaking, babe.'

'You went so fast, Ben. I actually came off my seat.'

'Aww, babe, I'm sorry. Are you OK now?'

'Yeah … it was scary. That lorry, I thought that was it.'

He cupped her hands in his and blew on them. 'We had loads of time, babe. I'd never put you at risk on the bike.' He kissed her tenderly on the lips and squeezed her chin.

Lucy opened the gate to the cottage, Ben followed her, and Mrs Pope watched from her curtain. She would be keeping a closer eye on Lucy Carter from now on.

Closing the door behind them to shut away the cold night air, Lucy made her way into the kitchen and opened the fridge. She took out a bottle of Bud and poured herself a glass of Malbec. Ben sidled up behind her and nuzzled into her neck. The knocker on the door rapped.

'Pizza first,' she said. Her eyes twinkled as she left him with his beer and went to open the door. He made his way through to the sitting room; his desire for pudding was burning inside him. He flicked on the television and searched through the endless channels. Finally settling on Netflix.

'Film?' he said. Lucy snuggled in next to him with the open pizza box on the table.

As the evening drew in and the moon lit the sky above, a splattering of white fluorescent lights surrounding it, the two lovers chomped hungrily on pepperoni pizza. Lucy snuggled her feet up against Ben and he stroked them. He wiped his hands on his jeans and closed the lid of the empty pizza box, sliding it away from the edge of the table.

'Now pudding?' The corners of his eyes crinkled. Lucy's eyes flickered as he moved in closer, he looked heavenward.

His hands wandered under her top and she rolled her eyes with a devilish smile, crinkling her nose. He unclasped her bra and traced his fingers around her breasts. As he pulled her down onto the sofa, the glow of the television shimmered in the background. She wriggled a little as he pulled her leggings off. His wandering fingers had taken on a magical touch.

Lucy brushed the hair away from her face as she lay gazing into Ben's eyes. He'd just made love to her on the sofa and now she needed to tell him about her phone conversation. She cast her look away from him, her eyes dipping to the floor.

'Hey, what's up?' he asked.

She exhaled deeply. 'Nothing, it's – it's just …'

'What,' he coaxed, 'it's just what?'

'DI Phillips phoned today.' Her voice dropped, her eyes caught his.

He shook his head, his eyes creased at the corners. 'OK … and?'

'He wants me to go to Spain,' she blurted.

'Why?'

'He's found Charlie. I don't know, I think he wants me to lead him to him. Use me to – kind of – trap him. Jo said entrapment. Jo said you'd understand. I'd have to take Simon.' She'd said it, it was out. Her breath deep as she waited.

'When? When do you need to go?'

'Tomorrow.'

'Do I get a say in this, or is it decided?'

'I have to go, Ben. If it means he's caught, then I have to go.' Lucy's eyes searched Ben's, looking for reassurance, approval, just anything.

'And what happens if something happens to you, have you thought about that? I can't go tomorrow. I'm a building a yacht.'

'It won't, Ben, I promise you it won't, but I have to do this. I have to face my fear. I can only be brave if I have fear. Will you take me to the airport, though?'

'Sure, I'll take you.' Ben moved his body off Lucy. He pulled his jeans up and went into the kitchen. She listened as the fridge opened and he took out another Bud. The bin lid clanged as he threw the top into it. She listened as the chair in the kitchen was dragged across the kitchen floor and he slumped into it. She listened to only the silence in the cottage, the clock ticking, the radiators gurgling and the guy she loved alone in another room. She turned the television off and sat staring at a blank screen. Was that it? Had she lost him all over again?

Chapter Twenty

Thursday, 20th March

Lucy's stomach churned as she held her wheelie suitcase close to her. Her other hand held Ben's tightly. He scanned the doors as they swished open near the departure lounge, needing to see the familiar face of Simon so he could entrust Lucy to his protection. Ben spotted him carrying a Nike sports bag and dressed casually in jeans and a sweater, his jacket hanging over his arm. They shook hands. Lucy watched them both. Ben seemed on edge: was it because she was leaving, or was it because of Simon?

'We're going to have to go through, Luce, are you ready?' Simon said.

'No ...' Her eyes began to swim with tears and her hand felt clammy in Ben's. She held it tighter, not wanting to let go.

Simon darted his eyes at Ben. He could see he was fighting back his own emotions, his own pent-up fears for the girl he loved.

Ben pulled her into his arms and held her, cupping her face. He crouched down a little and kissed her soft pink lips.

'I love you,' he said, his eyes searching hers.

'I love you too, Ben.' She fell back into him and cried, grappling at his collar, not wanting to let go.

Simon stood back and gave them time. He could only imagine how Ben was feeling inside. After a few minutes, he placed his hand on Ben's shoulder. Ben stood back from Lucy, and Simon shook his hand and man-hugged him.

'Look after her,' Ben said under his breath. 'Look after her.'

Simon turned to the door and showed his pass to the smiling hostess. Lucy went to follow, then stopped, turned, shouted.

'Ben!' She ran to him and kissed him one last time with passion, with fear, with love, with everything her body could give him. She touched his lips, wiping away her gloss from them. The tears were streaming down her face.

'Make a sail for me.' Each word caught in her sob. She turned and disappeared through the doors. He stood silently watching the last glimpse of Lucy before she was gone from view. The airport buzzed around him, but he heard nothing.

Ben slunk towards the escalator. He stood in the viewing deck, his hand pressed up against the window as he watched the plane on the tarmac. Service trucks trundled around it. Men in fluorescent jackets, looking like small Lego characters, waved huge great lollipop sticks. He swallowed hard, holding back the tears that would gush if he let them.

Lucy sat with her nose pressed against the window, her heart beating faster. She wiped her hands on her legs. Simon watched her, he watched her wipe away the tears that fell. She fastened her belt and held her tummy. It still churned. He took her hand and squeezed it.

'I won't let anything happen to you. I gave my promise to Ben.'

She looked at him, her eyes just a glaze of watery liquid. She nodded. As the engines rumbled and the plane started to taxi across the tarmac, the sign to fasten seat belts lit up. Over the internal speaker the voice of the flight attendant came in:

'Good morning ladies and gentleman, this is Emma, your chief flight attendant for this morning's flight. On behalf of Captain Hughes and the entire crew, I would like to welcome you on board British Airways flight 9743 flying direct to Valencia. Our flight time will be two and a half hours. Could you please make sure your seat backs and tray tables are in their full upright position and that your seat belt is correctly fastened. All handbags or laptops are tucked under your chairs. Please make sure all portable devices are set to airplane mode until our arrival. Thank you.'

Lucy gripped the armrest; she didn't like flying particularly and could feel her nerves bubbling up in her throat. The plane taxied down the runway, leaving behind the building where Ben stood watching from afar. Lucy leant forward and took the information chart from the seat pocket. She held her tummy again.

'Are you OK, Lucy?' Simon asked.

'I hate flying,' she said.

'When was the last time you flew?'

'Oh my God, I can't even remember. I hate it. I much prefer to go by train – that's just romantic, isn't it? I mean a proper train journey, not your commuter trains,' she said, a glimmer of a smile cracking across her face. 'You know, those trains each with a compartment. They are just dreamy, aren't they.'

'Do they even exist anymore? Or am I beginning to get a glimpse of the romantic novelist in you?' His eyes creased at the side as he teased her a little.

'Yeah, sure they do.' She elbowed him tenderly. 'I can remember taking the train from Italy to France a couple of years ago. It was magical. I could watch from the window, read, write and just float away. The clanking sound of those doors when they opened, the stranger that sits opposite you and offers you a smile. The sound of that deep mahogany leather that's squidgy and wide, that sighs when you nestle into it. My perfect way to travel. I'll take that any day.'

'You're adorably funny,' he said, his face loaded with warmth.

Their chatter was interrupted by the Captain's voice over the speaker.

'Cabin crew please take your seats.'

'Oh my God, Simon, tell me when we've arrived. Fuck.'

As the engines powered up, the plane accelerated across the tarmac.

'Oh fuck!' Lucy squeezed her eyes shut.

The engines opened up full throttle and the sound of deafening speed engulfed Lucy. Her body pressed back into the seat. She held her breath as the nose of the plane lifted and its wheels left the tarmac.

Lucy clasped and unclasped her hands over and over again as if in need of being touched and reassured. She began to chew on the inside of her cheek. As she pushed herself further back into the seat, she felt the warmth of Simon's touch on her hands, the gentle grazing of his thumb across her skin. Her eyes dropped to his reassuring touch.

As the plane climbed higher, the fields below became a patchwork of green, the tractors trundling along below like matchbox farm toys. Lucy watched the clouds buffeting past the wings of the plane. The engine noise diminished to a gentle hum and her eyes grew heavy.

The next thing she heard was the pinging sound of the fasten-your-seat-belt sign, waking her up. The mesmeric drifting of the clouds had allowed her to sleep the whole journey. Simon was dozing with his headphones in his ears.

'Cabin crew please take your seats for landing.'

The Boeing 737 tilted slightly and began a slow and steady descent. As it fell through the clouds, Lucy could see the Spanish landscape below. The tyres hit the tarmac and the brakes finally brought the jet to a halt.

Outside passport control stood a man holding a board with Carter/Mackenzie written on it. Simon greeted him and walked with Lucy to the taxi outside. The driver spoke little English but knew of the destination.

'Peñíscola,' Simon said.

'*Sí, sí,* I take, I take.' He ushered them into the taxi. Lucy went to open the window. The warmth of the air and her claustrophobia from the flight had made her feel a little light-headed.

'Non, non! Air-condition, air-condition!' the driver said gruffly in a strong Spanish accent, pointing at his air-con dial. Lucy hastily closed the window. She watched as they left the airport and drove the fast route to Peñíscola. The arid red earth of the rugged terrain ran parallel along the edge of the autoroute. Through the windscreen the main road seemed to undulate in the air as the sun's heat hit the grey tarmac, which had been bleached over time. Lucy blinked.

Spicy yellows and greens flooded the rugged slopes. Spiky trees grew in an abandoned kind of way, yearning for some water. It seemed odd to have a fast road running through such barren desert land, with intermittent random great wooden billboards with the name of the region, Castell*ón*, or another with Alicante, showing their distances in kilometres.

The sunburnt landscapes were gently reminiscent of the American Wild West, she thought. Her eyes were captured by the façade of a mountain where a bull had been etched into the rock, its horns low as if ready to toss itself through a red cape. There was nothing else to add to the landscape. Her eyes flickered as she sucked it all in, her nose almost pressed up to the window. There was only the odd derelict building half-hidden on the red, dusty terrain, or a solitary villa with no apparent access road. She looked on in wonderment, already building another picture in her world of make-believe.

The taxi slipped off the autoroute and followed the road that wound down through the high grounds of the Valencian region towards their destination. With an audible gasp she saw it. Like that moment when a child suddenly sees the sea on their never-ending journey. There it was, the bluest aquamarine she could imagine, the sun's rays glistening on the water. She nudged Simon to see what she had spied. The coastal road wove around each bend, gradually approaching the sea. It was beautiful, breathtaking, something only Lucy could only ever write about. The boats in the harbour bobbed on the gentle waves as they pushed up to the pier's edge. The taxi turned left into the market square. He parked under the palm trees and turned off the engine.

'I think we're here,' Simon said. The driver was already at the boot, taking out their luggage.

'Bonita Rosa, Bonita Rosa.' He gestured towards the passageway leading off the square. Then he pulled away, leaving Lucy and Simon alone.

'I guess he's been paid?' Simon said, taking Lucy's case and his bag and moving them onto the pavement near the bank.

'Are we staying at the Hotel Bonita Rosa?' Lucy asked, taking in the sight of the square and the terraced houses, cafés and shops that enveloped it. The wheels of the case wobbled over the cobbles and its noise broke the wonderful Spanish silence of siestas in the afternoon sun.

Lucy could almost smell the gorgeousness of the passageway that led to the hotel, through a labyrinth of passageways and a jumble of small plazas. Colourful flags bearing the names of the shops floated a little. A couple of bistro chairs sat empty outside the closed doors and shutters of an ice cream parlour.

'They really do have a siesta, don't they?' Lucy said as she turned 360 degrees, breathing it all in. She forgot for a moment why she was even here. The salty air of the sea snapped at her nose, the warm rays of the sun tingled across her forehead. If only Ben were here. She took it all in: it was spellbinding. A scruffy dog trotted past her, and scowled a little when she went to stroke it.

'Don't.' Simon took her hand and pulled her back. 'It's feral.'

The shutters of Taberna de José were down, but the door of Bonita Rosa was open. Simon lifted Lucy's case up the few steps to the reception desk. It was small inside.

'Buenos días,' said the girl from behind the counter.

'Buenos días,' Simon said, resting his arms on the reception desk.

'You are English?' she smiled.

'Yes, d'you speak English?' he replied.

'I do.'

'Thank God,' he sighed in relief. His Spanish was barely existent - schoolboy stuff, and even that was pushing it. 'We need two rooms. I'm not sure if they're booked, though.'

'Your name please?' she enquired as she scrolled through the computer.

'Simon Mackenzie and Lucy Carter.'

'Yes, you are booked. You are guests of Mr Phillips, I believe, he has sorted it all.'

'Yes, that's right, great.'

'So, your rooms are located on the first and second floor, number four and twelve. Mr Phillips has asked for a table for four in the dining restaurant this evening, at eight o'clock.'

'Is he here now?' Simon asked.

'No, I believe he went out earlier today, with his friend, and he will be back for dinner.'

'Right, that's great. Is there a lift?' Simon took the room keys.

'No, there is no lift, but the stairs here will take you to each, how do you say, umm ...'

'Landing?' Simon was hesitant to help her find the word. She spoke better English than he spoke Spanish.

She smiled. 'Yes, that's it, landing. Breakfast is served from seven o'clock until ten and then the restaurant will be open for lunch and dinner, but you must book if you like that. If there is anything else, please just ask. Enjoy your stay.'

'Thank you – oh, just one thing, what time does everything open again?'

'At five o'clock, mostly, so very soon.'

Simon carried both cases up the flight of stairs that curved around the walls. On the first floor, he stopped and handed Lucy her key.

'Fancy a drink at five?' he asked.

'Yeah, call for me at five.'

Leaving her alone, he climbed the flight to the next floor and let himself into room twelve.

Lucy threw herself onto the bed and lay there for a moment. She took her phone from her satchel and opened her messages. There were eight from Ben. She touched the screen as she read every one before replying.

Hey you, I've arrived ☺

Bubbles appeared below as he typed a reply.

Hey babe, I'm glad. How's the hotel?

Not the same without you …

☺

I wish you were with me …

Me too

I'm meeting DI Phillips at eight and I guess I'll know then what I have to do

You've got this Lucy, man I love you xx

Message me tonight at bedtime, message me until I fall asleep on you xx

I will, I promise, now I need to make that sail xx

I love you Ben xx

The bubbles faded away. He'd gone. She lay on the bed and reread his messages over and over again. It was as close as she was going to get to him. She could hear his voice in every one; she just needed to hear his voice next to her.

It was warmer in Spain and she felt all sticky in her winter wardrobe. She went to the bathroom and ran a bath. Leaving a pile of clothes on the floor, she submerged herself beneath the bubbles. She let the water soak into her body, catching the bubbles in her hand and watching them glisten and pop. Her thoughts were of Ben and her desire for him to be with her.

Wrapped in a soft, warm towel, she dried her hair. She rummaged through her case and pulled out a summer dress and pumps. Simon would be down soon. She stood at the open window, scanning the small alleys below. The town was romantic and archaic, full of mystery. A faint knock on her door took her from the balconette and its view of the rooftops of Peñíscola.

'Hey,' she said.

'You ready?'

'Sure, let me grab my satchel.'

She turned back into her room. Her shift dress floated in the lightness of her steps. Simon watched her awhile.

Closing the door tightly behind her, they left the hotel to explore the passageways of Peñíscola and find a café before meeting the DI for dinner.

Chapter Twenty-One

Thursday, 20th March

Peñíscola, Spain

Sipping his scotch on the rocks, DI Phillips sat with DS Murphy in the restaurant of the Hotel Bonita Rosa. Some American tourists sat at a table nearby, trying to decipher the menu. From the corner of his eye he spied Lucy and Simon enter. He pushed his chair back and stood, his arm outstretched to greet them.

'Simon, you made it, great. Lucy, you look well, please take a seat.' Lucy and Simon sat next to each other. Lucy fidgeted with the thin strap on her dress, her feet tucked under her chair.

'How was the journey, Lucy?' he asked, breaking the silence and appeasing her.

'Yes, it was OK. The taxi drive especially was pretty nice.'

'Good job. And Ben, how is he?'

'Yep, he's good, thank you. He couldn't come - he has to finish a yacht he's building. He would have come otherwise.'

'That's too bad.' Phillips beckoned to the waitress. 'Let's get you both a drink and then I can fill you in.' He asked the waitress for a glass of Rioja and a San Miguel.

Simon took a swig from the bottle. The chilled liquid felt good as it slid down his throat. The day had been long and full of anxiety.

While they waited for their paella to be served, Phillips made the astute decision to start without further ado. He could sense Lucy's tension. He took a sip from his water glass.

'Right,' Phillips began. 'Lucy, I don't want you to be frightened, first of all, but I am going to explain as concisely as possible what we have at the moment. We've had confirmed sightings of Charlie, the first a few days ago by the Spanish detective who is working on this case with the CID department. His name is Pedro Rodriguez. When those reports came through, DS Murphy, who has been following his accounts from London, was able to confirm a significant amount of money had been transferred from Charlie's UK account to a Spanish one that is based here in Peñíscola. Charlie was seen by our Spanish aide at the bank when this transfer took place.' Lucy wriggled in her chair as she listened to the information Phillips was giving her.

'DS Murphy and I have been here since Tuesday and all seems very calm. Yesterday, both myself and DS Murphy located his mother's villa along the coastal path, tucked away on the Iberian slopes. I was able to see from the RIB that Charlie is staying with Sofia Martinez, his mother.' Phillips spoke as if he was seated with the MIT. 'From what we have seen, the relationship between them appears non-confrontational. She takes Charlie to the village, and he doesn't leave the car unless he is going to another villa.'

'Another villa?' Lucy asked, her hand going back to the strap on her dress. She took a sip of water from her glass; her mouth felt dry.

'Yup, let me get to that.' His face was warm and appeasing.

'The villa, is it connected in some way?' Simon asked.

Phillips sighed deeply and put both elbows on the table, moving his body closer to the three of them.—

'I believe so. Experience here tells me that I don't think we are going to be greeted with the same Charlie I arrested in London or indeed that was presented to us in court. That's what I think. You remember what he was like, Simon.'

'Sure I do: angry with a violent temper, and that was just the phone call.' Simon shook his head at the memory and took another swig from his bottle.

'What d'you mean, not the same?' Lucy asked, her voice breaking a little.

Phillips tapped his fingers on the table before taking an unlit cigarette and twiddling it in his fingers like a pen.

'When I was within touching grasp of his arrest on the container ship, I threw him a lifeline: I'd do him a deal, if he came quietly.'

'But he didn't take it,' Murphy interjected.

'He didn't, but he thought about it.'

'Why?' Murphy asked.

'Good question. Why indeed? What would change the mindset of a man on the run, who wanted to hurt Lucy?'

'Dunno, guv. The family relationship?'

'Exactly. I gave him a picture of his father again. He didn't like it. That gave him his thinking time to surrender.'

'So his dad meant something,' Lucy said.

'Yes. Over the last few weeks Charlie has been on the run. He doesn't want to be found, which is why he's using the name Miguel. From experience I'd say he's making a new identity for himself and those around him. But ...' Phillips raised his index finger. 'He's beginning again as the son of Robert Wainwright. There will have been a shift.'

'But how does that involve me? He thinks I'm dead.' Lucy looked at Simon, confused by everything.

'I'm pretty sure Charlie is speaking with someone and that someone is the key to the truth, to the man we want and to his arrest. This is the villa.' He pushed a photograph of the villa Cueva Cascada and another of a woman towards Lucy and Simon.

'Who is that, his mother?' Simon asked. Lucy shook her head.

'No. A woman whose name is Ana.'

'Ana?' Lucy said. 'A girlfriend?'

'Nope, although I can't be sure whether there is an intimate relationship between them. Ana Pérez is a therapist and spiritual healer in Peñíscola. Charlie and his mother were followed yesterday and today they led Pedro, unknowingly, to her villa.' Phillips tapped his unlit cigarette on the table.

'But how does that involve me?' Lucy asked again. She wasn't a spy or part of the police network dealing with criminal minds; she was a writer. Her stories were make-believe.

'Lucy, he does think you are dead. However, I think if he sees you, he may come without pressure. I don't think his feelings want you dead. I need you to stay here with Simon for a couple of days, and when I am sure, I will use you as bait.'

'Bait … like live bait? Jo said this would happen – she was right. But what happens if it goes wrong, what happens if there is nobody there to protect me? What happens if it's like the beach, or worse? What happens if he is still the man he was?'

DS Murphy shot a look at Phillips. Lucy had a point, there was no guarantee. Simon fixed his look on Phillips, waiting for the answer.

'Because my gut tells me differently. You have to trust me with this.'

Lucy swallowed hard and took a large sip of her wine. The waitress appeared with a huge paella dish and placed it on the table. The four fell silent as she dished out for each of them and scurried away.

'I need to speak with Ana and determine what he is doing and who he has told, if anybody," Phillips said. "I need you to face Charlie, Lucy, to come to her villa.'

'OK, I'll do whatever.' Her hands held her stomach as it squirmed beneath her dress. 'When?'

'He has met with Ana for the last two days at ten on the dot for an hour. I would imagine these visits have been happening since he arrived. This is why I don't think it's a lover - it's too uniform, too precise. She's watching the clock.'

'Will Simon and DS Murphy be there too?' Lucy asked, the anxiety in her voice noticeable.

'Simon, DS Murphy and Pedro Rodriguez from the Spanish police will all be present, but it is only you and me who will face him. Should anything go wrong, we have backup.'

'Backup?' Lucy pushed the rice around her plate.

'This is not the first case I've covered where I've entrapped. Just as a precaution, we require backup. That's all.'

'OK, what time and when?' Her hands twisted around her neck.

'I need tomorrow alone with Ana. Be in the hotel reception at nine o'clock on Saturday morning. We'll wait and watch from the track near his villa before we approach. Pedro will tail us to the location.'

'OK.' Her voice trailed off.

The waitress cleared the plates and Lucy placed her scrunched-up napkin on the table.

'Is there anything else? I think I might go to bed, if that's alright,' she said as she pushed her chair out. 'I need to speak to Ben.'

As she walked away, she turned back to Phillips. 'Good night.'

'I think we have it all covered. Lucy …' Lucy turned again to the DI. 'You will be safe. I promise you that.' Phillips rose from his chair slightly to bid her goodnight. A reassured smile broke across her face. She left the men at the table, taking the staircase to her room.

Simon gestured to the waitress for another beer.

'How will you keep her safe?' Simon asked. He had seen the anxiety in Lucy bubbling up. He could almost feel it. She'd barely touched her dinner. 'I can't let anything happen to her, sir. I gave Ben my word.'

'Because, Simon, I truly believe we are dealing with a different man. I'm going with my gut.' He tapped the cigarette on the table again and swallowed the last of his scotch.

'Sir, this is like the butterfly trap, isn't it?' Simon was beginning to realise the genius and workings behind Phillips.

Phillips threw down his napkin and pushed his chair back, still with the unlit cigarette in his hand.

'That it is, Simon,' he said drily.

'Are you going to smoke that thing or just twiddle it all night?' Murphy asked.

Phillips mustered up a dry laugh. 'I'm going to smoke it and then I'm going to turn in.'

He went out to the cobbled passageway. The night was alive with bodies milling around the streets, enjoying the late evening. Music filtered out from the string of tabernas; bistro tables spewed out onto the cobbled streets, each one full, with sounds of laughter and frivolity. Hunched over, he lit his cigarette with a silver Zippo, which clicked as it snapped closed. He rubbed his thumb along the smooth, shiny curves of its edges before placing it back in his pocket. He mulled over the talk at dinner as he blew the grey nicotine smoke into the air and traipsed the labyrinth of narrow passageways and tiny alleys weaving off the market square of the fishing town. Locals chatted across balconettes as he passed beneath them. He eyed the feral fur creatures that lay low, their limbs close to their bodies, their faces menacing and scowling. He was closing in, although it was a different kind of man he would be cornering this time.

Lucy lay in bed, the cold white sheet pulled close under her chin. The shutters of her window were closed, dulling the noise of the revellers below. Her phone pinged in a message.

Hey, babe how's things?

Hey, I'm in bed. I had dinner with DI Phillips, DS Murphy and Simon tonight, they want me to be bait for Charlie

How?

DI Phillips wants me to meet him face to face … he thinks he's changed …

Changed?? Seriously, the guy almost killed you!!!!

I know but he seems to think he's seeing a therapist

Shit, Lucy I don't want you to go, just get a flight home!

I can't, Ben. I have to do this, just be there when I get back, just hold me when I get back. Promise me you'll hold me.

Fuck

Ben, promise me

I promise

I love you, Ben

Lucy

Yep

I missed you from the moment you were gone

Her breath caught in her throat as she read the words that came onto her screen. Her eyes swam with tears as she tried to type, so she could hardly see the letters ... she gave up. Her fingers and eyes weren't working in unison. He'd taken her breath away with the power of a text, totally thrown her into a place of serenity and caught up in a mist of love at its fullest power. Blown her mind with his words in a message.

Sweet dreams Luce xx

The screen dimmed – he'd gone.

She closed the messages and placed her phone on the bedside table. She wrapped the pillow under her head, then turned it again, trying to find a cool spot. She lay in the dark, her eyes adjusting to its deep black light, the discernible shape of the baroque-style chaise-longue a silhouette against the window. She turned again, moving her pillow and doubling it up, squidging it down so she could sleep.

Her mind replaying dinner over and over again. Why wouldn't the night steal her away? Lucy pulled in the pillow that lay untouched against the headboard and cushioned it against her body, holding it as if it were Ben beside her, his message swamping her mind. Her thoughts whirred away, not allowing her to fall into a sweet slumber. She wrapped the sheet closer, letting it find every inch of her naked skin to cling to.

She lay still for a while, until her hand stretched over to her phone. She opened it, the brightness of the screen causing her to squint. It was midnight. Lucy sat up in bed, fumbling for the switch to the bedside lamp. She narrowed her eyes and blinked rapidly as the dim light spoiled the darkness that had seeped into the room. Leaving her bed, dressed only in her pants, she rummaged for a cotton T-shirt in her case. Then she searched in her satchel for her journal and pen.

She sat on the velvety cushioned chaise-longue, her knees bunched up and her bare feet curled under her. She leant across and opened the shutters slightly, making way for the starlit sky to offer its wonder to her. Opening her journal, she rested it on her bare leg. It was cold to the touch on her soft skin, and she shuddered slightly. She wrote: Hotel Bonita Rosa, Peñíscola March 2019, and underlined it. She began to scribble each word on the clean page, taking no moment to pause, every thought, every feeling exploding in a ribbon of ink. Every feeling she'd had from when she was found by Bob on the beach, half dead. Every feeling of how Bob must have felt, to run despite the pain that jagged through his body, so he could find help and protect a girl who had become like his own daughter. The daughter he had lost and couldn't save. Every feeling she had when she allowed Ben to touch her for the first time without pushing him away. The feeling she had at his final text, which had swamped her with an emotion she couldn't keep hold of in Spain that night. Every feeling she had of writing the last word in her novel *War Torn* and allowing Jim and Peggy the happy ending they required. Every feeling of how finding that end in a brutal war, and her time sitting with Bob and their peppermint teas, gave her more hope than she'd ever thought existed. Every feeling she had of how the words from Doris' grandmother in Jamaica, used to calm the sadness and angst of a small child, had been passed on to herself. The words that stayed etched in her mind from Bob - "fear is a reason to be brave, until tomorrow dear Lucy" - the tomorrow for her was going to come. The ink swirled about the page as she wrote about the old typewriter and the fear of the room and the inked-ribbon-letters where she typed: "Affliction."

Lucy's eyes began to unfocus. She shook her head and rubbed them, willing her eyes to stay open. As if an ebony sky littered with white diamonds and the trail of words written onto a crisp, clean page were the enchanting spell to let her body drift away and the dark steal away her anguish.

The orange hues of the sun glowed across the far-reaching Spanish skies, breaking the night's shadow and allowing for a new day to begin. Lucy stirred from her sleep, uncomfortable from resting her head on the upright back of the chaise-longue. She rolled her neck around a few times, massaging the discomfort of the crick. She shivered a little, her arms pebbled with goosebumps from the lack of a cover and the warmth it brought. Her journal lay open next to her, the ink pen resting in the groove of its spine. As she went to close it, she brushed the tips of her fingers along the dried ink, as if allowing it all to fall back into her body and finding a sense of calm, a resting place. Her finger trailed along the last word she'd written. It read: *Atonement.*

The two detectives sat in the dining room of the hotel. Phillips, dressed in a soft pink polo shirt and chinos, stirred the deep brown treacle-like foam that covered the top of the cup. It disappeared with the swirl of the spoon. The ceramic cup was cold to his touch. A fleeting expression of malcontent crossed his face. He judged a coffee by the foam and its ability to persist on the cup. He took a sip of his espresso: the treacle-like liquid sat in his mouth, the strong flavour of Colombian beans permeating through every taste bud. His expression changed to one of rapture.

Murphy sat casually in jeans and T-shirt and tucked into a plate of Spanish pastries and a pot of tea. Phillips slipped the silver bracelet of his watch down his wrist. Holding it between finger and thumb, he watched the hand smoothly rotate around the face, without a jerking motion on each tick. He scanned the room, narrowing his eyes as he sized up the occupants. Murphy stopped eating his pastry for a moment; he wiped his hands on his jeans and watched his boss. Phillips continued to watch each table without anybody knowing. His detective style was as sophisticated as the timepiece he wore on his wrist. Most of the tables were occupied by European and American tourists browsing through maps and leaflets about the area. Smartphones all at the ready to take photos and upload them to the voyeuristic world of Facebook and Instagram. Phillips, like that silent voyeur, was on the outside looking in.

It was like any other Friday morning - the close of the working week for some, the last day of a holiday for others - or, for a small group unbeknown to anybody else, the closing of a case that had been at the forefront of Phillips' mind since the 2nd of February three years ago. His hand went back to his watch, his fingers in exactly the same position: it was 9.15. A gentleman entered the dining room as the second hand slowly rotated. He was ushered to a table for two in the corner. Phillips raised his hand for another espresso. The gentleman watched behind a copy of El País. Phillips' eyes followed each person in the room, falling back unnoticed to the gentleman. It was a built-in characteristic that he'd adopted early on in the police force, never taking his eye off the ball. Lie low, go undetected. Murphy watched him; he knew the drill, too. The gentleman ordered a coffee and a pastry.

After paying his bill, the gentleman lifted the paper, rustling and obscuring his view of the other diners. At 9.25 he pushed the empty coffee cup into the centre of the table. His left hand showed two fingers holding the paper's edge, a sign to all detectives to be ready. Murphy nodded at Phillips. The sign had been given. At 9.27 the gentleman left. He dropped his napkin on the floor.

'Murphy,' Phillips said, pushing his chair away from the table. They turned right out of the entrance and followed behind the gentleman, keeping a distance. He stopped in the square and checked behind to see if Phillips and Murphy were there. He stood long enough by the car for them to see which was his and then drove out of the square, taking a sharp left down a side street in the town. Murphy drove the hire car, following the blue Mercedes at a distance. It approached the roundabout where the wild dogs, by now a familiar sight, moved slowly. Their mottled coats were dusty from the arid ground, their tongues hanging from their mouths, salivating.

The blue Mercedes drove through the main street of the town, Murphy still one car behind. The car turned off down a small Spanish street lined either side by shuttered windows with Juliet balconies decorated by the early spring blooms. It turned again, leaving behind the string of houses and cobbled streets. This time only Murphy's car was behind. It slowed as it approached a track, and the driver looked in his rear-view mirror. It sped up a little and drove past the track. Murphy followed. The Mercedes drove until the track was no longer in sight, then pulled over onto the verge, the orange dust from its tyres funnelling away. Murphy pulled up behind it.

The men got out of the cars and walked towards each other. The area was desolate, untouched by humans, the ground the colour of saffron with a blanket of flora that could withstand the dry Spanish heat. It was 9.47. The men stood silent. Phillips could see Cueva Cascada and its track, the waterfall that fell alongside it, crossing the sunburnt landscape until it reached a pool. He turned away from the villa and viewed the orange roofs, a contrast against the deep azures of the Mediterranean. The eerie quiet was broken by the sound of a car on the dusty tracks. The men watched as a silver Beetle climbed towards the villa. Moments later the same car drove back down the track. It was ten o'clock. Phillips' breathing was shallow. He took out a cigarette from his packet, offering one to Pedro.

'The other side of the track, where does it lead?' Phillips asked, one hand in his pocket.

'The sea,' Pedro replied. 'We are surrounded here by the sea, on every side, almost.'

'Are there any other villas behind this one?'

'*Non*. Cueva Cascada is the only one here. Behind it are the olive groves and then it will lead to the sea,' Pedro replied, lighting his own cigarette.

'What are you thinking, guv?' Murphy asked.

'The container ship and Charlie's reaction – would he have fallen without being shot?'

'Dunno, guv, maybe jumped?'

'What might he do now? Run, come quietly or jump?' Phillips mused.

'If he is seeing Ana, he may have changed,' Pedro said. 'We see this happen here in Spain, many times.'

The men walked across the deserted land and watched the villa that was nestled above them, their bodies hidden by the vegetation.

Pedro stopped in his tracks. 'If we walk any further, we will be seen, that is sure. We must stop here.'

The men traced the ground, watching the villa for some time. There was no movement for a while, no further comings and goings from visitors. All was quiet. Some time had passed before Phillips took in one last look at the olive grove that ran down to the cliff's edge. He pursed his lips, his eyes narrowed. He flicked up his wrist: it was 10.55. They turned back. As they approached their parked cars, the silver Beetle came into view, driving along the track towards the villa. They waited a while until they saw it leave again and head away to the town.

'Do we visit Ana now?' Murphy asked.

'Yes. Pedro, we'll follow you,' Phillips said, opening the passenger door of the hire car. The red dust from the track blew up behind the tyres of the Mercedes. Taking the track slowly. Pedro pulled up by the olive grove. Murphy parked next to him.

The men stood at the front door. Phillips pulled the bell-rope.

'Ya voy,' came a woman's voice. A dog yapped in the background. She opened the door and recognised one of the men.

'Inspector Rodriguez. Is there something wrong?' she asked, perplexed by the company at her door.

'May we come in?' Rodriguez asked.

'Why yes, of course, please come through.' She led them to her room where she had sat moments before with her client. 'Please, take a seat,' she said, gesturing.

'May we speak in English?' Phillips asked.

'Of course,' she replied.

'Are you Ana Pérez?'

'I am, yes, why? Who needs to know?'

'I am Detective Inspector Phillips, from the Criminal Investigation Department of the Metropolitan Police in London. The Spanish police are assisting us in an investigation I am leading. I need to ask you some questions.'

'This sounds serious. Of course, I can try. I am not sure how I can help, though,' She took a sip of water from a glass on the table - one of two glasses.

'Do you always have two glasses of water?' Phillips asked.

'I'm sorry, I do not follow,' she said, her Spanish accent heavy in her voice.

'There are two glasses of water,' Phillips said.

'Ah, I see. No, it was a client's water.'

'Client?' Phillips pushed.

'Yes, I am a therapist. Inspector Rodriguez knows that.'

'And it *was* a client's glass?' Phillips left the question hanging, waiting for her to take it, divulge.

'Yes. I have just had a client; he has left now.'

'He?' Phillips said. Murphy watched on.

'My client is a gentleman. I'm sorry, I am not understanding this.'

'Can I ask his name?'

'You can ask, Inspector, but I will not tell you, it is confidential.'

His eyes narrowed as he rubbed his lips together. She was bright.

'But a man, you say.'

'Yes, a man. I said *he,* I will leave that with you, Inspector, to make up your own mind of the sex.'

'Does this client of yours - a man, we can assume - come here often? Does he pay you?'

She stared at him, her eyes not leaving his, 'Inspector, I do not know why you are here, but if you are asking me if I am sleeping with him, then please do not. I am a therapist. Please explain your reasons for this call.'

Phillips darted a look at Pedro, who spoke in Spanish to her. Her expression changed as she began to listen to him. They stopped abruptly, and she looked at Murphy, then Rodriguez, and then her glance stopped at Phillips.

'I knew he was tormented inside,' she said.

'His name?' Phillips asked once more.

She lifted an eyebrow. 'I will help you, Inspector, but I will not share his name.'

'Did he come often?'

'Yes, for a few weeks now, almost daily.'

'And he spoke freely?'

'At first, no. He was quiet, closed, tense, in my honest opinion,' she said, taking a sip from her water.

'And now?' Phillips pushed.

'Now he is relaxed, most of the time.'

Phillips mused on what Ana had said. He slipped the bracelet of his watch down his wrist, his finger and thumb holding the face, watching as the second hand swished round seamlessly. The corners of his eyes crinkled.

'So, you see Miguel often as your client?'

'Yes.'

Murphy smirked inwardly as he watched on. Phillips had done it again. Without realising it, she had confirmed his name. The smooth, meticulous, precise work of his boss in order to get the result - the name - was as smooth and precise as his watch, never faltering, flawless.

She gasped as she suddenly realised her error. A wry smile broke on Phillips' face.

'Miguel, yes, but that is all I know.' She was acute, sharp, her eyes bored into him. She shifted in her chair.

'Please, tell me about him.'

'He looked familiar when I first saw him. I thought nothing of it, only that his story was one which I know of.'

'And that is?' Phillips asked.

'A boy who was sent away to school, a boy whose relationship with his father was powerfully strong. I know of his mother.'

'Miguel, you mean?' Phillips questioned.

'Yes, that is correct,' she said, scorn slipping off her tongue. Inwardly angry that she'd shared his name.

'He is Spanish?' Phillips asked.

'He spoke fluent Spanish. Yes, he is Spanish.' She hesitated. 'Although ...'

'Although?'

'Nothing.'

'Was he English, Miss Pérez?' Phillips pushed.

'I said he spoke fluent Spanish, Inspector.' She twisted the feather in her earring.

'You also said he went away to school. Is this a common thing in Spain – boarding school, I mean?'

'I do not have children. I do not know these things.' She could play him too.

'What did he share with you?' Phillips needed to know the man he was now dealing with. The state of his mind.

'He told me how his father would tell him about the mermaids he would see in the sea. He asked if I believed in them ... he spoke mainly of his childhood. How he was now a monster, how his father would be ashamed of him. How he was ashamed of himself.'

Murphy chewed on the inside of his cheek.

'He said he was in an oblivion, which is a kind of peace. I let him talk, I said nothing. I just listened. He said there was nowhere out of hell.'

Phillips inhaled deeply and exhaled. 'Was he in hell?'

Her eyes caught his again, drilling to the back of his head.

'Yes,' she said. She took her glass and drank from it.

'What is hell for him?' Phillips asked, his approach softer. He remembered his own sister's hell.

'Do you want my answer or his?' She was clever, she was unwavering; she knew that her client was a damaged man who had once loved.

'What did he say?' Phillips pushed.

'He said, "the absence of people we love".' There was silence in the room, an eerie silence; only the wall clock ticked in the background. A bee buzzed between the almond blossom and the cicadas clicked outside. Ana continued, 'I asked him if that was his fault – had he failed someone? He said, "An educated, intelligent being chooses the life of a fugitive. Education, intelligence, these are only arrogant weaknesses."'

'Why did he say this, why a fugitive?' Phillips pushed a little harder.

'You tell me, Detective Inspector. It is clear you know what he is running from.' She could be as clever as him in her approach.

'He left a girl for dead in England. That's what he is running from,' Phillips offered. Ana's face didn't flinch.

'I wondered if something had happened. He was angry at women, his mother, school ... he felt he failed his father by his actions, although I did not know them. Maybe he will share them with me. He trusts me. I am perhaps the first woman he has trusted.'

'Right ...' Phillips stopped awhile. 'Ana, the girl he thinks is dead, is alive. She is here in Spain and I am here to arrest Miguel. He has already served a prison sentence because of this girl. We have been looking for him since he fled the UK and we believe him to be hiding at his mother's. We need your assistance.'

'So, I become another woman who he cannot trust? I do not betray people, Inspector. It is not my way. I have a code of practice,' she said vehemently.

'It's not about trust, it's about justice. I believe the man I am about to arrest is not the same man I arrested three years ago, who served time in an English prison. I have heard what you have said, and Miguel needs to know that Lucy is not dead. He needs to know to rest his own mind and to stop running, to give himself up. I need you to assist me. No harm will come to you.'

Ana swallowed, grazing her teeth along her bottom lip, pulling it in.

'He is coming tomorrow at ten. He stays for an hour. Please give him that time, please do not arrive until that time has passed.'

'Did you find out who he was?' Phillips asked as he began to get up from his chair.

'No, but I found out *what* he was.'

'And that was ...?'

'He was rational.' Her stare was fixed.

Chapter Twenty-Two

Saturday, 22nd March
Peñiscola, Spain

Lucy woke early. She had tossed and turned all night. The white cotton sheet had been ripped out from the tightly folded corners of the bed and lay strewn across it. The duvet was a mountain of chaos to the side of the bed, nowhere near her. The pillows lay haphazardly, with huge indentations in them where they had been pummelled through the night.

A message pinged into her phone. Bleary-eyed, she pulled it close.

Hey babe, how ya feeling?

OK, I think?

Think?

Yeah, I didn't sleep well, but I'm ready

I wish I could hold you, Lucy, be with you

Me too, I miss you

The bubbles stopped for a while.

Ben?

Yeah

Do you think you can forgive someone?

Dunno babe, why?

Just wondered …

Call me as soon as this is over

I will

Ben

Yup

Can we have pepperoni pizza and extra olives and then pudding when I'm back …

Pudding, for sure ☺

☺ *xx*

She rolled onto her back, the phone lying by her. Her tummy turned a little inside her, and she held it until the squirming feeling evanesced. She got up, leaving the crumpled sheets and duvet in a mess. She turned the shower on in the bathroom and undressed, leaving her pants and cotton vest in a pile by her feet. The steam misted up the mirror above the basin. She drew her hand across it and looked at herself in the mirror. The bruising was gone, the ugliness no longer on her – it was a face she recognised as her own. It disappeared as the steam took the smeared line she had made.

As she was dressing, her phone bounced and vibrated on the bed.

Hey you, are you ready?

Yeah, I'm ready Simon, give me five, just need to dry my hair

The knock on the door came quietly and then there was a silence. Lucy took up her satchel and brushed down her simple summer shift dress. She tied a thin jumper around her shoulders. She opened the door. Simon stood there, his arm leaning up against the doorframe. His smile let her know he was there for her and everything would be OK. She wiped her hands on her dress; she could feel the sweat forming in the middle of her palms.

'How ya feeling?' he asked, as she closed the door behind them.

'Nervous. Ben doesn't want me to do this.'

'And you? Do you want to do this?' She could feel the warmth in his voice.

'Yeah, I do. I have to do this. I have to let go.'

'Come on.' He took her arm in his and walked the short length of the landing, letting go as they took the stairs down to the reception.

'Can we eat somewhere else for breakfast? I feel I need to get some air, figure this out.'

'Sure, let's go to the square. I'll text the DI to meet us there.'

The door of the villa was left ajar. It allowed the fresh air to blow in, a gentle sea breeze, whilst Ana continued with her work.

He sat in the room, his hands held together. He hadn't noticed the door had been left open; she normally closed it. The room was furnished with an array of books on shelves, oodles of them, all shapes and sizes, arranged at random:

healing books, spiritual, self-help, and then a treasure trove of literature from the greatest to the unknown, new and old, all well-thumbed, all jumbled, no meticulous order, no straight lines. The antique sideboard flanked a wall. He'd got used to this space. It was less clinical than his London flat. Less formulaic than Sofia's villa. He felt a comfort here that reminded him of childhood, the vibrant autumnal colours of the décor, a huge tapestry of a Spanish bullfight hanging from a wall. Warm colours – or was that simply a memory of something he'd wanted but never had?

She poured a glass of water. The ice clinked into the glasses, its sound awakening the silence that surrounded them. He'd driven alone today. She opened the veranda doors and let the spring sun throw its warmth onto the room. The colours of the ground were a reflection of hues of reds and burnt oranges within the room. It gelled from interior to exterior. In the olive grove the leaves looked like silver shards of glass on the trees. The gnarly trunks hung low to the ground, their girths thick and old. He looked out to the sea. Its glistening colour of blue azure took his mind away from the room momentarily.

'It's beautiful, isn't it, the view of the sea? Gives you time to think,' she said.

'Yeah … it does.'

'What are your thoughts, Miguel?'

He sighed deeply. 'It's been good coming here, I needed it.' His eyes were still cast out to the deep blue horizon. The sun beat down, the sweet scent of the almond trees hanging around the sides of the villa. There was bougainvillea trained along the veranda's rail, the crimson flowers gently curling their petals, the deep green leaves holding them as they trailed around them.

'Tell me about it. What do you see when you look out at the view?'

'That nobody is ever brave enough to tell you that have to swim to shore by yourself.' The clock ticked gently in the background. The breeze murmured through the leaves of the grove. 'To climb the rocks that are sharp and pointed and jagged. Nobody tells you that bit, but once you realise it, you find your place, you know what you have to do. To learn how to go through the agony of walking by yourself again. Righting your wrongs - and only then you feel at peace with what you've done. To give in, confess.'

He turned from the window and looked at her. She was gentle to look at, the curves of her face soft, the tone of her skin like the olives in the grove. She had been kind to him.

'What wrongs, Miguel? You were just a boy.' The breeze caught in the feathered earrings she wore, and they fluttered a little. He watched them, mesmerised by their movement, free.

'I am a man, too, not just a boy. I hurt someone,' he said.

'Your mother?'

'No.' He swallowed. 'Worse. A girl I was to marry. Your books remind me of her. She would have loved this room.' He breathed heavily through his nose, letting the air reach his lungs. 'I didn't just hurt her. I did more than that.' He stopped, his hands wrapping around themselves before he brushed them through his hair, leaning forward in his chair, his head sunk low.

'More? Tell me, don't keep it in. Let it go. Why would she have loved this room?' she said, watching the clock.

'She read all the time. She was a writer.'

'Was?'

'I hurt her so much. I kept on hurting her, and then, as if that wasn't enough for me, I killed her. I fucking killed her and then I ran.' He closed his eyes, his head shaking from side to side at his own monstrous act. 'Why? Why did I do it, *what am I?*'

'You killed her? How, Miguel?' She was direct but soft in her approach.

'Not with my hands, but I pushed her so hard, she fell, she struck her head on a rock. That was it, I left her. What man does that, what monster does that? I am not my father's son. I am her son. I am her son, full of hatred and unloving. Evil. Why, why me?'

'Why do you think? You have told me of your childhood, of a little boy who wanted to see the mermaids with his father. You have told me of his letters. You have told me of the small boy you saw in the town who hopscotched through the cobbled streets, his father's hand holding his tightly with care. You have told me of the mother who hurried them along. You have told me of a mother who drank champagne, who didn't love you. You have told me of a girl who would have loved this room. You have acknowledged her love of books. This room would mean nothing to you if you didn't care about her. It would be just a room full of books. But it isn't. Is it? Now, tell me why, that answer is there already. It's there within you. Realise it, own it.'

He threw his chair back, making it screech along the floor like chalk on a board. Ana sat motionless. He paced to the door, the sun beating down on his face. His hands roughly brushed through his hair. His voice was loud, like a shout but louder, uncontrolled, full of sorrow, full of anger, full of remorse.

'Because of *her*, because of my own mother! She drove me to this. Jesus Christ, my own fucking mother, and now look at me, I'm nothing more than a monster. I have become her - selfish, unloving, unforgiving, worthless. I sat in a prison cell, and all that went through my mind was a fucking dormitory and a matron who was as unloving as her. I could hear the inmates taunting me. They thought I was a monster too.' He sank to the floor, his back against the veranda's edge. His knees bent up, his head in his hands, his eyes blurred and swimming with tears. Ana left him alone with the words, allowed him the silence. He didn't raise his head. The door into the room pushed open a little more. He was unaware of the presence behind it.

'Charlie.' Lucy stood, her hands clasping her dress, and watched him weep. She'd heard his words from outside the door. 'Charlie,' she said again, swallowing and brushing away the tears that fell freely down her cheeks. She'd heard all his words, his confession.

How did she know his name, yet her voice was like hearing a ghost talking to him? He looked up. The figure that stood by him was like a silhouette of an angel. He blinked through the tears. He was seeing things, like a mirage. He wiped his hands across his bloodshot eyes. She was still there.

Lucy moved towards him, her fingers tingling. As she bent down to him, he took her hand, he had to tell her he was wrong, he was sorry. He hated himself for doing what he had done. But then, in a flash, he panicked. He took her arm and dragged her with him down the steps of the veranda, through the olive grove, until he stopped, breathless, tired of running, tired of hiding. He touched her face. Her skin was soft, her eyes as deep as he had remembered them. Lucy was shaking. Then his mother's image flashed into his mind. He had to finish this. He had to end it.

He took her and held her close to him, the sweet scent of her hair, he inhaled it. He stood at the edge of the clifftop, the sea below moving in and out onto the shore. The olive grove was sheltering them. He held her in his arms, tightly. A stone tumbled, ricocheting off the edge of the cliff's face, drawing with it the crumbled dust and earth before disappearing into the sea below.

'Charlie, don't do it. Come away from the edge.' Phillips moved forward, his arm outstretched. 'Let go of Lucy. Charlie, please, listen to me.'

'I didn't mean it. I didn't mean any of it. I never meant for any of it.'

'Charlie, I know. Step away from the edge. We can talk, I will listen. I understand.'

'You don't understand. Nobody understands.'

'Charlie, please,' Lucy whimpered. 'Please, Charlie.'

'Charlie, step away from the edge. This isn't what you want,' came Phillips' voice again. Though it was cool and calm, his hands were beginning to sweat.

'You don't know what I want. Nobody knows what I want.'

'This isn't the way. Let Lucy go.'

Charlie took another step back. The sea crashed against the rocks below, showing its anger. Hurling each wave onto the rocks, ready to grasp and swirl around whatever fell.

'Charlie, please, it's over. You don't need to run. I will see you right, I give you my word.' Phillips' words were caught in the breeze.

The sweat dripped from Charlie's forehead and he wiped it, the sun now high in the sky. It blinded him. He tried to see, to make out the figures. Ana stood by Phillips. She stepped forward.

'Miguel, please, come back inside.'

'I trusted you. I trusted you. But you are like my mother.'

'No, I am not. Come back inside – you can still trust me. You needed to know the truth: that Lucy wasn't dead. That was important. You know, like swimming from the sea to the shore, finding your way back, realising by yourself. You are not a monster. You are not that.' Her words swept past him. He took another step back and his foot lost its hold. As the stones fell, he pushed Lucy to the ground. Then his body fell. Simon hurled himself across the dusty ground to the cliff's edge. Charlie was clinging on by his fingertips. Simon grabbed his hand, wrenching it, his grip slippery with sweat as the weight became too much. The grip loosened. Simon held him until their clench was ripped apart, Charlie's hand slipping through his fingers. His body fell, it tumbled like a mannequin, flightless. The screams of a man disappearing as he fell. Lucy screamed as she scrabbled to the edge, Simon grabbed her, his weight on her.

Charlie lay between the rocks below, the waves lapping around his body. Lucy scrambled out from beneath Simon and ran along the edge to a spot where the descent was easier. Her legs took her, she didn't stop running, her body tilting backwards, her footsteps ahead of her. Loose rubble tumbled down the steep, rocky slope. Lucy grasped at the spindly sea shrubs, which tore at her skin. She lost her footing, her breath rasping, a pain stabbing in her throat. She slipped again. Her ankle twisted, it throbbed, she ran through the pain, her legs grazed and bleeding. She had to reach him. The rocks tumbled ahead of her as she ran, as she ran to a man she *had* once loved, the man who remembered deep down she'd love a room full of books, the man who now lay on the beach below.

'Charlie,' she screamed as her body tumbled further, the stones and pebbles passing by her.

'Lucy!' She closed her eyes for a moment. The voice she heard wasn't Charlie's. Simon was behind her.

She fell to her knees, rolling a little until the momentum stopped and she balanced herself. She ran across the craggy, rocky beach towards him and knelt at his side. His head was bleeding, his eyes open – not a flicker, motionless. She lifted his head. Warm liquid seeped through her fingers. She held him in her arms, cradling him in her lap. Then she saw the lightness in his eyes, a softness she had once known, a feeling that she had thought would be there, just buried deep. His hand touched her knee, his thumb gently wiping away the blood from her graze.

'I didn't mean it. I'm sorry for everyth …'

'No!' she wailed, rocking him. 'Oh my God, no!'

The tears came fast and strong as she held him, rubbing her hands through his sandy, salty hair. Matted by the congealed blood.

Simon reached her, breathless, sweat drenching his top. Phillips and Murphy stood behind.

'I didn't want this. This isn't what was supposed to happen. He wasn't supposed to die.' She lifted his head and stared into his eyes – cold, grey, no life. She turned to the men, who stood still.

'This isn't what I wanted.' Her sobs hard, her nose running, the slime slugged across her lips.

'Lucy,' Simon knelt by her.

'This isn't what I wanted, Simon.'

'I know.'

She brushed her hands across Charlie's face and smoothed the sand away from his head. Her fingers gently moved across his eyes, closing the lids.

'I for … I for … I forgi … I forgi … I forgive you, Charlie. I forgive you.' The tears streamed as she sobbed, gasping for breath between each word.

A police helicopter circled the sky above, letting down a winch with a medic and a stretcher. Simon, Phillips and Murphy lowered the stretcher to the ground. Phillips' face was grave. He shook his head as the medic unclipped himself and knelt down. He placed his fingers on Charlie's neck, searching for a pulse. There was none.

Simon teased Lucy away from the body, allowing it to be carefully lifted onto the stretcher and taken up to the helicopter. The medic harnessed himself in, holding the stretcher. The sea's waves were now calm against the rocks. The gentle breeze buffeted the stretcher as it turned in the wind. Lucy didn't take her eyes off it; through the tears she watched. The helicopter dipped its nose and veered away from the scene.

Lucy fell to her knees, her cries relentless and then silent. Her eyes watched the surf of the aquamarine water ahead. On the horizon she caught the flash of a tail in the foamy waves. It disappeared. Simon pulled her up and held her close to his chest. Her cries came again, uncontrollable. Like the cries he'd heard when she'd realised she was being watched, that he'd found her. Yet now the cries from the same girl, the same howling animalistic noise, from a girl who knew the man she once loved was no longer here – it wasn't what she wanted, she had never wanted this. She clenched her fists and beat them into Simon's chest.

'No!' she screamed, 'no!'

Phillips stepped forward and rested his hand on Lucy's shoulder. He turned to Simon and led them back up the cliff face. Not a sound, not even the cries of the gulls could be heard. Perhaps it was nature's way of respecting the dead, whoever they were. Simon led Lucy back to Pedro's waiting car. Phillips stood with Murphy, looking out over the sea. The sky blue, the sea even bluer.

'I'll see you back at the car, Murphy.'

'Guv.'

His breathing heavy, Phillips took out a cigarette and lit it. The smoke caught in the wind. The white surf on the sea frothed. A flick of a tail showed itself in the surf. He watched it as it disappeared again under the foamy white crest. Maybe a dolphin, maybe a mermaid.

He flicked his cigarette over the edge and walked back to the car.

The drive to Peñíscola was silent, Lucy stared out of the window, her eyes darting back and forth as she tried to stay with the seascape. Simon sat next to her, aching to hold her, knowing her pain. She was just a writer, she was just a girl. She was just that girl on the beach, whom he adored.

In the square, the palm trees' leaves hung low as if to sweep Lucy back to the cocooned safety of the hotel. Every part of her body was churning. She turned to the tree and hurled. The sick splattered her legs and pumps, but she hurled again, propping herself up against the tree. Simon turned to Phillips and shook his head.

'Look after her, Simon, we need to go.'

'Go?' Simon questioned.

'His mother's, Sofia's,' Phillips replied. 'Pedro, please assist us.' The three detectives left the square.

They stood at the door and rapped. Sofia stood in a long dress that draped, flowing to the floor. Her hair caught up, her skin a honey brown. She looked at Phillips and she knew. Her howl echoed around the olive groves, a heart-wrenching howl of pain at the loss any mother feels when they are faced with the news that destroys your soul. It was the loss of Sofia's only child, whom she should have loved with every inch of her body, and yet she had failed. He died because of her. He was who he was because of her. He should have been like his father, a kind and gentle loving soul. She had made him who he was; he wasn't born evil. He was born a little boy with a bear called Hugo, who played in the surf with his father, who hopscotched along the rocks with his father, who believed in mermaids because his father had spotted them in the surf of the Mediterranean Sea.

The door closed and the detectives left. She stood with her back to it. Her bare feet walked step by step to the room, his room. She brushed the bed linen, feeling where he had lain. His clothes were still hanging over the chair. She sat by his trunk. Opening it, she took out the bear, his ears scraggier and more thumbed than the rest of his soft brown fur. She took out the letters, all of them airmail, all of them written by 'Daddy', none from 'Mummy'. She took out his pyjamas, a soft brushed cotton, and pressed them up against her face. A small torch was tucked between them along with an envelope. She opened it. Inside were some euros and a letter that read:

Mother,

Should anything happen to me, the money left in this envelope is to go to Santiago and his family to help with the renovations of his fishing shop.

I wish you had loved me, and I wish I had been the son you wanted. I failed you. Now I have only failed myself. I am my father's son. I am going to confess, to turn myself in.

Charlie

She placed the letter back in the envelope. She held Hugo and she wept: 'Oh Charlie, forgive me, I love you my child.'

Chapter Twenty-Three

Sunday, 23rd March

Lucy stared out of the aeroplane window at the bleached tarmac, a haze of sun rippling across its surface. She sat in her own oblivion, her own sensibility. The screams of a man, the grey steely eyes that had lost a glimmer of light. The words he spoke in Ana's room. She'd heard it all and now it was gone. She blinked, trying to make the blurry movement of the tarmac disappear. She held the buckle of her seat belt, feeling Simon's hand rest on hers, smoothing away her trauma. She rested her head on his shoulder and closed her eyes. Closed her eyes to it all and slept.

The pilot's announcement went unheard by Lucy. 'Cabin crew take your seats.'

The flight was silent. Simon held her hand throughout, letting her sleep. Every now and then he brushed her cheek as her head tossed on the headrest. They'd both seen something neither wanted to see.

Stansted airport was full, the noise, excitement, people bustling about, strangers trying to get home. She searched the throng of faces, looking for Ben's. Then she saw him. She dropped the handle of her case, and ran, ran towards him, his smile, his face, his arms. She ran into them and let her be held in his grip, her hands grappling at his collar, holding it tightly. Simon pulled the case behind and stood back a bit, allowing them their time. Watching whilst Ben's arms wrapped around her tiny waist, his chin resting on her head. Lucy had to stand on tiptoes to hold and cling to him. Ben held her face and kissed her, smoothing away the tears that trickled down her cheeks.

'Simon,' he said eventually, shaking hands. 'How was the flight?' Lucy was still nuzzling into him.

'Long, it felt long. Let's talk when we're back. I need to get some rest. Look after Lucy.'

Simon left them on the concourse and drove home.

Ben took Lucy's hand and walked her to the car park.

The drive home was silent. Lucy didn't break the silence until they were nearly at Wrabness.

'I'm hungry,' she said. He touched her leg, rubbing it gently.

'What do you fancy?'

'I don't know, something comforting and simple.'

'Pizza?'

'Yeah, I guess.'

He squeezed her leg. Her eyes glazed over.

Ben pulled up outside the cottage, the gate squeaking as he pushed it open. The familiar scent of the candle that had burnt away in Lucy's absence. She went through to the sitting room and fell onto the sofa, Ben sat next to her and put his arm around her. She snuggled into his chest. The sun was dipping in the grey sky. She tucked her feet under herself and sat curled up like a dormouse, ready to hibernate in the warmth of his arms.

'How are you feeling, Lucy?'

'Numb, just numb. Kind of helpless.'

'Want to talk about it?'

'He's dead, Ben. I watched the life leave him.'

'I know. Come here, baby.' He pulled her even closer to his chest, his hand rubbing her arm as she heard the beating of his heart. A beat that she never wanted to stop. Her tummy jiggled about and gave a soft rumbling gurgle.

'You're hungry,' he said. 'Let me order food.' He teased her out of his arms and left her whilst he found the menu, returning soon after with two glasses of red wine.

'Pepperoni and extra olives, Luce?' he called as he sauntered down the hallway and back to the sitting room.

'And capers,' she said.

'Capers? Are you sure, babe?'

'Yep, I'm sure. Lots of them.'

'Ooo-kaaay.' His voice was unsure and his eyes curiously questioning.

As the sun gave way to the night sky, the two lovers nestled into each other and ate pizza together.

'I think I'll go to the beach tomorrow and write,' she said as she tucked her body into his chest, cupping the wineglass in one hand and a triangular slice of caper-topped pizza in the other. He twiddled her hair and kissed her forehead. She was where she needed to be.

As the night closed in and darkness fell on the cottage, Lucy watched from the sofa as Gladys Pope took Barry out for a last trot of the evening. The candle flickered on the windowsill. The draught from the open front door whipped around the hallway. The street was dead outside, just the hooting of an owl echoing in the darkness and the screeching of foxes on the prowl. Ben rattled the lid of the bin as he threw the empty pizza carton into the recycling box. Barry barked. Gladys swivelled around abruptly, throwing the light of her torch down the street, ready to flush out the intruder.

'It's only me, Mrs Pope, just putting the rubbish out,' Ben called as the torch shone like a searchlight straight at him, dazzling him.

'No bother, young Ben. Come on now, Barry, do your business would you, me cocoa's sitting on the side.' She shuffled off up the street.

Ben closed the front door and locked it firmly. He drew the velvet curtain across before returning to the sitting room. He blew out the candle, the black smoke filtering up like a snake weaving out of its charm basket. The moon was high in the sky above number 8.

'Right, come on, bed,' he said as he pulled the curtains across. 'You look knackered.'

Lucy pulled herself from under the throw and moseyed up the stairs to the bedroom with Ben close behind her.

Leaving her clothes in a pile by the door, she climbed under the duvet, the sheet cold beneath her. He moved over to her and rested his hand on her tummy. It somersaulted inside with his touch. She tucked her leg into the crook of his, resting her head on his bare chest. Tiredness swallowed her whole.

She stirred in her sleep, letting out the faintest of murmurs. Ben stroked her hair as her muffling sounds woke him. She whimpered and moved her head further onto his chest, her hands holding him tighter. The duvet became twisted around her limbs and she let out a cry.

'Shhhh,' Ben breathed, brushing her bare back.

'No,' she cried, 'no … no!' Her cries louder. Her breathing faster, her heart pounding in her chest.

'No!' Lucy screamed. She sat bolt upright, searching in the darkness for a chink of light. The room was entirely dark. The remnants of the nightmare still clung to her mind.

'Hold him, don't let him go. *No!*' Ben eased himself up from his sleep, his arms around her, a cold sweat on her naked body.

'Hey, you're having a bad dream, shhh.' He brushed and twisted her hair.

'I saw him fall, Ben. I didn't want that. His scream. His eyes. A mermaid, I'm sure I saw a mermaid.'

'Shhhh, I know. Come on, lie here, come on.' She lay back into Ben, her hands clenched on his chest. He smoothed her hair, pacifying her memory of the frantic trauma she had witnessed. Easing away the nightmares she would have.

She felt the touch of his lips against her forehead and she nestled into him.

'I didn't want him dead,' she whimpered.

'I know, baby. You're safe here.' Twigs brushed against the window like a gentle lullaby.

The mist in the sky held back the sunlight from the crack between the curtains. Lucy stirred from her sleep, scrubbing her fists against her bleary eyes, stretching her arms out. She could hear the shower running and Ben whistling in the bathroom. The click of the lock and his footsteps dashing down each step on the staircase. She let out an audible yawn and pushed her body up from under the covers where she'd been hibernating. She leant over to her phone: it was seven o'clock. Ben appeared in the doorway holding a peppermint tea and a coffee, and wearing only a pair of Calvin Klein boxer shorts. He placed the tea on the bedside table and pulled the curtains open. It made little difference to the lightness of the room.

He sat on the side of the bed and wrapped his arms around Lucy.

'Are you writing at the beach today, Luce?'

'Yep. I have a new story to tell. I need to get it down whilst it's fresh.'

'Sounds good! What about the other one, what's the news?' he asked.

'Well, Jo has it at the moment. I'll see what she thinks and then play with it a little.'

'You make me smile ... Right, I need to go, I've got a yacht that needs to be finished for some rich guy in St Helen's. But I'm taking you out for dinner tonight. Wear something warm and no heels!' He tweaked her nose, affectionately.

'No heels? A bike ride? Like our first date.'

'Better than that. Be ready for six and not a second later.'

'Sounds intriguing. I'll be ready.'

He slapped a huge great kiss on her lips and licked her lips with his tongue. Then, once dressed, he raced down the stairs, leaving Lucy with a smile on her face that stretched from ear to ear and her eyes twinkling with wonderment for 6 p.m.

It was the brightness of the fresh page in the spring sun that brought a smile to her face. The mist had lifted, and the sunshine on the beach was pushing the wintery cold away. She spotted the little girl she saw regularly collecting pebbles and shells in her red bucket, her mother's hands close by, guiding her to another pretty shell. The bump the woman carried was growing rounder and protruding further. There was a friendly wave from the waggling stick as Bob approached the stone step, Archie finding another spot to cock his leg.

'Peppermint tea?' Lucy said, pouring two cups.

'And why not, my dear Lucy.'

She handed Bob his cup.

The sea was grey and murky, unlike the aquamarine blue of the sea that had blown her mind, in Peñíscola.

'He's gone, Bob,' she finally said as she cupped the tea.

He held her hand, his touch consoling and palliative.

'I heard his story.'

'And that, Lucy, has brought closure to yours.'

'It wasn't the ending I wanted.'

'Do what you do best.'

'And what's that?'

'Write about it.'

'Bob?'

'Yes, Lucy?'

'When you found me on the beach, what did you see, what did you feel?'

He watched the sea. The gentle melodic swishing as the waves washed up onto the shore. A robin perched on the beach wall near to them, where it tipped its head and trilled. He wished he had a pocketful of crumbs to throw for it. For a moment he was lost in a transitory memory of his time with his children, collecting white shells from the beach and feeding the birds with the stale breadcrumbs Olivia had stored for the weekends when he'd return from sea. The weekends that gave him the time to play with Robin and Lottie, and make love to his beloved Olivia when the children slept. His glance moved over to the pier where he'd found Lucy, that bleak morning. He sighed heavily.

'I saw a young girl I knew, whom I loved like my own, with a porcelain white face. Cold, motionless, gone. I saw my daughter's face in a fire, I saw my son's face in a fire. I saw Olivia's body lying on the landing to their bedrooms, trying to reach them, protect them. I saw two children asleep forever in a bed. I saw me running through the town to reach them and failing. I would not fail again. I would not let this be the end. I could not let this be the end for the girl who had restored my own faith in life, in a cruel world that can snatch away those most precious to you. I saw hope. I saw fear. I saw courage. And that, Lucy, is what you have now been witness to. You can now expel those memories.'

'I see his face in my dreams - not the face of the man who hurt me, but the face of him on the beach, where he fell. I saw the face of a man I had once loved, who craved the love of his mother. My mind see-saws between dwelling on the past and the resentment I had for him. The poison he poured into me - attacking me for what I wore, who I saw, hurting me, abusing me, locking me away, raping me. I lost my self-esteem and myself for so long. And then I heard for the first time his torment inside. I never knew - but I can't be blamed either, can I? He spoke of mermaids and his father and the love he had for him.' She sighed as she told of the last few hours of Charlie's life. Looking out to the sea and its restlessness. 'Can I have a hug, Bob?'

He opened his arms like the father she'd never had and hugged her with every inch of a father's love. He moved her away and cupped her face in his hands. 'The sea has so many stories and secrets yet to tell. Here we explore, admire the wonders and learn. And mermaids, a wondrous sea creature, a wonderful father to ignite such a memory for his child. Believe. Now, my dear, write about it and let go. You can never blame yourself for his badness but perhaps now knowing why can help come to terms and realise where it came from. It's not excusing his evil but instead allowing a resting place.'

He eased himself up from the stone step. She watched him as he walked the sandy shore of Harwich beach.

'Until tomorrow, my dear Lucy.' He waved his stick in the air as he whistled to Archie who trotted behind like his old faithful friend, cocking his leg at every spot.

Lucy opened her notebook to a fresh page. The lid of her ink pen popped as she opened it. The beach was now empty of dog walkers and young children running towards the waves in their brightly coloured wellies and giggling as they ran away from the chasing water. The nib rested on the first line. She scribbled: "Memories Forgotten", Harwich Beach March 2019, and underlined it twice. She brushed her hand down the page and gazed out to sea before she wrote. Every word she poured out onto the page, almost frantic with the ink on the paper. Stopping only briefly to tuck away the wisps of hair that blew into her face from the offshore breeze, momentarily looking up to watch as the gulls squealed about in the sky, looking for a discarded bag of chips or an unwanted sandwich.

She had finally let go, and although it was a pain that would stay with her, she felt freer, and now she would write about it. Her novels had always included a conflict that she would solve; today it was her own. Where the words on each page were honest, real, hers. A conflict where the ending couldn't be changed. Pages and pages of black swirling ink trailed across them. It was only the rumbling of her tummy that reminded her she hadn't eaten anything and it was way past lunchtime.

She undid the buckle on her satchel and took from it a brown paper parcel. It rustled in the wind. Wrapped inside were two chunky pieces of freshly cut bread, sandwiched together with lashings of tuna mayonnaise and capers. She had a thing about capers. She tucked into the sandwich, holding it with two hands. The mayonnaise oozed from the sides of the golden crunchy crusts, leaving a creamy mess around her mouth. She wiped it away and took another massive bite. The saltiness of the capers hit the spot. They tasted like the sea, just fresher. She devoured the lot without drawing a breath. Her appetite was on another scale, yet she gained no weight other than the few kilos she'd needed to gain after staying in hospital.

The mist began to seep in over the horizon, masking the blue Titan cranes on the horizon. It was four o'clock. She'd spent the whole day at the beach, writing, simply whiling away the hours filling her notebook with her newest novel – but she also needed to be ready for Ben and absolutely not be late. Jumping up, she wiggled the life back into her bottom, which was numb from the cold stone. She tossed the empty scrunched-up brown paper into the bin and meandered through the mews to where she had parked the car. A message pinged into her phone.

Hey gorge, awesome, awesome, awesome!!! X

What is, Jo?

Your manuscript. I love it. You gave Peggy and Jim a happy, ever, after x

Yeah I did, it felt right to … I'll message later, Ben's taking me out tonight, can't wait. x

Fab!! I'm down for the weekend to see Matt. Love you kiddo! Have fun!Xx

Back at you ☺ xx

Pulling away from the mews, she drove the long way home. She needed to warm up; her toes tingled as the heat came through the vents and blasted a hot noisy air onto them. She clunked the black lever to moderate the heat, but it didn't really work. It was either hot or cold, no in between.

She drove past the low lighthouse that sat in the still waters at Dovercourt, the sun casting its shadow like a runway across the glassy water. The neon sign flashed fish and chips. *Not tonight,* she thought. What had Ben got in store for her? A guy on a bike cycled past on the pavement. She smiled; it reminded her of the first time she'd seen Ben, the guy on the bike she fell for.

Once home, she plonked her satchel on her writing desk and headed straight for the shower. From the top of the stairs she could hear the motorbike's engine outside.

'Lucy, Luce,' Ben called from the front hall.

'I'm upstairs, getting ready.' The hairdryer blasted her hair and face. She was dressed only in a towel.

'Hey you, that's not warm clothes.'

'I know, I'm getting dressed now. I don't know what to wear, though. What do I wear?'

'Jeans, boots, jumper. Simple.'

She slipped on her skinny black jeans that had designer rips in the knees, a tight, black fitted polo-neck, and her ankle boots - no heels. Sitting in front of the mirror, she applied her make-up, drawing a liquid line across her already feline eyes. She smudged blusher onto her defined cheekbones, snatching them in further. Then she lined her lips with a chocolatey brown liner and even more chocolatey brown lipstick and gloss. Leaving the wet towel on the bed, she rushed down the stairs. Ben was in the kitchen, rummaging through the drawers for a corkscrew. He turned and eyed her up.

'Wow!'

'Is this OK?' she asked.

'It's more than OK - fuck, you look gorgeous. Right, come on, we've got to go. Helmet, bike, let's go!'

He took the lanes slowly down to Harwich and parked close to the boatyard.

'Harwich? The boatyard?' she teased.

'Close your eyes,' he said.

With her eyes squeezed shut, he took her hand and led her along the marina front and down the rickety pier.

'Step up and in.' Holding both her hands, he led her a few steps in. 'Take four steps down, hold my hands still.' She counted the steps. He stood her beneath the shelter. 'You can open them now.'

Lucy eased one eye open and then the other. She took in a sharp breath as she saw a table laid with a candlelit dinner for two inside the cabin.

'Oh my God!' Her breath caught in her throat. It was simply beautiful.

'Bob helped me,' Ben said as he poured her a glass of champagne.

'He did? Oh my …' Her heart skipped a beat.

'He said you'd never sailed before.'

'Oh gosh …'

'So, I'm going to take you now.'

'You are?' The smile on Lucy's face was infectious. Her eyes lit up and sparkled.

'I am.'

Ben untied the mooring and let the wind catch the sails as the boat cleaved its path across the water until it reached the halfway point across the harbour. He let down the anchor at the stern, so they drifted and bobbed on the sea close to a red buoy. The anchor light on the stern glowed as dusk fell.

They sat in the cabin together, illuminated only by a few simple tea-light candles in jam jars. Dressed crab as a starter, followed by langoustine and baby asparagus salad with a splattering of croutons and lemon mayonnaise, and homemade chocolate brownies from Betty's cake shop.

'I didn't know you could cook, Ben,' she said in wonderment.

'I can't. I commissioned The Pier and asked them to make up a hamper of seafood. And Betty, well, she makes the best chocolate brownies in Essex!' he chuckled. 'I wanted it to be special and I wanted to take you sailing.' He stood behind her, his arms around her. She held his hands in front of her.

'I love it all, all of it. And Bob – he said nothing this morning.'

Ben unclasped his hold and took from his pocket a small box. He turned Lucy to face him. He opened the box and took from it a piece of entwined sailing string with a carefully tied knot in the shape of a heart joining it together to form a delicate ring shape.

'Lucy Emma Carter … will you marry me?'

Lucy's eyes swam with tears. She bit her lip as a tear trickled down her cheek. She tried to hold it back. But in vain.

She nodded her head vigorously, her smile growing bigger and bigger. 'Yes, yes Ben, yes.' The tears fell and the smile ran across her face. He slipped the delicate piece of twine onto her finger and kissed her gently, finding her tongue with his.

The small boat swayed on the waves as their bodies wrapped around each other under the starlit sky, two lovers with nothing but the sound of their breathing and the waves that gently rocked them, becoming one.

Lucy rolled over, a little bleary-eyed. Only a blanket was covering their naked bodies. She opened her eyes and took out her hand from beneath the warm cover. Her left hand with an intricate piece of sailing twine on her engagement finger. She felt a warmth inside: her heart seemed to sing.

Ben's arm came out from under the blanket and pulled her in, nuzzling the nape of her neck, holding her tightly with his arm. She stroked the inked bracelet around his upper arm.

'We're going to have sail back,' he said. kissing her.

She turned into him and kissed his nose. 'I'm getting married!' Her eyes glistened and danced.

'You are indeed. Come on, gorgeous, get dressed, I need to get the boat back.'

The sun was just coming up on the horizon, throwing a red glow on the easterly corner of the world, its red and amber hue reflected over the still waters, turning the grey sea into liquid gold. The early morning breeze was enough to sail the boat back to the marina. The wind caught against Lucy's face as she sat close to Ben while he steered the boat gently into the mooring.

On the back of his bike, she held him tightly as they took the bends of the road, the red sky ahead of them. There was no traffic about, just the two of them riding in the early hours of dawn. Ben pulled up outside the cottage and tilted the bike so Lucy could climb off. The street was still sleeping; the only sound was the rattle and clink of the milk cart on its rounds. The midnight blue BMW had gone.

Closing the front door behind them, they made their way upstairs, undressing and falling into each other's arms in the bed, where they made love again and again.

Chapter Twenty-Four

Tuesday, 25th March
Wrabness, Essex

Ben rolled over and pulled Lucy in closer to him. She let out an audible sigh of pleasure as she snuggled into him, his body heat permeating hers like a hot water bottle.

'I need to go to work, gorgeous,' he said as he released his arm from her and headed for the shower.

Lucy reached out for her phone and messaged Jo, squinting as she cleared the predictive text.

Call me xx

She rolled the duvet back and climbed out of bed, grabbing her bathrobe from the chair and throwing it on. She padded across to her writing room and traced her fingers across the keys of her typewriter before turning the roller to a new line. She pressed down on each key and typed until it pinged. She rolled the paper up and smiled at the words she'd typed. They read: *Happily, Ever, After.*

The morning whizzed by. Lucy stayed in her cottage all day writing at her desk. Her thoughts were only disturbed by her mobile vibrating on her desk. She peered at the screen – it was Jo.

'Jo!' she squealed, hardly able to contain her excitement. 'Guess what!'

'Umm, you realised I'm the bestest friend you could ever have?'

'Well, of course, but … Ben asked me to marry him last night, on a sailing boat on the sea, with a candlelit picnic dinner,' Lucy squealed down the phone without taking a breath.

'Oh my God! Oh my God!' Lucy held the phone away from her ear whilst Jo screamed with utter delight. 'Fuck me, that is awesome. Oh my God, Lucy, that is best news ever! Who else knows - Simon?'

'No, just you. I think Bob may know. He helped Ben sort it all, and he told him I'd never sailed before.'

'My God, Bob is such a decent soul. Salt of the earth. Listen, I'm going to tie up some loose ends up here and come down Friday - we need to celebrate. Pick me up from the station, I'll look up train times. Have to dash now, gorge, I've got a meeting with Medusa to close the contract with Harper's. Fill me in with everything on Friday? Can't wait to see you.'

Lucy popped her phone on the desk and opened her laptop screen. She googled 'simple wedding dresses'. Pages of bridal sites flashed up: flouncy meringue-style dresses, straight figure-hugging styles with fishtail bottoms, A-line, short, long, second-time-around numbers, white, cream, gold, plain, ruffles, lace, sweetheart necklines, strapless, long-sleeved. None of them the slightest bit what she would wear.

She gazed out onto the street, remembering the first time she'd driven past the church and spied a florist busily arranging the archway over the gate for a wedding. She'd had an overwhelming feeling of escaping from a huge white wedding she didn't want, with no pang of envy as she passed the church. She'd driven to the police station that day with a box full of Margaret Arthur's belongings to return them to their rightful owner. She'd met Matt and Simon for the first time and forged a friendship like no other over the three years she'd lived in Wrabness. She'd fallen head over heels in love with the 'guy on the bike', who'd watched her cartwheel frivolously on the beach with Jo, had seen her get ridiculously drunk in Samuel Pepys, and now she was going to marry him. Finding love and friendships in a village that was now truly her home.

She picked up her phone and sent a message to the boys.

Supper at mine 7pm Friday x

The message bubbled below.

Sounds great, will bring wine Sxx

See you then, awesome Mx

Lucy smiled at the screen. That was the boys sorted.

The week whizzed by. Ben would come back to hers, snuggle up on the sofa with her, have supper and then flick through the channels for something to watch. He'd make love to her and leave in the morning on his bike for work with his rucksack and a change of clothes. So, on Friday morning, Lucy decided that it was about time she made space for him in her bedroom, now that he was officially her fiancé. She googled 'vintage chest of drawers' and found a quaint little shop tucked away in Harwich that sold odds and sods and furniture. She raced down to visit it.

The bell tinkled as she opened the door, and an old man stirred from the chair he'd been napping in. *He looks a hundred years old,* Lucy thought as she bid him hello. The shop was an Aladdin's cave of ornaments. It was dimly lit with tired-looking lamps and smelt musty. She sidled past the lamps, old school trunks, vintage cases, shelves and shelves of leather-bound books that you could blow a puff of dust from to leave you spluttering, silver candelabras, canteens of old-fashioned cutlery, tea sets, crystal decanters and a simple-looking chest of drawers with blackened brass handles that resembled tiny fairylike door knockers. It was just the right size for the space she had in the bedroom, too, although it was too big for her Mini. She paid fifty pounds for it and an extra tenner for delivery that day. Pleased with her purchase, she left and drove back to the cottage, stopping on the way at her local butcher's in the 'windmill village' and bought bacon, sausages, mince and five chicken breasts with the wings still on.

Once the meat was safely in the fridge at home, she dashed upstairs. *Now for the wardrobe,* she thought. In the bedroom, she rearranged her shoes and boots, making space at the bottom. She pushed her clothes to one side, allowing hanging space for Ben's. She nudged her dressing-table across the floor, pushing it further up against the wall. Her tummy tingled a bit with its weight as she shoved it with her bottom and hips. Perfect - she'd made space for the antique chest of drawers, which would be arriving at 1 p.m.

She changed the bed and made it with freshly laundered white linen. The only thing left to do was to rearrange the bathroom cabinet for a boy's shaving bits. *Perfect,* she thought as she closed the bathroom door and went back downstairs to prepare supper. She was picking up Jo at three-thirty, Ben would be back by about five, and the boys were coming over at seven.

Before long the mouth-watering smell of chicken in garlic and wine with an undertone of caramelising sticky toffee pudding filled the cottage.

A rat-tat-tat on the door led her away from her cooking. That would be the delivery of her bedroom furniture. Two burly men carried the chest of drawers upstairs and left it in the space she had made. Perfect. She ran back down the stairs for the duster and polish to give it a good clean. She polished it frantically until it looked a little less tired. She loved it.

Her tummy rumbled, reminding her it needed to be fed. In the kitchen, a medley of chicken in red wine and sweet toffee pudding dispersed heavenly scents around the small cottage. She sliced two hunks of bread and smeared a layer of butter on each slice, carving wedges of cheddar, with piccalilli and a spoonful of capers on top. She devoured the lot. She'd spent most of the day cleaning and cooking and making her cottage into Ben's cottage too. A message pinged into her phone.

Just at Colchester, be there soon x

On my way now x

Snatching her coat from the bannister, she left to pick up Jo. She sat at the level crossing as the train from London passed slowly by. The red lights stopped flashing and the gates lifted. Lucy's tyres bumped over the tracks.

As a collection of commuters taking an early exeat from London bundled off the train, Lucy scanned the platform for Jo. She spotted her: skinny bleached-black jeans, cropped woollen jumper with a large roll-neck that almost demolished her shoulders, black beret on top of her swish clean-cut bob, black leather jacket with pointed studs, luscious glossed lips, oversized Jackie Onassis glasses and studded biker boots to match the jacket that was flipped over her shoulder, carrying a bag with Bollinger written down it and wheeling her weekend suitcase. She swaggered down the platform, allowing the men in their staid suits to turn their heads and be caught up in a moment of sexual allure. She looked every inch an object of desire and she knew it.

'Hey gorge,' Jo said as she held out her arms for a heavenly hug. 'Show me, show me, show me.' Lucy held out her hand, beaming from ear to ear. 'That's just the cutest thing, it's sailing twine - oh my God, how romantic. Come here.' Jo hugged her tightly again. They chatted all the way back to the cottage.

Leaving the suitcase at the bottom of the stairs, the two girls made their way through to the kitchen. Lucy took a quick peek at the chicken and turned the heat on.

'Is it too early for champagne?' Jo asked, flinging the Bollie bag at Lucy.

'Let's save this for tonight and the others, I have one in the fridge already.' Lucy opened the fridge and took a chilled bottle out, placing Jo's Bollinger on a shelf below. Jo unlocked the kitchen door before rummaging through her bag for her packet of Marlboro Gold cigarettes.

'Want one?' she said, thrusting the open packet at Lucy.

'Actually, I might join you.' Lucy poured two glasses of champagne and stood outside with Jo.

'So, does Simon know yet?' Jo gently asked, blowing a plume of smoke out of the corner of her mouth.

'No. I don't know whether I just blurt it out or tell him quietly. But if I tell him quietly, he's going to know that I know he's always cared for me, isn't he? Which is the lesser of the two evils?' The nicotine taste caught in Lucy's throat; it felt harsh. She stubbed out the cigarette in the flowerpot, unfinished.

'I guess you have to tell us all and Simon will celebrate it. He loves you, Lucy in more ways than one – but knowing Simon, he'll be happy for you.' Jo squeezed Lucy's arm reassuringly. Lucy nodded her head, knowing that Jo was right. She adored Simon like the brother she'd never had. He'd always been there for her, and now Ben was the main feature in her life, she was scared she would lose Simon. He looked out for her, protected her. He'd even basted a turkey at Christmas with her, when she didn't know the first thing about Christmas lunch. He'd been a policeman and a friend and she loved him for that.

Back in the kitchen, Jo pulled up a chair and crossed her gazelle-like legs.

'Simon will be OK, Luce. Come on then, I'm dying to know – tell me how he proposed and show me that ring again.' Lucy recounted the evening of utter fairy-tale romance to Jo, smiling at every part where she said Ben's name or what he did or how he held her. Her eyes sparkled with delight as she recounted the sailing boat, the sunrise and the ride home.

As the evening drew in, Lucy and Jo danced around the kitchen, laying the table for the five of them. Then came the sound of Ben's bike and the key in the door.

'Hey babe, I'm home.'

'We're in the kitchen,' Lucy called out.

'Well, congratulations, Ben!' Jo exclaimed, throwing her arms open and giving Ben an almighty hug.

'Thanks, Jo, I guess Lucy's filled you in with everything?'

'She certainly has – just awesome news.'

'Yeah, I've been grinning all day!'

'I bet. You better go get in that shower. The boys will be here soon,' Jo said, smiling with delight for them both.

Ben strode up the stairs to shower and change.

'He's a dream,' Lucy said, totally starry-eyed. Jo got out three champagne glasses.

The knocker on the door hammered as Simon and Matt stood outside with wine. Lucy left Jo in the kitchen, calling to Ben to come down quickly too. She flung the door open and gave them both a humungous hug.

'Jo's in the kitchen, Matt,' Lucy said as she almost skipped to the kitchen. Ben raced down the stairs.

'Simon, Matt, good to see you both.'

He followed them through to the kitchen.

'Something smells good,' Simon exclaimed.

'Coq au vin!' Lucy told him, and then, 'Sticky toffee pudding.'

'Wow, you've been busy. And champagne glasses, too – what are we celebrating?'

'Well ...' Lucy's smile stretched from ear to ear. She took Ben's hand. 'Well ... Ben asked me to marry him and I said *yes!*' she squealed.

Simon watched Lucy's face as it lit up with those words.

'Mate, that's great news, congratulations.' Simon extended his hand and gave Ben a solid handshake. He turned to Lucy.

'That's amazing, Lucy, come here.' He wrapped his arms around her and squeezed her in his hug. Jo's eyes held Simon's and she smiled at him as if to say, *hang in there.*

Matt threw a smacker on Jo's lips. 'Let's pour that champagne!'

Five friends sat in the cosy kitchen on Lambourne Terrace, with laughter, chatter, tunes, scrumptious food, oodles of champagne and a page of new beginnings.

Chapter Twenty-Five

Friday, 11th July (a few months later)

The crude sound of the alarm woke Lucy. She'd slept through the noisy cheeps of the birds outside her window. She rolled over to snuggle into Ben's pillows, her tummy jiggling and bouncing about as she held them tightly to her, breathing in the scent of his aftershave. A rat-tat-tat on the front door hastened her to get a move on. Climbing out of bed, she grabbed her bathrobe and wrapped it around her. She pulled back the curtain and unlatched the front door. Her eyes widened and her nose scrunched up as she stood barefoot on the doorstep, confronted by what looked like a human walking bouquet. A head peered around from the beautiful flowers. 'A Miss Lucy Carter,' he chirruped. The foliage of ivy, gypsum and ferns cascaded over the pink and white tissue paper.

'Yep, that's me.' She took the bouquet from him, her brows knitted, her eyes glistened in the morning sunlight.

'Someone's a lucky girl,' he chirped with a twinkle in his eye.

The scent of gardenias and daphnes was intoxicating. She stood with her back to the door and drew in the scent, the smile on her face becoming a beam of happiness. She peered inside the bouquet as it rested on the worktop and tucked her hand carefully inside, retrieving the envelope that was nestled between the ferns. She placed it on the worktop whilst she searched through the cupboard under the sink for a vase that was big enough to contain the gorgeous medley of pink, purple and white flowers.

But as she untied the bow, the envelope fell to the ground and slipped under the counter. *Damn,* she thought, and knelt on the floor. It had slipped right to the back. She went to the under-stairs cupboard to grab a broom so as to prise it out. Kneeling on the cold kitchen floor, she levered the broom at an angle. A pile of dust and cobwebs came out from under the counter along with the small white envelope with 'Lucy' scribbled in biro.

There was something else, too: a half-opened envelope addressed to her. She hadn't been expecting to find another one – and why was it half-opened? She brushed them both off and left them on the table whilst she flicked the kettle on. It was gone ten o'clock and her persistent tummy-rumbles were pushing her to making breakfast before she opened the card. She poured the hot water into her mug and let the peppermint bag bob about. She buttered a piece of warm toast, not bothering with Marmite – she'd gone off it, she wasn't altogether sure why. Her tummy squirmed a little more; she was starving.

Sitting at the table, she pulled the two envelopes closer to her. The letter was postmarked London and dated the 16th of February 2016. It was years old. How could she have missed it – was it important? At least, was it important now, three years later? All her bills were up to date and she'd had no red reminders for anything she could think of. Taking a bite of toast, she sighed and took the small card. It had to be from Ben. Who else would send her such a gorgeous bouquet, with flowers that made her heart sing? She opened the envelope and pushed the card out. It read: 'with love, hope and forgiveness'. She stared at the card. The writing was that of a florist, not of the sender.

Her phone pinged in a message.

Hey gorgeous girl!!! I'll be with you at 4pm with champagne xx

Hey Jo! That sounds great, I can't wait, I actually can't wait. Xx

Me neither, kiddo xx

Jo?

Yes, gorge xx

Did you send me any flowers? X

No, why? X

I've got a bouquet, pink and white flowers and pink tissue paper…

Right, probably Ben. He's missing you already! ☺ Xx

They're not from Ben x

Why not, of course they are, or da-da-da OMG you've got a secret admirer LOL xx

No, the card says "with love, hope and forgiveness" that's it??

Hmm, dunno maybe the wrong card in the flowers?? Maybe Rachel? Don't think about it, they're probably from Ben. It's your birthday tomorrow, silly xx

Yeah, you're right, they're beautiful xx

Listen, I'll see you later, love you, kiddo xx

I'll pick you up from the station, see you later ☺ xx

Lucy sighed inwardly as she read the card again. The florist was in Clacton, so she'd phone them and ask – yes, that's what she'd do. The line rang and she patted her tummy, suddenly wishing she'd made herself another slice of toast.

'Emily's Flowers, can I help you?' came the friendly voice on the line. It sounded as bright and cheery as the flowers that sat on her worktop.

'Oh yeah, I wonder if you can help? I had some flowers delivered today and I'm not altogether sure who they're from. Is there a chance you could let me know who sent them? I'd just like to be able to say thank you to whoever it was.'

'Um, sure. Emily isn't in the shop at the moment, she's in the cold room making up some hand ties. Can I take a number and get her to call you back? Oh, and the address for the delivery.'

'Sure.' Lucy left her name, number and delivery address with the girl on the phone. She could only wait now for the call back.

She turned the tap on and let the water run ice cold before filling the vase half full. She snipped the string that tied the stems and carefully placed the bouquet in the water, trying to keep the spiralled shape that the stems formed from the florist's arranging. The flowers fell open a little more now with the freedom of space and no tissue paper to bunch them in. Their scent punctuated the room with an instant hit of meadow freshness and summer haze. The particles of dust in the air caught in the beam of light that shone through the cottage window and flooded the kitchen with a burst of summer light. She stood back and smiled. It looked dreamy just there on the worktop.

She went through to the sitting room, where the curtains were still drawn. As she pulled them open, the door of number 8 opened and Gladys Pope waddled out with Barry in tow. It had to be gone eleven, because she always walked him before lunch – his mid-morning whoopsie walk, as she called it. Lucy pulled the bathrobe around her waist and darted upstairs to shower and dress. Never before had she been quite so lazy with a morning, and it had almost disappeared. She let the robe drop to the floor in the bathroom and turned on the shower taps. The hot water steamed up the mirror, the boiler hummed in the cupboard as she drenched herself in the warm water. She'd see Ben tomorrow and she couldn't wait. He'd been away for the past couple of days on a strictly-no-girls-allowed boys' rampage of Amsterdam. All the boys had gone, and Jo would arrive that day ready for a girlie evening in. She smiled to herself as she thought about it all. She couldn't wait for this birthday. It was going to be the best one ever with the guy she loved and her friends around her.

As she was dressing, her phone rang in the kitchen. She raced down the stairs, catching it just in time. It was a local number.

'Hello,' she said, pressing her mobile against her wet ear.

'Oh, hi, this is Emily from the florist's. I've got a message to call you about a flower delivery?'

'Yes, I had some flowers delivered this morning, but there's no name on the card. I wonder if you could let me know who sent them …' Lucy asked, turning the card in her hand.

'Was it to 3 Lambourne Terrace, Wrabness?' Emily asked.

'Yes, that's right. Lucy Carter.'

'They came from a Sofia Martinez. She didn't want to add her name.'

The line went quiet. Lucy stared at the card.

'Hello … hello …?'

'Oh, right, OK, that's great, that's perfect, thank you.' Lucy hung up and sat down with the card, turning it again in her hand. She hadn't heard from Sofia, not even to let her know about the funeral. She put the card on the counter by the flowers. The unopened letter still sat on the table. Looking more closely, she saw that the postmark was just before her court date. She pushed it away – she couldn't open it. She left it on the table and grabbed her jacket from the bannister and left the cottage. She needed to get wine and champagne and beer and food before Jo arrived.

Jo chucked her case onto the back seat and let out a huge sigh as she buckled up.

'Bad day?' Lucy asked.

'Long day, and bloody awful journey. Anyway, how's you? Been busy?

'Yep, I've done the alcohol shop and mammoth food shop - not sure if my fridge is big enough - and I phoned the florist, too.'

'Florist?' Jo turned in her seat.

'Yeah, I needed to know who the flowers were from,' Lucy said, tapping the steering wheel and indicating right towards Wrabness.

'And ...?' Jo asked, her eyes narrowed.

'Sofia.'

'Charlie's Sofia?' Jo's ears pricked up and she fidgeted on her seat. 'Why?'

'Don't know.' Lucy exhaled. 'I guess she's lost her son.'

Jo squeezed her friend's leg. 'Enjoy them, Lucy. You can do nothing more. Now we need an early night, strictly no alcohol, too. We've got a birthday to celebrate tomorrow without a hangover.'

Lucy passed the police station. Both squad cars were parked outside the front door, which was firmly closed, and the overhanging light was off. She drove past the church. Gladys Pope was outside, tending to the flowers on the wooden archway, replacing the dead and wilted ones with posies of cosmos and large white daisies tied up in gingham ribbon. Barry lay next to her, his ears flopping on the pavement and his soppy eyes closed, napping whilst she busied herself with her community work. Lucy tooted her horn and waved before pulling up outside her cottage.

The girls unloaded the boot, the little red Mini seeming to let out a relieved groan as it was unburdened of the weight. They began to pack away the food for the weekend.

'So, those are the flowers?' Jo said passing the bottles to Lucy. 'They're beautiful.'

'I know.' Lucy rammed the last bottle of Bud onto the fridge shelf.

Jo twizzled the half-opened letter on the table. 'Feeling indecisive, Luce?'

'What d'you mean?'

'The letter, it's half open ...'

'I was waiting for you, actually. It's years old, I found it under the counter this morning.' Jo picked it up and held it up to the light, her lips pursed. 'Shall we open it?' she said, trying to make out its contents.

'Sure. Can you?' Lucy said, flicking the kettle on.

Jo teased her finger along the broken edge, ripping it further until the envelope gaped open. 'It's a letter,' she said, taking it out and releasing the creased folds.

Lucy watched her hands, then her face. Her eyes went back to the letter in Jo's hand.

'Jo, who's it from? Jo?'

'It's from Charlie.'

'Charlie?'

'He must have written it when he was in prison, in custody,' Jo said, letting her eyes trace across the words.

'What does he say?'

Jo drew in her breath as she read the words. She cleared her throat.

Lucy,

I never imagined I'd end up like this, to be faced with prison because of a woman. But which woman – you, my mother, the judge that will make her decision? Which one of you put me here to serve a sentence behind bars, locked up like an animal? I sat in a chair, handcuffed. I will face a judge, face you, never facing her. My lawyer will fight for me, because I will pay him. You will not ruin me. I will get three years out of the five because you know I am going to screw up? Screw up like I've always done ... I didn't take that from your life, I didn't take three years. Am I trying to justify myself and escape my guilt? Who is guilty? I ask myself, whilst you'll live your life in freedom. I will be out one day and then Lucy, and then ...

Charlie

Lucy sat and let the words seep in. She swallowed. She knew his story now. She'd heard Ana in Spain and witnessed Charlie break down, overcome by a past that had led him to become the person who had caused her so much suffering. She'd told him she forgave him, but did she? The letter was real, his venom was real, his hatred all too real. She didn't want him dead, that was no lie. But now what? It was a letter from before Ana, before she'd heard him break down. Was it all just an act? Was he just evil? Wouldn't he have taken her over the clifftop if he were evil? But he had planned on coming for her – that unfinished sentence – "and then, Lucy, and then …"

She got up from the table, took the flowers from the vase, opened the bin and threw them in, the petals toppling from them, bent and crushed. She pushed them down further, breaking the delicate stems, as if pushing Sofia under water until she breathed no more.

'I don't need her flowers.' She ripped the card into tiny pieces and chucked it into the bin. The lid clanged shut. It was over.

Epilogue

Saturday, 12th July
Wrabness, Essex

A message pinged into Lucy's phone.

HAPPY BIRTHDAY TO THE MOST BEAUTIFUL GIRL IN THE WORLD … I LOVE YOU!! ☺☺☺ xxxxxxxx

'Happy birthday, gorge!' Jo said, falling onto the double bed and thrusting a beautifully tied box into Lucy's hands and a card. Lucy pulled the ribbon from the neatly tied bow and slid her finger along the wrapping paper, breaking the sealed edges. She slowly unwrapped it, beaming. Excited and intrigued by such a small, intricate package. Her eyes widened with delight as she held the turquoise box with *Van Peterson* embossed in gold on the lid. She opened the box and gasped. The prettiest of bracelets with a threading of blue, almost topaz-coloured precious stones, knotted around the silver wristband.

'Jo, it's beautiful.'

'Here, let me.' Jo took the delicate piece of jewellery and slipped it around Lucy's tiny wrist, pinching the clasp together. Lucy let it fall a little down her wrist and gazed at it in wonderment. The stones caught in the sun's light. She threw her arms around Jo.

'Thank you, thank you, thank you. I love it.'

The letterbox rattled with the midday Saturday post. Lucy scampered down the stairs and opened the solitary letter. A handwritten note in black ink was enclosed inside a formal printed letter. Her eyes swam with tears as she read it.

Jo bustled down the stairs and stopped short. She sat on the stairs, watching Lucy. Was it another letter from Charlie? Or Sofia?

The tears began to run down Lucy's face. She brushed them away, trying to read the words.

'Lucy?' Jo paused. 'Lucy, what is it?'

'It's my grandfather's lawyers. I'll read it later. It's fine. Each year, they send it, a birthday cheque and a pre-written letter.'

Placing the letter on the hall table and wiping her teary eyes, she went back upstairs. The girls bustled about the cottage, sorting their outfits for the celebrations. They were going to The Pier - or so Lucy thought.

As soon as Lucy was safely in the shower, Jo grabbed her phone and messaged Matt.

Hey babe, is the boat sorted? X

Yep, sexy!

Keep on track here! Decorations in the right place? X

Yep, super sexy!

Matt, seriously, behave! Have Ben and Simon got the bubbly chilling? X

Yep! Listen, gorgeous, we are on this. She's going to love it!

Have you called The Pier for the cake? X

Yep, babe. Simon did it this morning and the food is arriving as we speak. ☺

Perfect, she's got no idea, she still thinks it's at The Pier. See you at 1pm! Don't be late. Got to go! xx

Stay cool, sexy x

You're so bad! But I like it!! xx

Everything was going to plan. The bathroom door unclicked. Hurriedly Jo threw her phone back onto the bed and smoothed down her hair.

Lucy sat in front of her dressing-table mirror. Her skin glowed: there were no longer any blemishes to remind her of a past life. She drew the brush through her hair. Jo sidled up next to her.

'Let me, Luce. I think simple, understated, a little boho-chic.' She stood behind Lucy and brushed her hair, the heat of the dryer pushing its warmth on each strand of hair as it fell into a gentle ringlet. Jo caught the back up and rolled it into simple twists that sat along the nape of her neck, a few strands falling about her face.

'There, what d'you think.' She bent down, with her cheek almost touching Lucy's, and looked at her reflection. It was one that showed the prettiness of Lucy, now a year older.

'I love it,' she said, her voice soft and warm.

The girls were still in their leggings and sloppy vest tops. It was gone midday and they'd had a lazy birthday morning. They were meeting Ben and the boys at 1 p.m. and only Lucy's hair was done. Now for her make-up.

Jo had opted for a silk emerald-green and silver tunic-style dress, blocked short sleeves, with an open teardrop shape at the back. Bare legs and killer heels. It was now quarter to one. Lucy's tummy knotted itself with butterflies and she was starving hungry again, but resisted the urge to snack so as not to spoil the celebratory meal.

From the sitting room window, Lucy spied Gladys Pope and Stanley. Rarely did she see them out together. Perhaps there was no darts today. Gladys pushed him along. He was dressed in a shirt and tie, and she brushed him down as he ambled by, doing what he was told. Nudging him as they went. Gladys bounced her hair with the palm of her hand, making sure her rolled look was in place, still chivvying him up. Lucy smiled. Would she and Ben be like that one day?

Jo was struck by Lucy; she took her breath away.

'Oh my God, you look stunning. Here, wait, I forgot.' She opened the front door and took a small posy of summer flowers that were hand-tied. 'Ta-da, birthday flowers. I had to hide them outside so you wouldn't see them.'

'Oh wow, they're gorgeous, Jo. Thank you.'

'Right, come on, let's go. We need to meet the boys.'

Lucy and Jo crossed the road outside the cottage and walked a few yards. There, sitting with a bow tie around his scruffy neck, was Archie and by his side, Bob, in full naval attire, his black shoes polished to a gleaming shine. Jo kissed Lucy and, taking Archie by the lead, she left her with Bob.

'Happy birthday, my dearest Lucy. I wouldn't have missed this for the world.' He wiped away the solitary tear that trickled down her cheek and put his arm out for her to link it. He walked her through the open gates, where posies of cosmos and daisies smiled in their gingham ribbon, hand-tied by Gladys Pope.

Bob walked her to the door of the church. The light beamed in through the stained-glass window. Lucy gazed ahead at the pews full of villagers. Matt sat next to Jo on the front pew and Simon on her other side. Archie lay at the end of the pew on the cold stone floor with his head in his paws. Gladys Pope and her Stanley nestled close to the front. And there by the altar, with his best friend Rob at his side and the boys from the yard in their pews, was Ben. Ben's parents and his sister were on the front pew, sitting as proud as punch.

Lucy walked down the short aisle, her thin white satin dress, which fell onto the smooth lines of her figure with simple spaghetti straps, shimmering and blowing a little, like chiffon as she walked. Its length just caught the floor as she went. Her back was bare to the base of her spine, with the straps criss-crossing it. A few strands of hair fell about her face. Silver diamantés sparkled in the twists. The silver bracelet with something blue and a small summer posy rested in front of her tummy, hiding the tiniest of bumps, unbeknown to anybody. She turned to her left and smiled gently as she drifted past DI Phillips and DS Murphy. They watched on and nodded at her serenity. She caught Simon's eye as she came closer. His eyes were following her with adoration. Jo held his hand and squeezed it.

And then there he was. He held his hand out towards her, Ben, her Ben. She'd found her happily, ever, after.

The confetti fell about them like soft petals of pastel snow, catching in her hair. Ben kissed her as the bells chimed, gently brushing away the strands of hair from her beautiful face. As she laughed into him and another photo was snapped, she took his hand and placed it on her tummy. She whispered, 'Here, feel, that's why I love capers.'

THE END